AT FATE'S END

AT FATE'S END

CHRONICLES OF TAROTLAND

KILLIAN WOLF

ISBN: 978-1-951140-31-1

Copyeditor: Dan Edelman
Cover design: Logan Keys - coverofdarknessdesign.com
Conlanger: Christian Thalmann - twitter.com/thalmach
Map designer: Zentra Brice
Header designer: Etheric Designs - etherictales.com/etheric-designs
Formatter: Michael Davie - grimhousepub.com/plans-pricing

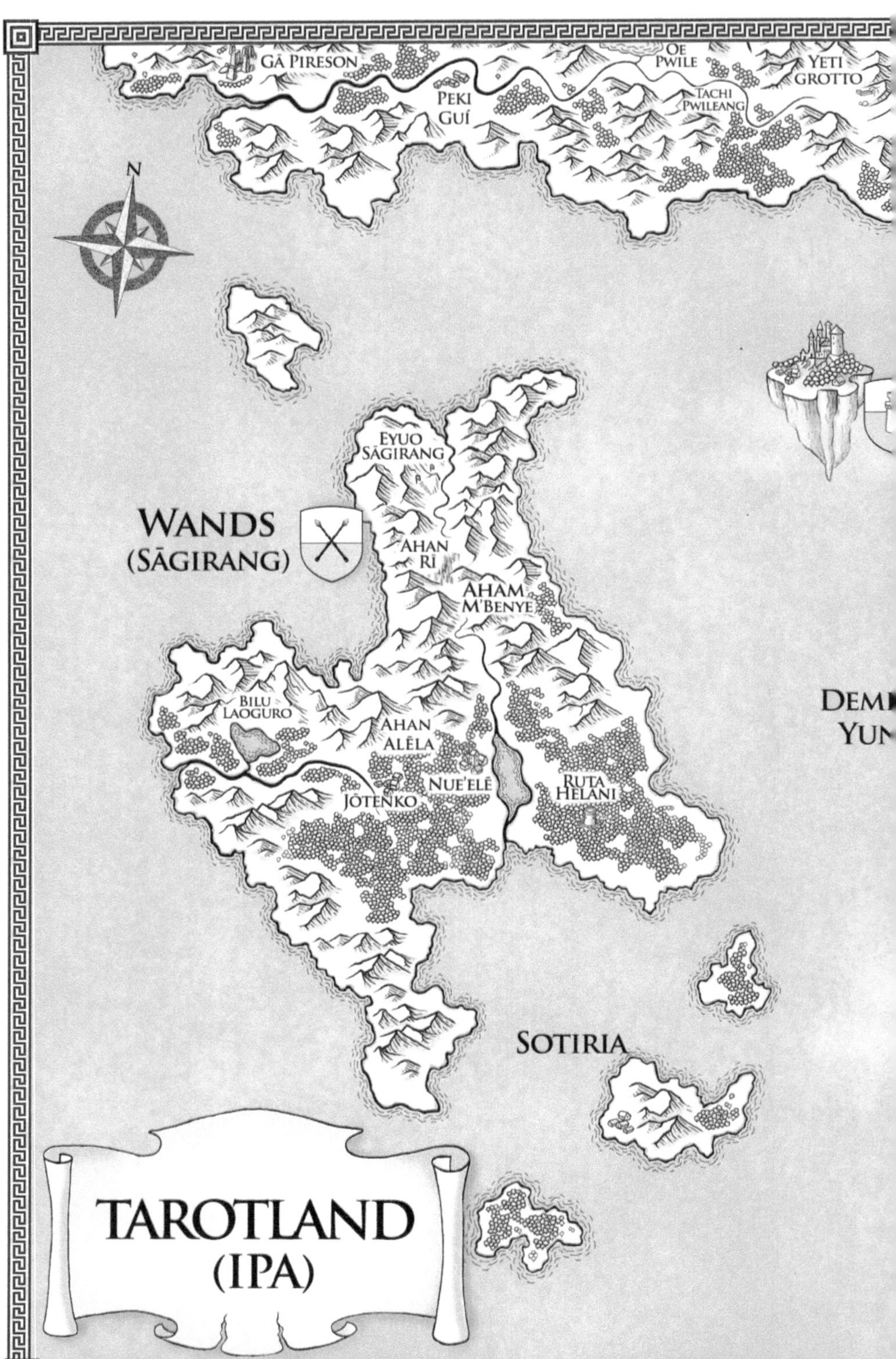
GĀ PIRESON
OE PWILE
YETI GROTTO
PEKI GUÍ
TACHI PWILEANG
N
EYUO SĀGIRANG
WANDS
(SĀGIRANG)
AHAN RĪ
AHAM M'BENYE
BILU LAOGURO
AHAN ALÊLA
NUE'ELĒ
JŌTENKO
RUTA HELANI
SOTIRIA
TAROTLAND
(IPA)

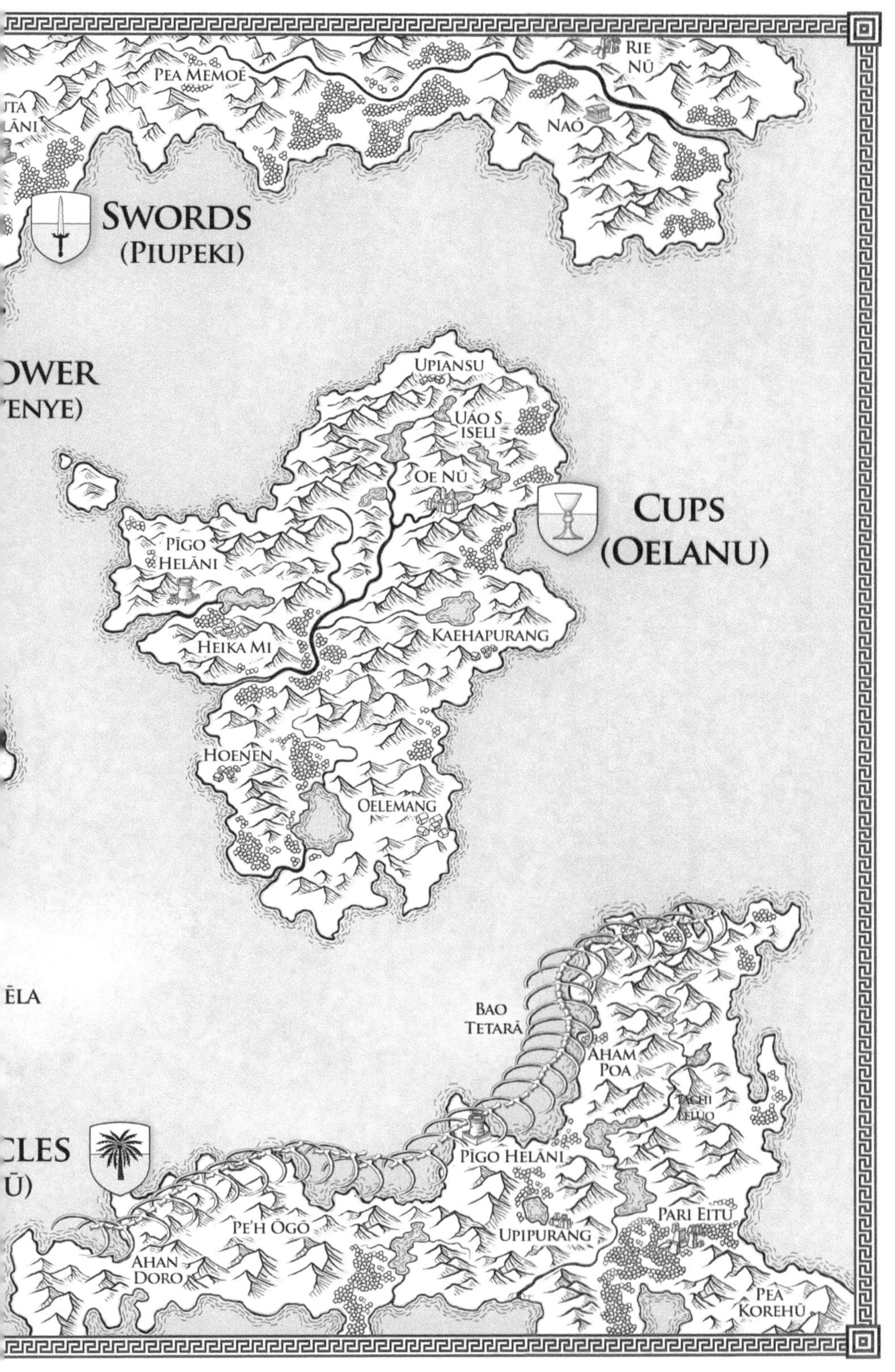
PEA MEMOE
RIE NŪ
NAÓ
SWORDS
(PIUPEKI)
OWER
ENYE)
UPIANSU
UÁO S ISELI
OE NŪ
CUPS
(OELANU)
PĪGO HELĀNI
HEIKA MI
KAEHAPURANG
HOENEN
OELEMANG
BAO TETARĀ
AHAM POA
TACHI LELŪO
CLES
PĪGO HELĀNI
PE'H ŌGŌ
UPIPURANG
PARI EITU
AHAN DORO
PEA KOREHŪ

1

SOREN

Bony fingers scrape along my scalp, pulling at the tangles like some nightmare version of a queen's handmaid. I grab the brush and slap it into his hand. "Use this, asshole."

Even though I'd prefer the oddly gentle reanimated skeleton to not touch me, I can't risk being late.

Dinner with Tetalla is bad enough; slipping away to meet Philo on the way is risking him finding out about it. I have a message my little spider friend needs to get to Nkella, and lining this up took more luck than I'm comfortable with.

My nerves buzz like a live wire. If we get caught, there's no telling what Tetalla would do.

Bobby, my skeletal handmaid, starts working through the knots. I gave up fighting him days ago. Tetalla has us on a routine, and like everything else here, it doesn't stop because I hate it.

I still won't let a skeleton dress me, though.

His joints and bones rattle with every move, making my teeth grind. There are skeletal guards all over the castle, but this one wears a deep red, velvety sash, placed here specifically for me. I should be used to him by now. He's always here, tending to my every need. And I do mean every need. I can't even bathe alone. He watches me sleep. It's unnerving —Tetalla's spy, tracking my every move.

The sockets where his eyes used to be are as hollow and dark as the eyes behind the masked Minor Arcana soldiers. Tetalla uses his powers of the Death Card for more than war.

My gaze falls back to my reflection. The bags under my eyes have deepened. I haven't slept in days, maybe weeks, since before I got here. Drinking the water from the Ace of Cups goblet took away my hunger and exhaustion, but after Nkella and I got back, it caught up to me quickly.

My aovate.

My heart sinks to my stomach.

The way he looked at me. Like I had betrayed him, but he has to know I did it to save him.

You are my aovate, not his. I would rather wait an eternity here for you to come back to me than for you to submit to someone else.

I shake my head. No, I wasn't going to just leave him there. That would have ruined everything. Nkella's alive and belongs here. I did what I had to.

Bobby gapes, gurgling in protest at my movement, and I roll my eyes.

"I can brush my own hair, you know."

He moans something back that sounds like a whine. I roll my eyes again and glimpse my bronze shackles, Ipani scriptures glowing on their surface. I close my eyes, digging deep for any trace of my Fate power, but I hit a wall. With these on, I can't summon spiderwebs, nor even look back into the past. A token from Tetalla after I covered him in webbing when he tried to kiss me the other day.

He singed it right off, but I hurt his ego.

"I cannot have you using Fate powers until I am ready for you to use them," he said, but I know the truth.

It's the same type of ouma used to block Ipani from their powers. Somehow, Tetalla learned to use it against Fate magic. He's grown stronger. I don't know how, but he has.

If Tetalla were to get near the Empress, he might dull her powers. As much as that could solve many of this world's problems, it would bring something far worse. Possibly make Death the emperor.

Bobby moves back, letting go of my hair.

"All done?"

He moans.

"I'll take that as a yes." I stand and walk to the open window shaped like a teardrop. My room sits high in one of the corner towers of Danū Castle, buried deep in the caverns beneath what's known as the Royal Mountains. It overlooks a drop so far down I can't see where it ends. A fall would probably kill me before I hit the bottom. Heat rises from somewhere far beneath, carrying the acrid tang of burning that clings to the stone around the window.

The window faces the back wall of the castle, and if I stretch to the right, I can see the houses carved into the mountain across the divide.

This is the castle I saw in the Deep.

Now I'm here, but in the real Danū. The heat isn't as bad as I expected. This castle has old airways that keep it bearable. Outside, though, it's hot as hell.

Bobby moans by the door. I clench my fist around a tiny hidden scroll beneath the windowsill, keeping my back to him.

Philo checked on me once before. She let me know in an oumala vision that it's too dangerous to continue, but the crew is worried. I told her I wanted to see her again, but with no oumala connection this time. It takes too long, requires too much focus. And with Tetalla watching through Bobby, I can't risk it.

The scroll is small, barely the length of my finger, but it's big enough for one simple sentence.

I did it to save you. I'm still yours.

I slide it into my bronze shackle, keeping my movements slow and casual. Tetalla watches everything.

It's the only thing I can do. There is no way out of here.

I'm not even allowed to walk the castle grounds. Tetalla doesn't trust me, and it's been challenging to play the part he expects. If I could bring myself to get close to him, have him trust me, then maybe he'd at least walk the castle halls with me. It would allow me to case the joint, figure out how I might get a message to Nkella without endangering Philo. To let him and the crew know I'm okay. To tell Talia I'm okay. I just want to know what's happening outside.

I can't escape. He'll kill Nkella if I do. We have a deal, so I wouldn't really leave. He just doesn't want me interacting with Nkella at all, to forbid romance between us.

Bobby disassembles into a pile of dust, swiftly moves through the air, and rebuilds by my feet. He grabs my arm and moans as he stares into me. I gasp and snap my arm away.

"Fine, I'm ready."

He grunts.

"Don't grunt at me. I'm going."

Taking one last look at myself in the mirror, I tug at the tight, criss-crossed, deep-red garment, snugly covering my breasts and crossing at my hips to reveal my stomach in a V. My pants, the same shade of deep red, are open at my hips, swaying as I walk. A gift from Tetalla, to be worn at dinner tonight. I sigh and walk out the heavy brass door, Bobby close behind.

We descend the spiral staircase, going down two more floors until we reach the hall leading to the dining area.

My pace slows on the landing, and I bend down, pretending to fix my slippers. My eyes scan the stone wall for a flicker of Philo's mosaic glass pattern, but there's nothing.

Bobby stops short behind me, letting out a low moan.

"Go on," I mutter, waving him forward. "I'm not going to run."

He creaks past me, joints cracking as always.

I don't move, quickly searching the tiny crevices of the wall. Where the hell is she? My stomach knots.

If she came through already, I missed her. Or she's late, which isn't like her. I check the scroll tucked in the shackle, then keep walking.

Maybe something distracted her.

Tetalla's skeleton soldiers stand at attention on either side of the tower doorway at the far end of the corridor. Each pair of hollow eyes stares at me as I pass. Bobby's clattering bones echo through the space.

The sound isn't what alerts Tetalla that we're coming. He can sense the dead at all times.

"You're late." Tetalla's dark, snippy voice makes my skin crawl as I step through the large, ornate brass double doors.

"We don't have to eat together every night," I mutter as I walk past the skeleton pulling out a seat for me next to Tetalla at a long rectangular table. I opt for a seat farther away. The skeleton quickly moves the plate from the original setting over to me.

Tetalla scowls as I sit, but his expression shifts into something nauseating. His sharp fangs peek from his lips as he drinks in my body with his gaze, and suddenly, I feel vulnerable in this outfit.

"What a vision of red you are, my vicious one."

I notice he's also wearing a deep red tunic that splits at the collar, dipping into a wide U at his chest, paired with black pants—the colors of Danū. He has his hair pulled back, showcasing his pointed ears, and Ipani stripes reaching up from his neck.

My cheeks heat, and I look down at my empty plate as the rattling of bones approaches the table to serve my dinner.

"I'm doing this for you, and I do not like to wait," he says.

I squint at him. Doing what for me? Dinner? Forcing me to spend time with him in a sorry attempt to get me to like him?

"You know, I wouldn't take half as long if I were allowed to brush my own hair and didn't have to wait for some dead guy to do it for me. Not to mention how much quicker I'd be without these." I hold up my shackles.

A sly smile spreads across Tetalla's face; his dark eyes don't leave mine.

"My princess must be cared for at all times, lest she wander off."

"I would never," I say, holding the snort to myself, though he doesn't miss the sarcasm in my voice.

He leans in, and I swallow.

"You know," he mimics my tone, "I would love to take those dampeners off you. But not yet. I can only trust you to be vicious, *Uoko yani,* my vicious one. For I know your loyalty is still with your pirate crew."

He sits back in his seat, eyeing me with a lifted chin. "But you will come around."

"Don't hold your breath."

He reaches for his drink and snaps his fingers with his other hand. One of his skeleton minions approaches, holding a small plate, too small to be dinner, covered by a dark amber dome. I squint as the skeleton sets it in front of me and lifts the cover.

The blood drains from my face. Philo floats in the air, her eight little legs motionless, eyes fixed on nothing.

"N-no. Philo!" I grip the table.

"She is still alive. I won't martyr her and have you hate me."

"I already hate you," I hiss.

"I told you, no little friends, no little spies, or our deal is off. Be grateful for my mercy, or I'll squash her anyway."

My heart hammers in my chest. That's why she wasn't where she was supposed to be. She got caught because of me.

"Please...don't. I didn't know she came," I lie. Tetalla's guards inside the Aō must have caught her. Poor Philo. She doesn't deserve this, and I won't forgive myself if he hurts her. "Let her go."

He clicks his tongue and waves for his guard, who comes to take Philo away. My eyes sting as I watch the dome close around her tiny body, carried off. At least she's alive.

"I will when I can trust you," he says. "And then your dampeners will come off."

"You only put them on me because I rejected you. You're using your powers to compensate for your tiny dick."

His eyes narrow, and a silent beat passes between us.

Shit.

"Do you want to test this theory?" His voice is calm, unbothered by my insult. "If you shared my bed, there wouldn't be any need for your watchers." He nods at Bobby, who stands behind me.

I grip the fork instead of balling my fists and watch as his skeleton servant finishes serving him and leaves.

I play with my food, the silence heavy. His gaze stays on me.

"The sooner you get over the pirate captain, the sooner you can move on with me and be happy."

A laugh escapes my throat.

"Laugh, my vicious one. Fill this room with your jest. But deep down, you know that little lover's mark never appeared on your wrist."

My throat dries, and all laughter drains from me.

"Your connection is severed, is it not?"

I chew my cheek.

"Hnn." He lifts his chin and smiles down at me. I hate him with every fiber of my being. My gaze drops to my wrists, where my marks should be, hidden beneath the dampeners. The lover's mark never appeared. The connection Nkella and I felt when we professed our love is gone.

At one point, I did feel it, but it was so faint I was afraid I severed it for good when I made this deal. Now I think I might be right.

I hate how we left things.

"Uoko Yani, do not despair, daí?"

My eyes narrow as I glare at him.

He stands, calm as always, and my body stiffens as he approaches. My breathing shallows as he sits beside me, taking my wrist and pulling me onto his lap.

My heart pounds, and the temperature drops around me, sending goosebumps rippling down my spine. My entire body is tense. I hold my chin up, refusing to meet his gaze this close.

"Do not be nervous, my uoko yani. If I meant to hurt you, I would have already."

I swallow. "Why have dinner with me? Don't you have a war to fight?"

He ignores my question, a slight smirk in his eyes. "We do not have to fall in love, you and I."

My mouth dries. I avoid licking my lips, afraid any action might give him the wrong impression. If I move away, he'll hurt me at this range. Without my powers or any weapon, I'm completely vulnerable, and he knows it, especially in this outfit.

"What I mean is, I could give you back your powers if you do one thing for me. So I know you'd never leave and would always be beside me as I rule."

I blink and glance at him from the side. "Do what?"

He pulls out the Death Card from inside his shirt and flips it around in his hand, glancing at it, then at me.

"I have been recently confiding with the Aō," he says.

My features scrunch. Confiding *with* the Aō? What does that even mean?

"It appears I can make space enough for two."

I squint at the card. "I don't understand." Space for two Deaths? Has there always been space for two Deaths, or is he changing the rules?

The last thought makes my hair stand on end. No one, especially not an Ipani, can change the rules of the Tarot. Only the Fates can. Right?

He must see my confusion, because he chuckles softly. His fingers brush my rear, and my body stiffens again.

"We would share the card, but I wouldn't let you go if you decided you didn't want it anymore. We would be as one."

It's as if everything slows around me. We would share the card. My heart thunders in my chest at his words. He's changed the rules. Somehow, he's managed to gain power from the Aō, enough to alter the Death Card so that we would be "as one."

"Hell no," I whisper.

"Do you not want your powers back? Your freedom? You could see your captain, your sister, your friends."

"And you'd let me?"

He shrugs modestly, still eyeing me. "You'd give me what I want, the counterpart to all your Past Fate powers. Together, I would be unstoppable, and you would be free."

Together, I would be unstoppable. Right.

I stare off at a tapestry near the entrance. A devil wearing a crown stands with his queen, black palm trees surrounding them atop a volcano.

Nkella would hate this deal, but maybe it's the only way. Then we can finally be together and take Tetalla down. Nkella never liked any deals I've made.

"I'm offering you a great bargain, Uoko yani. Take it." He places the card in my hand. "Hold it, a token of my good faith."

I stare at the card, a purple glare flickering over the image of Death by a boat at sea.

"All you have to say is, I accept the position."

Something is off. How is he changing the Death Card's rules? Just like I haven't figured out how he dampened my Helāni magic. By consorting with the Aō? What does that mean?

He moves a strand away from my face, and I glance at him, reminded I'm still sitting on his lap.

"What do you say?" Tetalla purrs. "Say yes, and get your power and freedom back. Only come when I call you to use your power."

He wants the Empress dead, his revenge—and for me to take the Empress Card, since only a Fate can replace her, or the world crumbles. The Hierophant, Demitri taught me this. Tetalla believes that with me, he can become Emperor. Just like Demitri wanted for himself.

I lean into him. His eyes ignite, reminding me momentarily of Nkella. I whisper in his ear, "I can only trust you to be unpredictable. So I'm gonna pass."

I rise from his lap just as he pushes me away.

"Take her back to her room."

A skeletal hand grabs under my arm and drags me toward the double doors. I catch my footing, pulling my arm away and straightening myself. "I can walk, thanks."

Bobby protests with an annoyed moan.

Tetalla's pissed-off glare doesn't escape me as I turn away, and a smirk tugs at my mouth. My stomach rumbles. I should've eaten at least a few bites of food.

Behind me, Bobby rattles with every step as I walk briskly back to my room, wanting as much distance between us as quickly as possible.

And now I have to find another way to send Nkella a message. My stomach twists at the memory of Philo's little body floating over the plate.

Inside my room, I throw myself onto the bed and bury my head in my arms. The sound of running water fills the space, and I'm actually grateful Bobby's here to draw a bath and help scrub Tetalla's touch off me.

I scoff into the pillow. I must be losing it if I'm actually thankful a skeleton is here to draw my bath.

Once I'm submerged in the hot water, one of the few perks of living in a castle inside a volcano, I curl my knees to my chest while Bobby pours water over my head. The scent of jasmine and vanilla floats up with the steam, calming me as much as anything can right now. The special blend is apparently a staple tea in Danū, so I lean into it, letting myself get lost in remembering Nkella instead of Tetalla.

He doesn't come in here anyway. This is my time.

Nkella always had a faint scent of vanilla and hickory from his favorite rum. I wonder if he chose it because vanilla grows on this island.

Did I make a mistake not accepting Tetalla's offer? I could be with Nkella right now. Would he take me back? And if he did, would he accept the new deal—me lending Tetalla my power?

It's better than promising my betrothal to Tetalla. Thankfully, he isn't forceful about that. As creepy as he is, he wants me to choose him. He wants to be certain I'd never abandon him, so he can get what he wants. He'd only trust me if an aovate mark showed up on our wrists, or a different kind of allegiance like the one he's offering. It's all strategic to him.

But to get the aovate mark, he would have to love me too. Maybe this loophole with the Aō exists because he knows he'll never love anyone but Adara.

Bobby hands me a freshly soaped cloth and adds more steam to the water, which rises around his skull.

I know better than anyone—if something sounds too good to be true, it probably is. Tetalla even said it himself. Together, *he* would be unstoppable.

That wasn't a slip. He doesn't outright lie, but he's manipulative and unpredictable. He could promise something and then change his mind, all while having technically told the truth.

He's tricky.

It's better that I didn't accept his offer, no matter how badly I want out of here, no matter how much I miss Nkella. Tetalla could decide later that he's grown tired of our arrangement and kill Nkella for fun.

Forget it.

Bobby lifts a soft blanket and holds it out for me.

Back inside my bedroom, I dry off and dress in a comfortable, long tunic to sleep in.

Bobby moans as his bones clatter toward the door. He opens it to allow another skeleton carrying a tray inside. The aroma of tonight's heated dinner wafts toward me, and my stomach opens up again.

The skeleton places the tray on my vanity. Tetalla knows keeping me hungry won't change my mind. The skeleton remains still until I wave him off. I can always tell when Tetalla is puppeteering them, watching through their eyes. He isn't right now. He hasn't for weeks—not since I first arrived. I made him agree to a bargain: if he kept spying, I'd never consider him more than my captor, never trust him.

Never is a long time for someone like Tetalla, so he took me seriously.

Bobby moves to sit by the door, settling into stillness until I need him again. It doesn't take much. All I have to do is stand, and he'll stand.

I take a bite of dinner, a roasted grain dish topped with honey-glazed roots and slices of spiced sand-antelope, drizzled with a tangy red citrus sauce, and immediately start eating ravenously.

Something hits my window.

At first, I think it's just the crackling fires rising higher than usual. But when something hits again and bounces off the glass, I turn.

I catch the tail end of a black-and-white feather as something drops through the window and lands on my bed. My eyes widen, and I glance at Bobby. He hasn't moved.

My pulse quickens.

There's only one person who could have made it down here, badass enough not to get caught by the oumala guards inside the Aō.

Lāri.

The crew is trying to reach me. Sending Iéle would've been too risky, same for Gari.

This isn't good.

Tetalla didn't kill Philo because he knows she matters to me; he's using her to get me to submit. But the crew?

I can't risk their lives.

I rise from my seat, and Bobby rises too, joints cracking at knees and hips. His hollow gaze settles on me.

"I'm ready for bed," I say.

He walks toward the bath area to prepare my toothpaste of charcoal and mint, and I make a quick dash to the bed. I lift the covers and slip my hand beneath them. A quick glance out the window shows nothing.

I find a crumpled ball of parchment and quickly unravel it before Bobby returns. He'll wonder why I'm not already waiting for him. Inside the parchment is a tiny vial filled with a pale violet solution. I blink, then read the note.

It's written in half Ancient Greek and half Ipani script. Whoever wrote this can't write perfect Ancient Greek. My pulse quickens as the translation potion kicks in, working through the Greek sections.

> *Drink the invisibility potion. You need to make it to the top of the northeast tower. Once there, jump. Will be there to catch—*
>
> *Three days.*
>
> *Lāri*

I suck in a breath. They want me to *jump* off the tower?

I stare at the invisibility potion. Who will be there to catch me? I've never even been to that side of the castle. How would I get there?

Three days. They're improvising. Of course they are. How long has she been flying around here, risking her life for me?

My throat tightens. Philo nearly died trying to help me. If Tetalla catches the others, he won't show mercy.

No. This is insane. I'll write Lāri a letter. Warn them, somehow.

Because if they come for me, they won't make it out alive.

Bobby moans from the bathroom as I tuck the potion away.

I need to stop them before Tetalla turns their rescue into a massacre.

2

NKELLA

She's the only one who can quiet the Devil inside me. Even when we clash, her voice alone can drag me back from the edge.

But all I hear now is the devil, clawing relentlessly at my insides.

My vision blurs, the walls bleeding red at the edges. Thirteen days, and we still have no plan, no way into Danū. And she's trapped in there, with Tetalla.

Each breath burns in my throat. I'd already be inside if the Kings weren't holding me back. But they're not wrong. Tetalla would tear me apart and make her suffer for it.

My knuckles crack. My arm begins to shift.

"I don't think the Kings will appreciate you putting holes in their walls."

I turn to face my cousin Kae, now standing at the doorway. "How long have you been there?"

"Not long."

An annoyed howl comes from the bed. I glance back to see Iéle stretching across my sheets. Rohaka, the gray-coated wolf who seems to be Iéle's favorite, stirs beneath the window, ears twitching but otherwise still. The other two huddle together in the corner, barely lifting their heads. They've all stayed close since I returned.

My arm returns to normal as I grab the flask from my side table and take a swig.

The rum burns going down, soothing the tension in my throat. I've always enjoyed that burn.

"Spoiled wolf," Kae says, holding out a shell of water. I stare at it. "They announced the Empress is on her way," he continues. "Sober up."

"She's coming now?" I narrow my eyes. "She was supposed to take Soren and me to her tower for failing to report immediately when we returned. As the Fate of the present, I'm sure she's known I've been here since the last full moon." However... she can't detect the presence of another Fate; their powers cancel each other out.

"Koj. The King sent Arcana to tell her Soren was captured."

I wince at the mention of my aovate being taken but bite it down. Deal or not, Soren is still a prisoner.

"I doubt me being here has her unbothered. What's taken her so long?"

Kae shrugs. "We'll soon find out."

I pass Kae and his water on the way out. He scoffs and chugs the shell while I take another swig of rum.

Iéle jumps off the bed and pads after us. Rohaka's ears flicker as he lifts his head, but none of the others bother getting up.

Walking these halls feels strange. Almost like a memory I never got to live. The twisted shell columns. The polished arches. Everything so clean and... royal.

What would it have been like, growing up here? Traveling between castles. Parents alive. No Empress.

But then Soren's mother wouldn't have met Sehu. She wouldn't have grown up in these halls either.

Maybe it's the familiarity of being in a castle, reminding me of being a boy in the Empress's tower that is conjuring this surreal feeling.

A sigh leaves me when I find Tessa, my sister, and the Kings talking in the garden grounds. Kae and I exchange a glance. He's as tired as I am of talking in circles.

The Kings, with their endless stories, lavish grounds, and robes dyed in the blues, greens, and golds of Cups, are a maddening contrast to how I feel inside. Every day that passes with senseless pleasantries makes me the more angry. I need to rescue Soren.

We take our seats at the table. A servant hands me a drinking shell. I accept it out of politeness, then pour some of my rum into whatever fruit concoction they've given me.

My sister's smirk at my action doesn't go unnoticed but I ignore it. She sighs with her arms crossed as the kings talk, her eyes fixed toward the fountains in the garden.

They're still talking about the story I told them.

The same conversation. Again. I'm about to lose my mind knowing the deal Soren struck puts her in as much danger as me and my crew.

And with Tetalla's guards slipping in and out of the Aō, it makes it harder to infiltrate.

Why couldn't she just listen?

She had to save me.

My aovate. My skin crawls at the thought of his hands on her. She must think I hate her. But I'll never stop fighting for her.

I throw the drink back, the fruit and rum settling the fire in my throat. My hand tightens. The Devil in me stirs and wants out. I take a breath.

Think of something else.

Like how I'm going to wage war against Tetalla.

"Captain?"

I glance at Kae. He motions downward. I follow his gaze.

The shell cup is crushed in my hand, pieces scattered across the table.

I set the shards down and wipe my blood on my pants.

"Are you okay, Captain?" Tessa's voice is soothing despite the current mood.

My frown doesn't waver. "I'm fine, Tessa. Didn't even feel it."

"That's not what I mean. How are you doing with... everything?"

I stare at her, then at the two Kings standing behind her, watching me.

"I don't have time to worry about me, daí? How are we waging war against Tetalla? We're wasting time. We should be—"

"We cannot do anything, my prince," King Bako says. "Not without the Empress, and remember that she still believes we are on her side. She's on her way, but..." He glances at his husband, King Mayi —Soren's uncle. It wasn't too long ago that she found out not only was her father from Ipa, but that she's related to royal family of Oleanu.

The Kings exchange a glance, and a muscle jumps in my jaw. What are they not telling me?

King Mayi clears his throat. "We were hoping we'd have a plan by now to offer her. Something I was hoping you would do."

My eyes narrow. "Daí?"

Silence falls over the garden, and my anger rises as I stare at the Kings, then Tessa, then Kae. "What is it?"

"They want you to take the Danū throne," Tessa says softly.

I let a breath out through clenched teeth as I pinch the bridge of my nose.

"... Soren didn't tell you," King Mayi mutters as more of a statement than a question.

Kae buries a laugh in his hand as he leans back in his chair.

"Kh. Soren keeps many secrets." After a beat, I add, "This doesn't surprise me."

"We had a feeling she hadn't," King Mayi continues, "which is why we waited to bring it up. We were hoping you'd agree to take the throne. It was part of our deal, in exchange for the Ace of Cups to bring you back."

I sigh. "She must've known I'd overreact to another promise she made."

"And now?" King Bako presses.

My back straightens. "How am I supposed to take the throne, hn? I can't control the royal flames from here."

Tessa squints at me. "But you said you did."

"In the Deep. The difference between fire and the royal flames is that the royal flames come from the Deep itself, and only the Danū royals can call on them. At least, that's what Soren and I figured out while we were there. And it's not easy to get them to obey, Daí? That was another dimension. We don't know if they'll listen from here."

"What about Ipani fire?" Bako asks.

"It's nothing compared to what Tetalla can command. For the royal flames to obey me from here, they'd have to betray their current master."

I never wanted to be called prince, let alone ever be king. That was Ntaoru's destiny—to be Queen of Danū. After our parents died, and after she was taken and made into an Arcana soldier, I took to sea. Most thought I died. For a long time, I kept the secret, but news travels fast. I chose not to stay in Danū. I left to save my sister, and in doing so, abandoned everyone.

"My people hate me. They'll never see me as their king."

"So you'll give up?" King Mayi asks.

Tessa shakes her head at me, but I ignore her. I'm not in the mood for people trying to console me.

"Never. I intend on stealing her back."

"The only way you could do that is by controlling the royal Danū fires. Especially if you're so certain she's in Caverns Castle beneath Pupipurang."

"With your army, daí? Kh. Where are they?"

Agitation spreads across his face, and shock crosses his husband's. The Kings aren't used to someone speaking to them this way, but they don't know what to do with me. The estranged Danū prince. The one they too failed to save. I don't blame them. They had their own people to protect.

But they still betrayed Ipa by siding with the Empress. Even if it was just a performance.

"With the Arcana," he says.

"Using the Arcana is the same as handing Tetalla more ammunition." I take another sip of my drink. "Or have you not been paying attention?"

"Soren still has the Ace of Cups," King Mayi says, agitation reaching his voice. "If Tetalla gets a hold of that card... if he has it already..."

King Bako places a hand on his husband's shoulder and stares at me. "You are our only hope now, Prince Nkella."

Ntaoru leans toward me, cutting away her gaze from the garden. "It cannot be me anymore, little brother."

I shoot her a glare. "You shouldn't even be here."

"I will leave before the Empress arrives."

I nod at her. I don't want her anywhere near the Empress.

"It's as if our parents named you Nkella, meaning hope," she continues, "because they knew you would be the last chance our people have at survival. For them, for Cups, and for all of Ipa."

I have to stop myself from rolling my eyes. Soren would do that. Roll her eyes at something stupid or cheesy. I shake my head instead, and glance away from my sister.

"Know that whatever choice you make, I will be there to fight by your side, brother."

"You think I should take the throne?" I ask, snapping my gaze back to her.

"I won't tell you what decision to make. But I trust you will make the right one."

"What would you do in my position?"

She smiles at me. "Go save the one I love. Of course."

Iéle raises her head and I scratch behind her ears. If only I could send Iéle to deliver Soren a message. But he has guards all over the Aō.

"But wouldn't that be easier with controlling the royal flames? Being King?"

"Kh. And how am I to do that exactly, daí? Walk into the heavily guarded castle and demand the flames to listen to me? They listen to Tetalla." I glance at Ntaoru. "Any word from Lāri?"

She shakes her head.

"It is dangerous for her out there. I don't like this."

"You know how she is, Captain," Kae says. "She has a hard head."

I sigh behind my teeth. "She is going to get herself killed."

"I don't think she feels she has anything to lose," Ntaoru says. The moments of silence that pass between us speak loudly. AJ's passing has taken a hard toll on all of us, but especially Lāri. And even considering, she remains loyal to me and to Soren. She still risks her life to find her whereabouts.

The grief comes in waves. Even though I saw him in the Deep, he is gone. Never to resurface. The Deep is in another plane of existence. The only reason I came back is because I am... a Devil. And it kept me alive, trapped—but alive. That is the only reason Soren was able to bring me back to the surface.

The playing of horns disrupts my thoughts, and Iéle growls. They're announcing the Empress. I flick my gaze back to Nta.

"I better go," she gets up and heads away from the garden moments before the Empress appears in a gust of smoke, surrounded by ten Arcana split on either side of her. I glance at their hollow stares behind their pearl-white masks, then return my gaze back down to my rum.

The Kings move over to greet her, motioning for us to stand. Kae does as he's told. I reach for my flask and stay seated.

I make eye contact with Tessa. She has an excuse as to why she can't stand. I wink at her. She shakes her head at me.

The Empress's annoying tone makes me take another swig of my rum. "Mayi, Bako, how long has it been since I've spoken to you in person?"

"Too long indeed." They switch to Imboe so she can understand with her translation potion she must have undoubtedly drunk. No matter how many centuries she's lived here, she has never cared to learn Ipani.

"The garden looks marvelous. You must send your servants to tend to mine—I'll admit my Arcana can't do much of that."

I take another swig of my rum.

Her eyes fall on me, her gold mask reflecting the bright sun and the flowers around her. She walks slowly over, and I stay put.

"Captain. It is a relief to see you well. Alive."

"Kh."

"Come here," she demands.

I take another drink of my rum and slam the flask down at the table. "You have been the bane of my existence. Why would I take demands from you?"

"I've come to offer a truce." She wastes no time. "We have a common enemy; I believe we can work together to stop him."

"Another who thinks I can do anything. I only have one agenda.

And that's getting Soren back." My eyes narrow and I look past her. "Soren's sister—where is Talia?"

"She's safe, in my Tower. I keep her plenty busy, and I'm too wise to bring her here so you can try to indoctrinate her into joining you bandits."

A smile spreads on my face. "There's the awful queen we all know."

She balls her fists. "I won't tell you again. Stand for your Empress and come here."

Slamming my hand on the table, I stand, but when I do, the blood rushes to my head all at once and the ground spins a little. When steady, I walk over and face her eye to masked eye.

She takes a step back and holds her hand up.

My eyes narrow. "What is the matter, daí? You told me to come to you. I am here."

"You're a disgrace. Get yourself cleaned up." She whips her stature to the Kings. "He's meant to be strong, and in control of his Devil? How do you expect him to do anything drunk?"

"Kh. I am not drunk."

"Believe me," Kae says from behind me. "He is functional."

"Fine." Her shark eyes flick with hesitation. "You once did something to my Arcana that I hated to admit you had enough power to do. But now, it is crucial you lean into your powers."

"I already have."

"Quiet."

My eyes burn. How badly I would love to fill her with air until she pops.

But she cannot die.

It could still be fun.

"Pay attention."

I lift my chin, motioning for her to continue.

"You once killed—and I mean truly killed one of my Arcana." My stomach twists. I want to look away but I let her continue. "It would have been impossible for anyone to do it under my magic, but you managed it."

"I was told this, but I have no recollection of doing it." It was when Soren was still my prisoner aboard the *Gambit*, and I lost control of myself during one of her raids. When I came to, my crew said I had killed an Arcana soldier. Not just made them disappear to return later, but truly killed them. "The Arcana are people stripped of their ability to make choices, thanks to you. They did not deserve for me to kill them."

Her eyes roll behind her mask. My fists clench. "I now know it was because they cannot withstand your Devil curse."

"It is not a curse." I don't know why I care to correct her. Who cares what she thinks of me? She's the one who had me believe my true nature was a curse. Yet, ever since I learned the truth about my family, I want the world to know it.

"You would still be able to defeat his army. And only a Devil can defeat another Devil."

I consider her words. Half his army is made up of Arcana he's collected from her throwing them at him. The other half is the raised dead. "And what about his Death Card? It is your own magic making him all that powerful, daí?"

"That part I am still working on. But it is why we must work together."

"Kh." Working with her would be treason.

"We have worked with her before," Tessa says as if interpreting my hesitation. "In order to bring you back."

I turn to her. "Under deals and conditions. This is bancha, daí?"

"But it might be the only way," King Mayi says.

"And yet," I flick him a glance, "I cannot control the royal flames above the Deep. I have tried."

"You will convince them," the Empress says.

"Them? As in the fire?" I guffaw in her face, and her eyes narrow at me from inside her mask. "How?"

"This is something you're going to have to train to do. If you want Soren back, the way to her is to take out Tetalla."

"You think I don't know this? I may be able to match him in strength, but he is powerful. Probably more powerful than you, Helāni."

"Nkella—" King Mayi starts but she cuts him off.

"You hate me, and I've given you reason to. But, just this once, we're on the same side."

I lean in closer to her emotionless mask and lower my voice. "Let us not pretend that after this, you are not next on my list, daí?"

Her cold green eyes say she hides something else behind her mask. She is not afraid of me, but she should be, given what she just told me about my ability to kill her Arcana. So what else is she keeping?

We lock eyes like wolves, waiting for the other to back down. She's the one who speaks first.

"You'll get to see her. I can promise you this because I need you two to work together."

My heart skips a beat, but my frown deepens. "There's nothing you can offer that would make me follow your command. I'd sooner turn the fires to my side and let them burn the world behind me, just to reach my aovate, than take one step in your direction." I turn my back to leave.

She giggles, and I pause, agitation stirring the Devil in me.

"Has your feathered friend not told you yet? We've already made our way inside Cavern Castle."

My eyes widen. Lāri is the only feathered friend she could mean. I spin back to face her. "If you hurt her—"

"Care to listen to my plan now?"

3

SORREN

“He canceled dinner with me?”

I make a fist around the bottom of my tunic and start pacing the floor. Guards have been circling my window since I woke up this morning, and the only reason for it I can come up with is they’re searching for whoever trespassed here last night. Something must have tipped Tetalla off, or worse, Lāri could have been spotted by one of his guards in the Aō.

I twist the fabric between my fingers.

And now he’s canceled dinner, which is something that despite being at war, he always works into his schedule as part of his strategy. If it wasn’t for the fact Lāri could be in danger, I’d be glad to be eating alone tonight.

Bobby opens his mouth, letting out a gurgle as if trying to form a word. The tray of food shakes in his hands as he makes an effort to portray his emotions.

Agitation builds at my temples, and I move aside. “Just set it down already. Don’t hurt yourself.”

Bobby moves past me, his bones rattling as he sets my dinner on the vanity table. He moves the seat back so I can sit and stares at me expectantly.

I oblige, tired of hearing his moans and grunts to get me to do stuff. I grab the fork and poke at the meat, then drop it immediately, letting it fall on the table with a clatter.

A large dead bird, burnt to a crisp, stares back at me on the plate. Bile rises up my throat, but I swallow it down.

It's too small of a bird to be her, but the message is enough to lose my appetite.

Tetalla definitely knows something's up.

I shudder a breath as Bobby goes to sit by the door, blocking my exit.

Relax, Soren. If he knew someone was here last night, he would have marched his ass up to my room, or at least had Bobby drag me to him. I need to calm my nerves, or it'll give everything away. For all I know, Lāri is alive, and they're looking for someone else.

I still need to figure out how to warn her.

It's been two days since I received Lāri's message with her escape plan from the crew. So fact is, the guards are most likely looking for her. This is why I never would have accepted help from the crew. I hate to disappoint them, I really do, but even if I were on board with their plan, which I am absolutely not, there would be no way I could leave this bedroom, let alone this castle.

Tetalla hasn't given me free range. I'd have to lose the skeleton somehow, which, seeing as how he can turn to dust and reanimate at the speed of the wind to grab me, is seemingly impossible.

Maybe if I start complaining to him about being bored he'll let me walk the grounds with my morbid chaperone. Then, once I find the tower, I can jump. He'll try to grab me, but by the time Gari catches me, it'll be too late.

Assuming it'll be Gari who catches me.

But that might be too dangerous for him.

And hoping Lāri isn't already captured and dead.

This is stupid to even think about. How does she expect me to jump off a tower? That's insane.

I push my tray of food away and rest my head on my arm.

I am tired of being locked up though. All I've done is pace this room, do push-ups, leg lifts, squats, and fight the skeleton.

Bobby moans behind me, and I know it's because I'm not eating. I ignore him.

He moans again, and my eyes land on a polished volcanic stone by the window. Hiding my smirk, I quickly run to grab it and throw it at his head, full force, with no warning. He catches it like a programmed dead Terminator, and I swear his sockets furrow somehow, making him look evil.

Fighting Bobby might be kind of fun, but it's also keeping me trained up and on my toes. Nkella would be proud.

"Relax, I was just having some fun," I lie. "And you can forget about me eating. I'm not eating that."

Bobby stands, walks over to my vanity, and sets the stone back where it was, his dark sockets fixed on me the entire time.

I need to get out of this room. If I'm not going to have dinner with Tetalla, I need to find out what he's up to, and make sure he's not killing my crew. Maybe I'll get a chance to make it to the west wing, if nothing else, to leave a note warning her not to come back. I face the skeleton.

"What do you say we pay your ol' puppet master a visit?"

He responds with a groan in question, his features somehow now relaxed.

"Let's go see what he's up to, shall we?" I stand, unsure if Bobby will let me leave the room or let me get close to Tetalla when he's decided whatever he's doing is too important for me to be around. But I have to at least try. If Lāri is in danger right now, or if he's planning something that can hurt my crew, or get my sister killed, I need to know about it. He's promised to keep them safe as long as I'm here, but that could vanish with a whim.

I stand in front of the door, and Bobby moves to block it.

"Move."

He huffs at me.

"Come on, I'm bored. Can't we just... go for a walk?"

His sockets fix on me, unmoving and unreadable. I'm not even sure he understands me when I talk. I try stepping past him, batting his bony hand away when he reaches for me. That earns me a full shove backward, and I nearly land on my ass.

"Seriously? You're an asshole."

He crosses his arms in front of him.

"Isn't there anything a skeleton would want?"

An empty stare.

"No? Nothing?" I look around the room. What could a dead thing ever want, anyway?

Besides probably being alive again. Or rest. My eyes fall to the bed.

"What if I let you sleep on the bed?"

Bobby follows my gaze, and I walk over to a silky pillow and pick it up.

"Feel how soft it is." I hold the pillow out for him to touch as I squeeze the feathers inside it. Bobby stares at it blankly, and I grab his skeletal hand to make him hold the pillow. "See?"

At first, he freezes, and I pause. I have to be careful. I don't know if there are any trigger words that would cause Tetalla to look through Bobby's eyes like he has in the past. But then Bobby grabs the pillow and squeezes it, his sockets soften, and a glimmer of hope sparks in me.

"Let's go for a walk on the grounds. We'll be back soon."

He lets out a low moan as he holds the pillow. I walk slowly to the door, but this time I take his wrist and pull him with me. I'm not sure if he understands the trade I'm trying to make with him, or if I should have just tried pulling him with me in the first place, but I think this is working.

We walk out of the bedroom together, with Bobby still holding the pillow. At least we're making it down the stairs without him protesting.

Now, where in this castle could King Creepo be?

We first stop at the dining hall; it's where I'm used to seeing him, so I half expected him to still be here, eating without me. Or hosting a dinner that I wasn't invited to.

A loud thump spins me around to face the long, dark hallway. Bobby doesn't flinch, which tells me it probably came from Tetalla. Did he throw something? Keeping close to the wall, I move swiftly toward where the sound came from. Bobby grunts behind me, his bones rattling over the scuff of the sash against his ribcage as he moves to keep up.

Hoping to God Tetalla doesn't hear the rattling of Bobby's bones and that the iron double doors block it out.

A deep, almost gurgling voice becomes clearer as I reach the front of the tall iron doors. It doesn't sound human though. The gurgling reminds me of Gari, except this voice is deeper. I press my ear right outside the wall, next to the door.

The fact that Tetalla can find me without opening the door is still in the back of my mind as I try to be quiet. Any little noise, and he'll find me with his mind. Or use his spy. Either way, he always knows where I am and what I'm doing, so long as I'm still in this castle. Again, King Creep.

That's another reason why sneaking around to leave the castle is a waste of time. And stupid. He'd find me if he had any inclination of what I was up to.

And if I do manage to leave, I'll always be on the run. When I was searching for Nkella and on the way to Oleanu, he was able to visit my dreams, although it took him a long time to find my exact whereabouts.

I take a deep breath and let it out slowly. Here's to being stupid. I push at the heavy iron door with my foot, hoping it doesn't make a sound. It budges silently, opening up enough to let the voices out more. I stare at Bobby and press my finger to my lips. Please don't moan or grunt, you idiot.

"You said the feather was white?"

"That what was reported before it got singed in the flames," the gurgle continues.

The blood rushes to my ear. A white feather? That could be from Lāri's underbelly. I mean, what other birds would be flying around down here?

None. No birds come down here.

Damnit. I knew she was in danger.

"No matter. Even if one of the Undead Crew made it through the entrance in the volcano, they'd never make it inside the castle. Soren is still here, but I'll have to keep an eye on her. Perhaps I'll have to send another guard if her current one is being compromised."

I swallow and stare at Bobby. He has a blank look on his face, and again I'm not sure of how much he understands.

A gurgled chuckle follows. "Are they still the Undead Crew now that they're alive? I think not, eh, sire?"

Silence comes from the room, and I wish I was able to see his expression.

The gurgle starts again. "Shall I continue the search for any Ipani shifters inside the Aō?"

"Yes. If an Ipani is sneaking in for Soren, they are a traitor."

"What about the new Arcana? Would you rather keep them here to guard the castle perimeter like you've been doing?"

A pause. "No, turning them to dust is more efficient."

"Sire?"

"This ends sooner than the Empress thinks. Enough foreplay. Obliterating her army is the way moving forward."

My eyes widen. Dust? How? A memory of Nkella killing one of them, when it was deemed impossible by the Empress's magic, returns. Of course, the Devils must be strong enough to kill them. And Tetalla being Death, can easily kill them without having to touch them.

Bobby's bones rattle as he reaches for my shoulder.

"Did you hear something?" Tetalla says.

I hold my breath and freeze as Bobby's hollow eyes blank and stare back at me. A chill crawls up my spine as I recognize that look.

The door opens wider, and Tetalla steps out, a serious look on his face.

"Why are you not in your room?" His gaze falls on the pillow Bobby is holding, then at me.

My heart thuds in my chest. "I—I was wondering why you canceled dinner."

He squints at me. "Do you actually care?"

"To have dinner with you? No."

He grimaces.

Why is he not questioning me about Lāri? "I care to know why you would just kill Arcana. Many of them are Ipani who had no choice."

"In war, there are casualties. You should know this better than anyone, Uoko yani."

I blink. "These people don't deserve it."

He stares at me, devoid of emotion, as if trying to read me, but then he speaks. "I don't like it, but it's a necessity." He looks at Bobby. "Take her back, and I'll deal with you later."

"What? No witty jokes? No trying to lure me to linger after your meeting?"

He says nothing, and something sinks in my stomach. He isn't done for the night. There's more he has to do that he's refusing to tell me.

Black and white fur poke out from the room, and I get a view of the drakon he was talking to. A long mustache of gray and sparkly hair reaches halfway to the floor. Since when does Tetalla work with drakons? They come from the Empress's world. I figure he'd be against them. Although, he made friends with the serpent.

Tetalla stares at me, then at the drakon, and smirks. "Even the Empress's pets are teaming against her. Imagine that."

Bobby grabs my shoulder and I let him pull me away.

Back in the room, I pace. Bobby sits at the foot of my bed, holding two pillows now. He better enjoy them, but I just ensured his obliteration. Any minute now, a new skeleton is going to come in to take his place, and I'm going to have to start over.

Damnit, Lāri. You've put us both in danger now, not to mention the double surveillance he's placed for any kind of Ipani on the perimeter.

But it doesn't look like he was certain my crew came for me, or if an eagle, or bird for that matter, is part of my crew.

Something else twists my stomach.

Someone like him doesn't keep promises for long, just long enough to get what he wants. Maybe I do need to make it out of here. Maybe Lāri is desperately trying to get to me because they've learned something that can help.

Nkella knows the deal I've made. If they're risking everything, then they've thought of something. Maybe jumping off the tower is our only hope. For all of us.

Either way, I have to at least go and warn her that he found her feather.

I stare at Bobby. He looks the same, not the blank stare into space he has when Tetalla watches through him.

"How long do you think until you're replaced?" I ask him.

Bobby's jaw cracks as he opens it to moan something at me. Is he really so busy that he hasn't replaced him yet? Something is amiss. He did say he'd take care of Bobby later, but I expected it to have been done by now.

I barely catch a wink of sleep. I sit by the teardrop window and stare down at the cavern walls, with empty homes carved into them. I don't even have a view of the native Ipani from here. He wants me isolated, not having people stare at me from below. The terrifying drop of darkness never fails to tilt my world on its axis, so I avoid looking down.

But how am I going to feel jumping off a tower? Especially if Gari is there and invisible.

The better question is, how am I going to get myself through the castle and to the east tower with Bobby watching me?

I have to hope Tetalla's busy again, and that Bobby is still here with me to take my bribes, given that he hasn't been reprogrammed.

All this uncertainty gives me a headache.

I'm used to living with uncertainty. But with Tetalla, he's too unpredictable.

I'm just going to have to wing it. I can't form a solid plan like this. The only thing I can do is stay out of his hair all day. Let's see if he has dinner with me tomorrow. If we do, I'll act like nothing happened, and hopefully that's enough to make him not replace Bobby.

Bobby lies down on the bed, and I wince. I did promise him he could sleep on the bed. It looks like he can understand a lot more than he lets on.

The aroma of fresh bread and spices wafts under my nose, making my eyes open. Bobby has come in with breakfast. Surprise flickers through me as I squint at him, making sure it is in fact still Bobby, and not some other skeleton that looks like him.

He lets out a groan for me to get up. It's him.

Tetalla must have been really preoccupied last night. I wonder what he was up to.

The light in the room is still the same. Being underneath a volcano brings the burning glow from the controlled Ipani fires, but it never gets bright, no matter what time of day it is.

It isn't hot though. The castle has a unique cooling system that circulates throughout. Harold would have found that interesting. Probably would be nerding out over it the entire time.

I push myself up from the floor and rub my sore neck. There was no way I was sharing the bed with Bobby last night, but I kept a pillow and covers. Wishing there was coffee, I reach for the cup of some kind of juice. It's sweet, with a tangy finish, like a mix of orange and strawberry.

"Did you enjoy the bed last night?" I ask him.

He stares back at me and looks at the bed. I'll take that as a yes.

"How would you like to sleep inside the covers tonight?" The lie is sour on my tongue. I don't like my bony guard, but I've gotten used to him being around. Knowing that we'll most likely get caught and him obliterated makes this a tad hard.

Just a tad. He's already dead.

He grunts at me. I wonder if he gets scared. He was there when Tetalla said he'd be dealt with later. Is he aware enough to know I'm putting him in danger?

I quickly dress and pull my hair back into a braid. Bobby follows me around as I pace, trying to avoid him sitting me down to do my hair for me. It takes too long.

His grunting makes my eyes roll. The more I take jobs from him, the more frustrated he gets.

"You want to help me?" I ask. "Take me to the east tower."

"And you can sleep inside the covers tonight, and always." I hope I don't regret saying that out loud. If Tetalla is listening in, I feel that's something he'd use against me.

I stare down at the magic dampener on my wrist. I can't even use my web power for protection. He's stripped me of my weapons, not because he was "afraid" I'd use them on him, but because he said I wouldn't need them. He also took the Ace of Cups Card.

I swallow, missing the dagger Nkella gave me.

Him taking the Ace of Cups is a problem, but I have bigger problems to worry about. I start making my way to the door, watching Bobby. When he doesn't move to stop me, I open the door and step out.

My eyes narrow on him as he follows.

"So, you'll sleep inside the covers tonight?" I say low, as if someone might be listening.

He grunts back.

"Alright then, I'm going to take that as we have a deal."

I walk briskly down the steps toward the hall that takes me to the dining area, but Bobby stops me. When I'm about to protest, he points to the other set of stairs that keep spiraling in another direction.

Oh.

Cautiously, I start climbing them until they stop at another door. I twist the knob and open it, causing the hinges to creak loudly. I wince and search around, but it looks like we're the only ones here.

Tetalla really has no idea.

Inside is a long, dark hall with nothing to light it. I step inside and immediately get hit in the face with cobwebs. A cold draft passes through me as we walk all the way down, with Bobby's joints cracking as we move.

"What is this place?" I whisper.

Down the hall to the right is a door slightly open, with a red light seeping through it. A cold chill runs down my spine as I get near.

Something dark and nefarious is happening inside; I can feel it in my bones.

I stop in front of the door. Bobby tugs at my arm to direct me toward the end of the hall, but curiosity makes me push the door just a little, enough to peek inside.

My eyes widen, and I swallow a gasp.

I'm caught.

Only...

Tetalla floats in the air; his eyes are white, and his palms are spread open. He doesn't see me. He looks like he's in some sort of trance.

Is this what he gets up to every day? What is he doing?

Bobby's cold skeletal hand pulls at my skin, and I quickly step away from the door, then try to move the door back exactly the way he had it.

My breathing picks up as what I just witnessed hits me.

"I have been recently confiding with the Aō..."

That's what he told me during dinner that night. This has to be what he was doing just now. That's how he found a way to create a magic dampener for Fate magic.

My heart thumps loudly in my chest. Okay, I'll deal with that later. I start running through the dark hallway toward the door at the end.

Once through it, I start to climb the steps of the east tower.

This is it. I've made it.

I run all the way up the stairs, with Bobby on my tail. Once we're at the highest door, I open it and step outside, letting Bobby out with me. If I were to slam the door on him, this all would be ruined. After I jump, he can do whatever he'll do.

He groans at me and stares down at the height. This tower is higher than my room in the west wing, and the dark drop to the abyss doesn't even show the sparks of fire down below. I press my back against the door. From this angle, the cavern walls are a lot farther, making the height somehow feel worse.

Now, how the hell do I know if I'm supposed to jump now or later?

Bobby drops down to pick something up, and that's when I see the eagle feather. I walk to the edge.

This is crazy. I never should have come.

Something grips my shoulders and a yelp escapes the back of my throat.

The last thing I see is Bobby reaching for me as I'm pushed off the tower. A scream lodges in my throat. Everything becomes a whirl of darkness, robes, and—

Feathers.

4

SOREN

I'm dropped onto rough gravel and block my fall with my arms. My chest aches from having held my breath so intensely. Every muscle in my body stiffens, expecting the worst from Tetalla right now. My eyes fix on a hard stone floor as I move slowly to get up. My hand touches something cold and wet, and I pause to look at it. Snow?

Tall walls of green shrubbery and flowers surround me, no other snow in sight.

"Finally," a familiar orotund voice makes me pause. "Quite honestly, I doubted she'd be here. Good job, bird."

"Again, my name is Lāri. And I knew she'd come."

I slowly lift my head, eyes wide as I gape at Lāri. It worked. I can't believe it. Lāri stares at me with a grim expression. Her eyes are sad, and my chest squeezes. She must have gone through hell to get to me, with AJ on her mind. She offers me a weak smile.

"Well, stand. What are you still doing on the ground?" the Empress demands. "We haven't much time, you need to get back soon."

"Get back?" I pick myself up and dust myself off. The Arcana soldier who dropped me stands idly behind me. I move to hug Lāri.

"I thought the crew were the ones catching me," I whisper.

"In due time, Soren. This was the best method."

I pull back and nod.

"What am I? Chopped liver?" Talia's voice spins me around, and I slam into her, draping my arms around her small frame. A sob, more laugh than cry, escapes my throat.

"Ow."

"I was so scared I'd never see you again," I say into her dark curls.

"I know," Talia's voice breaks as she hugs me tighter. "Me too."

"This is very touching," the Empress interrupts with a strained voice, "but we really must hurry to get you back before he knows you're missing."

I let go of Talia and stare at the gold mask of the Empress. Her green eyes stare back at me.

"You don't understand. I can't go back. I'm guarded by my keeper, a skeleton, at all hours of the day, and he watched me disappear from that tower." I shake my head and look at Lāri. "I was only hoping to warn you. He found one of your feathers and has guards all throughout the Aō. If he finds you, he'll torture you before he kills you."

Lāri doesn't even flinch and offers a shrug. "I did what had to be done."

I narrow my eyes at her. "Are you kidding? I made a deal with Tetalla, I can't have you losing your life for me. And," I glance at the Empress, "how is it you're working together?" I walk a few paces, lowering my voice despite the Empress standing right there. "You hate her. How can you be here, after everything?"

Lāri lifts her chin but stays quiet.

"She did what is best for this world, Soren. As should you."

I turn to face her, taking in my surroundings. We're standing inside the garden maze outside of the Tower. I recognize this place from a vision I had of Adara with Tetalla.

Snow prints lead into a hole in the shrubs. I squint into them, but it's too dark to see anything.

"Listen carefully," the Empress states. "I need you to go back to be my spy."

My eyes widen. "Did you not hear me the first time? He already knows I'm gone. How did you even get past his guards?" I look at the Arcana, wondering how he wasn't obliterated.

"It appears your crewmate's abilities to sneak around proved useful."

I glance at Lāri, still unhappy about her risking her life for me, but pride swells in my stomach at how good my crew is.

"Tetalla wants you alive," the Empress says. "You can still do what I ask of you."

"I haven't been allowed to leave the room he stuck me in," I raise my voice. "What makes you think he'd give me enough free range to spy on him? I can't even use my power to see into his past." I raise my wrist, showing her the magic dampener.

She comes closer and takes my wrist. "What is this?" Her voice lowers, concern tinging it, but I know it's not for my safety. If he can control my powers, he'll be able to control hers.

"Only one of our problems. He's somehow been able to speak directly to the Aō." I try to explain what I witnessed before coming here. "And because the Fate magic and the Aō intertwined so long ago, he was able to create some sort of dampener for me. He's getting more powerful."

She drops my wrist and steps closer, her eyes boring into mine. "This is how he's had the castle protected against my magic," she mutters to herself. "This is why, Soren, you are the only hope of Fateland."

Lāri coughs.

"Ipa," I correct.

"Everyone's lives depend on you learning Tetalla's motives," she tells me. "You are the only one in that castle with him. I need to know his plans so we can defeat him."

I laugh. "Do you think I haven't been trying to figure out his motives this whole time? He doesn't trust me."

"Because you haven't given him reason to. It'll be up to you to convince him."

That would mean being nice to him, possibly flirting. My stomach turns at the thought of his hands on me again.

"Where is the World Card?" the Empress suddenly demands.

"Tetalla took everything from me. The Ace of Cups too."

Guilt twists in my stomach as the memory resurfaces of the first day he took me from the ship. The last day I saw Nkella. Tetalla took me into a cold room and had me stripped of my clothes. I was completely naked while two skeletons dressed me in what he wanted me to wear. I tried to fight him off, tried to save the cards, but he had them and my weapons confiscated.

The Empress visibly deflates. It's not like I'd ever let her have them, but I understand losing them.

"He can't use them," she says. "He just doesn't want you to have them."

"I know."

"You'll have to get them back."

"It's been on my to-do list. He just doesn't let me go anywhere without eyes on me, not to mention he can see through any of his dead guards in order to watch me."

"You'll just have to try harder then, won't you? And while you do, try to find the Ace of Pentacles. Despite his own power, that card will take ownership of Danū's currency; it will help the people and feed them, but it will also challenge Tetalla. He who holds the Ace of Pentacles will have the sway of the people."

"I don't know how having more sway will be worth anything against Tetalla. But I'll do it."

"Good," she says.

I refrain from sighing out loud. Hopefully, this is the last time I have to work with the Empress. The crew and I worked with her to get to Oleanu, and now they've been working with her to try and save me. I know the Empress's only plan is to defeat Tetalla, and the crew wants the same, but... I walk to Lāri.

"How is he?"

Her eyes flash. "I haven't been around them lately. I've been here."

"But have you spoken to him?"

"Yes."

Why is she being so cryptic? "He's mad at me, isn't he? He hates me."

"I doubt it, Soren."

The Empress interrupts. "Never mind all of that. It isn't important now. You will see each other soon though." A butterfly explodes in my stomach, and I turn to face her. "I'll need you two together while I do something."

"What? When? What are you going to do?"

"All in due course. Right now, all you need to know is that I will have someone pick up your report in the form of a letter in a week's time."

"What if he changes my room?"

"We'll find it. Is there anything you can tell me now?"

My eyes widen. "Yes, don't send any more of the Arcana. He has the ability to kill them now. Straight dust. He doesn't care to reanimate them to be his army anymore."

"It was a matter of time..." she trails off. "The Devils can kill my Arcana."

I take a sharp breath.

"We can lose many in this war," she says, more to herself than to me. She snaps her eyes back at me. "Have you seen him control the fires?"

I shake my head.

"Make sure you report to me if he does."

Something inside the shrub rustles, and I move away in time for a white drakon to slither out. She stares right at me, shimmery silver streaks flowing from her white coat. She lifts off the ground and soars toward the Empress, playfully wrapping around her neck before flying off. I blink as a few flakes of snow fall from her feet and onto the ground.

"It's time to take you back." The Empress looks at the Arcana who brought me here. My gaze moves to Talia as she runs up to hug me.

"Be careful," she says.

"You too."

The Arcana grabs my shoulders. In a whirl of consciousness, I land back in the tower inside the cavern castle, and he's gone before I hit the ground.

I expect guards to surround me, but no one is here. In fact, it's eerily quiet. I walk through the tower door and head down the steps, the same way I came in with Bobby. I swallow as I reach the long, dark hallways. This time, there's no red light coming from a half-opened door.

This is strange. No skeleton guards? Not even Bobby?

Dread slithers into my stomach at the eerie silence of the castle as I climb the steps of the west wing tower to my room. When I get there, I slowly push open the heavy iron door and suck in a breath.

The sconces are lit, and Tetalla stands at the far end of the wall, his hands crossed in front of him, a bored look on his face. A small gasp escapes me. His shoulders rise and fall as he scoffs to himself.

"Sit," he says.

I swallow and do as he says.

The rattle of bones fills the room, and my eyes widen at the door. Bobby walks in.

"I—"

"Silence," he cuts me off.

My heart pounds in my ears.

"Retrieve what's in her pocket."

My brows furrow. Bobby walks up to me and reaches into my pocket, and I start to rise, confusion swarming me.

"Don't make this difficult."

"But I don't have anything in my..."

A large skeletal beetle crawls out of my pocket and jumps onto Bobby's hand. My eyes widen. A bug? My gaze lands on Tetalla as he takes the skeletal bug from Bobby. He holds it to his ear to listen.

My jaw drops. "You knew..."

The corner of his mouth curls. "Did you really think I would allow your guard to be fooled? I needed you to think you were on your own in your little quest."

Blood drains from my face. He always manages to one-up me. This is why Bobby led me to the other side of the castle so easily: he was allowed to do so the whole time.

"Now listen carefully." He turns his attention fully to me. "You will continue to report to the Empress, and you will tell me everything she tells you."

5

NKELLA

"You might be overthinking this, Nkella. The Empress has us waiting to retrieve Soren from a specific, hidden location." King Mayi stands in the grand hall of his armory while Kae and I look over what weapons to borrow. The armory, like most of Shell Castle, is built from sharpened mollusk shells, and it feels as though these dead mollusks were braver than the cowardly kings who have ruled from within them.

A guardsman helps Tessa fit a new cannon to her wheelchair while Ntaoru tries on a belt. The room is impressive and practical, every weapon within easy reach. I doubt these kings ever made use of it.

I select a longbow from one of his displays. "Perhaps the Empress is telling the truth, or perhaps she's only making it seem that way so she isn't blamed if Soren gets killed. Whatever she has planned, I don't want Soren in that castle."

The king turns to look at my cousin, as if he'd take his side.

"If my cousin believes we need to go now, I trust him," Kaehante says, spinning a hand cannon in his hands.

King Mayi inclines his head, his cloak brushing the stone floor. "I confess, I'm uneasy sending you to the wolves."

Iéle lifts her head.

"We are the wolves," I say, strapping the blue sheath to my side.

The king's jaw clenches. "Give me more than your word, Nkella. Assure me that refusing the Empress's signal will not leave us broken on the reef."

I drop the bow and spin to face the king, chest to chest. His eyes widen as he meets my gaze.

"Why do you suddenly want to follow the Empress again, daí? Your people may have been spared by her, but everyone knows it was out of cowardice. The moment you learned I was alive and Soren could retrieve me, you seized the chance to use the Empress, and me, to free Oleanu later. And now you want me to wait? Why? Are you afraid she'll punish you for letting me go? Kh. Try to stop me. No one stands between me and my aovate. Now move."

Ntaoru grips my arm. "Easy, brother. Be respectful, daí?"

I glance around. The Cups Arcana in their blue masks have gathered at the armory entrance, joined by Ipani soldiers. I smirk. I could take them all at once, but Ntaoru's right. The king has loaned us weapons and a dozen soldiers to aid our mission.

The king motions for them to stand down. "I truly want what's best for Soren and for you, Nkella. But I won't apologize for being an opportunist if it benefits my island and my people. You are right that I have ruled with fear in my heart, yet every choice I've made was out of love for my people. Perhaps I have been a coward and an opportunist. But if we act too rashly, it could be fatal for us all. I only ask that you make sure you know what you're doing."

I stare at him for a beat. "I do not trust the Empress. She is vengeful; this could be part of her plan. Soren once told me that through one of her visions, she witnessed the Hierophant telling Tetalla that the Empress killed her own sister Adara—his aovate for their treason. The Hierophant had brought him proof of a body, but it was a false corpse made to look like her. This was orchestrated by the Empress out of anger and jealousy, all the while, she was keeping Adara locked up in one of her dungeons.

"Tetalla believed the Hierophant and retaliated by attempting to kill the Empress by burning the Tower to the ground with her in it. Do you know what happened next?" I ask the King, knowing no one else knows the true story. When he doesn't answer, I continue. "Tetalla found out that she had orchestrated it all, and by his own retaliation, he killed his own aovate. Adara burned to death, locked up in that dungeon. Only I can attest to how deep that anger would reach our Devils. When his Devil took hold, its fury dragged him and everyone he slaughtered that day down into the Deep. That's why the Death Card chose him and he took on the role as Death, ruler of the Deep. But do not forget the cards belonged to the Empress. It was her magic that cursed him as Death with no escape. Until now."

"So it was vengeance and cruelty from both of them," King Mayi says.

"They have been at war with each other for centuries. All they care about is vengeance for Adara's death. Ipa and its people comes second to that."

"Do you think she'd sacrifice Soren?" he asks, eyes wide. "For whatever she's planned for Tetalla?"

"Why else would she not tell us her plan?"

"But Soren is the Past Fate. The Empress needs her..."

"Kh. That is what she tells Soren. The Empress has ruled for many years alone. I doubt her needing anyone is true. I won't waste any more time."

"It's not like we're leaving so many days ahead of her schedule," Tessa calls over to us.

"Getting a head start is a good idea anyway, given anything can happen at sea."

This makes my heart race. "We should have left a week ago."

"The Empress is occupied; she will not be watching for your ship to arrive early," King Mayi tells me. "Some of my soldiers are mer-Ipani and will ensure you have safe passage from below."

I give him a nod, and turn to my crew. "We set sail at sunrise." Being so far from Soren and not having consecrated as aovate above the Deep may have lessened our connection, but my vow to her holds true. She is mine, and I will stop anyone who tries to keep her from me.

SOREN

I stiffen after reading the letter a spider dropped at my windowsill a few minutes ago. This is the third one that's been delivered, and it's always this late in the afternoon, about an hour before dinner. Hence, Tetalla's already here in my room. He wants to be here when the letter arrives to make sure I don't meddle with it. Nothing of value has come from them. This one is the worst yet.

"Well?"

"Hmm?"

Tetalla lets out a sharp sigh, his patience growing visibly thin. He starts toward me, and I take a step back.

"Fine, I'll read it."

"Spare me no details."

I take a deep breath and hold the paper in front of me, knowing this day is about to escalate.

> *Soren,*
>
> *The Empress told me to tell you that the weather in the Tower is brighter for this time of year, with a pleasant chill. She hopes it isn't too hot where you are. She also wanted you to know that the palace peacocks have resumed their morning promenade, insisting on nothing less than emerald plumes for their display.*
>
> *Talia*

I bite my lip and stare up at Tetalla. The last two letters asked about decoration plans in the castle and whether he was keeping Nkella's parents' decor. She's clearly just trying to get under his skin, and it's working.

I suck in a breath when Tetalla rips the letter from my fingers. He squints at it, but it's written in English, and he can't read the translation. The page bursts into flames in his hand, and my eyes widen as it turns to ash.

I'm meant to be trying to find out where he's hiding the World Card and the Ace of Pentacles. I'm not going to get anywhere with him like this.

He turns to leave my room.

"What should I write back?" I ask.

"Respond in two days. Tell her I'm still waiting on color swabs for the dining interior."

I stare at the back of his head as he walks away. Great. I'm stuck in a high school note match between Death and the Empress.

"She isn't stupid, you know."

He pauses and looks over his shoulder.

"If you want her to open up to me and say something of value, you need to let me talk to her as me. She can read between the lines if you curate all my words."

"Hn." He spins around to face me. "If only I knew your allegiance, truly." He takes out the Death Card and holds it in front of me.

"Nice try," I smirk.

But he's right. He knows that even though I hate the Empress, I might join forces with the current lesser evil. Especially seeing as how she's not the one holding me captive here. He is. Taking the position as a second Death he's offered me would mean tying our fates together. Betraying him would be betraying myself.

"Maybe it would be better to send me over there with one of your bugs again. That way I can see what's going on, and you'll have an extra pair of ears and eyes."

A smirk stretches his lips. "I like your deviousness, vicious one. But no. I will see you at dinner."

"Same place?"

He scoffs as he leaves the room.

I throw myself on the bed. Bobby sits in his usual chair next to the door. Ever since he slipped the bug in my pocket and went along with

Tetalla's plan, pretending to be working with me, I've banned him from my bed.

I should have known the skeletons couldn't be compromised.

The Empress wants to know about the royal Danū fires. But aside from him setting her letters on fire, which is by his own ouma, I haven't seen him do anything with the royal ones.

I'm going to have to up my game tonight.

I have an hour to get ready. This time he didn't have any specific requests for what he wants me to wear, but I pick out his favorite outfit anyway. Deep red, with high slits on both sides of my legs, and the top hugs my curves, giving just enough cleavage to leave the rest to your imagination.

I'm right on time, but if he notices, he doesn't show it. I guess he only likes to make a remark when I'm late. I take my seat next to him as a skeleton pulls out a chair for me. It's going to take everything in me to resist being defiant today.

The skeleton holds up a crystal decanter filled with what I assume is some sort of red wine, and I move to the side so he can pour it.

Neither of us speaks, and a smoky aroma wafts in the air as one of his animated skeletons serves us a heavy stew with chunks of meat and what appears to be some sort of root vegetables.

Nothing but the sound of our chewing and the movement of bones fills the space. My shoulders tense. I have to think of something to say before dinner is over, or before he takes over the conversation. Or worse, he leaves and I lose my chance.

I clear my throat, and he quirks a brow.

"I think it's cool that Ipani have ouma."

His brows furrow, and he stares at me.

"I mean, the fact your people are born with abilities to make fire and wind and turn into animals is amazing to me. People can't do those things where I come from." That's right, keep it real so he doesn't feel I'm lying. This is all true. No matter how long I've been in Tarotland, I have never gotten over the fact that there's magic here.

"This has always been obvious to me. A fact of life. The humans who came with the Fates were useless. And do not belong here. They tarnish the Aō."

I chew on my cheek, refraining from telling him to fuck off. Keep your eyes on the prize, Soren. Taking a deep breath, I let it out slowly.

"So, the fire you used today... that was your ouma, right?"

He stares at me blankly, as if bored of me bringing up obvious things, so I get to the point.

"What would happen if you used the Danū fires?"

"It would remain burning."

"So the letter wouldn't have gone out? Or the flames would just burn in place...or?"

He takes a sip of his drink. "Why are you asking what you already know, hn?" He flicks his eyes back on me. "Was it not only a moon cycle ago you witnessed a Devil control the royal flames?"

My throat dries. I knew he had been watching Nkella and me down in the Deep, but I didn't expect him to admit to it.

"I was just making conversation... and... I don't know how it works, so I was curious."

"Curious about what, vicious one? If I can control the royal flames?" He smirks at me, and I swallow.

"No... I was only interested."

"In?"

"Y-you."

He quirks a brow. "Oh?"

I pick up my drink. Some alcohol would be good right now. I swallow, the sweet wine softening the knot in my throat.

He eyes me like a cat watching his prey as I put my cup down.

"Tell me more then."

I study his features, unsure if he's just waiting to trap me in my own game.

"I—Honestly, I've been thinking that if I'm going to be living here, I might as well try to get to know you. I mean, you're never going to let me go. Whether I take up the Death Card or not... and I thought maybe you're not so bad..." Bile rises in my throat, and I swallow it down.

He sits back in his chair and brings his hands together. "Not so bad..." He chuckles. There's no way he's buying this. "What about me is not so bad, my vicious one?"

I fight to steady my breathing. "You're really going to make me say it?"

His smile widens, showing his sharp Ipani fangs.

"I mean... you can be nice... and... you're..." my cheeks heat, and I look down at my plate, "handsome."

Which is not a lie, but to me, he'll never hold a light to Nkella.

"Why don't you come closer to say this?"

"Closer?"

He motions for me to sit on his lap, and I swallow, slowly getting up and moving over to him. He takes my arm and brings me down to drape my legs over his.

And once again, I'm uncomfortably close, and I hate myself for doing this. I already feel horrible that Nkella thinks I've betrayed him, and here I am willingly sitting on the enemy's lap. But this is my chance.

I bring my hand up and plant it on his chest, feeling the raw silky fabric of his maroon tunic. He arches a brow, and I lick my drying lips.

"Can I see the Death Card again?"

His lip curls upward as he reaches into his tunic pocket to show it to me. "Rethinking my deal?"

"Maybe." I take it from him and stare at the skeleton standing by the boat on the water. A purple glare swipes across the image, making the nautilus swirls come to life on the card. "Where are the other cards?"

He guffaws, and I wince at his breath.

"You must think I am a fool. You are not getting the World Card back, vicious one."

"No," I say quickly, "that's not what I mean—"

"You have two seconds to exp—"

"The Ace of Pentacles. I was only curious because I know of the rest on the other islands. I only ask to know the lore, that's all."

He brings his head back, the wide grin still on his face. His hand curls around my thigh, and a shiver runs down my spine.

"The truth is, I do not know."

Now I quirk a brow.

"I'm being honest. I haven't an idea where the Helāni Card is. It was not in the castle when I arrived, and I have not heard of its whereabouts. Usually, my people know these things, and they would be too afraid to lie to me."

I study his features, not that I'd know when he's lying. He's good, too good. But I think he's telling the truth. I open my mouth to speak when a ground-shaking quake makes the castle roar around us. Both our eyes widen, and he stands, pushing me off him.

He spins around. "Where are my guards?"

I look around and realize they're all gone. What the hell? The guards are always at the doors. A quake like that should've brought them in.

Another quake, and I grab onto the table.

His eyes narrow on me. "Was this you?"

"Me?"

"How did you do it?"

"N-no! I have no idea what's going on..."

His features relax, but he grabs me and ushers me out of the dining hall. Bobby is nowhere to be found.

"I don't have time to lock you in your room. Go there now and stay there."

His eyes glow as he stares at me, and I already see his body starting to shift. I've never seen him shift to his devil form before. And if he loses control...He'll kill me. I can't bring him back like I can bring Nkella back from it. I start running back to the tower.

As I sprint, I realize this is the first time in weeks I'm on my own. Not with Tetalla, not with Bobby, or any other skeleton. And since this is unexpected, I know there's no bug on me.

This makes me run faster in case one of the Empress's guards is waiting in my room.

When I get there, I swing the door open. The room is empty. I look around and walk in, closing the door behind me. What could have caused the castle to shake like that?

It sounded like when the Arcana would land on the ground nearby.

But why would the Empress send them when she knows she'd just be throwing away her army?

A cold wind hits the side of my face, and I pause, touching my cheek. A cold draft all the way underground, beneath the volcano?

Sticking my head out the open arch, I gasp as snow falls inside the volcano.

6

NKELLA

"THE SPEED POTION IS HALFWAY FULL, AND WE STILL HAVE about a day's journey to Danū." I straighten from behind the wheel, one hand gripping the railing as the ship cuts through the waves. Wind rushes through my coat, flaring it open, the salt stinging my skin. Kae spreads the map beside me, his fingers steady despite the spray. The heat rolling off Danū rides the air now. We're close. My skin hums, tight with the need to see her again.

We sail against the wind. Without the potion, we wouldn't be able to make a straight cut to the south. "The winds are against us," I shout, "but if we keep the same speed through the night, we will make it by sunrise."

"I will take night shift," Kae tells me, fighting with the map. I give him a nod.

"Tessa and Ntaoru are making progress with the potions. The kings supplied us well enough to start an army. Tessa says they'll be the most potent she's ever made."

"It won't matter. No explosion will be enough against Tetalla."

Kae shrugs. "It might help with his army of dead."

"This is true. Anything that gets in my way to her, I will blow up."

I rest my hand on the wheel, ouma crackling faintly inside my bones. "We don't need potions to break through everything," I mutter more to myself. "Not when Nta and I have fire and wind."

I keep my eyes on the sea, but I can feel Kaehante's stare. When I don't say anything else, I expect him to leave. Hopefully to go sleep so he can take watch tonight. Not that I will be able to sleep.

I don't remember the last time I had a good sleep.

Yes, I do. It was in the Deep after I made love to Soren for the first time. There was an acid rain shower outside, so we found a cave to take cover. I fell asleep with her in my arms. Despite the dangers that awaited us, I didn't want the moment to end.

Kae's hard stare is still on me, and I glance at him. His jaw muscles are tense. Something else is on his mind. "Was there something else?"

His gaze narrows on me, and I squint back at him.

"What is it, daí?"

"And what if Tetalla puts innocents in your way?" He keeps his voice low and deep enough for my ears only.

"Kh. What are you trying to say, Kae?"

"You tell me, Captain."

"What is this, daí? Are you trying to get me to say I will put our own people at risk?"

"Koj. I want to hear you say you will not."

My grip tightens around the wheel. "You insult me, cousin. How could you think I would hurt our own people?"

"Weren't you saying you would destroy anyone who got in the way of you and Soren?"

"I meant Tetalla's undead. You know this. Why are you picking a fight with me?"

"I am not." He sighs. "But we are headed to Danū for the first time in..." He wipes the back of his bald head and looks over to the side before staring back at me. "In years. What are we going to do about our people? About the current situation? Anything at all? What are we doing after—"

"After we get Soren," I say. "I will think of a plan."

"You will think of a plan after we get her? Not now?" He grunts.

"Nkella, even though you hate it, you are the Prince of Danū, and you are going back. Danū may no longer be under siege by the Empress, but they are still prisoners unable to leave, with a cruel king."

"You think I don't know this?" I let go of the wheel and shove my cousin hard, my fist landing on his chest. I step back from him, and he stares at me.

I grab the wheel again and fix my eyes ahead.

"Do you think you can just stand up to Tetalla, call on the royal fires, and take the throne?" he says calmly. "Is this your only plan?"

"I never wanted the throne."

"*Rōkan*, Nkella," Kaehante curses through clenched teeth.

"Ntaoru can still take it while I defeat Tetalla. I was able to call on the royal fires in the Deep. I know it will be difficult to do it from here, but once I do, it won't matter who I appoint after I defeat him. As long as I defeat him."

"And have you asked Nta how she feels about this?"

"Koj."

He chuckles and wipes his face. "Kh. I have always taken my role in our family seriously. You know this." He raises his wrist to show me his Knight of Danū mark. "So much that even the Helāni magic knows it."

"What is your point?"

"My point is, do not make me have to choose standing with you versus standing with our people. They have suffered enough. I have suffered enough."

I stare at him. His eyes are bloodshot, and my chest aches. Kaehante lost his aovate at the hands of the Empress, helping me try to take her down to defend our people of Danū. He lost her to save the many, and he doesn't want it to be in vain. Hell, this crew was made of rebels against the Empress, together against the tower. But I've always felt it was a lost cause.

I bow my head. "I understand you, cousin."

"I trust you, Nkella. I always have, but sometimes you can be rash. Promise me you will think things through."

"I will." We hold each other's gaze for a moment before a whistle makes us both turn to look at the water below. One of the mer-Ipani swimming beside us in our Aō bubble holds onto the side of the ship, trying to catch my attention. A pool of blood surrounds him as he struggles to carry someone over his shoulder. "Stop the ship!"

Reaching beneath the wheel, I yank the speed potion out but keep the invisibility up. This will lose us time.

Kae and I move quickly, grabbing rope and tossing it down. I'm already halfway down, taking the injured king's guard on my arm as Kae helps to carry him up.

Back onboard, we carry the injured guard to the main deck and lay him down. The man grimaces in pain. Burn marks slash over his eyes down to his chest. They cut so deep he's bleeding. His friend grips his hand.

"Get Tessa," I tell Kae. He runs below deck. Looking up to the king's guard, I ask, "What happened?"

"Tetalla's Aō security comes closer than expected. A wide range of electricity surrounds the island. Veloru was speeding before me and got caught in it before I could."

"Was anyone else down there?" Meaning how soon do we have before his army of dead come for us.

"Koj, but we cannot get through. We don't know how high the security fence goes. It can cut the ship in half."

Rōkan. I stand, facing the bow. "How far away was the electric fence?"

"About a mile south from here."

I squeeze my eyes shut, thankful I didn't send Iéle toward Danū. But if Lāri went this way, how high could the skies have security? Dread twists my stomach. Footfalls make me spin to find Nta and Kae running up the ramp.

"Tessa says to bring him down," Nta says. Kae is already scooping up the injured to take him to one of the rooms.

I turn to the guard. "We will care for him. What was your name?"

I'm Taremu." He points to himself. "My injured friend is Veloru."

"Iá. I'm Nkella, captain of this ship. Help me drop the anchor."

He nods, and we walk toward the bow.

"Drop the anchor?" Nta shouts over the wind as she runs after us. "Is someone going to tell me what's going on?"

Taremu explains to her what happened, and she gives me a worried look, but I say nothing as I grab the anchor and drop it overboard.

"Looks like you didn't need my help," Taremu states. I stare at my arm, which had shifted to my devil form without my awareness. My brows furrow. This is becoming second nature to me, and I hadn't noticed it happening.

"Looks like it," I say, then start back to the main deck. "Nta, call a meeting. Have Kae and Tessa meet me in my room when they're finished tending to Veloru."

I head to my cabin to grab my scope and look through it.

A popping sound draws my gaze downward. Iéle stands at my feet, and a sigh of relief escapes me. "You couldn't have shown up at a better time, my girl." I bend down and scratch behind her ears.

"Good thing, too," a gurgling voice echoes around us as the drakon's face appears from the Aō.

"And you found the drakon, Iéle. Well done."

"Or maybe," the drakon zooms in front of me and I grimace, "I found her."

"Kh. Where have you been, daí? Soren was taken."

"As I understand it, she made her choice to go." He spins his head. "To save you."

I bare my teeth at him. "Do not begin to argue with me, drakon."

"Come now, you know my name."

"Kh."

"Looking good back in your dark, brooding suit." He swims through the air around me, poking at my leather, and gurgles a laugh. "What can I do for you?"

"If you care about Soren, you will help me save her."

"Is Soren in need of saving?"

"Somebody once told me you care about your fur." I take my knife from my belt. He wiggles back, and I smirk.

"What would happen if you did save her? Would the bigger, meaner Devil in that castle just let her go?"

"Kh. He is not bigger."

The drakon laughs as the fins on either side of his neck wave in the air.

"I will not allow her or myself to be imprisoned. There is a way out of this, and I will find it. You can either help or stand—or float idly—by. The choice is yours."

He bows his head. "I'll help. But it's your funeral. Hopefully not hers. I like her very much, I do."

Tessa's motor comes up the ramp, followed by the footfalls and chatter of the rest of them.

"What do you know about the electric perimeter around Danū? How high from the sea does it reach?"

Katergaris turns his head toward the south, looking up. "I know he extracted the ouma from a dozen eel Ipani, so it cannot reach higher than this ship."

I ball my fist. "He's killing Ipani?"

My small crew gathers around us, followed by Taremu, falling silent to listen.

The drakon moves his head from side to side. "It's my only guess. Every Arcana the Empress sent him, he has not only killed but utilized their ouma."

Killed?

"How do you know this?"

"Drakons talk, you know. I do have friends."

I bring my fist to my mouth in thought. "How deep do you think it goes?"

"I haven't a clue. You might want to test it if you really want to go through."

"Or go around," Kae adds.

"That could take a long time," the drakon says.

"He's right," I say. "We don't know how wide the range is."

"So what do we do?" Nta asks.

I lock eyes with her. "What can cut through electricity?"

Her eyes widen. "The two of us can."

I smile. "So we go through."

7

NKELLA

My sister stares daggers at me as I pull the anchor back up.

"Have you even practiced your ouma lately?"

"Koj." I frown at her. "But now is the time to do it." I drop the anchor on top of a pile of ropes and jump down the bow.

"This is going to hurt," I hear Tessa mutter as she drives down the ramp to get the raku bombs I told her to grab.

"We don't even have time to prepare," Nta argues.

I spin to her. "Nta, what other choice do we have? How else can we get to Danū? With your ouma of volcano, and mine of air, we can do it together. Trust, daí?"

Her face pales. "And what if there's an army waiting on the other side? There are only five of us, and one injured below deck."

"That's what the bombs are for."

She breathes hard as she stares at me.

"Unless you have a better plan?"

She groans behind her teeth. She knows I'm right. There's no other way to Danū that won't require navigating around the perimeter, and without knowing exactly where it is or how far it goes. Time isn't on our side.

"When was the last time you connected with your ouma?" she asks. "Because it's been a long time for me, and there's no room for error. Any one of us could be hit—me, you, Kae, Tessa..."

"We won't fail." I squint at her and step closer, keeping my voice low. "Ntaouru, our ouma is second nature to us, daí? It's time you let it in."

She takes a deep breath. I don't blame her for hesitating. She wants to be strong for the crew, but I see the torment behind her eyes. I don't know how often she used her ouma while I was away, but it's clear she avoided it. The last time I remember her using it, she boiled Soanalo alive from the inside out and had no control over it. It pains me to think what else haunts her while she sleeps.

She licks her lips, something she does when she's nervous, and I touch her arm. "Never mind, Nta. I can do it. I'm strong enough."

"Don't—"

"Koj. I'm sorry I asked. I'm sure I can handle it on my own. Air can cut through electricity. I just need to form a barrier around the ship and turn up the speed." I leave her standing there before she can protest.

I stand at the wheel and open myself to the Aō, letting my ouma bond with its element. Immediately, whispers of the spirit of air surround me. I search within them for the right one. There are multiple spectral colors, visible only to me. But I look for a specific one, a feeling —the one strong enough to bring the Tower down if I was ever close enough. The one that comes around every season and devastates our buildings.

I hear my crew shouting from somewhere beyond the colors. I can't feel them, but with a thrust of my arms, strong winds circle the ship. My winds are the hurricane, and the ship is the eye.

With me directing them harder as we cut through the sea, I reach down and turn the speed potion all the way up. A mile should give us the momentum we need to break through. How far in we'll get... that's the question.

A calm settles in my chest. For the first time in a long time, I feel peace. It's just me and my element in the Aō. I spent so long bound, unable to connect with what makes me Ipani, that when I got it back, it almost felt alien. But I was already at war with myself as a Devil, back when I thought it was a curse—before I knew it was a trait of my family. I never stopped to lean into it.

Voices whisper around me from within the Aō, low and ancient. I'm pulled by the echo of spirits drifting on every current.

Have I reached a part of my ouma that connects me directly to the Aō dimension?

"Mikiroro..."

A warmth spreads from my chest to the rest of my body. The voices growing louder...saying my...name? The spirits have never spoken before.

"Nkella...Mikiroro..."

"I'm listening." I say it inside my mind.

"The royal flames of Danū speak to you."

"Fight."

"Fight." I repeat. "I will always fight."

"Yesss. Fight Tetalla and you will win. Make your father proud."

A rush of primal fury and adrenaline pulses through my veins. Fight Tetalla and I will win. "How do you know this?"

"Do you deny us, Nkella Mikiroro? We are the royal flames. We choose you to rule. Fight and you will win."

"I will fight."

"Then this is what you must do..."

The spirits speak to me all at once and it is as if those thoughts come with electricity sparking me with the urge to fight. To win.

And now I know exactly what I must do.

The ship vibrates, and light whips through the air as we pass through the electric barrier. I hold my ground, gripping the wheel as bolts of lightning slam into the wind shield.

I raise more winds, spinning them faster than I can keep up. My head spins with them, and my knees give out. I clutch the wheel as I hit the ground. A scream tears from my throat as more electricity tries to pierce my barrier.

A crash hits the ship. The mainmast has fallen over the deck, whipping violently. I fear it'll snap free.

I try to ignore it and keep the winds steady. Another bolt strikes and panic rises in my chest as the ship shakes. Fighting the urge to stay down, I stand, hands still gripping the wheel.

I catch sight of Ntaoru on the deck, and something that looks like the knee mounds of cypress trees rises from the sea. Another pokes out. It takes me a minute before I piece together that my sister is the cause of this. She's creating a volcanic wall from the sea floor to help disrupt the electricity.

I maintain my wind barrier until no more shocks come. We keep it up a little longer, then I ease the cyclone so we don't spin out from a sudden stop.

Finally, she turns to me, and I let the winds die.

Nta drops her arms and meets my eyes. A nervous smile lifts her mouth, and I give her a nod.

My gaze moves to the fallen mast. Tessa, Kae, and Taremu come up the ramp with weapons, ready for any undead from Tetalla's army that may be waiting. They stop short at the mast, and Kae bends down to lift it. I jump in to help.

"What do we do about this?" Kae asks.

Katergaris emerges, wrapping himself around the mast. He grows larger, starting to lift it into place.

"It'll have to be replaced, but for now grab my tools from my lab," Tessa says. "We can hold it together with some *omute* potion and rope."

"We can't go anywhere until this is fixed," Nta says. "We're sitting ducks."

I walk to the bow and scan the horizon for Tetalla's undead. The sun is dipping under the sea. Now that we're through the barrier, a battle can start at any moment.

My fingers curl over the rail. My pulse spikes with every mile that brings me closer to Soren. This delay will drive me mad.

My sister steps up beside me, and a muscle in my jaw tightens.

"Even under a cloaking, his Aō guards can still spot us. This isn't like the Empress—she doesn't know how to look into the Aō."

"I know this," I snap, then grit my teeth. We share the same worry, but I don't need a reminder of the obvious. "Be ready for a fight. I don't think we'll go unnoticed for long."

Will he be the one to meet me here? If he does, it'll be under the guise of his dead. I'll burn them all just to get to him. I'll be the one to watch the light leave his eyes. Then she'll be mine, alone.

"I know I'm strong, but this is getting boring," the drakon gurgles behind me. I sigh into my hand. Nta chuckles, unaware of the bloodlust scratching at the surface.

Kaehante and Taremu come back up the ramp with the tools. We turn to mend the mast while Katergaris holds it steady.

Two hours later and it's as good as we're going to get it. With the omute potion, it should stay intact until we can replace it.

I straighten and give my crew their orders. As few as they are, they're all I have.

A sharp pop cuts through the air. "Iéle?"

My wolf stands before me with her head bowed. I know that call. She wants to show me something. I lean down and press my forehead to hers.

A white drakon swoops from the direction of the Tower, snow trailing behind it. The Empress must have sent a drakon to Danū. But I can tell by the pull of the Aō that it isn't regular snow. How is it possible a Helāni drakon has ouma?

She must have sent that drakon to steal Soren and take her to the Tower, leaving me to deal with Tetalla. She knows if I see him, I'll kill him. And once the oumala snow has covered Danū, and Tetalla is dead, she'll come down and claim it.

This won't go the way she planned.

I won't let it.

Iéle skips forward in the memory. Oumala snow begins falling over the island.

No one will be prepared for this. Danū means "six suns." My people are unprepared and will freeze to death, especially with unmeltable snow.

I tense as Iéle follows the drakon to the castle. She defied my orders. If she'd been caught—

Iéle nips at me, drawing me back to the vision.

The drakon dives into the volcano, and Iéle follows. Something strikes the top, and boulders crash down. The undead guards are distracted, and the oumala animals in the Aō move to investigate. Meanwhile, the white drakon drops a sheet of snow over the castle, and it falls into the moat of royal flames.

She's going to reveal the way in. A secret I've kept from the Empress since I was old enough to know what she wanted from me.

She has always been after the Danū fire.

I knew she would betray us—me, Soren, my people. I knew from the beginning she only served herself. But it was the only way to save Soren.

She knows Soren is my weakness, and now she'll try and take Danū.

The white drakon slips into the caverns unnoticed, freezing everything in its wake.

Iéle backs away from the castle, and the vision ends.

My wolf licks at my face and I tap on her head.

This must have just happened.

"Captain?" Kaehante approaches. There's concern in his voice.

I have to move fast. I don't know how the Danū fire will react to oumala snow—or how Tetalla will use it. But one thing is certain. If Soren's still in that castle, she'll freeze to death.

"Captain?" Kae says again, louder.

Iéle whimpers. I stand and turn to him. "Take the wheel."

"Daí?"

"Just do it. Head for Danū."

After sprinting to my cabin to retrieve my bow and arrows, I head straight for Katergaris. He's already floating toward me, a wide grin showing from his silver-and-blue swirls of hair, with Tessa and Nta close behind. Taremu stands near the mast, scratching his head.

"Did something bad happen?" Tessa asks. "Is Soren okay?"

Nta crosses her arms. "I don't like that look in your eyes, Nkella."

I ignore her, but she follows me.

"Tell me you're not about to ditch all the plans and improvise."

When I don't answer her, she grabs my arm. "Tell me, brother," she says, stepping closer. "What's changed?"

I give her a solemn glance. "No time to explain. We have to act now."

My eyes lock on the drakon. "Katergaris," I command. "Take me to Cavern Castle. We're getting Soren out."

His pupils dilate. A wicked grin spreads across his face. "That's exactly what I've been waiting to hear, captain."

8

SOREN

I DUCK UNDER THE OPEN WINDOW AS A BOULDER CATAPULTS from the top of the volcano and lands on empty homes, rolling over them. My eyes squeeze shut and I hold my breath as the castle floors shake beneath my knees. Any minute now, another boulder is going to hit, and it's going to punch straight through the wall I'm leaning on.

A moan makes me open my eyes to Bobby crawling toward me, his bones rattling as he moves on his hands and kneecaps.

"What's causing this?" I ask him, knowing he can't form actual words. He reaches for me, and I grab his bony hand, letting him guide me away from the window. Tetalla is busy dealing with whatever war might be knocking on the castle doors, so Bobby, for the moment, is just himself.

I crawl to the bed and prop myself up, staring out the window from a safe distance. Or at least, safe enough. Nowhere is safe right now. What do I do? There's no way out of here, but I can't stay either. Staying here is a one-way ticket to plummeting into the royal fires.

First, it's snowing inside the volcano, and now this? Snow doesn't cause earthquakes. Someone else is out there hitting the castle, and I doubt it's the crew. They wouldn't aim for the place I'm staying at. They know it could kill me. This is definitely related, and there's only one other person I know capable of this.

Something white and sinewy flashes past the window and I jump to my feet. A blanket of snow has draped over most of the inside of the cavern during the last few minutes and I blink at it. There are pockets of red flames underneath the snow...

Because that's not weird at all.

The sinewy serpent comes back around, dropping more snow, and I immediately recognize her as the drakon from outside the Tower. Her big eyes lock on me and she swoops sideways toward my window. Her silver strands almost glow in the reflection of the snow she's left behind.

I knew the drakons were half Helāni magic and half oumala, but I didn't know they could possess ouma. Gari doesn't.... All he can do is go into the Aō.

She presses her body against the wall and lowers herself just below the window. "Come with me," she whispers.

"The Empress sent you." It isn't a question.

"Yesss.... And we haven't much time." Her voice sings like a whisper. Unlike like Gari's gurgling nonsense... even though I like his nonsense.

"I knew it had to be the Empress doing this. I was starting to think she meant to kill me too. Then again, I thought she needed me alive, so..."

"Are you coming? The Arcana won't be able to distract much longer."

"Right." I glance at Bobby, who's now standing and staring at the drakon, unmoving. Is he calling Tetalla? Either way, he'll know I've left. It's now or never.

Stepping through the teardrop window, I grab onto the drakon's soft fur and carefully let myself drop over her body. She shifts slightly upward to catch my weight.

Bobby stands at the window and moans something, lifting his hand to me.

"Sorry, Bobby," I tell him. "It's been fun, but I can't stay here."

The drakon swoops down toward the dark abyss, and I clutch her neck. "Hang on tight," she says.

Cold wind lashes my face as the bottom of the abyss looms closer than it ever has. Freezing air replaces what should be boiling heat.

"Wait! Why are we going down? Aren't we meant to be getting out of here?"

"Trust me," she sings.

"Not exactly my forte, drakon lady. Start talking."

"You have no choice but to trust me now, darling child. Can't go anywhere, can you?"

I cringe. She even sounds like the Empress.

"And my name is Krua."

Krua.

She makes a sharp turn to the left. Molten lava appears in clumps along the rock walls. Blue and red streaks send waves of heat over my body, quickly replaced by frost. Hold up.

HOLD THE PHONE.

"How is your ouma snow putting out *royal fires?*" These are royal fires, aren't they? Not just ouma fire. Pretty sure that's how it was explained to me by Nkella, Sehu, his father, Tetalla himself.... This doesn't make sense.

"My ouma snow is royal." She makes a hard right inside a tight opening that leads to another dark cavern.

My lips press together at the drop in temperature. My heart pounds. Royal ouma? This drakon?

My mind races as we slither through the air somewhere under the castle, deep inside the volcano.

How does a drakon possess royal ouma?

Would royal snow come from Piupeki, if royal fire comes from Danū? That would make sense but... "H-how?" I manage to ask.

"Hold on tight." She ignores my question.

"You already said tha—" A yelp escapes the back of my throat as the drakon jerks upward, climbing into what feels like a ninety-degree angle.

My thighs burn as I tighten them on either side of Krua's long body, my fingers slipping.

I squeeze my eyes shut, waiting for it to be over.

My chest aches from breathing in the cold wind. I try to bury my face in her fur. Krua veers sideways, taking a wicked turn, and I swear if she makes one more move like that, my fingers are going to let go.

The air around me stills as her body begins to level, and I no longer feel like I'm about to fall. My eyes open, and I let out a sigh of relief as the dark ocean view and the Nautilus stars span around me.

I'm out.

I feel like I can breathe again.

But for how long? Once Tetalla figures out that I'm gone and he beats whatever battle with the Arcana he's fighting, because he will—he'll come for me.

As we fly over Danū, Krua keeps spreading her snow over the ground below. I squint at how empty everything looks. It looked empty when I first arrived with Tetalla as well, so this can't be because of the snow. It's fuller in the Deep, unless the people are hiding somewhere...

Krua takes us higher, and we fly above the giant serpent skeleton barrier.

"We're going to the Tower?" Stupid question. Where else would she be taking me? "I can't hide in the Tower forever... Did the Empress tell you how long I'd be there?"

"She doesn't tell me anything, only what she needs me to do."

"Th-that doesn't surpr-ise me..." My teeth chatter. "Why d-didn't s-she have an Arcana soldier just t-take me there? Would've been quicker. I'm f-freezing." I know what I sound like right now, but seriously, I'm so cold, my voice is shaking.

"Because all the Arcana are being wasted to act as a decoy. To save you."

"To s-save me?"

If fury could literally boil my blood, I'd be back to warm right now. All her Arcana? No. I don't believe she'd use up all her Arcana just to get me out. Obviously the snow was the plan, and she needs to keep me alive for her little scheme of wanting me to join her one day so this world doesn't collapse.

"So the quakes were the soldiers?"

"What did I just finish telling you? I know as much as you."

I bite my tongue.

"The Arcana was sent to take out his dead while you two were at dinner."

My eyes widen. So those messages she was sending were good for something. She was timing when we'd get them and knew what time of day we'd sit together.

"She knew eventually he'd realize something was amiss and send you to your room, but by then it would be too late. I would have already spread my snow and gone to collect you while he fights Arcana. I thought the quakes came from his defenses."

"Not that I know of. Could Arcana have been throwing boulders at the volcano?"

"No. That wasn't us. We think they're earthquakes, but that has never happened here before."

Earthquakes?

Something whips past my ear and I scream. "What was that?"

"What is what?"

"I don't know." I look around me but don't see anything. Then something brushes against my arm and I gasp. Turning my head slowly, I catch a view of blue fur with silvery streaks, and then they come into focus.

Nkella's fierce eyes pin me in place, and my heart stops. His black leather coat billows behind him as he grips Gari's fur.

"Nkella?"

"Soren, our potion is wearing out. You're going to have to hop on."

"Give her the invisibility potion," Gari gurgles in his singsong voice.

My legs begin to shake.

Krua snaps her head to look at them and swings us to the side. Gari takes a dive as they go out of focus again. They scream something, but I can't make it out through the winds that are picking up around us. Krua seems to be having trouble flying through this new turbulence, and I scream as I accidentally catch air when she makes a weird move with her back, before I realize Gari has wrapped his tail around hers.

Nkella's arm wraps around me, and I grab onto him.

"No!" Krua yells. "You don't know what she'll do to me. Please. Come back!"

I stare at her, then at him. "She's right. I can't let her take the rap for me leaving with you." I sit in front of him, but look back at his gorgeous face I missed so much. I want nothing more than to kiss him right now.

"I am not letting you go," he says sternly.

Krua hits Gari's side, trying to knock us off.

"Hold on, you two!" Gari calls to us. A wave of silvery force flies out of him, knocking Krua back. I forgot he could do that, but he explained to me once that it wasn't ouma.

Gari nose-dives, and I bury my face in his fur, catching a glimpse of Krua being blown backward.

Guns start shooting at us, and my heart lunges into my throat. Over in the distance, rows of undead aim their weapons at Krua.

"We are still under invisibility," Nkella reassures me, handing me a small vial. I chug it so we don't look weird, me just floating in the air. As long as nothing gets close enough to us to break the barrier, we won't be seen.

"But not for long," Gari singsongs.

Nkella wraps his arms tighter around my torso as we speed away from Danū. I'm afraid to look behind me. I'm afraid Krua got hit. Not that I'd be able to see it—if she got hit, she'd be badly wounded and in the ocean. She may work for the Empress, but just like every other one of her soldiers, or "pets," they're all her prisoners. I heard her when she said she didn't know what she'd do to her.

She was only doing her job, and now because of me, she's going to be punished. If she didn't get shot down first.

Nkella's hands fall to my thighs and I shiver at his touch. He grips my skin, and I take his hand, holding onto Gari with the other. I could let go of Gari altogether, and Nkella would never let me fall.

Suddenly, despite the gunfire and my escape from Cavern Castle, a sense of peace washes over me. He found me, and I know I never want to leave his side again.

But this isn't right. By now, Tetalla knows I'm missing, and he'll kill—

Wait a minute.

He'll think the Empress took me. He'll have no idea the snow drakon was overtaken by Nkella.

The *Devil's Gambit* comes into view.
I'm finally going back home, with my family. My crew.

9

SOREN

The cold wind bites at my cheeks as Gari's long body slices through the sky. The ocean glimmers far below us under the bright Nautilus swirls among the stars, but my focus isn't on the horizon. Nkella's arms embrace my stomach, holding me tight and I'm so afraid of waking up back in the castle, all of this having been a dream.

I want to turn, to face him, but I can't bring myself to. My chest is tight, my pulse beating louder than the wind in my ears. He came for me. I was so afraid he stopped loving me because he thought I betrayed him. But he still came.

The *Devil's Gambit* looms closer, its dark silhouette rising from the waves. I feel his breath against the back of my neck as Gari dips lower. I should feel relief. Now that we're almost back, I know we're going to have to talk about what happened.

Gari lands hard on the deck, the ship groaning under his weight. My body lurches forward, but before I can steady myself, Nkella's arm tightens around my waist, firm and unyielding. He holds me there for a beat too long, his touch searing through the light fabric of the outfit I'm made to wear in the castle. I swallow hard, forcing myself to pull away.

I slide off Gari's back, landing unsteadily on the deck. Before I can take a step, Nkella is there, dismounting behind me. He reaches out, his hand brushing against my arm as he steadies me. The contact is brief but electric, sending a pulse of heat through me.

I look up, and for the first time in weeks, our eyes meet.

The sharp edges of his cheekbones are shadowed, his jaw tight, his eyes burning with the beast he hides inside. Anger? Relief? Pain? It's all there, layered beneath his stoic mask, and I so badly want to reach for him, to say something, but the words tangle in my throat. My fingers twitch at my sides, desperate to close the distance between us, but the weight of the crew's stares keeps me frozen.

Nkella's gaze drops to my lips for a fleeting second, and my breath catches. He looks like he wants to say something, but instead, his eyes dip down to what I'm wearing, and my cheeks heat.

A flash of anger crosses his eyes, but he quickly hides it. I can imagine what he's thinking, wondering if Tetalla's touched me. He knows I wouldn't wear something this revealing on my own accord.

He takes off his coat and hands it to me. "It's snowing in Danū," he says quietly." I swallow at his words and wrap his jacket around me, immediately taking in his scent of smoke and rum.

"Captain," Tessa calls from her wheelchair, her voice cutting through the tension. "Welcome back, Soren. We missed you, and I'm glad you're safe."

Her grin is wide, but her voice carries an edge. Memories of AJ flood in as I force myself to look at her, and I push through the haze of emotions threatening to swallow me whole. The last time I saw Tessa, I promised to bring AJ back from the Deep. But bringing back the dead isn't possible. His situation wasn't like Nkella's. AJ really is... gone. "I missed you too, Tessa." My voice trails into the thrashing of the waves against the ship.

Kaehante stands a step behind her, his tall frame silhouetted against the brightness of the moon. He nods once, his expression unreadable as always. Ntaoru is beside him. Neither of them says a word, but their presence is enough to stir the guilt clawing at my insides.

A mer-Ipani walks up from the stern. He's tall, with bluish green shimmering scales tracing his arms and neck over his stripes, and his golden eyes glimmer in the moonlight. He takes a glance toward me but looks away, the tension probably making it awkward for him. "I'll be checking on Veloru," he tells my crew and continues to walk down the ramp.

Nkella doesn't look at me. His focus is on the horizon, his shoulders stiff, his jaw clenched. The silence between us is unbearable, a living, breathing thing that wraps around my throat and squeezes. I want to reach for him, to close the gap, but the crew is watching, and the weight of their eyes pins me down.

"I'm sorry," I say finally, the words spilling out before I can stop them. I'm not even sure what I'm apologizing for... they know I'm sorry for AJ; they went through it as well.

For accepting Tetalla's deal and saving Nkella?

Or for making them worry about me.

Tessa drives a little closer to me. "You did what you thought was best. You brought our captain back from the Deep. And you're here now."

My shoulders drop. "You know I can't stay though, right? I made a deal so that Nkella stays alive and out of the Deep. If I break it, Tetalla will send Nkella back."

He snorts and I stare at him. "I did not make that deal, Soren. I didn't want this, you know that."

"I didn't have a choice."

He starts to pull away but I follow him. "I still stand by my decision. I wasn't going to leave you in the Deep—"

He spins around. "I told you I would wait for you."

"In the Deep," I snap. "And I would have to live out the rest of my life knowing I could have saved you? That I could have brought you back..."

"And now I have to stand by and be fine with another Devil taking you as his?" Moonlight glints off his sharp canines as his grimace deepens. His eyes fall to my body and his voice cuts off. I shake my head at him, a tear threatening to run down my cheek. "You were my aovate, Soren. We promised ourselves to each other."

Were. There, he said it. The reason why our aovate connection has been cut off. It's my fault. My heart feels like ice has stabbed it, and I don't even care that we're having this conversation in front of everyone.

Tetalla never touched me. He wanted to, but I never let him, and he won't force himself on me because he knows he needs me to submit willingly. Forcing me won't get him my power. But how would Nkella believe me, especially wearing what I'm wearing?

"I just wanted you back here, safe, and alive," I say above a whisper.

"What good is it if we can't be together?" he says.

My heart skips a beat. "Maybe we can be," I mutter. "I don't think Tetalla is going to keep his end of the bargain, so I'm not going to keep mine."

His brow quirks but his frown deepens.

"We would have to be careful. I won't risk him killing you, or sending you to the Deep."

Ntaoru clears her throat and I glance at her. She's leaning against the rail with her arms crossed, waiting for us to finish arguing, but she catches me looking at her. "What do you mean he's not going to keep his end of the bargain?"

Tessa and Kaehante lean in.

I lick my lips. Nkella is still staring at me, and I can tell he's more bothered by what I'm wearing than he's letting on. I wrap his coat tighter around me.

I wipe my face, my nerves on end. "Maybe we should go inside and I'll tell you about it."

"That's a good idea. It's cold out here." Tessa reverses her chair. Nkella walks past her, heading for his captain's room, and the rest of us follow. The ship rocks as we make our way up.

Inside, a gas lantern and candles light the room enough for us to see. It's warmer in here, but I make sure to keep his coat wrapped tightly around me.

I turn to the crew and tell them all about the conversation I overheard between Tetalla and the red drakon, about him demanding any soldier—no matter if they're Ipani—to be obliterated. He only cares about his bottom line. Eventually I'll just be a pawn in his way.

I also tell them about my visit with the Empress, and how I'm a double spy.

Nkella huffs and I stare at him. He lets a chuckle leave his lips and my eyes widen.

"Did you just chuckle at me?"

A gleam I'm happy to see in his eyes twinkles back at me. "We have come full circle, daí?"

"It's not funny."

"You are right. It's not. The only utwa I want you being, is my utwa." His tone darkens again.

I swallow but rip my eyes away from him. "There's something else. The drakon that took me out of the castle said those tremors weren't caused by the Empress. It was something else."

The crew exchange glances among each other. "Where did it come from then?" Tessa asks.

"I don't know. And also, I can no longer check." I hold up my wrist to show my magic dampener. "We have a bigger problem."

Gari, now shrunken down in size to fit in the room wraps my wrist with the tip of his tail, and brings it up to his nose to sniff. Speaking of sniff, I scan the room for Iéle but don't see her.

"What does this mean, Soren?" Nkella now pulls my wrist away from Gari to inspect it himself.

"It means I have no powers. Tetalla has found a way to communicate with the Aō, more than I've seen any Ipani do... He's found a way to pause my Fate magic with this dampener..." I stare at Nkella, who looks deep in thought. "Like the rikorō dampeners, but not for ouma... for the Fates.

"How? An Ipani cannot control Helāni magic..." his voice trails.

I shrug. It was through the Aō. I saw him floating over the floor once, deep in some sort of meditative state. He usually sees me coming, but this time he was so deep into it that he had no idea I was there."

"The Aō mixed with Helāni magic," Ntaoru reminds everyone. "If he has somehow convinced the Aō to do his will, we have a bigger problem."

I stare at her. "Exactly. He's getting too strong. And soon, he might not even need me there at all."

Nkella's eyes harden and now there's fear in them.

"I should go back," I say. "He knows I'm gone, and even though he'll assume the Empress took me, the next place he might look is around the *Devil's Gambit.* Last thing I need is for him to come whispering around me or send his dead and find that I'm here, and then you're all in danger." They already are all in danger with me being here. Especially Nkella. "I was never meant to be on this ship. I was supposed to be at the Tower."

Being with the Empress I could have explained to Tetalla, as his double agent. All while trying to find a way to put an end to it all. But this is dangerous.

"I'm not sending you back to him, Soren." Nkella's words sound final, but I can't let him keep me here like this.

"I have to. You know the deal."

"I don't care if I go back to the Deep."

This again. I clench my jaw. "We have to be smart. Remember, you're here to save your people. Who will fight him?"

"Exactly," Kaehante mutters and I nod at him.

Nkella lifts his chin. "Kh. Let him come find me."

"He won't have to, Nkella. You've been in the Deep; I'm sure he can just sense you. Not to mention all the oumala guards he has in the Aō searching for our familiars." My stomach coils at the thought of Philo.

"Kh. I was not dead."

That's true.

He turns to Gari. "Send word out to the rabbit, Sapphire, to stay away. I will say the same to Iéle about the pack."

Gari's fins on the sides of his head flutter in response.

"One night," Nkella says coming toward me. My brow quirks at him. "Give me this night, and tomorrow, you will go back as my utwa."

"Great just what I needed to be. A triple spy."

"Except your loyalty is to me, is it not?"

His deepened voice has me licking my lips. "Of course it is."

"While you're there, try to find where the citizens of Danū are in hiding. They are cave people and won't be out on the island. They will freeze to death with the snow drakon spreading ouma snow everywhere."

"They weren't in the empty homes by the castle either," I say.

"There are more caverns and volcanoes across the island," Kae says. "Cities of them."

My eyes widen. "I'll try to convince him to let me walk around." Although, I'm not sure how I'll do that, especially not now after this escapade. "But you should know, staying in touch will be hard."

"Leave that to me," his eyes flash with the gold veins in a crimson glow. "I plan to infiltrate."

I stare at him. "Why am I not surprised?"

"Kh. This needs to end. Am I not the one that has to fight him?" We lock eyes for a beat. He's not wrong. He does have to fight him, and take him down. Only a Devil can fight another Devil...and there aren't any others alive.

"What about the tremor?" I ask. "If the falling boulders weren't caused by the Arcana, could the volcano be erupting?"

"Koj, not with royal fire."

"What could it have been then?" I ask.

Silence befalls the room.

"Well," Tessa starts, "we're not going to figure it out tonight, I know that much. We'll leave you two..." She eyes Kae and Ntaoru.

"Oh yes, we should see to the injured mer-Ipani below deck, and our new friend." She elbows Kae who stares at her for a second before realizing they're leaving the room.

Nkella approaches Gari, and whispers something. The drakon's eyes bulge so wide they look cartoonish against his shrunken body. Kae glances at them and his brows knit together. Gari hurries away after him.

Whatever Nkella told him, he doesn't want the rest of us to hear.

I follow them out with my gaze, grateful to have been able to see them again, even though it was dangerous, and only for a night.

Nkella locks the door right after they leave, and we're finally alone. The dim lights of his room give him almost a sinister allure, and it reminds me of how he looked in the cave in the Deep.

I want to ask him what that was about, but decide against it given the look he's giving me right now.

He walks toward me slowly. I bite my lip as he grabs his belt and undoes it in one simple movement, tossing it to the floor. My breath hitches, and he pulls his shirt over his head and tosses it. His tribal tattoos over his Ipani stripes decorate his chiseled arms and torso, and I'm yearning to touch him.

He's on me before I can say his name. He stops before me and his eyes dip maliciously to my sheer clothing. With both hands he grabs at the fabric of my top and rips it in half, a loud tear coming from the cloth as he pulls it apart like a savage beast, exposing my breasts for him to see.

He pulls me up from my waist and my legs immediately straddle him as he sets me down on his bed. "I want to hear you scream my name, my Neyuro."

The way he's dipped his tone has my heart racing.

His head dips down to my nipple and he takes it in his mouth. A loud moan rips from my throat and I hope the thrashing of the waves on the ship will be loud enough to muffle the screams he's promised to draw from me.

He moves lower and takes the sheer pants I have on in his hands and rips them up as well. He isn't gentle when he rips my panties away either, and I swallow a yelp. He doesn't hurt me, but he definitely wants the garments Tetalla has made me wear destroyed by his hands.

"You will go back wearing my clothes."

I swallow.

He lowers his lips to my pussy and his tongue comes out, forked—the Devil he keeps at bay coming out to play. His tongue wraps around my clit and squeezes as he opens his mouth and sucks on me. I moan loudly, wrapping my fingers through his hair until I feel his horns protruding out. "Nkella—" I call out his name and it makes him lick me harder, pushing on my sensitive area, sending a wave of heat tingling up my legs and up my spine.

"Louder, Soren. I want him to hear it."

I bite my lip, and start to sit up. He's pissed and I get it, but this isn't okay. He pushes me back down.

"Wait," I tell him.

He glances up at me.

He has to know nothing ever happened. I tilt his chin to bring him up to face me, and he obliges.

"What is it?"

"Listen... Tetalla and I—" he winces but I keep going, "I never had sex with him."

His gaze fixes on me and now he sits up.

"He never touched me, Nkella. He wanted to. Maybe he still does, but I never let him."

He stares at me.

"I belong to you."

"Yes, you do," he says and pulls me lower by my waist. I yelp and a chuckle escapes me. This time he lowers himself on top of me, and I feel his girth slip inside me, stretching me. My eyes roll to the back of my head as Nkella's cock grows inside me, shifting to his devil form as he pushes in and out. But I'm not scared of him. I haven't been for a long time now. My nails dig into the muscles in his back as my body moves up and down with him, almost to the rhythm of the ship.

His body is warm against mine, and as I kiss his chin, and his neck, sparks of our ouma connection start to pulse through my body. And suddenly that familiar feeling of him inside my soul is back. I can feel him physically—oh god, how I can, but I can sense all of his emotions at once. His desire, his lust for me, but also his love.

I try to look at him as his body thrusts inside me, and he catches my gaze, immediately taking my lips in his.

He deepens the kiss, driving harder into me, slow enough that I feel every inch. My breath catches, trapped somewhere between our mouths. I wrap my legs around him, pulling him closer, feeling his hips press firmly against mine. Every thrust fills me completely, stretching me again, making me ache in the best possible way.

Nkella breaks the kiss, trailing his lips down my throat. His subtle fangs scrape gently against my skin, sending a sharp pulse straight down between my legs. I tilt my head back, exposing more of my neck to him, craving the bite of his teeth. His breath warms my skin, ragged and hot, matching the rhythm of his hips.

His hand slides down my body, gripping my ass, holding me in place as his thrusts quicken. I arch beneath him, nails scraping along his back. He groans softly, burying his face into the crook of my neck, each breath heavy and harsh against my ear.

I rock my hips upward, meeting his movements, matching his pace. The friction between our bodies builds relentlessly, each stroke bringing me closer to the edge. My body trembles beneath him, my breath coming out in short, uneven gasps.

"I feel you," he murmurs roughly against my skin. "Everywhere."

His words drive me further, pushing me closer to release. My muscles tighten, pulling him deeper. I can feel him tense above me, his movements growing sharper, more urgent.

Pleasure rolls through me in waves, leaving my thighs trembling as his body shudders, hips pressed tight against mine, and his breath tickles against my neck.

He grips me tighter, hips snapping forward one last time, hard and deep, pushing me over the edge. My body clenches around him as he follows, his body now quivering.

For a long moment, neither of us moves as we lie tangled and warm, our bodies still joined. Eventually, he lifts his head to meet my eyes, his gaze heavy.

"Mine," he whispers, and kisses me softly this time, gentle and slow.

10

NKELLA

SHE SHIFTS BENEATH ME, GAZE DARK AND HUNGRY AS HER hands trail slowly down my chest, sending heat pulsing lower. Her fingertips skate along the edge of my hip, then sink down, her hand wrapping firmly around my cock. My breath catches, and I grip the sheets at either side of her.

"What are you—" I begin, but the words dissolve as she moves her body lower, her lips brushing softly against my abdomen, my hipbone, and then lower still.

"You've only done this to me, and I don't think it's fair," she says.

When her mouth closes around me, my whole body jolts at the slide of her tongue. My muscles tense as her tongue slides along the underside of my cock. Her eyes never leave mine, watching me closely as if she enjoys my reaction as much as I do. The soft moans she makes around me send vibrations through my entire body, drawing out a low, ragged groan from my throat.

Her hands grip my thighs, holding me steady as she moves faster, taking me in deeper, guiding me into pleasure I've never felt before. Her tongue swirls around the tip, pulling another groan from my chest.

"Soren," I whisper, voice rough and broken.

She hums softly, the sound rippling through me, driving me dangerously close to release. I grip her hair, careful not to hurt her, but desperate for something to hold onto as she works me expertly with her lips and tongue.

"I'm close," I manage, my voice strained, breath shallow. But she doesn't slow down; she moves quicker, more insistently, driving me to the edge. Heat tightens in my core, pulsing, building, until I'm unable to hold back. My hips buck involuntarily as I shudder into her mouth, pleasure washing over me, sharper and deeper than anything before.

When the trembling subsides, I collapse back onto the mattress, my chest heaving. She moves up beside me, resting her head on my chest. Her breath tickles my skin as her hand lazily traces my stripes along my stomach.

Eventually, our breathing slows, and our bodies relax into each other as sleep pulls us under.

Sunlight filters gently through the window when I wake. Her soft breaths warm my chest, her red hair tangled across my skin. I glance down at her peaceful face, a warmth settling deep in my chest.

I didn't think anything could feel better than last night, but waking up with her curled against me beats it.

I wrap a leg around her slender form and flip her onto her back. She looks up at me through those dark lashes, her breath quickening beneath my touch. My fingers brush along the softness of her cheek, sliding gently into her red hair. Golden flakes of the Aō's ouma shimmer faintly against her fair skin, tracing the lines of her collarbone.

The Aō is bonding us together again. If only she could see what I do, feel me the same way I feel her. But this is the caveat of being with a human; only one of us will feel the bond more intensely.

The reflection from the brass royal Danū coin glistens under the

Aō's influence. A purple wave sweeps across it, catching my gaze and irritating me slightly for diverting my attention from her beautiful face.

"What are you thinking?" she whispers and I stare back at her.

"How do you feel, my aovate?"

Her eyes light up when I call her this and I smile as her cheeks grow a pink color.

"I feel…" She breathes in deep, looking around her. *AJ used to tell me that he felt some of the Aō with Lāri, or at least what he thought it felt like.* "Like the world around me is made of magic. She bites her lip and now I want to feel them again. I dip my head down and reclaim her bottom lip, sucking on it gently before I ravish her mouth.

She moans inside my mouth and I feel myself getting hard again.

Maybe our love is strong enough for her to experience the ouma harder than anyone. Makes me want to keep her in my bed forever.

The sound of the crew's voices come from the direction of the wheel and I grimace. Soren chuckles close to my lips.

"Koj."

"Koj what?" she says with that bemused voice of hers.

"We are not leaving here. Not yet."

Her heart rate picks up in her throat, and I sense a shift in the air. Reality is starting to seep in and she's nervous. Anxious about having to go back to Tetalla. How I wish I could prevent that.

"Nkella—"

I sigh and pull myself off her, regretting it the moment I do. My eyes drop on her naked body and the regret is growing worse. "Killing my enemies is the only way I can be with her and take back Danū, which is exactly what I'm going to do. I just can't let her, or my crew, know just yet."

"Nkella?"

Soren snaps me from my thoughts of the day's plans and I meet her eyes. She grabs the sheets and sits herself up. I fight the urge to push her back on my bed and take her again. Instead, I get up and swipe up what I need off the floor.

"You need clothes to go back today."

Since I ripped them off her last night.

I turn and hand her a pair of my pants and the smallest tunic I own.

Black on black. With her red hair, she looks sleek. Sexy. I have to tear my eyes away from her so I can get dressed.

Once done, her arms wrap around me. I hold her in place and lean down to kiss her.

"I love you," she tells me.

Turning around, I continue to hold her and look into her eyes. "I will kill anyone on the planet who thinks they can keep me away from you."

Her lashes flutter. "A simple I love you back would have been enough, Nkella." She lets go of me and opens the door. "So intense," she mumbles. I chuckle and follow her out.

The air is crisp with a biting wind, quickly bringing me back to what happened yesterday with the snow drakon. My gaze lands on Kae who is at the wheel wearing his thick Piupeki coat. Soft chatter comes from Tessa and the two mer-Ipani from below. Soren climbs down the stairs to meet them but I stay up here. This ship used to be filled with AJ's dumb jokes and laughter.

Forcing myself away from those thoughts, I stare out at Danū. We're far enough to not be seen, especially with the cloaking, but close enough to see the peaks of the mountains covered in snow. The people are underground hiding from it; this I know only because I know my people, and snow is not something they are prepared for. But are they snowed in? I already know they've been starving under the Empress's reign. What about under Tetalla's?

Closing my eyes, I search for the connection I had made with the royal flames when they spoke to me, reaching for their wild, raw power. Silence fills my mind. My ouma of air rises up, knowing I'm searching for something... But I bypass it. The Devil inside me stirs. Yes... That's closer.

Silence.

I'm too far still.

"Captain?"

My eyes open to Kaehante approaching from behind me.

"The seas are quiet, Captain." He leans next to me overlooking the rail. "Too quiet."

"Yes." We are both thinking the same. After what happened last night, it is far too quiet for comfort. What is Tetalla planning?

"Do we have a heading?"

I turn around to look at him. He has a black bandana wrapped over his bald head and is wearing his winter coat.

"Soren goes back to distract Tetalla while we infiltrate and catch him off-guard. You will rescue Soren while I fight Tetalla."

He stares back out to sea. A crinkle forms in his temple as it does when he's thinking hard. "How are we going to get past his guards within the Aō?"

"We won't need to worry about it."

His brows raise.

"First, breakfast, daí?" I push myself off the rail. "I could eat a drakon."

If I tell any of them what I plan to do, they'll only try and stop me. As of now, Tetalla doesn't know the extent of the power I reached in the Deep. He thinks that because he governs the Deep and holds the Death Card, he knows all. But what he does not know, is my advantage.

The aroma of the warm spices the Hermit left us with makes my stomach growl and I turn to see my aovate walking up the ramp with a steaming cup of something delicious. The way my pants hug her hips stirs something inside me and I want to drag her back into my bed. She turns the corner and her cheeks redden when she sees me staring at her. Tessa rolls up behind her with Taremu following behind.

"Here," Soren hands me the cup in her hand. "This is from the stash the Hermit left for Harold, it's the dark coffee with chocolate he likes.

I take it from her and take a sip. The hot beverage warms my throat and instantly gives me a jolt.

"Do you like it?"

My brow quirks. "Hn. It needs something." I hand it to her and she gives me questioning look as I pull out my flask and pour a few drops of rum.

"Seriously? That's going to give it the opposite effect."

"Koj." I take my mug back. "Not to me."

"And, I meant for us to share that."

I hand it back to her. "Do you want more?"

She rolls her eyes. "No."

"Kh."

Tessa's chair motor interrupts my fixed stare on Soren and I turn to look at her as she drives up to us. "Nkella, I tried to give Soren a bandolier with at least a few weapons, but she refuses to take anything."

A muscle in my jaw flexes. "It is wise she goes back with none. Tetalla will strip her of any weapons and make her pay the price for bringing them in. He has already taken her power; let's not push him more than we already are."

"And how much more are we pushing him, Captain?" Kae asks, adjusting the pistol at his hip.

I turn to him. "Do not think for a second that Tetalla does not know where she is, daí? We may be cloaked with transparency potion, but it is temporary until he sends his dead to find her."

"Or he comes himself," Tessa mutters.

"That would only be a gift to me, Tessa."

They share an unreadable look among one another and I can only guess it's because they're not sure if I am ready for a fight with Tetalla or not. I don't let this bother me, and instead, continue my plan.

"The Empress is the other to worry about now. She didn't just cover Danū with snow to allow us a reunion." I brush my hand to Soren's wrist, where she has the dampener. "I know you cannot use this, so you cannot see the immediate past, meaning we do not have the upper hand against the magic they wield."

She grimaces, but I squeeze her hand.

"We will get your power back, Soren. I promise you. But we need to prepare for more than one fight, one that includes the Empress."

My sister walks up from the ramp, fully prepared for battle.

"I just wish I could help," Soren says. "I hate feeling useless." She tugs on it.

Ntaoru walks up next to Soren. "Just like you returned the Ipani their ouma, we will help you remove that dampener." I give them a nod but don't miss Tessa's brows furrowing at Ntaoru's bombs on her bandolier.

"Should we be strapping up?" Tessa interrupts.

"You should all be strapped up," I say. "Always."

Tessa flicks her gaze at Kae and then they quickly leave to get dressed. I don't like leaving my crew in the dark, but in this case, anything can happen. And that means, if Aō forbid, any of them die, Tetalla will leech the information out of them. Ntaoru was a risk, but I needed someone in the know.

"Taremu."

He turns.

"How is Veloru?"

"Healing well. He can walk but he's resting until he can swim."

"How long do you think that will take?"

"It's up to him. Are we infiltrating now?"

"Koj. Not yet."

"Wait," Soren grabs my arm. "You're *not* infiltrating yet. I'm going back. Now."

"Everything will happen at the right time," I tell her. She frowns at me. "Is there anything you can tell me about the Empress's plans?"

She shakes her head. "No, but I'm sure Lāri has to know something."

The drakon emerges into the light with a pop from the Aō. "Are you ready?" Soren nods, thinking he's talking to her.

"It's time, everyone," Soren declares, and I smirk to myself.

"Says who, daí?"

She stares at me with an arched brow.

"Are you our captain?" I ask her, keeping my voice steady, but I'm still fighting the pull of my lips threatening to break into a smile.

"You're the captain, Nkella. But it is time for me to go back..."

I take her by the arm, and pull her in the direction of my cabin. "First, we talk. Then you can go back."

She sighs deeply. "We're stalling," she mutters.

Yes, we are.

11

SOREN

He shuts the door behind us and I spin around to face him. "Nkella, what are you—

He pins me to the wall and lifts me up. My legs immediately straddle him. He wastes no time in kissing me, devouring my mouth as if my lips will be his last meal.

I moan into him as I let my hands wander his back, allowing me to get lost in him. Just a little longer before I have to go back. He tugs on my hair and my moan grows louder. "Nkella—" I breathe. "We have to stop."

"I'm not letting you get far from me again."

"I know, but I really have to go—" Far from him? My eyes open and I stare at him. Those crimson flakes glow in his irises as a lustful smile plays on his face. As if we had all the time in the world. My fingers dip at the corner of his pants, forcing me to want to forget the words he used...

He lowers me enough for my feet to touch the ground and he starts tugging on the pants I'm wearing. My breathing picks up. I guess we still have some time. The cloaking is still disguising us.

Nkella's tongue slides inside my pussy and a gasp gets lodged in my throat.

Okay. He has my full attention. Other guy out of my mind now.

His hands clench my ass hard and I arch into the wall, and my legs start to shake. Without taking his focus off my region, he takes my legs and sits them on his shoulders with my back sliding down the wall. At some point we end up with my back on the floor but I don't care. His tongue draws circles around my clit, and it starts to throb. I grip onto his hair and gaze down at him. I bite my lip as he stares up at me, his sinful eyes pinning me down as he works. He sticks his forked tongue inside me and I bite down harder to keep me from screaming out his name in broad daylight, with the crew working outside on the ship.

The waves rock us back and forth and it only helps him to move his tongue in and out of me. The throbbing intensifies and my stomach starts to convulse. I grip onto his shoulders and squeeze my eyes shut as my back arches. My orgasm crashes through my body, sending a ripple of multicolored specks through my vision, and I think I literally see waves crashing around me.

I blink and the waves crash away onto the floor. I blink again and look around, my hand touching the dry floor. He follows my movement, a brow quirking.

Must have been my imagination. I chuckle. "I think that one made me hallucinate."

He laughs, but his eyes keep me pinned in place. "Good. I wanted one last taste of you to keep with me."

I swallow and get myself up, bringing my pants up.

I regret having to leave to go back to Tetalla. I know it kills him that I have to go. "I'm sorry, Nkella... I hope this will all be over soon."

"I'm the one who's sorry, Soren. Truly."

"Sorry for what?"

There's an edge to his voice, and a darkness flashes in his eyes that tells me he is planning something...

"Nkella, what did you do?"

The devilish smile he just had becomes a frown and a chill runs down my spine.

"Nkella, answer me. What. Did. You. Do?"

He licks his lips as he stares into my eyes, and the back of his hand brushes my cheek. "Do you remember what I called you when we were down in the Deep?"

My brows furrow as I search his face. The nicknames he's given me have gone from utwa, spy, to Neyuro, brave. But when I found him in the Deep, fully shifted into his devil form—back when we thought it was a curse—I brought him back to himself. And from there, he was able to take control of his Devil, and the fires it brings. "Light of your fire," I whisper.

"Roé yani," he smiles, repeating it in Ipani. "I love you, Soren. Pa che."

I swallow. Unease filling my gut.

He dips back down to plant a kiss on my lips, then his eyes flick up toward the window of the cabin.

I turn around to see the crew pointing their weapons out to sea, and my pulse quickens at the sight of another pirate ship closing in. I reach for the door but Nkella stops me, moving me behind him as he walks out, without a weapon.

That's unusual.

A gust of cold air carries flakes of snow through the doorway. Why is he walking out casually, without his bow and arrow, or a gun?

My gaze flicks to Gari holding the cloaking potion in his hand. My eyes widen as he nods to Nkella.

"What the hell, Gari?" I yell.

"I told him to unlatch the potion and carry it out to the sunlight," Nkella says. Tessa and Kaehante share surprised looks, but Ntaouru doesn't budge from staring out at the enemy ship covered in lichen.

Nkella puts his hands up in the frosty air and walks over to the edge. My mouth gapes open. No he didn't.

"Nkella, this is not how it works," I tell him.

"It isn't what you think, Soren. Stay close."

I squint at him, wrapping my arms around myself.

Their ship thuds against ours, making the *Gambit* lurch. Skeleton pirates encrusted with algae and barnacles haul thick ropes across the gap to lash the two vessels together.

"Hold your fire," Nkella instructs our crew.

A tall feminine figure stands close to the algae-covered rail of their ship, she flickers in and out, and in one flash, she's standing before us. I jump back.

"S-Soren," it says.

Now Nkella produces a knife in his hand and walks toward the undead woman, searching around as if having expected for Tetalla to have come himself. Disbelief reaches his face when he gets closer.

"Soanalo?" he says, looking back at the ship she came from.

I startle when I realize he's right. It is her. It isn't the first time I see her walking dead... But it is the first time I see her in front of everyone else, and this time she's covered in algae. I step forward. "What did Tetalla do to you?"

Nkella lowers his knife. I'm guessing this was not in his plan right now. Tetalla threw us a curveball. But why? Just to fuck with us?

She turns to face me. "You both need to come with me."

I step forward, my mind wildly searching for an excuse to give Tetalla. "No. Just me. Tell him I had no idea what the Empress was planning. Nkella saved me from the white drakon." Not that I was in imminent danger with the drakon, I did go with her willingly, but he doesn't need to know that.

"He received this ship's signal. If you do not both come, he will make me kill Nkella in front of you. Please don't make me do that."

Ah. There it is.

"I was never going to resist." Nkella steps toward the armed dead who all grab at him at once.

"What are you doing!?" I shriek and Soanalo steps in front of me.

My ears tune out the crew screaming behind us as reality dawns on me with what Nkella just did. I stare at Gari and realize he's no longer holding the cloaking potion; he's holding a potion that would transmit an alarm to the Aō. I turn to Kaehante.

"Kae, what did that alarm say?"

Kae bows his head, fury in his voice when he says, "It declares capture."

My blood rushes from my face to my toes. "It what?"

"He basically called war on Tetalla," Tessa finishes for him.

I bolt to the edge of the rail to call after him. "This was not our agreement, Nkella!" I don't even know if he can hear me now that the undead have taken him below their ship. I stare at Soanalo. "So what happens now?"

Her eyes go dark and Tetalla's voice seeps through. "It wouldn't have sufficed for your captain to solely declare war. He had to make the theatrics and declare your capture as well. And for that, your deal has been broken." Which I'm sure was Nkella's plan all along.

That's why he apologized to me. I ball my fist. That idiot.

"Soren," Soanalo's voice comes back. "We have to go." She extends her decaying, algae-ridden hand, and I decide not to take it. Instead, I follow her onto her ship, passing a look to Ntaoru and the remaining crew instead. Tessa and Kae look lost, but Ntaouru has a stern look on her face. Seeing Soanalo like this must be hard on her too. They were childhood friends and the Empress used Ntaoru as a puppet in order to brutally kill the princess.

Ntaoru nods at me once, and a bit of me relaxes, hoping that as soon as we leave, she'll let them in on some secret. I hope to god there's a better plan here.

Once aboard the ship, I step onto a deck slick with seaweed and bone fragments. Lanterns sway overhead, casting flickering shadows on planks scarred with old bloodstains. The skeleton crew forms a loose circle around me, their seaweed-wrapped ribs creaking as they shift to give me open ground.

"Where is he?"

"In the brig," one of them rasps, algae clinging to its jawbone.

"Can I see him?"

"We have been instructed not to allow you near him," Soanalo responds.

Steeling myself, I push through the skeletal pirates guarding a narrow set of ladders. They push back hard, causing me to fall back and be caught by a pair of skeletal hands. The undead crew in front of me unsheathe their sabers and cross them in front of me. Bony fingers dig into my arms so hard a yell tears from the back of my throat. "Let me go!"

Soanalo steps forward. "Please do not resist, Soren. He is not happy."

"We did nothing wrong! Nkella only saved me from going back up to the tower! That's it!"

Her face twists and she grips onto her jaw as Tetalla's voice rings through her. Her eyes fix on mine and her lips speak: "You test my limits, vicious one. You're beginning to prove to be a hindrance to me rather than a use."

My throat dries. Soanalo's foot forces forward despite her visible attempts to try and fight him. Her hand quickly wraps around my neck and I get pushed back into the skeleton holding me tight. Soanalo's eyes are black, filled with Death's echo as he infiltrates her body.

"If it is true that your pirate captured you and you did not willingly go to him while the Empress acted to destroy Danū, I will take into consideration his punishment for your sake. If it is a lie, I will know it. And you have not yet seen what vicious is, my vicious one."

Soanalo's body drops to the broken floorboards and this time I hold my hand out to her, ripping my arm free from the undead guard. She looks up at me and takes it as I pull her to her feet.

"Soren—"

"Stop. It's okay, Soanalo. I won't try and fight you. I know this isn't your fault." The fact Tetalla has now used a dead Ipani princess as a way to make Nkella yield from starting a fight, or whatever psychological mindfuck he intended to use on him, or us, tells me he has completely lost it. He doesn't care about the Ipani anymore. He only cares to win.

I could kill Nkella myself.

My mind races to find if we have broken the deal I made with Tetalla in any way. I promised to go with him, to be his wife if I left Nkella... and he'd let him live. There's no way to prove anything happened between us, though it might take some convincing... but I was technically rescued and did not seek him out for my escape. I had every intention of coming back. Okay, I think I can handle this.

Nkella declared war on him.

That may have thrown a wrench in our agreement.

He has absolutely no right to ever call something I do "bancha" again.

Something in my chest stirs and it feels familiar.

It's our aovate connection… He's letting me know he's okay. Rage coils inside me as I fight back the tears.

"Our arrival will take a few hours. Please make yourself comfortable."

My gaze drops to the barnacles growing on the inner walls, and algae- and seaweed-ridden floors.

Gross.

Snow continues to drizzle over the sea and I warm my nose with my hands. I decided to take a seat near the bow of the ship, away from all the skeleton guards. Not that it would stop them from moving up here if I decided to jump, but I didn't feel like sitting anywhere in the inside of this death trap. Soanalo drapes an itchy wool blanket over me, and I can't be bothered to move to grab it. Anxiety has my gut twisted into a knot.

Ice starts to emerge in the water as we get closer to the island. "I knew the snow drakon caused the snow, but I didn't realize just how much snow. How is it possible?"

"The snow drakon only had to cover a small portion. Ouma snow will keep on giving without stop."

"And fire ouma can't melt it, can it?"

"It cannot. It appears this drakon somehow has royal snow ouma from Piupeki."

So Tetalla knows then.

My eyes narrow to the distance. Soanalo must know what I'm thinking because she continues.

"The royals of Piupeki have long been deceased but their royal snow was hidden away, promised to an heir. That heir does not exist, but it was passed on to a creature of the snow spirit's choosing."

"And it trusted the Empress?"

Soanalo shrugs a bony shoulder. "It trusted something. Perhaps the drakon. And the drakon trusted the Empress. Either way, only royal fire can melt it now."

It should have been melted by Tetalla now *if* he had control over the royal fires. I keep this to myself, knowing he'll hear me. But I thought he did have control over them— no—he definitely does because he was King of the Deep.

Or, is "was" the operative word here? Has he been up here too long? Would it matter with him being Death?

No, it wouldn't. So what happened? Why hasn't he melted the snow yet?

Soanalo peers down at me and I look back to the sea, afraid Tetalla is now looking in, knowing what we're talking about and wondering if I'm plotting against him.

He can bet on it. I'll always be the pirate against oppression.

The large skeletal remains of a giant serpent that cages the coastline of the island comes into view. The first time Tetalla brought me here, I refused to come topside so I missed the entrance everyone talked about. Danū looks different in the Deep, mainly dead and barren, and some parts such as this area looks like before the arrival of the Fates. We sail in silence as the ship rocks in icy waters. I shiver at the cold blanket of oumala snow drifting through the cavern. The natives of Danū, acclimated to the volcano's heat, must be suffering from this chill.

We step beneath the giant drakon's ribcage, where rusted iron cages hang from the bones on frayed ropes. Inside each one, a body sways. I half expect them to moan with the sounds of the eternal torture, but that was before I set them free in the Deep.

I glance at Soanalo and she flicks her glaze to me.

"Can I ask you a question?"

Her eyes widen, warning me to be careful what I ask. He's listening.

"Have you seen anyone we know in the Deep lately?"

"I don't have any messages for you, Soren. We're almost there."

I look away from her and try to avoid the bodies hanging inside cages from trees, now that we're through the drakon's giant skeleton. Something else different here than in the Deep's version of Danū is the fortress wall is ruined on the ground. I imagine hundreds of years ago, the drakon that lays dead must have destroyed it before the Ipani caught the drakon on fire. There are streams and creeks flowing from the tall volcanic mountains, instead of dead plains for as far as the eye can see. Everything in the Deep is dried up and dead. Danū is a beautiful place, just like the other islands. Partly sandy desert, and deep forest with running water.

But I still don't see anyone around. Beside the dead that are hanging in those cages that is...

"They were all the ones who tried to escape and fight the Empress before the siege, and were posted as examples for the rest," Soanalo tells me, she must have noticed how I was trying to avoid looking at them. Who could miss them anyway?

"Why haven't they been taken down now that Tetalla is here?"

"He leaves them there as an example of what the Empress did to them."

I almost scoff at that. It's like he knows he's being a terrible ruler so he wants to remind them all how bad it was before he got here.

My fingers curl over the fabric of my tunic and I had almost forgotten I'm wearing Nkella's clothes. I had already expected to come back to a fight with Tetalla over it, but now this is all going to be worse. Maybe he'll be too distracted by Nkella's declaration of war that he won't notice and just banish me to my room. What are the chances that he won't even be there to get me himself, and send Bobby instead?

The ship enters a shaded alcove by trees, some of the Mikiroro palms sprouted around. Despite the ones in the Deep, these are alive, but suffering from a thin layer of snow.

Skeleton guards start climbing the bow where I'm seated and I bring my legs up. One of them grabs onto the anchor and tosses it overboard with ease. I swallow, my anxiety kicking in. We're here. I stare toward the red stone pathway, lit up by fire poles on either side all the way through ruins. I know this structure from my time with Nangraku in the Deep. Pari Eitu was where they kept Nkella to fight in the Devil fighting ring. But it used to be an Ipani ritual site, destroyed by the Ancient Greeks during their wars. I remember looking at it in the map, and seeing markings for tunnels somewhere around here—which I'm guessing is an entrance to the caverns.

Patches of snow are on the ground, lit by burning fire that doesn't go out. Ouma fire, but I don't miss the fact that if it was royal ouma fire, the snow would be melted.

Tetalla is definitely having trouble.

A skeleton reaches for me and I stand, avoiding its touch. I'm led off the ship, with Soanalo behind me. Before I step away, I turn to face her. "Where's Nkella?"

She stares back at me, too much algae on her face to be able to read her expression. "We have been instructed to leave him in the brig of the ship. You will be taken inside by yourself."

"No..." I step toward her. "Where is Tetalla planning on taking him?"

"I can't know that, Soren."

My shoulders drop. "He isn't going in the prison inside the castle?"

Soanalo dismisses my question and signals for the skeletons to take me away. I dig my heels into the ground, making them drag me. The thought of me leaving Nkella in this ship and being taken who knows where... has my bones stiff. I start to run back to the ship, only to be caught by a tall guard. I'm pulled off the ground and I start kicking and hitting his nasty bones. I know kicking and screaming won't help but I can't help it. I have no weapons. Nkella is about to be taken from me. I might never see him again.

I'm carried all the way up to the mountain until I convince them to put me down. I have ten skeletal guards surrounding me as we walk, as if I were some dangerous fugitive capable of getting past one of them.

It's a long walk, and I was right about Tetalla not being here to greet me himself.

We enter into the volcano through a set of giant-sized iron double doors with brass handles. Inside, sconces light a dark path that descends into the caverns, and I gaze up at the stalactites high above us, dripping a steady beat of water as we make our way down a dangerous slope. The snow is no longer as present as it was on the surface, but there are still piles of fallen snow in the areas where the drakon had passed through.

As we walk, I study the walls of lit up passageways with what looks like house openings along all the sides of them. This is a different way than the last time I was brought through here.

About a dozen Ipani are gathered in a clearing in front of those houses carved in the stonewalls up ahead. A few children stare at me and point, and one of the little boys with dirt covering his forehead and chin gets a little too close to the edge of a cliff. One of the men puts a hand on his shoulder, moving him back. Their eyes are glued to me as I'm escorted down the cavern.

They're all so skinny. And glancing down, I know how far that drop goes and to what. Royal ouma fire that burns forever. The good news is, none of them down here are actually freezing, but where do they get their water from if the water on the surface is frozen? How often do they go up there now that there is a war?

Technically, they've been in danger, starving, and under siege for a long time, so who knows how often they manage to go up there at all.

I scan the tops of the walls and see more windows and openings from which Ipani stare at us as we walk.

Cavern Castle comes into view and I steel my spine to face what's to come. I can see the tower where my room is from here, and I never realized just how close I was to the rest of the Ipani in hiding. I've never entered the castle from the front entrance before.

Once at the castle gates, more skeletal guards await at the big iron doors. They step aside to allow for Tetalla to walk through them. He walks at a brisk pace, his eyes look tired but they're seething with anger when he looks at me. He scans me up and down, and the fiery glow that lives beneath the royal Devils of Danū flashes in his eyes, and his whole face twists in disgust.

"Search her," he orders them.

Skeletal hands are instantly on me and I can't fight them. One of them reaches into my pocket and takes something out. The guard hands it to Tetalla and I'm squinting to see what it is.

He holds out the skimpy outfit he makes me wear while I'm here. The same one I wore when the snow drakon carried me out. And then was torn by Nkella's hands last night...

How did I not notice he put it in his pocket before giving it to me to wear?

How could he do this? It was clearly to send Tetalla a message—and there goes the lie I was forming to tell him.

Tetalla makes a fist and catches them on fire.

My hands start to shake.

His eyes fix on mine. There's no lying to him now. Nkella wanted him to know I belong to him, and only him. I hold my breath, waiting for Tetalla to do something. His breathing is deep, but the silence that befalls the space around us is deafening. His features relax.

"To think I was worried about you." His voice is calm, collected. My heart rate increases.

"Tetalla—"

"What was I to do? You had been kidnapped. Taken from your bedroom by the Empress's pet while it rendered Danū a frozen wasteland. So while I was here, trying to save the cold and dying, you were breaking our deal." He licks his lips. "You should have considered my offer, Uoko yani. It was the only one you were ever going to get."

I open my mouth to speak, and he grabs my throat. My eyes bulge as he lifts me above the ground.

"Maybe you're right." His gaze is dark as he stares into me while I choke. "You and Nkella belong together. Forever." He tightens his grip, and my vision blurs. Then he drops me, and I land on my knees.

"Take her away."

I clutch at my chest and throat, gasping for air. He spins on his heel to head back to his castle, and guards grab me from both sides. I start to scream.

A heavy bag gets put over my head as I'm restrained with my arms and legs tied by heavy clasps.

12

SOREN

THE DARKNESS IS SUFFOCATING, COLD AS THE CHAINS BITING into my wrists and ankles. The stone wall presses hard against my back, and every part of me aches, from my arms straining against the restraints to my throat raw from yelling.

I've tried reaching Sapphire with our bond, but she hasn't reacted to my calls. Who knows if I can even reach her from here... wherever I am. I've been sitting here, replaying the conversation I had with Tetalla.

Maybe you do deserve to be together. Forever.

A groan cuts through the silence, low and faint. But the voice is unmistakable. My heart stutters, and I stop breathing. "Nkella?" I whisper.

Another groan. Then, a rasping breath. "Soren?"

Relief and fury crash over me in equal measure, leaving me trembling. I pull against the chains, the metal scraping against stone as I try to see him. "Where are you?" My voice is sharp, too loud in the quiet, but I don't care.

"I'm... here." His voice is hoarse, weak. A clink of chains follows, and I realize he's restrained too.

"How long have you been here? I'm surprised you didn't hear me screaming hours ago."

He clears his throat and then I hear the rattle of his chains. "Rōkan—they shot me with a suppressor. It knocked me out. He put you in here?" Surprise tinges his voice.

"They shot you!?"

"I'm okay... I heal."

"Nkella," I snap, fury rising again. "Why did you do it? You declared war on him. You practically handed yourself over!"

He doesn't respond right away, and when he does, his voice is quieter. "I knew he wouldn't face me otherwise."

"Face you?" I hiss, my voice trembling with frustration. "What exactly was the plan, Nkella? Get chained up so he'd have the advantage? Brilliant."

"I didn't expect—" He cuts himself off, his voice strained. "You weren't supposed to be here."

"What? You didn't expect me to be dragged into this? You knew, Nkella. You knew he'd take me too." My chest tightens as my voice cracks. "And then you had the nerve to slip my ripped clothes into my pocket. You wanted him to know."

His breathing stills. "Yes."

"Why? Why would you do that?" My voice rises, echoing off the stone walls.

"Kh. He already knew, daí?" Nkella says, his tone raw. "I was not going to let you just be his." He slams his chains hard, trying to get loose. These chains were obviously meant to keep a Devil incarcerated.

I bite down hard, shaking my head even though he can't see it. "Well, he was furious. He threw me in here, told me our deal is broken. What now, huh? What's your grand plan now?"

The chains clink as he shifts. "Let me explain."

"Please." My voice shakes, hot tears pricking at my eyes. "You put a target on both of us, and for what? To get under his skin? To prove a point?"

"The fires," he murmurs, almost too soft to hear.

I still. "What?"

"The royal flames," he repeats, his voice gaining strength. "They spoke to me."

"What does that even mean?" My anger wavers, confusion creeping in.

"I'm not just here because of Tetalla," he says. "I'm here because the flames told me this was where I needed to be."

A bitter laugh escapes me. "The flames told you? They talk now?"

"They're alive, Soren," he says under a cough, and "they… chose me. Or, I thought they did but now…"

I blink into the darkness, my heart pounding. "Did they ever speak to you in the Deep?"

"Koj. It took me by surprise, but now it is apparent they mean for me to challenge Tetalla. Assuming, he also spoke to them, he had the upper hand this whole time."

I exhale sharply, trying to process his words. "And what happens if he never gives you that chance to fight him? He's a Devil too, so he knows how to constrain you. What if he just keeps us here, rotting in this place?"

"That is his intention. But we will not stay here. Trust me, daí?"

He bangs loud against the wall, and I take it that he's shifting and trying to free himself.

I shake my head, disbelief and anger swirling inside me, and part of me is glad I can't look at his face right now. "And what about me, Nkella? Did the flames tell you to get me caught too?" I'm honestly not mad about being here with him. I'm relieved he's alive, and with me. But what the hell was he thinking? He wouldn't be so reckless with me, usually.

"No," he says quietly. "That was my mistake. I thought he would lock you back up in the castle."

I freeze, the rawness in his voice cutting through my anger.

"I didn't want to lose you," he admits. "Not again…"

The vulnerability in his words pulls at something deep in my chest. I want to stay angry, to hold onto the fury that's been keeping me upright, but it slips through my fingers like sand. He must have really trusted the fires…

The pain I've had in my chest since he was taken to the brig on the ship comes back. The way he hid his plan from me, and used me to give Tetalla a message.

Now we're chained up in a cave somewhere in Danū, and he has restraints on him to contain a Devil, and no one knows where we are.

"I can't do this," I finally say. A sadness pulls at my insides, and I feel our aovate connection swirling in the worst possible way.

A pause tells me he felt that too. "Soren? What do you mean by this, daí?"

"I'm not a piece on a game board, Nkella," I say softly. "You can't just move me around to suit your plans."

"I know," he whispers. "I am sorry, Neyuro."

"Nkella I—" I swallow the tears forming in my throat. "I feel like I'm always afraid for your life. Or mine. Now, I'll never see Talia again. I won't get to touch you again... Nkella, I—" My arms break into goosebumps and a lump forms in my throat. "We're never going to get out of here."

"We will. Trust me, daí? You said I was the only one you could trust. Me and the crew. I am asking you to trust me now."

"Trust you? How can I?"

I hear his breath hitch. This is the worst time to break up with him. And I love him, I do... but, being with him means always being in danger. I readily went to the Deep for him, and now we're imprisoned in a cave somewhere, with no way to reach the crew, Gari, or anyone else. Even Philo is gone.

A warm sensation reaches my chest and I swallow. He's trying to talk to me through our Aō connection.

"Not all is lost, roé yani."

"How do you know that?"

"I am asking you to trust me as your aovate, but also as your captain."

I lick my dry lips. "What are you not telling me?"

"I am not keeping anything from you. Ntaoru knows I have been captured. They are looking for us. Be patient."

A flicker of hope sparks in me but then dies down. "We've been here for hours, you even longer since before I got here. Why haven't they found you yet?"

"I don't know."

"Because Tetalla could have gone after them?"

He doesn't respond. Really great plan. I let my head rest against the cavern wall and hit it a little too hard, sending a searing pain to the back of my head. I grunt and let the silence engulf me while I think.

"So you really can't reach the royal flames?" I finally ask.

"I've tried. They want a duel. Tetalla is stalling by keeping me here, because he can no longer reach the flames either."

"What's his game plan then? Making you weak by keeping you chained up here and starving?"

Silence falls between us.

"Great. Guess that answers that question."

"Rōkan."

I stare in the direction of his voice. "What is it now?"

"That is why he imprisoned you here. He was afraid of me convincing the royal flames to make me ruler."

"I don't understand."

"With you here, he knows I will not burn you to release me and melt the snow."

My jaw drops. The royal flames won't burn his skin. So without me being here, chained to this wall, he'd be able to free himself and help Danū. "Wait. Do the royal flames know this? They must..."

He curses.

Shit. I have a sinking feeling this means Tetalla won.

If the royal flames take Nkella as standing down in order to let me live, then Tetalla will claim them, making him the rightful ruler.

"So we're really stuck here forever?"

"Koj, Soren. Relax, daí?"

"Relax?!" my chest starts to pant again, and sweat drips down my brow. Panic starts to course through me once more, the relief of having Nkella here and being able to talk to him again dissipating as the realization that we are practically buried alive comes crashing into my reality.

A tremor makes the walls shake and a few rocks come bouncing down.

"Why does that keep happening?"

"I have been trying to figure that out as well. I thought at first it was the Empress doing it."

"It still can be... but if so, then why? And how?"

Another tremor hits, but harder this time and a yell escapes my throat. If we have an earthquake hard enough to bring this cave down to hell, we're dead.

The minutes turn to another hour and my mind rolls into another cycle of how we've been buried alive. We're never leaving this place.

A tear rolls down my cheek. It's been over an hour since Nkella and I have spoken a word. Prisoners, the both of us.

A laugh escapes me.

"Daí?"

I was in jail back when the Tarot card opened the portal. Then Nkella stuck me in the brig.

Then he was a prisoner in the Deep, and I saved him.

And now? We're both prisoners together. I burst into a fit of laughter.

"What is so funny, daí?"

"You're a gembella. I'm a gembella."

"Kh."

"We're both gembella."

"Don't lose it now, Neyuro. Remember, you are strong."

My abs hurt from the laughter rolling through me, when a hard quake makes me swallow air. The walls are starting to shake, and the ground moves under my legs. "What's happening?"

The ground beneath us rumbles, the sound deafening as the cavern shakes violently. My chains rattle against the stone wall, and I press my back against the surface, trying to steady myself.

A jagged crack splits the ground between us, bright flames licking upward from the depths. The heat brushes my face, stark against the cold air. I squint through the light, and for the first time since we got here, I can see him.

He's slumped against the wall, his wrists and ankles shackled like mine, but there's a look on his face that sends a chill through me. He's smiling.

"Nkella," I call, my voice shaky. "What the hell is going on?"

"Ntaouru found us."

13

SORREN

THE GROUND SPLITS FURTHER, SENDING A WAVE OF HEAT and light through the cavern. Flames roar upward, casting sharp shadows across the jagged walls. My chains rattle as the ground trembles beneath me, and I press my back against the cold stone, trying to steady myself.

A figure rises from between the split ground, and my breath catches when I see Ntaouru balancing on a rising boulder. It reminds me of when she was in the fighting arena, forced into combat for the Empress's enjoyment.

Her presence is steady, commanding, like she hadn't spent years as the Empress's agentless soldier. She has full control over her ouma as she's controlling the land effortlessly. Relief floods through me, I can't believe she found us.

Ntaouru steps forward, her voice cutting through the roar of the fire. "This was too close. I almost did not find you."

Nkella shifts in his chains, the clink of metal against stone breaking the brief silence. "You're late," he says, his tone dry but lighter than before.

She arches an eyebrow, and her smirk drops. "Your plan was bancha, daí?"

"Completely agree," I tell her. She shakes her head at me, and hops over to Nkella and lifts his chains.

"They are meant to keep me restrained, so they will be tough to break."

"Strong for your strength, but not for the earth." The metal from which the chains hang breaks apart as molten rock starts to grow outward and pushes it off. Nkella tugs on the cuffs, and this time, they break apart. He steps free.

Ntaoru's brows raise. "Without the metal being intact, it loses its ouma?"

"Kh. Good. And the crew?"

"We're docked. The crew is waiting inside the caves."

Relief washes over me, and my shoulders sag. "They're okay?"

"They're safe," she confirms, her tone firm. "But something's wrong with the land. It keeps shaking, sending tremors, and I don't know why." She walks over to me, jumping over the split ground, and does the same with the rock formations to break my chains.

Ntaouru doesn't hesitate, turning to me with a steady gaze. The wall I'm leaning against vibrates as rock formations start forcing their way through the metal chains. Moments later, the chains clatter to the ground, and I sag forward.

Nkella's expression tightens as he reaches me to pull apart the cuffs. Our eyes meet, and my breath hitches. I'm still mad at him, but want to jump into his arms at the same time. Moments ago, I thought we were buried alive, but now that we're free, his decision has my stomach in knots.

I step away, but my knees buckle.

Nkella catches my arm, steadying me. "Neyuro..." His eyes soften as he brushes my cheek, but I turn, pulling away from him.

"I'm fine." My voice comes out steadier than I expected, and I nod at him. "Thanks."

His lips part but he steps back, giving me space. We'll talk later.

He pulls his gaze away from me to face his sister. "What does your ouma tell you about these tremors, then?"

Ntaouru's gaze drops to the gaping hole she just came out of. "The ground feels... unsettled. There's something else at play here."

Since Ntaouru has volcanic ouma, and can cause rock formations sizzling with molten lava, I'm guessing she can sense when the land is off with the Aō. "Think we can get out of here now and talk about this later? Before Tetalla knows we're escaping."

Nkella shakes his head. "Tetalla will think it's the Empress. He won't suspect us escaping. At least not yet."

Ntaouru's gaze flicks back to him, her voice grim. "Most of the snow has melted, by the way."

My stomach twists at the words. I glance at Nkella, whose expression darkens as the realization sets in. "That means Tetalla controls the royal flames," I say softly, my voice barely audible.

Nkella doesn't respond immediately, but his silence speaks volumes. The tension in his jaw, the way his shoulders stiffen—it's enough to confirm what we're both thinking. If Tetalla has the flames, our fight just became infinitely harder.

Ntaoru steps closer, the flames parting around her like obedient servants. It's clear to see why Nkella always felt Ntaouru should have been ruler of Danū. This is her natural ouma. Nkella has wind, and he never thought it was as valuable a power as hers.

It is though, and if he governs the royal flames, he'll be unstoppable. Together, they make a great team.

Ntaouru folds her arms, the fire dimming slightly around us. "We need to move. Even if Tetalla suspects this was the Empress, he might think to check on you."

His expression sharpens. "Then let's not waste time."

14

SOREN

THE GUSHING OF WATER GETS LOUDER AS NTAOURU LEADS us to the cave's exit, which is undoubtedly a gaping hole overhead leading directly to a waterfall above ground. Of course it is. It couldn't have been a normal, dry cave exit; that would have made life easier.

I place my hands onto the cold wet rock, when Nkella steps in front of me, "Climb on my back, Neyuro."

The familiar magnetism from our aovate connection pulls me into him. It feels calm and protective. Even though I would gladly take the easy way out and climb on him, instead of climbing through a cold waterfall, it takes everything in me to resist.

"Soren?" Hurt strikes his voice. Behind him, Ntaoru is already halfway up, she's keeping her head tucked to her neck as the water gushes over her. I step past Nkella and start climbing the rocks after his sister.

I know he can easily and safely just carry us both out. And I want to get out of here as quickly as possible, but I can't help but to resist him right now. I can't keep depending on him to get me out of dangerous situations. That's never been my style.

He had no right to keep me out of the loop of his plan, as if I couldn't handle it. I'm not the same girl he met when I first fell into Tarotland. I went and got him out of the Deep by myself for fuck's sake.

Not to mention, he put us all in danger. I need time to think without being distracted by the aovate connection.

Water gushes over my head and I can barely feel my fingers through the freezing stream. Nkella screams something behind me, but I don't turn around to listen. My only focus is to climb up. Don't look down. And don't fall.

"Soren!"

My name is called over the sound of the thunderous waterfall, but I struggle to focus on anything with it cascading over my eyes.

"Soren! Reach up!"

And let go? Are they nuts? I arch my neck, trying to find a pocket of air through the gushing water. I officially hate waterfalls. A blurry image of Ntaouru and someone else pops in through the exit just above me. Taking a breath, I let go of my hand and reach above to grab Ntaoru's.

My fingers are like ice and they slip the moment I touch her. I lose my footing and swallow a mouth full of water as I plummet backward. Nkella catches me and pushes me up. A set of two arms pull me to the surface, and I gasp for air before breaking into a fit of coughs.

Tears burn my eyes as my vision struggles to focus. My heart is in my throat.

"Soren!" Nkella crawls out of the cave's entrance and makes his way to me. "Are you okay?"

So much for handling myself.

I grab my chest and nod. Water drips off his brow and torn shirt.

"Do all the caves here have waterfalls for entrances?" I gasp.

Lāri shakes her head and I just now realize she was the other person helping me up from the waterfall. "No, but revel in it because it's the last water source for miles."

I blink up at her. "Where have you been?"

Her features twist.

"And what do you mean this is the only water source?"

"Look around," Ntaoru whispers. My brows furrow at her and then glance at Nkella as I stand. Tall purple flames surround us. I walk a bit closer as the fire brims over the streams. The snow has melted, and even though we're surrounded by fire, it isn't hot.

It's a cool flame. Controlled in temperature. Controlled like the royal flames are when someone commands them.

I stare at Nkella.

"I lost," he says.

I grab his hand. "No." He whips around to look at me. "He only thinks he's won. He doesn't know we've escaped, remember? You can still fight him. Command the royal flames, Nkella. You can do it."

"I never wanted to be king..."

"Nkella..."

"But now I do." He stares at me. "Danū needs someone who will put the people first. And I have put myself first for too long." He looks at Ntaoru. "I'm taking the throne, Ntaouru. Now because I want it."

Ntaouru walks up with a teary smile on her face, and reaches for him. "Finally, brother. What's first?"

He turns toward the purple flames, dimly burning over the streams. "This cave is the only water supply left?" he asks

I follow his gaze and search the area. Not a single person in sight. I guess it's true that the locals stay underground. "Why do people stay inside the caves? Do you think they can't get to water?"

Nta shakes her head. "They are afraid to leave because of the Empress. And now with the war between her and Tetalla, they rather stay below ground."

"Where does the stream in the cave lead to? Does it connect to where they are?"

"No," Lāri chimes. "That's the problem, mei?" She points to the stream with the purple flames. "The cave you were in doesn't connect to where the locals live."

"That's why it's a prison. I somehow thought we were still in the castle vicinity."

Nta shakes her head. "If it wasn't for Lāri, I would still be looking for you."

"It was a hope," Lāri adds. "This is the only cave not guarded by royal flames."

Nta plants her hand down on the ground. "And then I heard voices through the rumbles of my ouma when I would move the ground in search of you."

My eyes narrow at the waterfall. "Why wouldn't Tetalla have guarded us with royal flames?"

My focus shifts to Nkella who's passing his hands through the fires without getting burnt. He turns to us.

He stares at me. "If he tried, the royal flames spared us. Maybe because they know I'm concerned for you."

I turn from his gaze.

"But wouldn't that mean you can command them?" Nta asks.

"Koj. I just tried. I need to fight Tetalla for control, but they do recognize me. At least for now."

"For now?" I ask.

"It can change."

A tremor rumbles beneath our feet and I spread my hands out to keep myself steady. It stops and I stare at Ntaoru.

"That wasn't me."

"It's been happening, daſ?" Nkella says. "Why? Can you find out?"

Nta shakes her head. "The volcanic spirits aren't saying anything about it. It happened while we were searching for you and I tried to ask why. It went silent."

A beat passes between us as we exchange glances.

"We need to move," Nkella says.

"To find Tessa and Kae?"

"Koj," he says and my eyes flutter. "We need to get the people to safety, away from the castle, and lead them to water."

"Where do we bring them?" Nta asks. "Out here? There is no shelter. They like the caves."

"But they have no water, daſ?"

"We have to convince them to set up camp, at least until the war is over," Lāri says.

"But what if it lasts for years?" Nta raises her voice.

My blood runs cold. I hadn't considered this war lasting for years.

"It won't," Nkella states in a low growl.

"Good luck convincing them, daſ?" Ntaoru says. "I doubt it will happen."

"What do you suggest, Nta?"

After a moment, she shakes her head. "Fine. We can at least try."

Long wings spread on Lāri' back. "I'll find Tessa and Kae and let them know of the plan. We'll meet you at the entrance of *Ruvanta*." Lāri unbuckles her canteen and hands it to me. "For your journey." I take it from her and then she gracefully lifts one leg into the air as she shifts into her eagle form, and flies toward the horizon.

Ntaoru takes out her canteen and grabs mine before walking to the waterfall we just climbed out of. That's two canteens of water between the three of us since Nkella and I were prisoners and don't have any of our belongings.

My gaze falls to Nkella who is now walking over to the waterfall and cupping it in his hands. I follow suit.

I press in close to him, and our aovate connection stirs. My heart squeezes. I don't like how we left things before Ntaoru rescued us, but this isn't a time to talk about it.

Ntaoru hands me the canteen, but I pass it to Nkella so he can carry it. His eyes soften as he takes it from me, maybe interpreting this as a symbol of an olive branch, or trust between us. I honestly just don't want to carry it, and I obviously trust him.

He holds my gaze and for a second, he looks like he wants to say something, but I turn away.

"We should go," I say.

Ntaoru shifts her gaze between us, and I feel like she's picking up on awkwardness.

He doesn't respond, but his jaw straightens, and eyes narrow at me. He takes the lead so that I'm staring at the back of his head. He's mad *at me?*

What the hell is he mad about? I'm the one he didn't tell his plan to and he put us all in danger.

"Ruvanta isn't on the map you've been studying, brother, daí?" She passes him a look. "I am hoping I can even remember where it is."

He doesn't respond to that either. Great. Here's to hoping we don't get lost.

Ntaoru walks beside me in silence, the awkward silence blossoming between us three. This is going to be a long journey to the caves.

A warm breeze tickles my nostrils with scents of citrus and vanilla, and for a moment the area surrounding us makes me wish I could just sit here and enjoy the view. The mountain scapes are covered in black and green leaves, with deep purple hues from the giant leaves, a stark contrast to what it looks like in the Deep, where everything is dead. I pick my hair up as we walk. They weren't kidding when they said Danū was hot, and this is with the sun setting. Kae said the meaning of the word Danū was six suns, not to be taken literally.

Why is Tetalla lighting the rivers with his royal flame? Is this just to show he's won? And for how long will he keep his people thirsty and hot?

Crickets start to chirp in the distance as the sun sinks down behind the highest mountain ahead. Tetalla has been quiet, unlike the past when he had searched for me before and during the time I was in the Deep. The entire time he had me imprisoned, he didn't try to speak to me. I guess he finally did give up. At least his silence now lets me know he still thinks I'm chained up in that cave.

We keep a brisk pace as Nkella takes long strides. This is more about him being upset than about us getting there quicker. I ball my fist. He has some nerve being upset. He should be apologizing for not having told me his plan, and for sticking my shredded clothes in my pocket. Using me to give Tetalla a message.

And he's called *me* reckless before!

The more I think about it, the more my blood boils.

I keep a steady pace beside Ntaoru, my boots sinking slightly in the softened ground. The snow may have melted, but the soil is still damp and cold, clinging to my soles as I walk.

A distant rumble runs underfoot. The ground shudders and I stare at Ntaoru. She stiffens beside me

A deep, guttural groan rumbles beneath us, like the earth itself is shifting. My heart slams against my ribs.

Nkella turns sharply. "Move! Now!"

The tremor surges into a violent quake. The ground jolts, splitting with jagged cracks.

I stumble, nearly falling as the world tilts beneath me. Dust and debris rain from above, the tremors sending loose rock tumbling down from the cliffs.

"Shelter!" Ntaouru shouts, her voice barely carrying over the deafening roar of the earth breaking apart.

I spot an overhang from a thick outcrop of stone, and sprint toward it. The ground shifts beneath me, and I barely manage to throw myself under the cover of rock before a boulder crashes down where I was standing.

Nkella and Ntaouru dive in beside me, pressing against the rock as the quake rages on. The sky is choked with dust, and the sound of the ground ripping around us overwhelms my eardrums.

Then, silence.

A ringing fills my ears. My chest heaves as I press my hand against the rock, waiting for the world to settle.

Nkella exhales sharply, his brows furrowing as he turns to stare at his sister.

Ntaouru nods, brushing dust from her hair. "That was longer than the others. But still no sound from my ouma connection."

I step out cautiously, scanning the destruction. Cracks zigzag across the terrain, and new fissures cut deep into the ground.

"We need to move, daí?" Nkella tugs at my arm, and I stare at him, still shaken by the violent tremor. Worry creases his forehead, and I momentarily push aside our issues. "No time to inspect this. People need us and it's getting dark. We need to find somewhere to make camp."

I nod, and we quicken our pace, but I keep glancing over my shoulder at the boulder that fell. Where did it come from? We're not walking alongside a mountain. It's almost as if it was thrown at us. To my side, I catch Ntaoru looking behind her as well, and I can tell we're both wondering the same thing.

My gaze drops to what looks like a concavity in the ground, with something sticking out of it. Then, something catches my eye. I frown, taking a step forward.

"What is it?" Nkella asks.

I don't answer right away. My fingers tighten around my necklace as I kneel beside the strange shape half-buried in the dirt. I bend down for a better look at it, having almost recognized it instantly but... no, it can't be what I think it is.

I reach for it and touch its rugged surface. Rubber, with soft rubbery bumps over it. Half the words in white spell out *GOODYEAR* across the tire's side.

I pause for a brief moment, reading it over. Is this real? I brush off the mound of dirt over it, and a heap of it falls on the ground. I turn my face into my arm as an explosion of dust and dirt goes everywhere, and then step back to see the rest of it appearing from the rocks. The Hyundai logo reflects from the black vehicle.

I blink, my mind struggling to process what I'm seeing. What the hell?

I feel Nkella's presence behind me before he speaks.

"What is this, daí?"

I swallow, my throat dry. I mean, it's not like they don't have tires here. Tessa has a wheelchair, and the Hermit builds things all the time... but, nothing near what a car is.

Ntaouru steps closer, her eyes narrowing. "I have never seen anything like this before. Be careful—"

I look up at her sharply. "I—I don't know how to say this, but... this is from my world."

Nkella arches a brow. "Daí? From your world? How?"

I shake my head. "It's called a car." My mind is fuzzy. I can't even explain how this got here. My eyes widen and I run to look inside the broken window, trying not to get cut from the glass.

What if someone was inside when the car crashed here?

I feel Nkella's hand brush to pull me back but he stops. I brush the window off with my hand and look inside through the twilight. A lavender bow sits on the driver's seat, but the car is empty.

At least that's good news. I think? I search the rest of the concavity. It doesn't look like an open hole or anything, so if there was someone in the car, they didn't fall into a cave.

Ntaoru meets my gaze, her expression unreadable. "This isn't just an earthquake. Something is shifting."

Yeah, no kidding. A cold shiver crawls down my spine.

The tremors. The land breaking apart. A freaking car. Demitri's warning back when he was training me with my power shakes my memory.

The Aō should never have adopted new magic, and the more those different magics tries to overcome the other, there's a possibility it might collapse one day.

Demitri had warned me that with only one Fate ruling magic that doesn't belong here, without the balance of the others, the Aō would be constantly struggling to stabilize, and the collapse of both worlds was bound to happen.

What if that day is today?

15

SORREN

THE THREE OF US STAND THERE, STARING AT THE CAR.

"Hn."

I flick to Nkella who's rubbing his chin.

"This had to be the Empress. She has the rest of the cards, daí?" His eyes flick to mine. "She went to your world to find you once; she could have done it again to bring weapons."

"So this is part of the war?" Ntaoru says, more of a statement than a question.

I scratch at my temple. The Empress didn't go back home to throw a car into Ipa.

The worlds might collapse one day.

I lick my dry lips. But why is this happening now?

Unless Tetalla got to her. And she's hurt. Or dead.

My eyes widen. What if the Empress is dead and now there's no Fate taking the throne at all?

And what would that mean for me? I can't take the throne. I don't even have my powers with this stupid thing on. I grab at the dampener on my wrist. I wish I could take it off.

And what if I could take it off? What then? Would I take the throne to save this world?

Holy shit, I would have to.

I would become... the Empress...

The world starts spinning around me.

"Soren?"

"Neyuro?"

I glance up at them, staring at me with concerned faces. Nkella steps toward me, and his eyes search mine. His hair touches his sharp cheekbone as he stares at me with those dark eyes of his. How am I about to tell him we're all about to be royally screwed?

"What is it?" His voice is low, and tired.

I blink rapidly. I can't even begin to process what that would mean for us. I, myself, would be at war with Tetalla, because he wants to kill all humans, and get rid of the Fates. He only kept me around hoping I would help him defeat the Empress, but with her gone, he still has to get rid of me... Or, he thought he already did.

But why keep me alive?

Was he saving me for later? Or for insurance in case he couldn't kill her?

Snap out of it, Soren. I don't know if she's dead yet.

"Neyuro?!" he calls again.

"Sorry." I clear my throat. "I have something to tell you."

He quirks a brow, and I can feel our connection stirring, but it's not affection. It's the familiarity that he feels I'm about to reveal something I've been hiding again. But it's not something I've intentionally kept from him.

A lot has happened since we were aboard the *Ghost of the Sea*, okay?

Ntaoru steps forward. "Go on then," she says.

I tell them the whole story of when I trained with Demitri aboard the ship. The visions, the cards, the Past Fate before me, the Empress, Asteria. Everything, including the rules of the Tarot cards. Because they came from their magical ancient Greek land, and then combined with the Aō, Ipa needs a Fate as ruler. Or, with the cards here alone, the Aō will encompass all the magic without direction of a Fate, and the worlds will collide. Ultimately, because they never belonged here to begin with.

Nkella's face goes rigid. "The Empress needs to be alive for the rest of us to live." His voice is filled with hatred and disbelief. He's wanted her dead for as long as he could remember.

I nod. "We actually need all three Fates. The world has been weakening for a long time, which is why Demitri wanted me to take over its rule, in order to get rid of her, and possibly bring back the Future Fate, Asteria. There really should be all three to rule.

Nkella falls silent, and Ntaoru wipes her face.

"I know," I say. "It's a lot."

"We don't know this is the reason for this... " He motions to the disaster behind me.

"Car," I finish.

He blinks at it.

"But it makes sense," Ntaoru says. "Neither you nor I have heard from our ouma about any of this. It is as if there is no knowledge about it in the Aō."

What she just said brought me back to having seen Tetalla floating, connected deeper with the Aō.

"And there have been so many tremors, daí?"

"So what then, daí?" He whips around. "If the Empress is dead, Soren takes the throne and continues to fight the war?"

Hearing him say it out loud sends my heart pounding in my ear. "I can't." I say. "I could never be..." the world starts to spin again, and my knees grow weak.

Oh my god, and Talia is still in the Tower.

I let myself fall to the ground, and now sit on the dirt.

Nkella leaps to help me, but I don't budge.

"Soren..." He takes my cheeks in his hand and looks me in the eye. The fiery flakes dance in his irises. "We will figure this out. We don't know if she is dead or alive, daí? If she is dead, we will handle it."

I nod.

"I think it would be worse if she was dead. Arcana would fall from the Tower, no?" Ntaoru says.

That's probably true.

"So maybe she's just hurt?" My voice comes out weaker than I expected.

Nkella sighs deeply.

I agree with that sigh. Wanting the Empress to live is the last thing any of us ever thought we'd want. I don't know why I hadn't thought of the dangers of her dying before.

"But Demitri did say the world would collapse with her still Empress too," I state, remembering fully. "Which is why she wanted me to be her "sister."

"Kh."

Ntaoru picks up her pack. "We need to rest, come on, we will continue tomorrow."

My eyes have slowly adjusted to the falling night. My mind was so occupied with all this, I didn't realize it was already pitch black. And despite it having been so hot during the day, the temperature has seriously dropped.

We find a half-cavern nestled in the woods, and make camp. Silence blooms between the three of us, and Ntaoru leaves to find food. Nkella stays back with me. Normally, he'd go, but I think we all knew we needed some time alone.

The fire flickers and cracks in front of us as we sit side by side. The latest revelation has almost made me forget about his reckless behavior that got us both thrown into the prison cave.

"I'm sorry."

I stare at him. "Why didn't you tell me your plan?"

He sighs. "I didn't trust you to not try and stop me. I needed to get close to Tetalla to fight, and doing what I did would give me the upper hand. I believed that because the royal fires spoke to me."

"Because it wants you two to fight."

"Yes." He winces. "The flames played us both. Had us both believe we had the upper hand over each other."

"Tetalla found a way to communicate with the Aō, much, much deeper than anyone else. I think he's always had the upper hand." I hold up my wrist to show the dampener. "Somehow, he knew he needed my Fate magic out of the way, and it was about more than just me using it against him while in the castle."

Nkella stares at me.

"What if he wanted me out of the way to keep me from becoming the Empress? Like, he knew what would happen, so he led me to believe I betrayed him, but that's not the only reason he kept me close and then put me in that cave." I close my eyes. "I should have known this would happen... Demitri told me I could replace the Empress Aleitha." I swallow. It's the first time I call her by her name, but I felt it right to address who she is. Or was...

In case I am the next.

That last thought has my head spinning again. I reach for the water and take a sip.

Nkella places his hand on mine. "Tetalla is a warrior, daí? He secured every angle."

I lick my lips and rest my head on his shoulder as he pulls me in. With his other hand he lifts my chin, and kisses me. My stomach flutters.

It feels good not fighting with him.

After Ntaoru comes back, we eat what she's foraged. We don't have enough water to clean and cook an animal, so this was the best bet. Ntaoru decides to sleep far away from us. I don't blame her.

Nkella grabs me by my waist and pulls me into him. A yelp escapes me, but I don't protest, wanting his protective embrace tonight more than anything. I let my eyes close with his arms wrapped around me.

Warm hands clamp around my waist and pull me back against him. My eyes fly open to Nkella's body pressed hard against mine and I gasp.

"Nkella... your sister—"

"She's out finding breakfast," he growls, voice low and husky against my ear.

"But—"

He silences me with a fingertip on my lips. "Shhhh. Neyuro, you think too loudly, daí?"

He captures my mouth in a fierce kiss, lips bruising mine. His tongue sweeps across my lower lip before slipping inside, matching each desperate pulse of mine. His hands explore my back, fingers tangling in my hair, and heat blooms between my legs.

A clearing of throat makes us both stop, our lips separating, but only an inch from each other. His eyes stare down at me from heavy lids and I lick my lips.

"Don't mind me," Ntaoru huffs. "I will be here doing everything myself. Kh."

Nkella huffs a chuckle and I wince, getting up.

"Sorry, Nta," I say.

"Hn." She glances at me and hands me a thick leaf bearing a single, bulbous fruit; its skin a pale blue streaked with silver veins.

"Where did you find *saechi,* daí?" The excitement in Nkella's voice has my pulse racing. She tosses him one and he catches it. Turning to me, he says, "This is the fruit I told you about, Neyuro. Do you remember?"

I sniff the one I have in my hand. It smells like vanilla custard. "How could I forget?" It's the one he told me he'd give up forever to be with me. I glance at Ntaoru. "He told me of when you were kids and you would climb up the highest tree on the volcano for them. "

Nkella bites into it and closes his eyes. He moans and my brows raise.

"Still think I'm better than that?" I tease.

He opens an eye, and a grin threatens his lips. Then he's on me before I could blink. "Neyuro... even now I would give up ever tasting another bite of this fruit, so that I could always have you to bite into."

My lashes flutter.

He takes another bite of his fruit. "But today, that is not in question. So let me indulge, daí?"

I scoff. I love this side of him. And I hated knowing he was trapped in the Deep, away from all his favorite things. He's suffered for too long without getting to have what he wants. I take a small bite and my eyes widen. The flesh melts on my tongue like a fluffy vanilla-custard cloud, brightened by a sharp tang of citrus.

We each drink some water and continue on our way. But we're all thirsty. And we're getting low. The flames are still alight on the river, and we stop for Nkella to try and control them.

He sits there with his eyes closed, trying to communicate with the Aō, but this is worse than when in the Deep. Tetalla has the Aō bending to his will, and the royal flames are listening.

Ntaoru puts her hand on Nkella's shoulder. "We have to go. Our people need us."

"Not if we die of thirst first," he says.

"Are we still far?"

They both shake their head, but regardless, there won't be water over there, so people will already be parched. And it's only morning. It's going to be hot as a Devil's balls.

Ntaoru takes the lead but we try to maintain a pace that won't tire us out but that isn't strolling either. I can already feel a headache coming on.

We make it halfway to the caves before the ground starts shaking. A deep, rolling tremor rumbles beneath us, and the three of us stop moving.

Ntaouru curses, grabbing onto a boulder for balance. Nkella plants his feet, scanning the horizon.

I stumble forward, catching myself before I fall.

Nkella grips my arm. "We need cover," he says just as the tremors worsen.

We start to run.

The shaking gets worse. Cracks splinter through the dirt, loose rocks tumbling from the hillsides. Dust kicks up around us, stinging my eyes.

"Over there!" Ntaouru shouts, pointing to an outcrop of stone ahead.

We make it just as the land heaves again. I press my back against the rock, breath ragged, hands braced on my knees.

Nkella is beside me, his shoulder brushing mine. He looks at me but doesn't say anything.

The quake slows, then stops.

Ntaouru exhales, brushing dust off her arms. "That was even stronger than the last."

I push off the rock, glancing around. Everything looks the same—dry, cracked land, patches of purple flames flickering where water should be.

Something sticks out from the ground and I slowly go to it, swallowing a lump forming in my throat.

At first, I don't realize what I'm looking at. It's half-buried in the dirt, bent at an odd angle. Rusted metal.

I step closer. My stomach tightens.

It's a street sign.

The words are faded, but I can still make them out.

SUNSET DR.

A freaking street sign and a car has now fallen from the sky. I really wish I could call Talia right now and find out if she's okay… if the Empress is still alive, and if they know anything about this.

My throat tightens. "Nkella."

He's already walking toward it, eyes narrowed.

"What is this?" Ntaouru asks, running a hand along the rusted surface.

I shake my head. "Something else from my world."

"It's getting worse," Ntaoru adds. "But we can't stand around or stop anymore. Our people are still trapped in the caves, and we have to reach them before Tetalla figures out you're free."

I pinch the bridge of my nose, knowing she's right. "Let's go."

He stops abruptly, holding out a hand. "Wait."

I follow his gaze.

There, half hidden behind an outcrop of rock, is a girl. She's curled on her side, motionless.

I gasp and we run to her. She has dark brown hair, mussed over her face, and a single dusty lavender bow half falling from the tips. Just like the one I saw in the car. So there *was* a survivor.

Her chest rises and falls, shallow but steady. I let out a sigh of relief. "She's alive."

I crouch beside her, shaking her shoulder lightly. "Hey. Can you hear me?"

She stirs with a groan, her eyelids fluttering. Then she jerks upright, eyes wide.

"Where—" Her breath hitches. She looks around, disoriented. "Where am I?"

Nkella and Ntaouru exchange a glance and I stare up at them. "She survived the car wreck we passed on the way here."

"Where is here?" she asks again, grabbing at her throat. "A-nd...do you have any water?"

I wince. "Yeah, here but... it's all we have." I hand her my canteen. "Water is a little scarce around here right now."

She takes it, cautiously but then hands it back, sitting up. "Sorry, I don't know you. I'm just... disoriented."

I get it, I wouldn't take water from a stranger either. Not at first, at least. I step back as she stands and dusts herself off. She's wearing a pretty green sun dress, and white sneakers like she had just been for a stroll at the park or something. I skim her various tattoos, one being a sewing machine on her left bicep. My eyes dip to the mark the world gave her, a ship wheel—the Wheel of Fortune mark.

My eyes roll to the back of my head and I sigh. Not again. The last time that mark showed up, AJ died.

That mark only shows up when there are things out of our control. And under the control of the Fates... I resist the urge to chuckle. Because, I'm a Fate. And I can do nothing, because I still don't have my powers back.

I glimpse down at my own wrist, checking to see if my mark has changed. Disappointment strikes me when I don't see the Lover's mark, but I push it aside. My spiderweb mark doesn't change, but the other is... "II." The High Priestess mark? I've been so busy, I haven't even stopped to check. I think I've also been avoiding looking. I gape at it momentarily.

"When did I get a new tattoo?" Her voice brings me back. "And what do you mean water is scarce?" Her eyes move over to Ntaoru, and then Nkella and her eyes widen, looking around us, frantically. "Where the hell am I?"

"Yeah, that's a little hard to explain," I say. "What's the last thing you remember?"

"Um..." She keeps turning around, trying to place herself. A low tremble comes from below us.

"We need to keep going," Ntaoru says.

"We can't just leave her here," I say.

The girl's face twists in confusion as she gapes at Ntaoru and Nkella. The first time I saw an Ipani, I too couldn't stop staring at the stripes on their skin, sharp canines, and subtly pointed ears.

Ntaoru undoes a strap from her bandolier, and loosens a small vial. "Here," she hands me what I recognize as the translation potion. "Tessa gave it to me in case you needed more."

I take it from her and pour the rest into my canteen and shake it. "Electrolytes," I smile at her. She's going to have to drink some eventually. I take a swig, then offer it back to her.

She takes it from me and drinks a bit more, making a face of disgust as she swallows the warm licorice potion. "I was... driving back from a work picnic at Tropical Park..."

I quirk a brow. "Tropical Park? What city and state are you from?"

Her brows furrow at me. "In Miami, wait— am I not in Florida anymore?"

I lick my dry lips and look around. Don't be sarcastic. She just landed in another world, which is a lot. I shake my head, no.

"Then where am I? Who—or what are they? Am I at a ren fair? Her eyes light up. Oh my God, is this Burning Man?"

That is actually a good guess. "No, sorry. Look, there's no easy way to say this but, you kinda fell into another world."

Her face twists and then she bursts out laughing. Ntaoru sighs behind me. I turn to them. "Look, when I first got here, I thought I was dreaming. It took Gari and the ship being attacked to convince me this was all real."

Nkella nods, and scratches the back of his neck. "It was strange for all of us, but it wouldn't be the first time this happens in Ipa."

"Ipa?" the girl asks. Good, the translation potion is working.

"What's your name?"

She grabs the bow hanging from the bottom of her hair before it falls. "Adriel," she answers, sticking the bow in the pocket of her dress.

"Cool dress, Adriel. I love a dress with pockets." I smile.

"Right? Thanks..." Her voice stretches the last word and trails as she continues to look around.

Adriel takes another shaky step back, her sneakers skidding slightly on the dry, cracked earth. Her eyes dart between Nkella and Ntaouru, lingering a little too long on Ntaoru's weapons, and appearances, before shifting back to me. "Okay. Okay, so you're telling me... I'm in another world?"

I nod. "Yeah."

She lets out a breathy laugh, but it's more nervous than amused. "Right. Another world. And let me guess, this is the part where I wake up, or I'm in some very elaborate prank show?" She presses a hand to her forehead. "Or maybe I hit my head in the crash and I'm hallucinating."

"You're not hallucinating," Nkella says.

She looks at him sharply, then back at me. "You're saying that like you expect me to just believe it."

This is taking too long. "I get it, it's a lot to process. But you don't have time to stand around debating whether this is real."

Adriel shakes her head. "No. No, that's not—" Her breath catches. "Wait. If this is real, what about my—" She stops herself, then turns back toward where we came from. "I was in my car—"

She starts to move, but I grab her arm before she can take off. "Adriel, wait."

She flinches, and I let go immediately, holding up my hands. "Listen. We already found your car. It's wrecked. You weren't in it when we passed by, but there was no one else, either."

Her face goes slack. "No one?"

I shake my head.

She sways a little, blinking fast. I recognize the signs of shock, the way her body is trying to catch up to what her brain refuses to process.

Nkella sighs, pinching the bridge of his nose. "We don't have time for this."

"She needs a second, Nkella," I snap.

"She'll get one once we're out of the open."

Adriel's head snaps up. "Out of the open?" Her voice pitches higher. "Why? Is there something out here I should be worried about?"

Nkella's expression darkens. "Yes."

She stares at him. "Okay, nope. You can't just say yes and not explain."

"There's a war going on," I cut in before Nkella can make it worse.

"And the guy who's currently trying to rule this land? Not great. So, unless you want to get caught up in that, I suggest we keep moving."

Adriel hesitates, and I see the battle play out in her head. She wants to argue, to demand more answers, but she also knows she's completely out of her depth.

She exhales sharply. "Fine. Lead the way."

The sun climbs higher as we keep moving, and the heat presses down on us. I keep an eye on Adriel, watching for signs of heat exhaustion, but she's keeping up surprisingly well for someone who just fell into another reality.

"We should find somewhere to rest soon," Ntaouru says, glancing at the sky. "Only for a moment though, daí?"

Nkella nods. "There's a ridge up ahead. It'll give us cover. But the caves is just over it."

"Good," I say. "We're almost where we need to be."

Adriel wipes sweat from her forehead, glancing at me. "Is there actually water where we're going? Or was that just to keep me moving?"

I grimace. "There was water."

She frowns. "Was?"

Nkella tightens his jaw but stays quiet.

I glance at him. "This ruler put fire over the streams so the people of Danū couldn't drink."

Adriel blinks. "I'm sorry—fire over the streams?"

"Yeah."

"Like... actual fire?"

"Yes."

"That burns?"

"No," I admit. "It's magic fire. More like a barrier."

Adriel rubs her temples. "Right. Sure. Magic fire. I'll add that to my growing list of things that make no sense."

I smirk. "You're taking this better than I did my first day."

She snorts. "I think my brain is just buffering."

Before I can respond, another tremor rolls through the ground, strong enough that I have to brace myself.

"It is happening again," Ntaouru mutters.

We pick up the pace, and I hear Adriel mumbling behind me.

"What now?" I ask.

She gestures vaguely with her hands. "Just wondering how the hell I went from driving home to running from magical earthquakes."

I snort. "Welcome to my life."

We reach a rocky overhang with enough space to rest without being completely exposed. And it must be the hottest hour of the day. Sweat drips down my back and I peer into the canteen. It's almost empty. "How are you with water?" I ask Nta.

"Almost out," she admits.

Adriel drops onto a flat rock with a sigh. "Please tell me I'm not about to wake up with another concussion."

"Doubtful," Nkella says, leaning against the wall.

She groans. "Damn it."

I sit down across from her, and try to think of how to put her more at ease. "So... work picnic, huh? What do you do?" I'll admit I'm also up for talking about anything else that'll get the Empress out of my mind.

She nods slowly. "I'm a paralegal."

Yeah, that won't help here. "Do you remember anything before you got here? Any signs of the sky ripping open, weird portals, glowing lights?"

Adriel gives me a flat look. "Yeah, totally. A huge neon sign that said 'Welcome to Another Dimension.'"

I roll my eyes. "I'm being serious."

She sighs, rubbing her face. "No. Nothing. One second I was on the highway, the next, I was here."

Nkella's eyes narrow and then looks at me. "What was it like for you?"

"I stole the World Card... then..." Skipping the part of being in a jail cell to avoid that conversation with the new girl, I continue, "a large hole opened on the floor, and winds pulled me in."

She shakes her head. "No, nothing like that. Not that I can remember anyway," Adriel mutters.

So portals are opening on their own now without use of the World Card, or by someone like Harold coming in. The balance must really be fucked.

Adriel stretches her legs out, fidgeting with the frayed edge of her dress. "So... what's the plan?"

I lean back against the rock, closing my eyes for a moment. "We keep heading for the caves. Once we reach the people, we get them out before Tetalla realizes what we're doing."

"And after that?"

Nkella folds his arms. "We get them, and you to safety. Back where there is water. Then we deal with him."

Adriel lets out a short laugh, but there's no humor in it. "Right."

Nkella watches her carefully. "Hn. You are handling this well."

She shrugs. "I mean, I'm freaking out, but I figure panicking won't do me any favors.

I smirk. "Smart."

She sighs. "So... who's this Tetalla guy? You said he's in charge?"

Ntaouru scoffs. "He took control of Danū by force, and has been at war with the Empress ever since he was let out of the Deep."

I swallow. That last part was my fault.

"It has been a battle for the throne between him and my brother, but the Danū royal fires have chosen him. We do not know why they are still covering the rivers."

Shortest explanation ever, but Ntaoru isn't one for long conversations. I'll fill her in the details as we walk.

Confusion crosses Adriel's face, and she glances at Nkella. "Wait, you're siblings? You've been fighting this guy?"

Nkella nods. "Which is why we need to move before he realizes we're free. He imprisoned us."

She runs a hand through her hair, visibly trying to process everything. "Okay. So... we get these people, get them somewhere safe, and then figure out how to deal with this guy." She pauses, looking at me. "What about you? Something about stealing a card and getting pulled in?"

I rub the back of my neck. "Uh... long story."

Nkella snorts.

Adriel eyes me. "Wait. It just dawned on me you fell into this world like I did, somehow. Does that mean there's a way back?"

I hesitate, my throat tightening. "I need to steal back the World Card from Tetalla first, before I can get you back."

Her face falls slightly. "So he's in the way of me getting home too? Then I'm coming with you."

I shake my head. "Trust me, you have no idea what we're up against."

She's about to protest but Ntaoru pushes herself up, brushing dust from her pants. "We should get going, the caves are up ahead."

I let Ntaoru lead Adriel out, but I hold Nkella back. He quirks a brow at me and I hold up my wrist.

"A new mark?" he asks.

"I just noticed it while talking to Adriel. It's the High Priestess mark. What does it mean?"

"You are asking me?" He scoffs. "You would know better than I do, Neyuro."

My brows knit together. Usually, it would mean to lean on my intuition. Remember my hidden strengths... but I can't even use my Past Fate powers. What good is this mark?

Nkella tugs at me. "Think while we walk, daí?"

We move out, keeping a steady pace toward the caves. The land is dry beneath our boots, and every now and then, the ground gives the smallest tremor beneath us. Nothing like before, but enough to keep me on edge.

Adriel stays close but quiet, taking everything in with wide eyes. The nautilus swirls are vivid in the night sky and we explain to her what it is. I catch her glancing at them every few minutes, staring up, and also like she half expects to see a road sign pointing her back home.

"How much farther?" she asks, shifting her hair tie from one hand to the other.

Ntaouru doesn't turn around. "Not long now."

Adriel exhales. "I swear if this turns into some biblical forty-days-forty-nights situation—"

I snort, but before I can say anything, Lāri's sharp cry cuts through the sky. A dark blur circles above us, and then she swoops down, shifting midair. Feathers fold into skin, talons stretching into boots as she lands in a crouch.

Adriel gasps and takes two full steps back. "What the—"

Her hand flies to her chest, eyes darting between us like she's waiting for someone to explain why the hell a woman just turned from bird to human.

Lāri dusts off her tunic, looking unfazed, and wipes away the dust from her short pixie cut hair. "The caves are just ahead. But you should know... this isn't what you're expecting, mei?" Her gaze stops at Adriel and she quirks a brow at us.

Nkella stiffens. "'What do you mean?"

Lāri gives him an apologetic look. "The locals aren't taking kindly to us being there."

Nkella falls silent, his forehead wrinkling. "What do you mean by not taking kindly to you? What are they doing?"

"At first they did, but when they realized who we are, and our association with you, Captain... they became hostile. But we must get to our crew, either way, mei?"

Nkella gives a slow nod. "It only confirms what I've known. They believe I betrayed them. I do not blame them."

I stare at Nkella who has a grim look on his face. Our connection swirls with his uncertainty. He's going back to his people after so many years, none of them really knew the reason he left after coming back from being kidnapped by the Empress. I reach for his arm.

"We'll get them to listen," I say. He stays quiet.

Lāri jerks her chin at Adriel. "And who's this?"

"I'm—" Adriel still looks shaken. "Uh, Adriel. And you just—" She waves vaguely at Lāri, still trying to process what she saw.

Lāri's eyes narrow at her.

"Adriel here is new to Ipa..." I tell her.

Lāri's eyes widen and she gapes at the new girl, then at me.

"We'll explain everything." I turn to Adriel. "And yes, she's an eagle shifter."

Adriel blinks rapidly. "Okay. Cool. Just checking."

Lāri doesn't give her time to linger on it, turning on her heel. "Come on. We don't want to stay out here too long, mei? I know a backway through the caves and into the city."

"Where's the crew?" Nkella asks.

"Inside. Dealing with... an argument."

Nkella and I exchange glances. An argument?

We follow her, weaving between the jagged rock formations. The landscape changes between forest with tropical trees and plants, to sandy oasis the deeper we go.

We reach a sheer rock face that, at first, looks like a dead end, but then Lāri moves to one side, pressing her hand against the stone. With a quiet click, the rock shifts inward, revealing a narrow passageway.

Adriel lets out a breath. "Oh. Hidden doors. Great."

Lāri steps aside. "In."

I go first, squeezing through the narrow gap. The air inside is cooler, and damp. A torch flickers ahead, barely lighting the stone walls. I hear the others following behind, Adriel muttering under her breath about secret passages and how this is some fantasy novel dream.

Oh, how far I've come from the days I thought this was all a dream.

We step into the main cavern, and my breath catches.

A very large man stops us at the entrance, and Nkella is already stepping between us. The man wields an axe with blades as large as his big head, his Ipani stripes wrap up his neck and around his ear, pointing over his eye brows. He grimaces at us.

"You are not welcome here, Helāni bitch," he says to me directly. "And you," he pushes into Nkella, almost engulfing his frame, "betrayed us all. You belong dead, just like the rest of the Helāni scum that cursed our land."

16

SOREN

The man's grip tightens on his axe. His eyes locked on Nkella through the dim cave lighting.

"Say that again." Nkella lifts his chin, squaring off with the guy.

A storm forms between our Aō connection and I reach for where I'd usually keep my dagger, forgetting I no longer have it. I flick a sharp gaze at Ntaoru who too has her focus on the man. Not the best time to be weaponless, but I'm not sure what'll be worse. Having to fight this dude, and how many others, or Nkella losing the control he has over his Devil and obliterating everyone in there.

And he was doing so well too...

The man's face is rigid, and unyielding. He looks like he wants to chop Nkella's head off. My heart breaks for him. This man has no idea what Nkella has been through. Shit, none of these people know the legends of the Devils of Danū are true. This guy has no idea what he's dancing with.

Before things can boil over, another voice cuts through the tension. "Haro, let them pass."

The man grunts as he looks over his shoulder. "Sokreni, you will allow the man who betrayed us inside?"

An older woman steps out from the shadows, wearing a thick wrap across her shoulders. Her eyes narrow at Nkella, but she gives him a sharp nod. "Let them in, and let them speak. The others are here. We might as well let these in too."

"Where are they?" I ask.

Haro's jaw clenches and he doesn't move. I look between him and Nkella. The pain he's banked for so long is festering and rising to the surface, starting to seep out and twirl within my gut as he's starting to lose control. He had a chance to stay and rule over Danū, helping to take the Empress down, helping his people get food, but instead he left to save his sister. How could anyone blame him for that?

He never knew he was trying to save one and sacrifice the many. He thought he'd always come back, but somewhere along the way, he lost hope in himself. Until now.

"We came to lead you to water," I say, loud enough for the watching crowd to hear. If I can take charge while he regains control over himself, that's what I'll do. "Tetalla sealed the streams with royal flames. We've come a long way to get you all to safety."

More shapes stir deeper in the cave. Whispers rise, and a few names pass between them that make me perk up. Nkella's, Tetalla's, mine?

How do they even know my name?

Sokreni steps forward and puts her arm on Haro's, pulling him back to let us through. Haro relents and gives us way. We walk past him but he stays close behind.

Sokreni's cheeks are sunken, her eyes sharp despite the hollow look in them. "This true? Royal flame on the rivers... risen from the Deep?"

Ntaouru nods. "Proof that they serve him now. We don't know why he's keeping us thirsty, or for how long, but we need to leave now and get to the only drinking source there is."

Haro scowls, but lowers his axe, "If Tetalla has won, that is only good news for us, daſ? This means he has taken what the Empress has wanted, final rule over all of Ipa, and now she will never have it." A smile crosses his features and he raises his axe, gaining a few cheers from the crowd behind him. I stand on my toes to see past him, but can't make out many others apart from shadows.

A small gasp comes from Sokreni. "The myths were a prophecy," she whispers. I stare at her.

"And you would want Death himself to have rule over the royal flames?" Nkella asks him. "How have things changed here since he's been back?"

"Tetalla, our patron god of war, has returned to save us all. We thank the Aō spirits every day for his return. It is in legend that the rivers would turn purple, for the royal flames of Danū will conquer. It is a temporary plight."

I swallow. "Legends?" I take a step back, the lit sconces along the cave shining over gorgeous, colorful imagery, far more colorful than when I first saw a few in the Deep.

He stares at me. "Did you think Helāni myth would wipe us all out?"

"No!" I gasp. "I just—I didn't..."

Back when Nkella and I first met, I remember a song people were singing at the campsite in Sagirang. I got it stuck in my head, and then Nkella corrected my words.

Haro turns to face Nkella. "You don't even recall your own legend, daí?"

I ball my fist.

Ntaoru steps up, pointing a hard finger at his chest. "The legend says *a* god of war. It does not specifically say Tetalla, daí? And my brother was kidnapped at a young age, and when he returned, I was then taken. "Besides, there is no prophecy. It is only legend."

Haro's brow arches, and his face softens at her for a moment, then his hard gaze returns. "He had many chances to return. We could have become stronger with the royal flames under him, if he so chose."

"I didn't know that was to happen," Nkella admits.

"Because you left," Haro spits. "And why are you here now?"

Nkella's voice stays even. "Haro is your name, daí? Your anger is justified. But know, I didn't run from my island. I was stolen away by the Empress long ago. My cousin's parents, and Soren's," he nods toward me, "risked everything to bring me back, and we paid in blood. Then she took my sister and cursed our crew. We lost everything."

He glances at me, and our aovate connection stirs with that weight of regret he rarely lets show. "But I'm back, stronger and wiser than I was," he says, taking a knee before his own people, and bowing his head. I keep myself from gaping. "Give me a chance to make it right."

The air shifts. I have never seen Nkella plead like this.

Ipani from all corners of the cave are coming out to watch Nkella bending his knee for them. My breath catches and my heart is heavy. Ntaoru smiles and nods and tears wet her eyes. Lāri comes forward with a proud smile on her face. She squeezes Nkella's shoulder, and I step in front of her as she turns to leave into the crowd.

"Do they really think the legend is a prophecy?" I ask her.

Lāri scrunches her face. "Some take the songs of our people literally, mei? I am going to go find the crew." She taps my shoulder and I let her pass.

A little girl walks between her parents and stares at me. I wave at her, but her mother places a hand over her chest to protect her. Just then I notice how many of them are staring at me too, not only at Nkella.

"And why should we follow you now, then, daí?" Haro asks Nkella. "What of Tetalla, then? Will you go up against him for the royal flames? Would they even listen to you now?"

"They have listened to him," I say, placing my hand on Nkella's shoulder. "It's hard to explain, but they want them to fight. Tetalla had me prisoner in the castle, so that he could claim my power as his own and wipe out all the humans. That is his end goal. As much as you hate the Empress, how many do you know who are either human, or half?" I stare at his face, and his eyes widen.

"Why should I believe anything that comes out of your mouth, Helāni?"

I pull out my mother's necklace, which my father gave her, and hold it up for him to see in order to show it's an old Danū coin, no longer used, and only passed through the royals. My voice rises for everyone to hear. "Because my father was Prince of Oleanu." It's the first time I say it out loud, and to a whole lot of people I don't know, but they have to hear this. I've come to terms with it, and don't care if anyone else does or doesn't.

Gasps come from all around, and Haro squints closer at my necklace until his brows rise to his hairline. Nkella stays in his place, and I don't know if it's Ipani custom, or what. Does he stand only when they let him stand?

"My mother was from my world," I continue. "And apparently we are descendants from the Empress and her sisters, but I never knew any of that. I was raised alone, with no parents, a lot like Nkella. And when I came here... I met the Ipani. The crew was a mix of human and Ipani, and they took me in. We became family. Believe me or not, but I care about all of you, and so does Nkella. This is his home, and it's mine now too. You're all his people... which means... you are my people too now." My voice shakes a little at the end. I swallow.

Haro's features have surprisingly softened, a little.

The cave silences, and some even take a knee to join Nkella, showing him their allegiance. Others still stand, which doesn't surprise me. Trust never came easily to me, so I can't expect a large group of people who feel betrayed by their monarchy to suddenly bend the knee to their estranged prince.

Haro finally lowers the axe. "Where's this water then?"

"We'll show you," I say, my shoulders relaxing.

Nkella glances up and sees half the people around the cave bending their knees, and now he stands. "We cannot wait long, daí?" he says with hesitation in his voice, and I know he's reluctant to let them all know everything that's at stake.

Haro grunts and steps aside. More figures move into view and my chest squeezes. Their faces are hollowed from hunger, and so skinny. So many years of them being under siege by the Empress. It's time they reclaim their island, and we put an end to any reign from the Empress, and from Death.

17

SOREN

A girl clears her throat behind me, and I spin to see Adriel. I had almost forgotten she was here.

"Oh," I hold out my hand and she takes it to help her down the steep step. "We also might have a bigger problem. The tremors."

People are now all coming closer to her, noticing her clothes. How different she's dressed than all of them.

"It is true," Nkella says. "No one is going to be alive if the world rips apart."

"Or collides with mine," I mutter under my breath.

Haro's brows furrow. "Rips apart? What are you saying, daí?" He looks back at Adriel. "You are not the first to come here in the past few moons. There are more of you inside."

My eyes widen, and Adriel and I exchange gaping glances. Lāri pushes herself through the crowd and reaches us, this time with Kae following her trail.

A wide smile tugs at my face when I see him. He and Nkella grip onto each other in a tight hug, and then Kae punches his shoulder.

"For being bancha, daí?"

"Kh."

I walk up to him and throw my arms around his neck. He picks me up in a hug. "Once again, you have brought our captain back."

I chuckle. "Always." He lets go of me, and I notice a solemn stare he passes from Lāri to me. My eyes widen.

"Where's Tessa?"

"Oh, she is fine. Back there... watching over the others."

"Others?"

He rubs the back of his neck. "A lot has happened. But first," he looks at Nkella. "I interrupted what you were about to say, and I want to hear it."

Nkella explains in full what's been happening, and the pieces that have fallen from Earth, while we're led to a communal area. I add in how Ipa is dependent on there being more than one Fate ruling in order to keep the balance between the Aō and the Fate magic of the Tarot cards controlling everyone's fates.

A few stare down at their marks and make resentful comments about me being a "Helāni bitch."

I can't imagine what they're all going through. Despite me being here, and having my life on the line too, their entire way of being was infiltrated by my distant, still living, ancestors.

Of course they hate me.

As soon as we reach the crew, we can continue on as a big group, for the journey to bring water. The sooner I can get out of these evil stares, the better.

"What does this mean for Ipa?" Sokreni approaches us and hands me a small wooden bowl of some sort of drink.

Nkella shakes his head. "We do not believe either world will survive the collision." He takes a bowl from her, and she turns to pour more into a new bowl to give to Adriel.

A few gasps come from around us, and Haro places his hand on Nkella's shoulder, ducking his head, leaning close. "We better not rouse panic among everyone in Danū," he whispers.

Nkella nods. "We need to get you to clean water first, or none of us will survive this, daí?"

"We have persevered since, Prince. But yes, I will gather a small group to go with us. What will stop the collision?" he asks.

Nkella passes me a look, our connection stirs between us, and I know he can sense my hesitation. "Me fighting Tetalla and winning," Nkella tells him, but I feel the lie stirring between us. A quick shift of his eyes on me, and back on Haro lets me know that's the story, and we're sticking to it.

I swallow a dry lump in my throat. Me taking the Empress's throne is what will stop the collision between worlds. She might even be dead already, and I'm here waiting for the end of the world. My gaze falls to my High Priestess mark, and it dawns on me that this card comes right before the Empress in the Tarot evolution.

Now my head starts to spin. Could my mark have been a premonition this whole time?

And Adriel's mark being the Wheel of Fortune, and we found her first. Circumstances without our control, or in the hands of the Fates.

A sinking feeling falls to the pit of my stomach, and it's telling me she's dead. And I'm going to be the one to become Empress next.

But no… I can't be.

"I will lead you to water, and then I will be off to find him," Nkella tells him.

My eyes widen. "You're not ready to fight him," I blurt. He's dehydrated, and just came out of a prison cave. How the hell does he think he'll be able to fight Tetalla like this?

"I will be," he says softly. "I will make sure I am ready by the time we return to the waterfall."

I shake my head slowly. "How—"

"Trust me, Neyuro."

I take a deep breath, and nod, tightening my grip around the wooden bowl as they walk away together, talking. I hold up the bowl to my nose and take in… neutral, earthy notes. I swish it around. "It looks like dirt and water," I whisper to Lāri.

"It is, don't drink it," she whispers. "It tastes nasty."

I quirk a brow at her.

"They have mixed some minerals that are nutrient rich with the little water they have. It is how they survived so long."

I frown and stare down at it. When I glance up, I notice Sokreni smiling at me and urges me on to take a sip.

"It will give you energy, Helāni. Go on."

I smile weakly at her and bring the bowl to my lips, glancing at Lāri, who frowns. I glance at Adriel who is nearly done drinking her bowl.

"I was thirsty," she says. She has a point. It might taste like dirt, but if these people have been drinking this for a long time and are still alive, then who am I to turn it down?

I take a gulp and swallow. It's like sand down my throat, and I cover a cough.

"Come," Sokreni says. "The others are in the living chamber."

The living chamber? Is that like a living room?

Lāri nudges me. "I'm going to fly back to the waterfall and refill your canteen. I'll be back."

I gape at her. "Hell no. What if you're caught?"

"I have survived worse than this, mei? It is better if I get a head start on you guys. I'll be their lookout while bringing you and the crew water. The group will only be able to bring enough water back for everyone—"

I give her my canteen. "Fine, you've made your point." She nods and leaves the cavern.

Adriel and I follow Sokreni deeper into the caves, over a bridge, with large, endless walls filled with homes carved into the stone. Lights illuminate the insides of many of them, and I remember Kae explaining to me how vast Danū was. It truly is like a city down here. I wonder how far we are from the castle.

"We all live here, but share quarters. It is not like other islands in Ipa, daí?" she says. "We all care for one another. Those who can cook, share, and those who can sew, make clothes for the many."

We walk in silence, listening to the echoes of her voice, and of Ipani talking and laughing in the distance. They've survived this long, away from being turned into agentless soldiers by the Empress. Away from merciless slaughter, to be stuck during the time of eternal suffering—when no one could truly die, away from it all. Waiting for a savior... like Tetalla.

Never meet your heroes, right?

We reach the end of the bridge and follow her down a dim lit corridor.

"Do you ever leave the cave?"

"Some of us, yes."

"It's just so... dark."

Sokreni turns and smiles. "There are some parts of the cave where the sun shines through strong from high above. It is beautiful."

We enter a large chamber draped with carpets of red, purple, and black with gold embroidery. Oil lamps hang from the ceiling and the walls, and a cozy fire adds ambience from a faraway hearth. People huddle around each other, telling stories, some drawing, and laughing.

It reminds me of our cozy home in Dempu Yuni. Not because of its comfort, but how everyone here is safe with one another.

"Soren!" Tessa's voice breaks my concentration and I nearly scream in excitement when I spot her light brown hair. I run over and throw my arms around her.

"Well, I missed you too!"

Tears sting my eyes and I let her go. Too much has happened since Nkella's crazy plan didn't pan out.

She searches past me. "Where's everyone else?"

"They went with Haro to get a group together to find the last remaining water," I tell her. "Tetalla won. The royal flames govern all the streams... and we don't know for how long. We didn't think we'd make it here."

Tessa's eyes are wide.

"I'll tell you more but—" I turn to Adriel and she waves at Tessa.

"Hi, I'm Adriel."

"I see you found one of them." Tessa quirks her head to two people sitting at the far wall. A tall white man, wearing what appears to be a pirate hat—not plain leather like Nkella's, but an elaborate one you'd find at a ren fair, with a feather and all—and upon further inspection, full-on pirate clothes, sits with his back against the wall. He stares out a the open, his hands semi-shaking. In the far corner of the cave, a slender girl around my age, with short brown hair, wearing jeans and a sage green tank, sits by herself. She appears to be doing something on the carpet, but I can't see what it is.

"Tessa, have you been able to speak to them? Have they said anything?"

"I gave them Indakepoa—the translation potion—but they still think this is all a dream. Like you did."

Yeah, I bet they do. I glance at Adriel. "Want to help me break the news to them?"

"I can try," she chuckles.

We carefully walk over to the man in the pirate hat. He glances at me as we approach him.

"Hi, I'm Soren," I start.

"Hello—Gibby."

"Hi, Gibby. Do you remember how you got here?"

His hands tremor but he stares at me right in the eyes. His eyes are crystal blue, and he must be somewhere in his fifties. "Uh, no," he says. I try to glance at the mark on his wrist, but it's covered by his sleeve.

"Where are you from?"

"Michigan."

My brows raise. "You were in Michigan before you got here?"

"No, I'm from Michigan, but I live in St. Augustine."

I deadpan. "Florida?"

"Yeah."

"And so is Kennedy." He points to the girl in the far corner.

"Do you two know each other?"

"Yeah, we have a lot of mutual friends within pirate crews and such."

Oh, right. Florida has a whole set of pirate re-enactors, and even mermaids. I get it now.

Adriel and I exchange a glance. "So, the rip between worlds is happening in Florida then?"

I shrug and look back at Gibby. "All right, Gibby. Just hang tight, we're going to figure this out. Are you hungry?" I don't even know why I ask, it's not like I have any food to offer him.

He glances at me and bellows laughing. "I'm sure I can dream something up if I am."

I give him an apologetic glance and then walk over to the girl. Now that I have a closer look, she has a collection of crystals that she's laying out in front of her. I get a quick glance at her wrist. The Magician.

She might be useful. And at least here in Danū, and with the war, we won't have to worry about the Empress going after her. Hell, we might even need her.

"Hi, Kennedy?"

She looks up at us.

"I'm Soren. This is Adriel. Are you doing okay?"

"No one has been able to answer me. Where am I? Why can't I leave?"

Oh good. "So, you don't think you're dreaming?"

"I'm not dreaming."

I sit on the ground in front of her. "Do you remember how you got here?"

"No, I think I must have been sleeping, but then woke up here."

I stare at her, and she stares at me back.

"Sorry, it's just anyone who comes here from our world usually thinks they're dreaming. And if you're telling me you were asleep before you got here—you must really be sure of yourself..." Definitely a witchy person. She knows herself better than a normal person would.

She shrugs. "I know when I'm awake. Don't you?"

I straighten my back. "Yeah, of course." I scoff a little. "What do you have there?"

"I found these outside the cave. I collect crystals. Wait—"

I quirk a brow.

"Did you say... 'our world'?"

There we go. I nod. "You guys... fell through a portal. Somehow." God, I'm terrible at explaining this.

"The same thing happened to me," Adriel said. "And no, we're not dreaming, so, you're right."

"If we're not dreaming," Gibby calls out to us. "Then why are there people with stripes, long ears, and sharp teeth?"

I smile at him. Wait until he sees the floating island. That one got me. "This is difficult to explain... but, other worlds are real. And, it's a long story but, our worlds are colliding."

"Yeah," Adriel adds, "I was driving when I crashed—and... ended up here."

Gibby's eyes are wide and now he's standing up.

"Gibby?" I stand walking to him as he starts to pace back and forth.

"I have to be dreaming. This has to be a dream."

"It's not...but it's okay—"

"No, it isn't okay. If this is real... my wife can be out there somewhere. Hurt. I have to get out of this cave. Now." He starts walking over the carpets, and heading toward the exit.

"Gibby, wait!"

Tessa reverses her chair, and blocks him from leaving. "Sorry, Gibby. It's safer for you if you stay here. You don't know what's out there."

Movement at the corner of my eye makes me glance at someone laying a scrawny boy to sleep as he coughs. I turn back to Gibby.

"Plus, there's a shortage of water, and out there is sort of a desert."

"That's worse then," he says. "What if my wife is out there?"

My shoulders drop, my heart breaking for him.

Kennedy now approaches us. "I don't know where my husband is either."

"I understand, guys. I went through something similar. A long time ago. The truth is, they can be here... given the circumstances. But you won't find them if you're dead. They can also be home, snuggled up in bed. What's your wife's name?" I ask Gibby.

"Rachelle."

I turn to Kennedy. "And you? What's your husband's name?"

"Brian."

"Okay, well, I bet Rachelle and Brian are at home. It's possible the portal is opening randomly, at inconsistent times and places. And possibly only around Florida. But I will say this: you're going to go home, but we all have to stick together and nobody panic. Can you do that?"

Gibby pinches the bridge of his nose and sighs. "I liked it better when I thought I was dreaming."

"I totally get that, dude."

"So what do we do then?"

"For now, try to remember the last thing you did before you ended up here."

"I ended up remembering that I was driving," Adriel reminds them, "so it is possible."

"In the meantime, I'm going to walk around and meet the Ipani here in this cave—that's what the natives are called, by the way. Tessa can give you a quick history of Ipa, because well, she's an Ancient Greek descendant."

Confusion sprawls on the new refugees' faces as I step away from them and let Tessa catch them up. This is all new to them, and it's going to seem impossible.

Which is understandable, but I don't have time to take care of them right now.

I walk over to the boy who was laid down, and is still in a fit of coughs. His mother stands and blocks my path.

"Hi, I'm Soren. I was just—"

"I know who you are." She crosses her arms. Ipani stripes cross with sharp edges right under her eyes, adding an edgy and sharp look to her already strong attitude. "Not all of us are for you being here. Helāni."

Sweat starts forming on the back of my neck. "I understand," I say, trying to look for the words that could make her see my side, but her eyes cut right through me. "I'm only trying to help. My friend is coming back with some water... I can share some until we find more—"

"Your kind has helped enough. Stay away from my son." She turns, whipping her long braid in my direction. I wince, looking around to see who else saw that, and if they agree. A few in the corner shoot me a smug smile and turn away.

Great. This'll be fun.

I stare at the boy for a moment longer, and notice his ears are round. He's half Ipani, half human. So by "my kind," she must mean the Fates, not humans. A low sigh escapes my lips as I turn to head back to Tessa and the refugees.

An elderly woman sits hunched over with her knees drawn to her chest, her skin looks sallow, and her long gray hair tucked under a woven scarf. Her eyes are half-lidded, barely open, and she's shivering, though the cave is warm. Beside her, two other women sit close. One is wiry with a sharp jaw and faded tattoos on her arms, and the other has a softer face, with rounded features. She tries handing the elderly woman some of what was in that bowl they gave me. She pushes it away.

Come on, Lāri... how long does it take you to fly there and back? One of the younger ladies with short, dark brown hair and soft Ipani stripes glances at me. What's the worst that can happen? They reject me like the other one did?

Steeling my spine, I approach slowly. "Hi," I say, bending down to their level. "Do you mind if I sit here?"

The round-faced one nods. The sharp-jawed one just watches me.

I sit. "Is she sick?" I ask quietly, nodding toward the elder.

"Yes," the kind one says. "And weak."

"If you want to help," the other one snaps, "find water."

I nod, swallowing hard. "We're working on it."

A rumble shakes the cavern walls and a yell behind me makes me spin around to find Gibby rubbing his head. Kennedy and Tessa go to him asking if he's all right.

"Yeah," he says. "Ow... Oh... I remember how I got here."

I jog over to listen as he looks over at Kennedy who's stuffing the crystals in her purse.

"We were at the Celtic festival, and we were both standing in line to get something to eat while Rachelle and Brian were getting drinks from another stand."

Kennedy's brows are furrowed as she looks down at her feet.

"Then, there was a rumble... like the one we just had... and when I turned around there was a giant rip in the sky."

Kennedy gasps, "And a big shadow. I remember. It was a black rip. I wasn't asleep."

"And then when I looked back down, there was a huge shake and you fell into me."

"Then I woke up covered in sand, with my jeans torn and wet."

"Yeah," Gibby says, looking at Tessa. "Then you and the tall dude," pointing at Kae who just walked in the cavern, "found us on the shore of a pink beach and brought us here."

I try to lock eyes with Kae but he's speaking to someone with his back to me. My eyes search for Nkella, but he hasn't come in yet, so I turn back to Gibby. "You've met my crew. You don't know how lucky you are that they're the ones who found you."

"Crew?" Gibby asks, and I smirk.

"Yep. Here, we have real pirates. These are good ones, but be careful."

Kennedy's eyes widen, but she stays quiet. I can tell she must be freaking out.

"Don't worry," I tell them, making eye contact with Adriel too. "We'll get you home." Somehow. I need to take this dampener off. And find the World Card. That's the only way I can get them all back, but with all that's going on, how the hell am I going to retrieve those Tarot cards?

Just then, footsteps echo down the stone path. I look up to see Nkella returning with Haro, Ntaoru, and a few others. A group of them, maybe ten, follow behind, carrying barrels, ready to make the journey.

Hurrying toward them, I jump over a few people sprawled out on the floor. "Are we ready to go?" I ask, itching to get out of this cave already.

Nkella's eyes soften at me and he brushes his fingers over my arm, I feel the tug of our connection, and I want to forget about our earlier disagreement. I want to kiss him, but it's probably the wrong time in front of everyone right now. During all this.

"Soren." He lifts my chin and stares into me. "Stay here, my aovate, daí?"

My features twist, but I let him touch my face. "Why?"

"It's too risky," he says. "We're already stretching our limits and—you are human. It is best only a few of us go and come back with water." I glance at the large, heavy barrels Kae and two others carry.

"I can keep pace. I'll pull my weight." I wish I didn't have this stupid dampener on me restraining my power. I could have easily reached into the past and brought out water. I tug on it, even though I've tried a gazillion times and know it won't budge.

"I know," he says softly, stepping closer. "But it's better you stay. Keep the others steady. Ntaoru too."

He glances over my shoulder and his brow furrows. "There are two more now. New ones?"

"Yeah. Gibby and Kennedy."

His jaw tightens, but he doesn't say anything more. Just nods.

I don't want to agree, but I'll only hold them back. "Fine, but promise me you won't drop everything to go fight Tetalla when you're not ready."

Nkella flicks a quick gaze to Kaehante who's busy talking with the others they've met. His eyes dip to my hands and he takes them. "Come, follow me."

I quirk a brow but let him lead me away from the chamber without asking him where we're going. I quickly glance over my shoulder to see if Tessa or anyone needs us before we go, but everyone seems to be preoccupied.

We walk down a long stretch of uneven ground, away from the bridge we crossed to get here. Our footfalls echo through the tall cavern walls, and it's the first time Nkella and I have been alone, and not in immediate danger, or on the way to somewhere urgent. I mean, there is still danger impending on us, but it's nice to just steal a moment.

He takes my hand again, and our Aō connection grows stronger at his touch, it's as if it tingles up my arms, urging me forward, wanting to touch. To be with each other. He leads me in through an archway and into a new chamber. He steps aside and helps me up the steps, his eyes not leaving me as I give him a curious smile. My mouth falls open when I step inside.

Soft beams of light cascade down from feet above, lighting the way through rows and rows of greenery, with small white-and-yellow flowers that almost glisten from where I'm standing. Dark, purple flames dance upon the once waterfall, and onto the stream of water that would be glowing next to us.

"We can't be here too long," he says. "Kaehante is waiting for me to leave, but... I wanted to show you this before I left. In case... something happened and I didn't get the chance to."

I gape at him. The shadows of the flames dance on his features in the dim lighting. So this must be where Sokreni was talking about. In broad daylight, this must be beautiful. "How did you know this was here?"

"Kaehante showed me quickly before I came to see you. He wanted to show me a place of our childhood. I remember playing in that meadow." He points with his chin. "I thought you'd like it too."

"It's beautiful."

He slowly presses into me. "Yes," he whispers, pulling my chin up as he dips down to take my lips. My breath catches as his kiss goes from sensual to devouring. I give into him as that sensation from our connection wraps around me, cocooning me in a deep euphoria, and I never want to let him go. Despite my eyes being closed, I can sense colors wrapping around us as I let my hands explore his body, and he pulls me in deeper. I feel the edges of his teeth nibble on my bottom lip as he slowly lets me go. My eyes flutter open, but my heart is still beating loudly in my ears. "I didn't want to leave without giving you a proper goodbye," he says.

My eyes narrow at him as I pull away a little. "You talk as if you're planning to meet Tetalla, and not just go get water."

He stares at me, and I push his chest. "Nkella."

"I wasn't, my aovate. But everything feels unpredictable, daí?"

"Fine."

He tugs me into him again, this time moving my hair out of my face and gently biting my neck. A moan escapes me, and my leg involuntarily wraps around him.

"You said we don't have time," I breathe out.

He kisses me again. "We don't."

Our breathing picks up as he dips to my chest, and I tug at his pants so he could get closer to me. I want to feel him.

The magic that infuses our bond starts to wrap around us again, and it forces a smile on my face. I could never ever feel this again with anyone else. Being with Nkella, it's more than just being in love. It's literal magic. A drug. And I never want it to stop.

Not that it would.

"Neyuro?"

"Hm?"

"You drifted."

I stare back at him. "Sorry, I was just lost in you. In us... in this... aovate ouma."

"Hnn." A smile tugs at his lips. "You seem to be experiencing it deeper than I thought you would."

"Because I'm human?"

He nods. "But that brings me joy, Neyuro. Maybe my ouma is strong enough for the both of us, daí?"

"Maybe." I lick my cracking lips. "And maybe you should spend a little time here trying to connect with the flames?"

He frowns. "We should go."

A wave of nausea hits me, reminding me that I'm dehydrated, but I don't ignore the way he evaded my suggestion. "Yeah, luckily Lāri is on her way back with my canteen. But still, we do need to go." I give this beautiful chamber one last glance.

"We'll come back, when this is all over." He raises my hands to his lips and kisses them.

"I'd like that."

"And… I have been trying to communicate with the royal flames."

"Oh? And?"

"They are cryptic."

"Figures." Why wouldn't they be?

"They are testing me. I need to be ready, and if they deem me fit, they will listen."

My lips part. So that's it? I'm not sure what there's to do with that information, but I don't want to add to his stress. "So we basically wait for when you and Tetalla are up to a fight, then see what happens?"

"Soren." He pauses, turning back around to gaze into me, the specks of his fire igniting his irises under the flickering sconces. "There is no escaping what needs to happen now," he whispers. His gaze looks almost solemn and now I realize why he's acting so weird. He's come to terms with a battle the royal flames will put him through, and he knows he might not win, because they've already taken Tetalla's side. "The flames don't care about what's just, daí? They care only about strength."

"I don't believe that." I stare up at him. "They've spoken to you before. They want you to rule."

"They told Tetalla the same things. He is the legend our people have sung about. No matter what means he's taking, the Aō wants to be pure, and if Tetalla's purge helps it achieve that, it won't matter to the fires of Danū how I see the world. Or how much I love you." His voice trembles, and it breaks my heart. "And how I do not want to lose you."

"You won't."

He pulls back. "I know." His breathing deepens, but we continue walking in silence the rest of the way.

We make it back out of the chamber and through the dark corridor, both of us in deep thought. And for some reason now, our aovate connection feels like there's some sort of invisible and physical cord tying us together. I like it, a lot. But I don't know if it's new, or if it's always been there, and I'm just feeling it now. Like if every time we share a deep moment, and a sexual one, it grows stronger. Or maybe the Aō is just letting me feel it more now.

A roaring vibrates the walls so loudly that I'm blinded by it. Nkella spins around and pulls me down to the ground as his body shields me from an intense heat. At first, I see dark, purple flames, and then darkness, before I realize I'm closing my eyes. A ringing sounds in my ear, and Nkella's shaking me as my eyes flutter open. He grabs my hand and I'm on my feet before I can ask what happened.

He has his coat draped over me as he runs me back into the chamber. I'm panting hard, sweat dripping down my neck. I scan the chamber. Everyone is staring at us.

"I thought the royal flames were cooler."

"Cooler, not cold. They're hot if they touch you," he says briskly, walking over to a group huddled in the corner. The blood drains from my face as I notice blue fur sticking out, swirling over someone. When did Gari get here? Kaehante and Tessa both have worried looks on their faces.

"Who is it? What happened?" I demand.

Gari lifts his head to see me. "...It's Lāri," he gurgles. "She's badly hurt."

18

SOREN

Smoke clings to Lāri's body, lying crumpled on the stone. Her feathers are half-shifted down her arms, and her body trembles. Burn marks snake along her legs, and her skin is cracked with purple lava simmering at the edges.

Ntaoru drops to her knees beside her, panic etched into every line of her face. "I know I can't do anything," she mutters, pressing her hand over the scorched flesh anyway. Lāri groans, teeth clenched. Ntaoru closes her eyes, and I think she's trying to reach her volcanic ouma connection.

Kaehante kneels beside them, keeping his palm steady on Ntaoru's back.

Gari's small claws twitch at his sides as he speaks: "I met her on the way to the waterfall." He lowers his voice to a low gurgling. "We didn't even make it. The waterfall's gone, dry, covered in purple flame."

Nkella steps forward, jaw clenched. "Was Tetalla there?"

"We didn't see him," Gari gurgles, bobbing his head from side to side. "But someone came down the pass. They were burned to a crisp, but... glowing from the inside, like a lantern, and he was... w-walking."

He lifts one claw and spreads his stubby arms as far as he can. "Boom. The whole basin was ash in seconds. I grabbed Lāri and flew her back here. Just in time... but another burnt dead followed us into the cave... and..." His yellow eyes go big.

"Exploded," Tessa finishes for him.

Lāri coughs hard, wincing as Ntaoru brushes a cloth over her wounds. "He knows we're here," she says through gritted teeth.

A heavy silence falls. My stomach sinks. Gari lowers his head and I stare at him. "I'm glad you were there, Gari..."

"I was looking for all of you. It wasn't hard to spot an eagle when no one dares fly these days."

I swallow. Lāri was risking her life for me. Guilt twists my gut and I bring my hand over my mouth. After AJ... "I shouldn't have let her go."

"S-stop it," Lāri coughs out, sitting halfway up. "We all have a job to d-do, mei? Stop blaming yourself."

I shake my head, tears burning the corners of my eyes. A ball gets lodged in my throat preventing me from saying anything else.

"Kae," Tessa whispers and he turns to her. "Grab my bag for me. Let me see what I have to help Lāri."

Haro scratches his head. "And now what do we do about the water, daí?"

A few people cough, others groan.

Nkella and I share a glance. His expression is serious, his jaw tight. "So he's filling up corpses with royal fire, and using them as explosives. One at the waterfall, and then another that followed them in here."

I glide over to him. "Do you think he knows we escaped?"

He gives a tight nod. "He must be securing every entrance. Sending out attacks."

I look over my shoulder at everyone carrying on with what they were doing. Our three refugees are talking amongst themselves. Adriel glances over at me and I offer her a tight smile.

"What are we going to do?" I say. "There could be more from my world, and people here don't have water."

He leans over and kisses my head. "My aovate cares for all, daí?"

I stare at him. "How can you be so calm?" A chill runs down my spine. "The last time you were this calm, you were planning something."

"Kh. You are the one with the more secrets, daí? We cannot move anyone now. Not with Tetalla's warriors walking around, and the Arcana in the skies. There is a full war outside. Leaving is too dangerous for them."

"So they stay here?"

"We stay too, until it clears." He glances at Kae who is now walking over to us.

"We should make a break for the ship and head for Sāgirang," Kae tells us. "Take as many as we can."

Nkella shakes his head. "Koj. We don't know if he dried out the other islands."

"We have to try. We also have water on the ship, but..." Kae lowers his head, "not for everyone, daí?"

"I will not leave my people again," Nkella states.

"But we can go, make trips?" Kae rubs his head. "What do you think Tetalla is doing? He does not want to kill his own people." The last sentence sounded more like a question, and I frown.

"No," I say. "He wants the humans gone. He's trying to smoke us out."

Nkella nods. "He knows Ipani will survive this, but the humans won't."

I lick my cracked lips; my throat is starting to burn. I wonder what would be happening to me if I didn't have this magic dampener on my wrist.

Would I be weathering this better with my Fate magic?

Lāri coughs and I glance at her. She's looking at us. "Yes, it is true."

Nkella, Kae, and I walk to her. "What's true?" Nkella asks.

"Smoking the Greek descendants out," Lāri says. "To be extinguished. Even..." she gulps, grabbing her chest, "even half-Ipani."

Gasps and cries circle around us as panic ripples through the chamber.

Nkella turns to Lāri. "How do you know this for certain?"

I grab at his arm. He better not be thinking to go out there right now, dehydrated and unprepared.

"On my way back, we were intercepted by the snow drakon. The Empress's spy, mei? "

"She and I didn't fight this time," Gari purrs.

A man in the back shouts, "It's true then. What they say. Tetalla means to drain us out. To let the humans die first."

"They know we can last longer without water," someone else says. "He means to wait us out."

My blood grows cold as all eyes are now on us. On Nkella. On me.

And suddenly, the walls of this cave are closing in on me. And I'm boiling.

Too close to collapsing. So much for not inciting panic...

Lāri struggles to lean in, but Kae helps her sit up. "She told me everything and needed me to come back to the Tower, but I couldn't do that without coming here first."

The chatter around this chamber has died down, and I can feel their eyes on us. I lower my voice. "So the Empress is alive?"

"Injured," she says. "And there is more Arcana now, more than before. They surround the caves."

I steal a glance to my wrist. The High Priestess mark is still there.

Shuffling noises come from all sides as people come closer. Haro's brows raise.

"The Empress is injured?" he asks, excitement in his voice. Nkella becomes rigid.

"The Empress cannot be injured, daí? If she is, it means Tetalla has become stronger now and can reach the Tower."

"Not to mention what we told you would happen to this world," I add.

Silence blooms the cavern walls.

A chill runs down my spine. Tetalla is even stronger. He's winning. But a wave of relief also washes over me. The Empress is alive. Bittersweet, but it also means Talia is safe, and I don't have to be rushing to take the Empress's place. But this confirms that she's injured, which explains the tremors—something that, according to Demitri, was bound to happen without all three Fates. But, if the Aō thinks she's dying... This must be why things are getting worse and fast.

I step away and Nkella follows.

"You're right, it's a war zone outside," I tell him. "We can't leave."

"The question is, how long until he sends his army into the caverns and starts taking people."

I narrow my eyes at him and search his face. What is he planning? "You can't go looking for him now, Nkella. He'll send his warriors to take people *while* you're out looking for him. You'd be falling into one of his traps, you know that right?"

He stares at me, but he knows I'm right.

Gibby stretches and yawns louder than necessary. "Think I'll go for a stroll," he announces to no one in particular, already rising to his feet. "Get a feel for these echo chambers."

"Gibby," I say flatly, "it's not exactly a tourist cave."

Nkella spins around to meet his gaze. "Did you not see what has happened? It is dangerous, daí?" I place a gentle hand on Gibby, and he reels back a little.

"I won't go far," he says, waving me off. "Promise."

I shift to intercept him, stepping just enough to block his path, and my hip knocks hard into Kennedy. "Shit—s-sorry," I stammer, reaching out to steady her, but something clatters to the ground.

A crystal, no bigger than a lemon wedge, slips from her purse and skids across the stone floor, landing on the corner of one of the carpets. It gleams faintly in the low light, translucent like quartz but edged in an eerie, luminous blue.

"Oh," Kennedy says, crouching. "Wait, let me—"

"I got it," I say, already moving to grab it. My fingers close around the crystal, but as I straighten my back, something wet slides out of my hand.

My eyes bulge as a shimmering stream of water pools in my palm.

I stare, mouth parting. "Kennedy," I whisper, stunned. "I... Wait, what the hell?" I stare at the puddle in my hand. "I'm so sorry. I didn't even know this kind of thing could happen here..."

I look up at her, and step back as now everyone is standing around watching me. My eyes move to Nkella, who's eyes are narrowed.

Kaehante stands frozen nearby, eyes locked on my palm.

"What?" I ask.

"That..." Ntaoru speaks first, voice low and uneasy. "That's not supposed to happen."

My brow furrows. "What do you mean? It just did."

Nkella steps forward slowly, eyeing the puddle. "Crystals do not burst into water, daí? Does that happen in your world?"

I gape at him. "No."

"Helāni magic?" someone asks, and the crowd shifts.

"It can't be," Tessa chimes. "Those crystals are from the caves. The Fates have nothing to do with what was here before they came."

"This is true," Kae says. "But then what is it?"

"I've had that one since the day I got here," Kennedy offers, her voice small. "I thought it was just... pretty."

"That was strange," says another Ipani woman nearby.

Kae kneels beside me. "It wasn't warm," he murmurs, running his finger near the edge of the puddle. "No heat from the royal flames."

"Could it be the Aō?" someone whispers behind us. "Hearing our plea?"

A murmur ripples through the onlookers. A mix of hope and disbelief.

I glance at the dwindling water in my hand, and I bring it up to my face. Smells like water.

"Don't—" Tessa's voice fades as I stick my tongue out, and I'm already drinking it.

"Tastes like water."

"Kh. That was bancha, daí? A stone turns to water and you drink it?"

Gari giggles beside me. "Do it again."

"Hey, out of all the weird potions you've all made me drink, you cross the line at crystal?" I wipe my hands clean. Gari glides over to Kennedy, his sinewy body loosely wrapping around her arms.

Her eyes go wide, and she holds her breath.

"Hmmm," Gari sings. "Do you have any more?"

"Yes," a woman says. "Let's test it."

Kennedy kneels down, unzipping her bag. "I've got more. I... I didn't think they were important. I just liked how they looked."

She pulls out half a dozen crystals, each shaped a little differently, but all with that same clear quartz base edged in a blue that shifts like flame or frost depending how the light hits it. She places them on the stone floor, careful not to let them roll.

Nothing happens.

I reach for one, fingers brushing its smooth surface, and hold it in my palm.

"Wait!" someone calls out.

I glance at a woman who steps forward, holding out a shallow wooden cup. "Try it in here."

I take the cup, and drop the crystal in.

We all watch in close silence at the rock inside the cup.

And nothing.

Gari slithers closer, craning his furry neck. "Maybe it has to be your hand," he says. "Like before."

Tilting the cup, I drop the crystal back on my palm. It's cool to the touch. Smooth. Still a crystal.

I shrug. "Maybe it was a fluke. Here, Kennedy, want it back?" But right as I grip it harder in my hand, a single drop forms at the edge. Then another. Water starts dripping into the wooden cup and my breath catches as the crystal dissolves completely, leaving the cup half full.

"Daí?" someone whispers.

Before anyone can move, Gari snatches the cup and gulps the whole thing down.

He licks his lips, eyes going wide. "That's water," he says. "Real water."

A murmur swarms through the room, and people shift closer.

"So it is the Aō," someone says behind me. "The spirits—they heard us."

I glance at Nkella. His face is serious as he watches me. I quirk a brow.

The crowd begins to buzz and scatter, so I catch up to him in a quieter alcove of the cave.

"What is it?" I ask. "You don't think it's the Aō?"

He shakes his head, slowly. "I don't know, daí? But Tetalla has been speaking to the Aō directly. And they've been silent for us this whole time." His jaw tenses. "Until now."

I swallow. "So... if it's not them..."

"Then who?" he finishes for me.

I look back toward the remaining crystals laid out by Kennedy's bag.

Whoever—or whatever—is answering us...

They waited for the right moment.

A tremor rumbles beneath our feet, and one of the sconces goes out, causing silence to spread in the chamber.

"We are running out of time," Kaehante says. He leans over to Nkella. "What do we do, Captain?"

I glance at Kennedy, who's now taking all the crystals out of her purse and putting them into cups. People circle around, waiting for something to happen.

"I have an idea." I look at the barrels, then back at Kennedy. "Where did you find those crystals?"

"They're everywhere."

"Yes," Kaehante says. "Along the entrance of the caves, other chambers." He scratches his bald head as he stares at the entrance of this cave.

"Hey, Gibby?" I call out. "You still want to go for a stroll."

He perks up. "Yes!"

"Okay. I say people split up to collect crystals and put them into barrels. That way maybe we'll have water." If I can get this to happen again.

Nkella squints his eyes, but nods.

"You're still skeptical," I say flatly.

"Captain," Kae says. "It is all we have. The drakon said it was okay to drink."

Nkella lets out a low sigh. "Fine. Let's do it."

Kennedy lays the rest of the crystals on a cloth while Kaehante and Haro break everyone into teams. Refugees, Ipani, everyone. No one's left out. Empty vessels are being gathered: barrels, jugs, canteens.

Some wrap their arms in cloth, forming padded slings for carrying heavier barrels. Others start forming lines, sorting the strongest from those who can help carry but not strong enough to lift.

Even Adriel helps, forming bundles of cloth to protect the more fragile containers.

I step forward, about to join in—

"My vicious one."

My body locks and my blood runs cold as Tetalla's voice grinds in my head, a hoarse whisper.

He found me.

No...

"You've stalled long enough. But my patience has waned."

I clench my teeth and step aside, slipping behind one of the stone pillars to get out of view.

"I won't rush my warriors in quite yet. I will not slaughter my own people. But the humans... they are the poison. You've felt the quakes. That is your doing. Helāni magic tearing at the roots of this world."

"That's not—"

"The cards. The descendants. You. The only way to stop the unraveling is to remove the thread. Wipe away every last human-blooded soul. Then Ipa will hold. The eruption will stop."

"I knew you were waiting us out."

"Yes. You will all run dry, and when the humans wither, the balance will return. The Ipani will see this truth in time.

"Get rid of the humans, seclude the Empress. That means you too, vicious one. Make your choice."

"My choice to what? Die willingly?"

"Rule beside me. You already know this world is broken. Fix it. With me."

"Yeah right."

"You know I speak truth. You feel it in your blood."

My breath grows short and my chest tightens. I know it's a trick. He must really think I'm stupid if he thinks I'll believe he'll spare my life. He needs me alive for my power. After that, I'll be useless to him, and he'll kill me. But he can't defeat her without me.

He doesn't know the world is falling apart because I'm not seated beside the Empress. And without all three... the balance is gone.

"Take the Death Card, and you will survive what I will do next. I am sending warriors to the entrances. You will all be surrounded. Leave them now and join me."

I gasp.

The Death Card.

I left it on the ship.

Damn it.

"Soren?" Nkella's voice makes my eyes widen.

I whip around. He's there, watching me with that familiar guarded intensity.

"Who were you talking to?" he asks.

I suck in a breath. "We have to get out now."

19

SOREN

"What are you talking about?" His voice is low as he walks into me, pushing me to a corner so no one else hears us. "Tell me you were not just speaking to Tetalla inside your head." Worry marks crease his forehead.

My voice catches.

Sparks ignite in his eyes and he grabs at his temples. I swear I think I see a shadow of horns flash on his head and then they go away.

"Nkella—"

He shuts his eyes, pinching the bridge of his nose. He opens them and with his voice still low he asks, "For how long has this been happening?"

"Just now."

His eyes narrow at me in question.

"I promise. This is the first time it's happened since I left the castle. He had left me alone until now."

His features relax but he lets out an exasperated sigh. I catch Kaehante and Tessa looking at us from behind him.

"I do not like this."

"Neither do I. I hate him being able to reach me telepathically."

He brushes the back of my head, squeezing my hair as I hug him. "How do you think he found us?"

Nkella pulls away. "It doesn't matter. Tell me what he said."

"He wants me to use the Death Card and take his side as ruler."

Nkella goes rigid.

"I'm obviously not going to do that. He's been wanting me to do it all along, and I've refused. He even let me keep the card."

"Where is it?"

"I left it on the ship before you boarded Soanalo's."

"Why would he want you to have that power? While suppressing yours," he says more to himself as he touches my wrist with the dampener on it.

"He only wanted to keep me from using my power against him. He needs me to take down the Empress, but I don't think he fully understands that if she dies, the worlds rip apart, and she's already injured." I swallow hard, hoping Talia is okay. "The world was going to rip apart without a third Fate to keep the balance. It was always meant to be three, but Demitri told me she is hardheaded. I guess until reality hit her."

He grimaces at the mention of the past Hierophant's name, but then whispers, "Have you thought more about taking one of the thrones at the Tower?"

I shake my head. "One thing at a time."

Because becoming a fake sister to the Empress, and moving up to the Tower is the last kind of goal I ever thought of for myself.

"What if it makes you stronger?"

"What do you mean?"

"What if... taking that position would make you strong enough to match Tetalla?"

My eyelids flutter. "So Tetalla wants me to take position of Death to help him beat the Empress, and now you want me to take the position in the Tower to defeat Tetalla?"

"Kh. I don't want you to do any of it. But be smart, Neyuro, daí? What is the best move to save your life, and your sister's? Hn?"

My shoulders drop.

"It will have to be a position of power. You have magic." He points to my wrist. "Do not allow someone to take it away. Or keep it from you like the Empress did to all of us."

I suck in a small gasp. He's right.

"Take your power back. Even if it is to pretend to take up a throne. Or a card, hn?"

Those are the two options, aren't they? Take up the throne as the Past Fate, next to the Empress… or as the Empress… but I don't want to think about that. Or, let Tetalla think I'm taking the Death Card. Pretending will let either one of them think I'm doing things for them, all the while plotting to get rid of them both.

I stare at him in the eyes, and nod slowly. "Got it."

Gari's large eyes come into view behind Nkella. I squint at him and he comes closer, swimming through the air.

"Is this a private conversation?" he purrs, moving from Nkella's right shoulder to the other. "Because it sounds serious, like you might need your crew."

"Kh. Who said you're crew, drakon?"

Gari's tail wraps around Nkella's shoulder. "Oh come on now, captain. Everyone needs a shifty drakon to do nifty things for them."

Nkella scoffs.

"You're part of my crew, Gari," I say. "And no, the crew should know what's going on, but not the whole room. Let the crew know we need to make it back to the ship as soon as we know there's barrels full of water for the villages here."

"There won't be enough," Nkella says.

"It's just for now. Until we figure things out."

A muscle in Nkella's jaw jumps but he gives a tight nod.

"What about the other-worlders?" Gari singsongs. I shake my head.

"We'll take them with us. Once I get my hands on the World Card again, I'll send them home." I just better get those cards, and get this dampener off.

"Okay, Captain. I'll let them know." Gari winks at me and moves back toward the crew.

Nkella quirks a long brow at the mention of Gari calling me captain and he can't hide the smile slipping on his face.

I slap his chest.

"Koj. I like it."

I roll my eyes.

Kaehante and Haro come back holding barrels, followed by more men carrying their share. Our three refugees are among the crowd, carrying bowls of crystals. I walk over to get this show on the road.

Here goes. If it can be done again.

"None of the crystals are turning into water," Haro says, turning to a woman who leans over one of them, lifting one up for inspection.

She closes her eyes for a second, and then speaks out loud to the Aō, to hear their plea.

Nothing happens.

"Soren's the water Magician," Gari purrs. "Let her trrry."

Great, thanks, Gari.

Haro locks eyes with me. "Any why is that, drakon? Because she did it the first time?" He picks up a crystal and holds it out to me. "Do it then. Helāni, use your magic. Maybe it *was* you."

"I—No. That wasn't me. It just happened."

Nkella stays quiet beside me, his expression still skeptical.

"It was already established that the Fates would have nothing to do with what was here before. And—" I hold up my wrist. "I have this dampener that Tetalla put on me to hold back my power. Not that I have much power, all I can do is look into people's past. That's all."

"Oh, that's all?" Gibby asks.

"All I'm saying is, I can't do what you're asking me to do," I say, making my way over to Haro and taking the crystal from him. I hold it over a wooden cup to show that nothing will happen, that the first time was a fluke and that any of them could probably make it work if they ask the Aō.

Immediately, the crystal bursts into water. I barely get any of it in the cup, and I gasp.

The room grows quiet and Gari giggles.

"So explain that then, Helāni," Haro says, with not much appreciation in his voice.

I shake my head and move back, but Nkella steadies me, and holds onto me from behind.

"This could be Tetalla, daí?" he says. I stare at him, silently hoping he'd take my stare as a question. They would have no idea as to why this could be Tetalla's doing.

"We should tell them."

"Tell us what?" Haro says, his voice rising.

"We have been in communication with Tetalla. He is sending warriors to all entrances of the cave, to come for the humans. This water might be meant for the Ipani only while the humans are… smoked out."

Commotion breaks out.

"We think this is going to happen in all of Ipa. It is to stop the worlds from colliding through all means necessary. But it is the wrong way."

"I knew Tetalla would supply."

My eyes widen. "But there is no way out."

Haro's smile widens. "Look around you. It is mostly all Ipani here; even the halflings will endure. None of us are leaving. This is all for you, Helāni. You and your friends can leave."

Kae moves to Haro and pushes him against the wall. "Tessa is human."

"Haro! Many here are human, daí?" Sokreni comes running up to Kae who keeps Haro pinned to the wall. "And there is no way of knowing the half-Ipani will survive. They are not well."

Haro slams down on Kae's arms, electricity sparking on his fingertips from his ouma, but Kaehante's arm shields don't seem to be bothered by it. Or he doesn't care.

"Our worlds are colliding, woman!" Haro yells. "Don't you see? The strongest will surv—"

Kae starts pounding his face in and I step back into Nkella, who moves quickly to pull Kaehante off of Haro.

Haro slides to the ground, blood pours from his busted lip and his head hangs over his clavicle. I blink, dumbfounded that that just happened. I stare at Kae. He's breathing hard. Nkella pushes him away, he looks at me over the shoulder. "Get them situated, we leave now."

"Yes, Captain," Ntaoru says beside me, before I can respond. We share a quick glance and get to work bringing the rest of the barrels in and lining them up. I don't know how long until the cavern entrances are blocked by Tetalla's warriors. Or if they will actually enter or not.

Or if these crystals are turning into water because of Tetalla, or because of the Aō, or what. But it can't be because of me. That doesn't make any sense.

How would it be because of me?

Ntaoru drags a barrel in front of me, and I lean over it, taking a crystal in my hand. Gari and Tessa come closer, followed by the refugees by their side. All eyes are on me as I stare at the crystal. How am I even supposed to do all of them?

Am I supposed to do one at a time? A loud sigh escapes me.

"You were the one," a frail voice comes from behind Ntaoru. I glance over and pass a look at Kaehante who's sitting next to Lāri on the floor. A grim expression is on his face, but he then catches me staring at him.

"I heard about you." My eyes follow the voice closer to where I had been sitting with the three ladies. The elder from before is staring at me.

"Did you say something?"

"Hnn. You were the one the birds sang about."

"What are you saying, ama?" the girl with the brown hair asks her.

"She gave the Ipani their ouma back. Took away our dampeners the Empress had put on us."

People are looking at me from all corners now, murmuring to themselves. "That was you?" one asks.

"Yes, of course it was her. Who else?"

I look at the crew.

"Word is slow to get down here since we have been under siege," Sokreni says.

I nod at her and look at the crew. They stare back at me expectantly. Now Kaehante is standing.

"Go on then," the elderly woman says. "You can give us water. I know you can."

I shake my head. "Even if I can, I want you to know it would have nothing to do with me being the Past Fate."

"Yes," she says. "These crystals are from here. You are not. But even still, it is you who is doing it."

Confusion flickers through my mind.

"It's okay, Soren," Tessa whispers to me. "Ignore everyone, just focus."

I bite my tongue. None of this makes sense.

"Try putting your hands on all the crystals," Kennedy offers. "To do them all at the same time."

Gibby and Adriel nod in agreement.

Great, now the refugee with the Magician's mark knows more than I do.

I do what she suggests and place my hands over the crystals inside the barrels. A few are the size of pebbles, others are larger than both hands combined. All at once, they turn to water.

My mouth gapes open, and people cheer.

We move onto the next barrel. Four more to go, plus a few bowls and cups. Kaehante walks out of the chamber, without looking at us.

I glance down at Tessa. "Is he going to be okay?"

"He will be. He just lost it a little."

"Can't say the guy didn't deserve it," I mutter under my breath. Placing my hands inside the next barrels, I wonder if I could do this with any other kind of crystal. Or is it just these? Can I do it with anything, or just crystals?

And why crystals?

Because they're clear?

I move onto the last barrel, trying my best to stay focused. Others stare at me as if I'm doing one of my sleight-of-hand tricks, but I can't even explain this myself. Wait until I tell Talia.

Nkella walks back in alone and glances at the barrels full of water, people lining up to fill their cups. Ntaoru hands me my canteen, and I take it.

I fill my canteen up and drink. The water soothes my throat, and my eyes widen. "Maybe I'm just parched, but this is the best damn water I've ever tasted."

Ntaoru huff-laughs in response.

"We're lucky we're in a cave full of crystals," I mutter.

Kaehante comes back carrying a barrel over his shoulder. He calls to

Nkella as he sets it down, "It is empty, shall we go find some more before we leave?"

I walk over and open it. A bit of dirt and some rocks sit at the bottom.

"Maybe clean it first?"

Kae takes the barrel and spins it over, dropping all its contents. He sets it down and I cover it while he walks over to grab his canteen from where he sat with Lāri. I scan her body as she rests, her eyes are half closed.

"Someone should clean her wound with fresh water now," I say.

"We can do that at the ship," Nkella says, his voice stern. A tight pressure wraps around us both. It's time to go. I lean over the barrel, and stare at everyone.

"At least we've left them with some water. Wish we could find food for them though. No one can leave to go hunt right now," I say.

"Believe me. We will be back."

I glance at him staring out to his people. It must be killing him to have to leave them. But we both know what awaits. I don't even want to think about it.

"Have you had any water yet?" I give him my canteen, but he takes his own and goes to fill it in another barrel.

"Only half. We have water on the ship."

I nod.

Kaehante comes back and I get off the barrel. He goes to lift it over his shoulder and drops it hard on the ground before he gets it too far.

Nkella scoffs. "What happened, cousin? Is a splinter winning?"

Kae shoots him a confused stare. "Did you add anything in it?" He removes the cover to look inside and he gasps, pulling out a loaf of bread.

I jump at the contents. A mixture of bread and sacks of dried meat... at least I think it is as Nkella opens one up. He stares at me, and I shake my head.

Kae stares at me. "Soren?"

"Don't look at me," I say. "I had nothing to do with that."

The elderly woman starts to laugh, and people start walking up, grabbing bread.

"Thank you," one of them tells me. I keep shaking my head, unsure of what to say.

"Why is this happening, Soren?" Nkella asks. I gape at him, but he moves in closer. "What did you just say a moment ago?"

My brows furrow.

"You were saying at least we left them with water. But you wished..."

My spine straightens. "I wished that we had left them with some real food." I stare down at the barrel, now emptying as people grab their fill. "This is insane."

"New power unlocked," Gibby says out loud, taking bread for himself. They must be starving too. I wave at Kennedy and Adriel to come back.

Nkella has his arms crossed in front of him, his gaze goes from the barrels, and back to me.

"I wish I could explain it," I tell him.

"I have a feeling we'll find out soon enough."

Tessa's motor nears the side of the barrel. "So does this mean the water and now food was not Tetalla's doing?"

I blink down at her. I don't have an answer. But no, this one couldn't have been Tetalla's doing. Unless... he can see through walls?

Even still, the timing would be just too perfect. I reach over and grab the barrel top from Kae.

He lets me have it, and now he and Nkella are watching me as I cover it up again.

"Only one way to find out."

Without saying anything out loud for Tetalla to hear—although the crystals had just turned to water—I put my hand over the top of the barrel. Please let it be a cheeseburger this time.

I open the barrel.

My mouth gapes open.

Not a cheeseburger. But bread and dried meat is their food, and they're starving. "Dig in."

Something burns me right on my chest and I rub it. *Ow.* What the hell?

"Your time is up, vicious one."

I drop the cover to the ground. Nkella's by my side in an instant.

"I have someone here that I am sure you would very much want alive."

"No." My heart stops. Talia. He must have gotten into the Tower somehow. Or Talia left the tower... "Don't hurt her."

"You know what you have to do."

"Do not hurt her."

"Hurt who?" Nkella is shouting. "Your sister?"

The ground shakes around us.

"Meet me at the castle."

He goes silent. I turn to Nkella. He wants me to meet him at the castle, but I need to get to the ship, where I left the Death Card."

"You're not going to—"

"I won't. But I'm not going to let him hurt Talia." I widen my eyes at him and point my finger to my lips, trying to cue him in that Tetalla might be listening. If he sees me without the Card, he'll know I'm fooling him. It has to look real.

Nkella nods, and looks to the crew. "Take the refugees with us, it's time to go." He looks to the crowd. "Feed as many chambers you can, share the water, daí? I will be back."

"Where are you going?" Sokreni asks and he stares at her, and half crouches to get to her level.

"I am going to go fight Tetalla, and win back Danū."

Her eyes widen.

"Tetalla first. The Empress next. Or I die trying."

"Then you better not die, we need our prince, Nkella Mikiroro." She turns to me and says, "and his Helāni princess."

20

SOREN

We hurry as fast as we can through the dimly lit corridors, toward the entrance to the cave, hoping the exit won't be barricaded by Tetalla's guards. Something burns on my chest and I rub it.

"What's the matter?" Nkella asks.

"I don't know." I had forgotten about it since Tetalla had spoken to me.

"I felt a burning on my skin right after food appeared inside the barrel."

"I'll look at it after we board the ship."

We move quickly, our footsteps echoing through the cavern halls. We reach the exit—a crack of light blooming at the far end of the tunnel. As we step out, the air shifts. Bright sun blinds me for a second before I adjust.

Pink sand stretches out before us, warm and shimmering under the afternoon sun. Waves roll in gently across the beach, and there, anchored not far from the shore, is the *Devil's Gambit*—a dark outline against the turquoise horizon. Which also means the cloaking has clearly run out, making it visible. Nkella and I share a quick glance, and we make a run for the ship.

Relief crashes through me as I step onto the gangway.

"It feels good to be on the *Gambit* again," Tessa says as she drives up full speed. Coming back up the ramp with Ntaoru, we both notice the refugees are still standing, dumbfounded on the gangway, eyes wide as they take it in.

Gibby whistles low, slapping the hull. "Now this is a pirate ship."

"We do not have time for this, daí?" Ntaoru whispers. I shake my head, skimming past everyone, and looking for my Devil.

Kennedy's mouth hangs open. "Were those ruby eyes on the devil skull in the front of the ship?"

Adriel trails her hand along the sleek outer edge. "It's so smooth."

Tessa wheels up behind them and gestures to the deck. "Welcome aboard the *Devil's Gambit*. Come inside quickly, we need to make haste."

I stare at the empty ship, then turn to Tessa. What happened to the two mer-Ipani who were with us?"

"They left as soon as we docked to report back to the kings about how you and Nkella were taken."

I quirk a brow. "Will they be sending reinforcements, do you think?"

"Ha," Kaehante scoffs as he walks by.

Tessa shrugs, then turns toward the refugees. She taps the edge of a compartment as I speed past her and head to the captain's quarters. Her voice trails behind me. "These slots here—those are for potion bottles. Some make the ship transparent. Others give it speed. Another can trigger auto-navigation. Some of them can even be mixed."

Gibby's voice follows. "You serious?"

"Dead serious," Tessa says. "You'll see. Stick with me, I'll show you where not to touch."

Kennedy laughs nervously. "Noted."

The door to the bedroom is open, and I step inside. The beige curtains move in the slightly open windows circling around the cabin.

Nkella stands in front of his desk, looking through notebooks and papers.

He doesn't look up at me. "Do you know where you left it?"

I head for the bed and dig through the sheets, still messy from the last time we spent the night in here. Before he made his lunatic decision. I uncover the bedsheets, and find a single card on the floor next to the side table. Not the best place for one of these Tarot cards.

But my clothes were torn off me, and then I had no time to get my things.

Picking it up, I hold it up for him to see. "Got it."

A purple sheen passes over the image of a skeleton holding a lantern, by a boat at a tranquil sea. The Deep.

Concern hits his face as I tuck it away in my pants. "I won't use it," I say to try and ease his worry, but his frown only deepens.

"You will do what you need to do. Just like I would."

My heart skips a beat. "I'm not leaving you to go to the Deep, Nkella. I'm not going to agree to be with Tetalla again."

He opens a drawer and pulls out a set of his carved arrows. "As I said. You will do whatever it takes to protect your family." He grabs his bow, and hangs it over his back.

"Just like you would."

"Yes."

"Nkella—"

He rushes to me, and moves my hair away, along with my necklace.

I gasp. "What are you doing?"

"Where did you feel burning? Has it gone away?"

"Yes..." My skin tingles as he runs his thumb over the center of my chest. "It isn't red or anything, and doesn't hurt... Maybe something fell on me and I didn't notice."

"As long as it wasn't a royal fire burn."

"It wasn't."

His eyes flick to mine, and my breath hitches right before he grabs my face and pushes me against the window. His tongue slides between my lips and I pull him deeper into me, my breathing picking up as my heart starts to pound. I need him badly.

A knock comes at the door. He pulls away and whispers in my ear, "Soon, I will have you to myself."

I breathe him in as we pull away from each other.

Kaehante pops his head inside. "Shall we go over the plan?"

"Yes, cousin, come inside. Call the others. "

I straighten myself up and lean against the wall. I'm too on edge to take a seat. My hand slides inside my pocket, and I fidget with the Death Card. I glance at Tessa. "What's the trio doing?"

"The refugees?" Tessa cranes her neck to look at me. "I whipped something up for them to eat in the kitchen, they're hanging tight."

I nod at her, and stare at Nkella. "I need to get to Tetalla so that he let's my sister go. But no one, especially them," I point to the door in reference to the people from Florida, "should come with me."

"Agreed that they stay." He looks to Kae and his sister. "In fact, the rest of you head to Dempu Yuni. We will meet you back when this is over. But I'm staying in Danū with Soren."

The crew starts to talk over each other, protesting that we're going to need back up. Nkella shakes his head, holding the bridge of his nose. A loud popping sound makes me jump as Iéle graces us with her presence.

Nkella places a hand on her head, and she looks at me. I smile back at her over the commotion.

"Soren," Ntaoru demands, and I sigh, "you should not go on your own."

"They're going to need your protection, Nta."

"You know where they come from better than we do; they probably still think they're dreaming," Tessa says. "It took you a while."

Nkella bends down and presses his forehead to Iéle's. I stare at Ntaoru.

"Lāri definitely can't come, she needs looking after. Not to mention, there is nothing any of you can do to help us with Tetalla. Nkella needs to fight him, and I know—*I can feel*, that with you guys here, it's something else for him to worry about, and he won't be able to fight to the best of his ability."

The room quiets, and they're all staring at me. Even Kaehante has a blank look on his face, because he knows his cousin and knows I'm right.

"And what about you?" Tessa asks me. I glance down at her.

"I have other plans."

Her features twist, and Nkella breaks his bond with Iéle to pass me a glance, eyes narrowing.

My brows furrow at him. He knows I'm going to pretend to take up the Death Card and make a trade for my sister. His lips part and he stands.

"We're about to have company."

I straighten myself from the wall. "What? Who?"

"Iéle has spotted—"

Gari pops into the room, his body floating over to a window. "Arcana are here."

"And we're uncloaked!" Tessa yells.

We all stand as the familiar deafening of whistles that sound like airstrikes fall around the ship. Kaehante runs out of the room first, and we all follow suit to the quarterdeck.

Seriously? Why are they worried about us right now?

Or is the Empress coming down to talk to me?

Could it be about Talia?

I lean over the rail as they start landing on the ship. The vessel rocks from side to side with each of their touchdowns.

Kennedy and Adriel walk up the ramp, holding cups in their hands and pause at the sight of the ten Minor Arcana soldiers, with pearly white masks, and the endless darkness in their eyes. Gibby stops at the edge of the main deck right next to the girls.

I gasp and nudge Nkella who is telling the crew to put their weapons down. Kaehante holds his gun to one of the Arcana, and Tessa loads her chair cannon.

"Nkella," I whisper. "Kennedy has the Magician mark."

He sighs. "We do not need this now."

I move past him to stand in front of Kennedy.

"What is this? Who are they?" she asks, eyes wide. "Where the hell did they come from?"

Adriel grabs her arm, pulling her back.

Before I can think up a response, the snow drakon makes its way down from the sky, her white coat blending in with the clouds as her long strands glisten.

"Oh no, not *her*," Gari says.

"This guy again," Gibby remarks gaping at Gari. "I'm going back to my theory that I'm dreaming."

Gari swims in the air and shakes his snout from side to side, now facing Gibby nose to nose. "If you're dreaming, then you wouldn't mind me having you for a snack." He inches his face closer to Gibby, his eyes narrowing. "Would you?"

"Gari focus," I tell him.

Gibby stares at the drakon, eyes wide as Gari lets his tail wander around Gibby while gliding near me.

I stare at him. "Do you know if Krua is going to pour snow everywhere again?"

"Who can tell with that one?" He spins on his head. "She works for the Empress, remember?"

Right.

"Soren," Krua purrs as she comes closer. "The Empress has sent me to retrieve an item from you."

"I grab onto the Death Card in my pocket and move back. "Not a chance."

"It is crucial you hand it over. She knows you have it."

I scoff. "Does she really think the Death Card would choose her? She can't force Tetalla out of it either, so I'm going to hold onto it." It's the most useless card to the Empress, if I think about it. She can't do anything with it. It only wants to listen to me, and Tetalla.

The snow drakon lowers herself in between the Arcana, and myself. The blank pearl faces of the Arcana stare at all of us.

"And did you really need all that back up?" I ask.

"She sent them with me." She spins around in the air, her eyes drift from Gari to me. "What do you mean, Death Card? She sent me here to retrieve the Ace of Pentacles."

"I definitely don't have that. And I haven't exactly had the time to look for it either.`

Now Nkella is walking down the steps to us, with Iéle by his side. The refugees jump back upon seeing her. I keep my focus on Krua.

The snow drakon hovers just off the bow, scales glinting like mosaic ice, her long tail coils and loops through the air like a ribbon through water.

"Give it to me," she says, her voice carrying on the wind. "The Ace of Pentacles. The Empress demands it."

My brows knit. "I don't have it."

The drakon's icy eyes narrow. "Don't insult the Empress, Soren. She sensed the card's magic from the Tower. It's here. And there is only one person aboard this ship who could wield it."

My hands curl into fists. "Are you not hearing me? I do not have a single Tarot card, aside from the Death Card. Now let us go—Tetalla has my sister."

She tilts her head. "How many sisters do you have?"

I pause. "One. Talia!"

Krua pauses, her tail end sinewing behind her. She stares at me blankly, then at Gari next to me who hasn't said a word to her. If a drakon could show confusion, this is it.

"Talia is with the Empress," she finally says.

"What?" I blink. "But Tetalla said—"

That lying bastard.

She comes closer and Gari swims through the air in front of me. The Minor Arcana each take a step forward at the same time. Gaze locked on them, Nkella's horns protrude from his head. I'm not worried about the Arcana, I once saw him kill one of them. And they normally can't die.

"Soren," Krua sings.

"Drakon," Nkella says. "Why does the Empress think Soren has the Ace of Pentacles?"

Krua flicks him a look. "The Ace of Pentacles takes care of the people. Danū used to be the Superpower. Creating abundance, protection for all. The Royals were of the strongest. The Empress is powerful; she sensed her magic being used."

"But what did she sense, daí?"

"She sensed stone turning into food."

I gasp.

The snow drakon shifts, her tail slicing the air. "You don't understand what more the Ace of Pentacles could do." Her voice is soft, almost like a whisper, so I move up to hear her. "If the Empress holds it, it tips the balance. The Aō will finally lean in her favor. It would diminish Tetalla's influence within the Aō. It may protect those who care for Danū's people. It may weaken him."

Nkella's eyes fall on me, but I shake my head.

"That's impossible. I don't have it. Even if I did have it, there's no way I'd give it to the Empress."

The drakon lowers her head, drawing close enough for her fur to brush against Gari's. He snaps at the air in warning. With feline grace, she slips back just out of reach, then mimics him—snapping at the empty space between them before swinging her head to meet me, nose to nose.

"I can smell it on you."

"That's creepy."

"She isn't lying," Nkella says. "And if she has it, she doesn't know she does."

I give him an appreciative smile. Him trusting—knowing that I'm telling the truth, and not keeping something from him or anyone right now—means more than I could ever tell him in words.

Krua opens her mouth to speak, and I'm about ready to smack her, but she snaps her gaze to look back at the island. My brows furrow.

Nkella tilts his head up. "The winds have stopped." Just as he says it, the sails slacken, and the swinging ropes still. Everything goes quiet, including the sound of the usual thrashing of the waves against the rocking ship.

"What the hell just happened?" I whisper.

Iéle lets out a low growl, crouched beside Nkella, her eyes locked on the shoreline. Her fur stands on end, her tail rigid. Gari shifts above, his claws scrape the mast as he presses himself low against the wood.

Figures move along the beach, and the all too familiar cracking of bones sends my hairs to stand on end.

"Nkella..." I start moving toward him and we both walk toward the rail overlooking the beach. In the corner of my eye, I catch Kae releasing a rope.

"Set sail," Nkella says just above a whisper.

I stare at the unnatural procession. Skeletal riders with their armor hanging off brittle frames. Men and women, or what's left of them, dragging swords, limbs twisted at the wrong angles. Some of them are crawling.

"Get the refugees below deck," Nkella orders, already turning. "All of them. Now."

Ntaoru hurries the refugees downstairs.

The formation breaks as something moves between them.

Tetalla. His sword hangs from his side as it sweeps across the sand. In his grip, a girl stumbles forward. She's barefoot, with wild brown hair; she struggles to keep up as he drags her by her wrist.

I squint trying to see if I recognize who she is. I think she's yet another refugee.

The snow drakon lands on the mast above with a soft thud, head lowered, watching.

"That's not Talia," I mutter. "Who is that?"

Tetalla stops at the edge of the surf. The girl sways beside him. He says nothing for a moment, just watches me with that same unreadable calm.

"She fell through the veil this morning," he calls out loud enough for us to hear. "I believe she is a friend of yours, daí? This world is not the only one unraveling."

His hand lifts, still holding her wrist in display.

"Use the Death Card. Or she dies."

"I don't know her," I say, glancing at Nkella standing close behind me.

"She's another refugee."

"It doesn't mean I want her to die though."

His gaze sharpens. "She is in danger, and he is using her to get to you."

My stomach coils.

Tetalla's voice slips through inside my head, and I grimace, my eyes fixed on him standing on the beach. His lips don't move as he locks eyes with me, his chin lifted.

"Would you trade her for the one you love?"

I don't answer him.

The ship jolts, and I grip the rail. Gari's shriek is sharp, panicked.

Something fractures above and Ntaoru points and yells for us to look up.

Clouds part over the ocean.

A jagged crack appears in the sky, and before any of us can scream, the ship jolts us all forward. My legs shake and I struggle for balance. Nkella and I find each other and I cling onto his arm.

The rocking of the ship worsens as we struggle to find somewhere to hold onto. I shut my eyes, waiting for it to end.

The deck jerks sideways so violently it wrenches my feet out from under me, and wood cracks beneath us. My shoulder slams into Nkella's chest.

The hull groans like it's about to rip apart.

Wind tears through the rigging, and a sail snaps, a rope whiplashing past my ear. Screams rise through the air but they're swallowed in the roar that follows. Something massive I can't see crashes onto the deck. A barrel maybe. My eyes are shut tight against the wind, debris, and the sea spray.

The quake turns to shattering as the sky splits with a thunderous clap that vibrates the world around us.

My fingers dig into Nkella as I hold on tighter. I can't hear the crew anymore.

A second blast hits, and the ship lifts like it's being picked up and dropped again. The sea slams over the side, and a scream tears from my throat, making me swallow a mouth full of seawater.

The next wave crashes straight across the deck, the force of it so hard, my body feels as if I just fell through cement.

Another rumble shakes the world around us, and we quickly grab onto the rail. My chest is panting hard as the ship rocks back and forth, and I hope to god the quaking has stopped. I place my hand on his chest.

Nkella lets out a soft gasp that makes my hairs stand on end as I watch the horror in his face. Nkella never gasps… I turn around to what he's looking at.

We now have a clear view of Rutavenye, where my sister is inside the Empress's Tower. The vibration only gets stronger, and I think my eyes are shaking because it looks as though the floating island is shaking too.

Nkella places a hand on my shoulder, pulling me back. I don't understand why… What's he seeing that I'm not?

The roar of something vast splitting engulfs my eardrums, then there's a deafening pause. And it's as if everything around me slows as I stand frozen, my mouth agape, as the island begins to fall.

The sea convulses, and a wall of water rises before I can get my head straight.

A scream shatters my ears, although, that may have been my own. I stumble but catch myself on the railing.

"TALIA!"

Her name rips out of me, and I'm sprinting toward the edge of the ship. Because of the war, she's not allowed to leave the Tower. She's stuck there!

Nkella grabs me from behind. His arms lock around my waist and pull me back hard.

"You don't know she's gone."

I don't believe him. He's just trying to hold me together.

I stop struggling.

"Now is your chance. Go to her."

I cover my ears in my hands, and shut my blurry eyes. I don't want him in my head. "Get out!" I scream.

"Take the Death Card. You can still save her."

Nkella spins me around, his eyes searching mine. "Neyuro?"

His lips are moving, but I'm not hearing him.

The Tower collapses. The whole island falls.

He shakes me. "Soren!"

My throat is clogged. I can't breathe. I did this to her. She came here for me.

"Take the Death Card."

My hands shake. Nkella still stands before me calling my name, but I can't form the words to tell him… I'm sorry. He knows what I would do for the ones I love. The same thing he would do. A tear falls down my cheek, and his face drops.

"N-no. Soren. Please..."

My fingers close around the Death Card in my pocket and I pull it out.

The moment I touch it, everything tilts.

The colors of this world drain around me.

The deck fades beneath me, and a cold chill fills my lungs.

Nkella reaches for me.

His fingers brush mine, and the world disappears.

21

NKELLA

Her fingers slip out of reach as the serpent rises from the Deep and drags her down with him. My heart hardens to keep from shattering. The waves thrash as I stare blankly at where she was just dragged, her necklace clasped tightly between my fingers. It snapped off her at some point during the quakes. I stare at the royal gichang, left to her by her mother and Sehu.

And now it is all I have left of her.

My breathing picks up and the Devil inside me stirs, wanting to rip out, but the gichang vibrates in my hand and I almost drop it. What is happening, daf?

I gape at it as it transforms into a Tarot card. My lips part and I study it. A purple sheen swipes across the image to reveal a large coin with the Mikiroro Crest. The black palm bent, as if swaying in the hot breeze. A large crown sits on top of the coin, with two horns sticking out from the inside.

The Ace of Pentacles is now in my hand, with my crest, yet only a Fate can use the cards. I recall it glowing on her chest inside my cabin, but thought it was from our connection.

It was her necklace all along. But she did not know it. Had her parents?

Sehu didn't seem to know what it was.

A warm sensation swirls in my gut. Our aovate connection speaking to me, telling me she is alive. A smile breaks on my face.

Winds pick up and my senses perk, listening to my ouma. Another calm before the worst of it to come.

Tucking the card into my pocket, I step over pieces of the broken mast and eye the ship. Where is the drakon when you need him? I whistle for Iéle to come out, and she does so, her head bowed as she explores the ship. Signaling for her to find Katergaris, she pops into the Aō dimension.

My crew stands staring at me with horrified expressions. Trepidation crosses their features like a wave. Waiting for me to react. To become the monster I now control inside me.

Kh. "Line them up."

Tessa and Kae look at each other before Kae asks me "Who, Captain?"

"The refugees." The three of them are scattered, probably hurt, as they've been thrown around from this...magical quake Adriel is lying beneath one of the masts. "Line them up on the main deck and have them clean up the ship. When Katergaris returns from his hiding, have him help fix the mast. We will return to shore."

Kaehante helps the girl up as Tessa turns to help the other two who have fallen below deck. He glances at me, worry lines indented deeply into his forehead.

"She is alive," I finally tell them.

Kae's eyes widen. "How do you know this?"

"I just do." My heavy boots creak the floorboards as I stride to the edge of the bow to see if Tetalla is still there and pause at Ntaoru, ignoring the concern she has on her face. "Check on Lāri, daí?"

"Of course, brother. But..."

"But what?" The agitation comes out harsher than I want. The sooner they help me pick up the pieces, the sooner we can have Ipa back. And the sooner I can have Soren back with me. Safe.

"Nothing." She leaves to do as I say, and I reach the edge of the bow.

Pulling out my scope, I lean forward to look through it. Tetalla is there, staring, waiting for me. He has a smug smile on his face, as he holds the girl in place. His face shifts to acknowledge me so I raise my chin.

His advantage is his natural ouma fire. I sometimes still wonder why I was given air. The wind wraps around me, and I keep it spinning.

"Captain?"

Tessa's voice rings from behind, but all their voices grow distant as I focus my energy and lean deeper into the Aō.

"Captain!" Kaehante yells at me. "What did he say to you?" I hear him ask my sister.

"Nothing. You heard his demands. Fix the ship! Be ready!"

Tessa argues. "Then why did it sound like he was going somewhere?"

I fight the urge to answer them. There is no time for conversation. The winds snap loud in my ears as they come together, stronger. Tetalla's features harden through the scope, and I bring it down, and whisper to myself.

"If you can hear me, my aovate. Knowing you still breathe is all that I need to go into battle. If I spend my final breaths fighting to bring you home, they will not be wasted."

I feel for the Ace of Pentacles in my pocket, making sure it's still there, but instead of the thick paper, it has changed shape. I pull the royal coin out by its chain. I clasp it around my neck this time and tuck it under my tunic.

The wind coils around my legs, up my spine, until it lifts me off the deck with a sudden burst, and I glide over the sea.

Shouts come from the *Gambit* behind me, but I ignore them. I knew they would try to stop me. And I cannot let them ruin my concentration.

As if standing in the eye of a tornado, I rise, arms tense at my sides, as I direct my ouma to keep the current alive. The sea churns below, as it resists me, fighting against my force of nature. My weight dragging behind each gust like a stubborn anchor.

Salt stings my eyes as I'm hurled forward, flung in wild arcs that I struggle to correct. My ouma wants speed, and I have to fight to keep my flight straight. I nearly fall once, my limbs tilting like a broken kite before I right myself again. My gaze fights to stay locked on my destination as my own ouma fights me for control.

I do not care if I don't look graceful. So long as I get there.

The aroma of hot spices of Danū and the pink sands cooked by the sun wafts under my nose, as the coastal dunes come closer, and I can almost taste it. Tetalla waits there, unmoving. The girl still writhes in his grasp. Purple flames coil around his free wrist, rising higher as I approach. His attempt at a taunt. A declaration that he's won.

The winds dissipate around me as my feet touch ground. I catch a quick glance at my ship. A mast has been lifted up and Katergaris's long drakon body works to keep it straight. I return my gaze to Tetalla, and keep my breathing calm. I need to get the girl to safety before we tear the island apart.

An amused smirk is plastered on his face. "Why have you come, Nkella?"

"Did I misread your invitation or were you just enjoying the fresh air?"

He scoffs. "Invitation to what? There is nothing left for us to do." A skeleton rises from beneath the sand and grabs the fidgeting girl as Tetalla casts a circle of purple flames around us. The air thickens inside it, and shadows dance between us, the roars of the fire masking the girl's screams as she tries to fight the risen dead.

"Let the girl go. She's done nothing to you."

"And lose my leverage?"

"Leverage from who? Soren does not know the girl. She is a refugee from her world. Soren's sister is presumably dead already from the Tower falling. Let the girl go, Tetalla."

He guffaws, and I make a fist.

"Wasn't that a sight to see? The Empress has once again damned herself. You should be celebrating with me. The Empress has fallen." He raises his arms. "Danū has a king. I have won."

"Koj. Not yet."

He takes two steps toward me. "Why resist me? Help me get rid of the humans and return our land to what it once was."

"I did not live when it once was. There are humans I care for, ones who have known nothing else but here. This is their home. Your fight is misguided, Tetalla. And the Empress still lives, daí? Even with the Tower fallen, she cannot die that easily. She is in the Deep."

"Yes, with Soren. Which is why I will not let the girl go. I still need my vicious one to do what I say. I still need her to comply."

My breathing picks up, becoming shallow. An ache ripples through my head as my horns protrude, and I fight it back down. Stay down. Not yet. Control.

Tetalla laughs. "You are not ready to lead, young Devil. It is truly admirable, if I may add. I was once as naive and full of hope as you."

"Use me as leverage instead of the girl."

"Ha. So that you stay here in Danū trying to win over the royal flames?"

"Afraid they'll listen, daí?" The purple flames flicker toward me, and I lift my hand up. They follow it. "Do not be so quick to think this is over, Tetalla. If you will not let the girl go, then fight me now, prove to the flames you are the one true royal ruler of Danū."

His eyes narrow and he strides toward me, his body shifting to his devil form as his fist meets my jaw. The moment before his fist touches, my body shifts to meet his strength.

My feet dig into the sand, heels gouging deep as my bones stretch, my skin hardens, and my devil form takes hold. Horns burst from my skull with a flash of heat. My wings tear free behind me, catching the wind as I lunge.

I slam into Tetalla, shoulder-first, and the air explodes between us. My ouma seeping out to help me. He stumbles, just a step, but it's enough for me to spin low, tail sweeping out, aiming for his knees. He jumps and counters with a jet of purple flame. It lashes across my chest. I roar through gritted teeth, wings snapping wide. The flames never hurt me before this.

"You'll lose her," Tetalla says, his voice calm, cruel. "I will not kill her. But I will break her."

Flames crawl up his arms as his form fully shifts, obsidian horns curl on his head, and his black wings spread.

"She'll kneel for me, Devil. You'll watch it happen."

My breath hardens in my chest. I lunge.

We collide in a crash, and his claws scrape my ribs, but I catch his wing at the base and twist. He snarls, fire biting at my side as he shoves me back.

We circle each other like predators.

"I've seen the kind of leader you are. Spine bent with guilt. Hidden from your own people. For how long?"

I spit blood, wings flaring against the rush of wind. "Say what you want. You're still the one standing alone."

Tetalla laughs. "I do not care about being alone. You left your people to starve."

My claws curl into a fist, and I lunge for him.

His fire lashes, burning across my side, but I drive a fist into his ribs and something cracks.

Wind escapes him but he keeps up his posture. "You are not fighting for Danū," he snarls, dragging flames down his blade. "You're fighting for an illusion of her."

"I don't need your blessing," I growl. "I need you dead."

The wind screams around us, and I let it carry me forward.

This fight is for more than Danū. Or for Soren. It is for my parents.

And it's for me. I don't care if I burn by the royal flames.

So long as I drag him down with me.

He blocks my blow, and counterattacks, and I block his, and fight him with every ounce of rage carried in my bones. The fury of the Devil in me comes to the surface, threatening to overpower me.

But Tetalla is my only focus and as long I do not lose sight of my end goal, I will not lose myself now.

"I agree to your bargain." He breaks the cadence of our fight while he sends a blow. I block it. "If I win, I will let the girl go to fend for herself. After all, I can tell Soren I have you and it will be leverage enough until she sees you down in the Deep, where you will stay forever this time. And so she too will never leave."

I barrel into him. Blow after blow, fast, savage, desperate.

He blocks some, grinning through a bloodied lip. He catches my wrist mid-strike, yanks me forward, and headbutts me hard enough to rattle my skull. I stagger. He grabs my horn, dragging me down, but I dig my claws into his gut and twist.

He screams.

Then he's on me, slamming my neck into the sand, pinning me down with the full weight of his body. I fight, and twist, but the royal flames rise too quickly around me, trapping us in a circle.

His face drops close and he grips my jaw, yanking it upward, and he begins to breathe down my throat.

Fire surges into my mouth.

I clamp my lips, but the heat forces its way in, searing past my teeth. My lips split. My lungs convulse. I choke, writhing as the blaze floods my chest.

Every breath is agony.

My ribs lock, and it feels as though my muscles are tearing.

I buck beneath him, my mind going blank from the pain. My claws find purchase on his forearm and rip deep, but he doesn't move.

The fire pours in deeper, and my scream dies in my throat.

I'm burning alive—inside out.

22

SORREN

I STIR AWAKE BEFORE MY SENSES COME CRASHING DOWN ON me and my chest heaves in a sudden fit of coughs. I hurl to the side, coughing up what seems to be an ocean in my lungs.

I grab at my chest as an unexplainable amount of water keeps seeping out of me. Tears stream down my face and I fight to collect my thoughts.

I'm out of breath, and I wipe my face, scratching myself with sand. Pink sand. I blink.

"Nkella?" My voice is hoarse from coughing so hard.

What the hell happened?

What's the last thing I remember?

I stare out into the horizon and get an uneasy feeling in the pit of my stomach. The sea is so calm. Too still... and the sky is... a deep red.

I gasp as it all comes crashing down on me. Rutavenye fell from the sky, into the sea... No one could have survived that. The Tower is gone...

Talia... "No!" I stand, and spin around. Dead black palms stand upon the shore of Danū. A vision of the serpent bringing me back to the Deep's version of the island resurfaces in my memory. I... I... Reaching into my pockets I search for the Death Card, and pull it out.

The blood drains from my face.

The card has changed. Death stands at the foot of a boat, next to still water, but now there's another Death. She looks like me, with red hair, wearing a long black cloak. A purple sheen swipes the image. I gasp and stare at the new mark on my wrist. *XIII* has replaced the High Priestess *II*.

Nkella...I clutch at my chest. I'm so sorry. I promised him I wouldn't leave him again. But he knew I would do what I needed to.

I swallow. If I'm Death... am I dead?

"Yes."

A voice echoes around me, and I spin around to gauge my surroundings. That voice sounded like Tetalla. Was he answering my question?

Several feet away from shore, the fortress still stands down here, as opposed to it now being a giant serpent's skeletal remains above ground.

Everything is just as when I left, except... I stare up at the surface of this plane. There are no longer the floating dead there once was, before we released them from their eternal torment. Although their spirits may be whole, they'll still be in the Deep.

So then where is everyone?

The sand circles in front of me, and carried by the wind, dark laughter comes with it. I take a few steps back, steeling my spine. Tetalla emerges, his shoulders back, and his chin held high.

"My vicious one, welcome home."

I purse my lips.

"Had I known your sister was your weakness, I would have taken her long ago."

I ball my fists. "I only took the seat next to you to find my sister. I still won't do what you want me to."

He strides over, calmly. His soft curls sway in the wind as he walks, showcasing his Ipani stripes. "You will have no choice. The worlds are tearing apart, but not with you here. After I have finished off the humans, you will take the Empress Card, and I will take the Emperor Card. It will be temporary, but will suffice until it is time."

"Time for what?" That unease at the pit of my stomach grows. Given his plans for me, I am still here... with the same powers as him. Why would he let me have this much power? One thing I know about Tetalla is that he's calculating. "Aren't I supposed to have powers here?"

His smile sends a shiver down my spine. He licks his lips, looking off to the side before landing his gaze back on me.

"The other seat of the Death Card will rule the Deep. So, yes, your powers will come in as you acclimate. But, my vicious one," he steps into me and I lift my chin, "to answer your question, yes, you are dead. The Death Card took your life to keep you in the Deep."

I fight to keep my breathing steady.

"And those in the Deep must stay in the Deep."

My lips part, taking in what he's telling me.

"Unless I raise you to the surface, which I won't until I need you to take the Empress Card."

My fingers start to tremble. And I would have to... because if I don't, our worlds will collide, and everyone I love will die.

Did I really give my life to find Talia down here? What was I thinking? That I could bring her back?

Yes, actually, that is exactly what I was thinking. I thought I could at least make her undead... She'd live in Ipa forever, but, at least she wouldn't be stuck in the Deep forever. My heart starts to race. She didn't even belong in this world!

Tetalla's smirk grows on his face as he studies me and I swing my hand to hit him, but he grabs it. I growl in his face and he laughs.

"You have eternity to make amends with yourself. Well, not really. Only until it is time."

"You keep saying that! Time for what?"

He shakes his head slowly. "Come on. You are a Fate, Helāni. Think."

My brows furrow. "What are you talking about?"

"You. The Empress. All who came before you and brought this... magic of yours are an infection in the Aō. To heal it? Destroy the Tarot cards. Make it so that you never came to Ipa, and I will replenish the Aō. Everything will be as it once was."

"That's why you need to be Emperor? To hit reset?"

He smiles. "And I cannot do it without you."

"Because I'm the Past Fate."

He nods.

"How is it you're even here? And I can't go back? Don't we have equal seats on the Death Card?"

He laughs. "I was unable to leave the Deep before, remember? I was trapped here until you released me. But now, I have the royal flames and have communicated with the Aō in a way no other has before. So, I am capable of more than you are. Not because of being Death. But because, I am me."

So he's not even after power, at least not forever. Only for enough time to get rid of it all. But to what end? Kill half the population. If he can't have Adara, none of them can live?

"Did you ever even really love Adara? Or were you just using her to do this very thing?"

His features twist into a nasty frown. "The cards were barely a thought when I met my love. Do not test me, vicious one. She is the only woman I have ever loved. And will ever love."

My throat dries.

"So kill half-Ipani and the drakons too? Every hybrid ever created here."

He shrugs. "Who knows what will happen once my plan works? Perhaps they will live here. Perhaps they will be ruled by you. Or the Empress, wherever she may be hiding."

My eyes flutter. I forgot about her. "Is she dead?"

"No."

"Is she..."

"Here? I cannot feel the Empress. She is the only one I cannot hear, but there was a rip into the Deep after the destruction. Perhaps she is here, or perhaps she is at sea somewhere." His smile widens. "Perfect."

With the Empress here, he can start demolishing the humans above ground. My heart hammers in my throat. "W-what about my sister? When will I be able to feel people's heart beats?" I wish I could stop my voice from wavering in front of him. It's bad enough I've lost. And he's won.

He leans in one shoulder, and winks at me. "She's alive."

"What?"

"When the Tower crashed, the Empress used her body to shield your sister from being crushed by the island's debris. The snow drakon tried to take them both, but lost the Empress due to the rip from the quake."

Disbelief overcomes me as I stare at him. "How do you know this?"

"I too have drakons as sources."

The red drakon I overheard in the room that day comes to mind.

"He watched the whole thing."

I blink. Why would she save Talia and risk herself?

"Do not grow a soft spot for the Empress now, vicious one. Remember why you are vicious. She is the reason why so many dead lived in eternal torture. Including babies and children. Do not forget what she did to Ipani up in her arena. She started all this, and I will end it."

"I want to end it too, but not like this. Tetalla, there has to be another way."

"There isn't. The only way to cure this infection is to remove it."

I suck in a breath.

"So you're okay with killing me too then?"

His eyes narrow at me. "Do not mistake the time we shared together as friendship. I have always had my goals set. Just like you had yours." Another smile. "You would have killed me had you had the chance. Danced in my blood while kissing your pirate captain." His pointed teeth gleam this time.

He's not wrong.

"By the way, he paid me a visit."

I still. Please don't tell me he lost his shit and went after him the moment I left.

Of course he did.

Tetalla ducks his head, his eyes still on me. "We fought. Like he wanted to..."

I'm going to kill him.

"You should know, he was admirable trying to save the girl from your world. He succeeded. I let her go."

"He succeeded?" My eyes narrow at him. The way he said it—

"I told him if I won, I would let her go. So I guess, he succeeded in losing. Either way, you won't leave here, and he is now burning with royal flames from the inside out." He looks around. "Right about here actually."

My heart shatters like glass. No... "No, that can't be true. The royal flames won't hurt him."

"They do now. They have united with the Aō and agree with me. The only way to reset the Aō, is for me to be in charge. That means over Danū as well—the rightful superpower over all of Ipa."

I keep shaking my head as if he's going to give up and tell me this was all a ruse. My heart is lodged in my throat. Everything happened so fast, our lives shattered in an instant.

"Yes," he says slowly.

A tear falls down my face. He can't be dead. Nkella can't be dead... He'd be here... He'd come down here. If it's true, I'll find him. The Devil inside him will keep him alive. This asshole is just telling me he's dead to leave me here to suffer. "You're a liar," I spit at his face. He smacks me hard across the cheek, sending me sprawling to the sand.

My breath is knocked out of me and I hold my cheek as I gape up at him. He stands backlit in the red light of the Deep, his frown deepened as he looks at me with disgust.

I hate him. I don't know how I'll do it. But I will find a way to take his ass down.

He dusts himself off. "I must be off. Take it easy as your new powers come. You will feel sick at first. And thank you for taking half the burden of Death from me. Enjoy the Deep." With a chuckle, he disappears in a swirl of sand.

I get up and step to where he had just been standing, and gawk at my surroundings. Then I open my mouth and release a long, loud scream that echoes across the mountainside, while also being swallowed by the waves.

I've fucked everything up.

I should never have taken the card.

Talia is alive! I never had to take the stupid card.

But she is alive. At least that's one thing that matters. Although, nothing will matter if Tetalla accomplishes his plan. And now I'm here, and can't do anything about it, not knowing if Nkella is truly gone... if I'll find him here someday... or if he's above ground, and burning forever, while his Devil keeps him alive.

Worst of all... I'm dead.

23

NKELLA

"SUBMIT ...

...to

us..."

The voice flickers in a hiss, each syllable sharp. Staccato. Before dying down to nothingness. Like the dancing flames. *"Where am I?"*

"Submit to the flames, Prince Mikiroro. Take up the line."

"I did. I have tried. You chose Tetalla."

"It is not choice, young Ipani. It is will. It has always been."

I spin but find only darkness covered in purple lights. "Where am I?"

"You are inside the Aō. Your body is protected. Give yourself to us, and you will have equal power to defeat your opponent."

"I thought I had. Then he moved you. Or, you allowed him to."

"It is true. The royal flames move as rivers in his blood. But to you, it does the same. He is more in tune with the Aō. You are not."

"What do I have to do to be in tune like him then?"

"Do you like your ouma?"

Why are the royal flames asking me this?

"All ouma are equal. You are connected. We are connected. Know this and accept it."

"—I do like my ouma. I didn't think it was good enough to lead before, but now I see. It is strong. It—"

"Yes—go on."

"It is me. It carries me, I give it direction. Like a captain on his ship.

"I have made men blow up from the inside out, I have ripped the tides to get the ship to a specific location, and I have trusted it to carry me over the sea. I now know I can do far more with it than I ever knew."

"And the flames?"

"I submit to them—to you. Fuel my blood, as my ouma of wind serves my lungs."

"Then you are ready for your duel."

I wake to a surge of water drowning me and I spit, sitting up.

"Cousin!"

"Brother!"

I stare at Kaehante and Ntaoru standing over me. Kae holds an empty bucket in his hands, relief visible over his big head. I wipe my face.

"Water on royal flames, daí?" Although, now that I am awake, the royal flames are no longer on me.

You are ready for your duel.

"We didn't know what else to do..." Ntaoru's voice is exasperated, breaking. I stand and take her into my arms. For the first time since we were children, her tears wet my shoulders, and she sobs. "I thought I lost you again."

I wrap my arms tightly over her. "Not yet, Nta. Not yet."

She sobs. "You had changed to your other form... and... you were not coming back. The fire was burning you. You were covered in royal flames, and your mouth was open... fire was inside you, and I was helpless."

I hold her tighter. I cannot imagine what that looked like.

Kae squeezes my shoulder. "You need to stop putting yourself in danger, daí? Your crew needs you. And every time something happens, we think the worst."

I let go of my sister. "I still have to fight Tetalla. You know this."

"But you weren't ready," Nta says.

I breathe deeply. "You're right. I wasn't, but I didn't understand why." I run my hand through my wet hair. "I went somewhere just now... the royal flames were speaking to me. They say I am ready to take him now, with equal strength."

"What does that mean?" Ntaoru asks.

I narrow my eyes to the ground and extend my hand. My palm warms until a single, purple flame comes out of the ground. My eyes widen and so do Kae and Nta's. I move my hand around, and the flame follows. With a gentle push downward, the flame flickers out.

A small gasp comes from behind Ntaoru. She steps aside, and the girl Tetalla had taken still stands there, shaking, having watched what I just did. Soren would say this doesn't happen where she's from. I'm sure none of this makes sense to her.

"You can control the royal flames..." Kae's voice trails, and I flick back to him.

"But so can Tetalla still. Only one will survive this."

"We need to get back to the ship," Ntaoru says pointing to the *Gambit,* now docked ashore. "And I guess we take her with us." We all turn to stare at the girl. She has light hair and a piercing under her nose. Her clothes are ripped and dirty.

The gangway is already lowered for us when we approach it, and Iéle greets me on the main deck. Katergaris is still here, and he floats around the new girl. Her eyes are wide and she clings to Kaehante. His brows furrow down at her but he doesn't move her away.

The three refugees stare at me, fear written on their faces. The tall one they call Gibby has lost his hat, and is holding onto a bundle of ropes. I stop at the other two. Adriel is leaning against a barrel sewing together a piece of the torn sail. Kennedy is sitting beside her, helping.

"Good. You are all being useful. We will make a crew of you yet," I tell them.

I turn to Tessa, who shoots me an agitated look, and I scoff.

"Did you miss me?"

"I'll deal with you later," she snaps while she drives her chair to the newcomer, holding up a bottle of the translation potion.

The girl takes a step back, and shakes her head. I turn to Adriel. "You, take care of her, daí? Tell her about the translation potion."

Adriel half smiles and stands, setting aside the torn sail. Kennedy takes it so it doesn't fall to the ground.

"Not sure a translation potion would make sense to her but..." Adriel takes the potion from Tessa to hand it over to the new girl.

The new girl yells something I cannot understand. The potion works to translate for us only. But between themselves, they will understand each other. Within moments, they're all talking at once.

Finally, the newcomer takes the cup from Tessa's hand and shoots it back.

She coughs and wipes her mouth. Most don't like the taste of licorice.

"Thank you," she says, and I nod. "What is this place? What are you all?"

The others once again start talking at once. I step toward her, and everyone silences.

"You are a refugee in my land and you are not the first." I look to the others. "What is your name?"

"Amanda."

"Amanda, what you just drank is a translation potion made with oumala plants here in Ipa."

She repeats the word oumala.

"Not everything can be translated. You hear I have an accent? It is because I am Ipani." I look to Tessa. "She is descendant from the first humans that arrived here more than two-thousand years ago. The Ancient Greek descendants, and they speak Imboe." I'm telling all of them this now, so they all understand. "Amanda, I am trying to explain this all to you, so you know this is not a dream. Do you understand you are awake?"

She nods.

"Good. The others will catch you up on all you need to know.

Welcome aboard the *Devil's Gambit.* I am Captain Nkella Mikiroro, and unfortunately for you, you are now part of the crew."

Amanda's eyes are wide as she takes everything in. Katergaris gets close to her, wrapping her body, loosely with his furry tail. She follows him as he turns her around.

"Tessa," I say. "Get this girl something to eat. She looks pale." I turn away from them and head to my room. I need to plan my next move.

"I think this is the most I've ever heard you talk to anyone new," Tessa says as I pass her by.

"I feel different." Turning from the steps, I give her a stern stare. "Be ready."

I start up the stairs.

"Do we have a heading, Captain?" Kaehante calls to me.

"Out to sea, away from shore. Anchor far enough away and put on the cloaking."

"We do have some left. Enough for maybe two nights."

"We won't be here that long. Have someone check on Lāri."

Kaehante quiets and I move up the steps, and into my room. Closing the door behind me, I lean my head against the door. Emptiness fills me, knowing she's in the Deep.

But she's alive. And that's all that matters. Now, how is she alive in the Deep, being human, and having taken the role of Death is another question.

24

SORREN

My throat burns for the long periods of time I've spent screaming and crying to myself.

For my life. For never being able to see Nkella again.

For Talia.

For failing everyone on Earth and in Ipa.

At some point, I think I fell asleep and woke up with sand inside my nose.

Now, my tears have dried up and I've cried everything I have in me. I think of the crew, and my heart starts to burn again. The only thing left to do now is try and find Nkella, if he really is here.

This can't be over. I refuse to believe Nkella is down here.

I'll go find AJ. Not sure how I can do that in this giant world... and without the World Card this time.

Loud buzzing screams into my ears and I whip around trying to find the cause of it. Bees? Here?

No.

The buzzing grows louder, stronger, shattering the inside of my brain. I start to scream myself. I grab onto my head and my knees buckle to the ground.

What the hell is this? "Stop!" I scream. "Make it stop!"

The buzzing intensifies, zipping toward me from all directions.

Drums start pounding all around me too. Loud, disorienting, out of rhythm. All at once, from different places. I can feel it in my bones. In my heart. As if my own heart still beat. But it doesn't. Or is it?

I can't tell with all this noise. Everything is vibrating.

"Stooooop!"

All at once, everything quiets.

My hands are on the ground and I'm facing the dirt. I somehow walked my way out of the sand and into the woods. I was too blinded by the noise to notice I moved.

"What the hell was that buzzing?" I say aloud, panting in place. After a few minutes of me staring at the dirt in silence, I stand. No idea what that was, but here's to hoping it doesn't happen again.

Now to find AJ. Somehow. I start walking toward the fortress until I find an entrance. Last time I was here, I snuck in with Snakebite—Nangraku—but now, should I be worried about the guards at all? How do I prove I'm Death?

The buzzing starts up again, paired with the drumming—it's getting louder, a rhythm of a heartbeat inside my head, and I can't hear myself think. Panic courses through me. "No, no, no. I can't take all that buzzing at once. Stop!"

The buzzing stops, but this time, I do hear a faint sound. Talking, but a whisper. I still, trying to listen.

"And then, I told her that I wanted to live back on my island. But she wanted to live in Oleanu. Guess a ship was the best place for us."

"AJ?" That was totally AJ's voice.

How the hell did I just hear AJ's voice?

And which direction is it coming from?

Oh. I roll my eyes. I think I understand what all that was. My powers of Death are coming in. I'm probably hearing people's voices, and their heartbeats. That makes the most sense.

I suck in a gasp. I wonder if I can zero in on a specific person's heartbeat. I pick a spot at the fortress and lean my back against the wall.

Closing my eyes, I listen for Nkella's heartbeat. I can do this, right? Our Aō connection should at least allow me to recognize him.

I take a deep inhale, and let it out slowly. "Where are you, Nkella?"

A beating heart thumps, loud and clear.

I think that means he's not dead. And he's above ground.

A smile crosses my face. That lying son of a bitch.

Now AJ. Just to be sure.

I'm met with silence, but it's an odd feeling... that of a dead silence only I can attribute to the absence of a beating heart. But I can still hear his voice. He's talking to someone.

A rumble shakes the ground, and I hold on to the wall. Another quake? Down in the Deep? This must be because of the rip Tetalla mentioned. The tremor grows louder and now the buzzing starts up again in my ears.

Shrieking mixes with it from above, and I hold my ears for dear life. Oh no... the Sirens!

They swoop down, their gazes focused on me. Why are they coming to me? I'm not alive for them to hunt and take away!

The rumbling grows louder and rocks start to jump on the ground. Confusion flickers through me. This isn't one of those quakes... It's starting to sound like... marching. I run out of the woods and back onto the pink beach where a formation of the undead army marches my way from the horizon.

For a moment, I freeze in place. Slowly, I turn around to see another formation headed my way from behind. The sirens start to circle overhead and I duck, but they don't seem to be diving down to grab me. They're just... watching.

What are they waiting for? I don't stick around to find out. Instead, I make a run for a tree to get a good footing. I pull myself up on a branch, using the wall to help me. The wails from one of the sirens rings in my ear as I scramble to get my leg over the wall. This was a lot easier with Nangraku. One of the siren's claws clutches at my back and I scream. The marching continues, getting louder as the siren pulls me off the wall. I kick and claw at her grayish arms. Her hair flails about her face as her sharp, needles for teeth glare down at me. I grab her wrists, now staring at the fortress wall growing smaller in the distance as she pulls me away, and toward one of the marching formations.

I'm brought down just as they stop in place, and I'm surrounded by both sides. Rows and rows of skeletons stand at attention facing me. They wear withered garments that look like they've been buried for centuries, some with a faded red, but their weapons still hang off their shoulders. The siren lets me go, and I grab my shoulder where she held me with her sharp claws.

The only thing I do is show my Death mark. I'm not sure if that's what they want, or if they were sent here by Tetalla to keep me in line, or... Am I meant to command them?

One of them move from the last row facing the calm sea. Its bones rattle as they move toward me, away from the formation. A small huff escapes me as I notice the red sash belonging to my handmaid.

"Bobby?" I choke. Bobby groans.

Of course Tetalla sent Bobby, and all of these too.

The skeletons behind me all move at once and I jump, spinning around to see them turning to face the opposite direction. They click their heels at the same time and start to walk.

Bobby grabs my arm, urging me to move, but I pull my arm away. He pushes me forward as the formation behind me starts to march with the others, forcing me to move in their direction.

The sirens wail overhead and continue flying above us in a formation of their own.

Is that really necessary? Where do they think I'll go? I couldn't outrun this army at this point if my life depended on it.

"Where are we going?" I ask out loud, as if Bobby could respond with anything more than a groan.

Inside.

I gasp and stare at Bobby. My Death mark tingles and I rub my wrist. Well, okay then. I guess we can speak to each other now.

The giant double doors leading inside the fortress are open as we arrive. Two minotaurs that tower over the walls stand on either side, each holding enormous axes.

As we continue to walk through the doors, and into Danū's village territory, the buzzing sound in my ears starts up again, this time louder than before. Words here and there stand out to me, and I realize that before I was picking up AJ's voice because I was thinking about him.

"So all I have to do is think of someone and I can hear them?" I ask Bobby as if he had already been tuned into my thoughts and knows how to respond to me.

"Yes," is all he says.

"And if I want to make all this buzzing stop?"

"Tell it to stop," he says simply.

I roll my eyes, "I tried that earlier. It didn't work.

"Focus," he says. "Focus."

Quirking a brow, I listen to the buzzing. It sounds like I'm in a crowded room, voices becoming more like voices and less like bees. I swallow, and tune into the rhythmic marching of the skeletal army instead. The talking starts to become distant, until all I hear is whispers. "Stop," I tell the whispers. All at once, they stop. And now I can hear everything around me as it is, and not in my head.

I gaze at my surroundings. People are staring at us as we walk. All eyes are on me, many are pointing and talking amongst themselves. I wonder if my father is anywhere in this crowd. Or if AJ is.

"Where are we going?" I ask again.

"The castle. Back to your chambers."

Of course we are. "What if I don't want to go?"

"You have to."

"Why? Because Tetalla says so? Why is he the boss of me? I took the position in the card too. I am Death too."

"Your job is in the castle."

Great. "And what is that job exactly?"

"To wait for Master."

"Master? You mean Tetalla? That's not exactly a job now, is it?"

Bobby looks at me but doesn't say anything more. He pushes my arm as we continue to walk. Tetalla made my job clear. Wait for him so he can use me to kill all the humans and get rid of the Tarot cards once and for all.

As we reach the caverns of the mountains, my memory goes back to the last time I saw Sehu and Nkura, Nkella's father. Weren't they going to stay and look after this place? Wouldn't Nkella's father be in the castle now?

"Hey, Bobby, is the castle empty right now?"

"It has not been inhabited since Tetalla."

"How do you know that? Does Tetalla know that?" As far as I know, he hears chatter, and living heartbeats. I heard AJ because I was thinking of him. How would he find the dead if he didn't know specifically who to look for? Nkura was trapped in his devil form all those years he was down here, put to fight in the arena. Would Tetalla know how to hear him? They were alive during different eras.

How did he know how to find me?

Maybe because I have the Death mark too... That's how he found me, and it explains how he used to find me when I was on the ship. He'd listen for my heartbeat, then hear me talking, or my dreams.

My heart flutters. That's how I can communicate with Nkella. Tonight, that's what I'll do.

"Death's abode is sealed. No one gets in. Except us," Bobby says.

I smirk. Does he still think Nkella's father is trapped in his devil state? Surely, he could get into the castle.

This is going to be interesting.

We walk to the rhythm of the marching, and I keep to myself, trying to recall Nkura's voice. I lean into it and hear him talking, but I can't make out where he is. Maybe that power comes later. Or maybe I'm too distracted to get a clear view of where he is.

More minotaurs stand guard as we reach the Royal Mountain. The entrance is perfectly and intricately carved from this direction. It isn't an entrance I've gone through above ground, so I can't say if it's the same. I've come to realize the Royal Mountain, being so big, has many entrances, secret and not. The army halts, and I almost buckle against the one in front of me. Bobby steers me forward, and we step out of the formation to enter a giant walkway of stones that lead to enormous arched double doors.

The minotaurs follow us with their gaze. They open the doors for us and Bobby urges me forward. It almost feels as if I'm being led to my own mausoleum. To be inside this giant fortress, to never come out until Tetalla arrives. I'll never see the sun again, and it's finally hitting me now that I've died. Like really hitting me.

With all that has been running through my head, I didn't get a chance to mourn my own life.

I don't feel dead though. That's the other thing about it. But I'm not feeling a pulse either.

Torches light the way through the narrow cavern halls as the doors slam shut behind us. The air is thick and it's cold, and dark.

Chin up, Soren. I'll see Nkella tonight. I promise myself I'll try.

We reach the winding bridge that showcases the castle built out of the rock from afar. The royal flames are somewhere down below the cliff, too far down to see them burning. I can see the tower I lived in from here on the east wing.

Bobby and I don't speak as we follow the winding path down to the entrance of the castle.

A roar breaks the silence and a flicker of hope ignites in me as a Devil comes soaring out of one of the Tower windows. It has to be Nkura, this is where'd he'd be.

Bobby immediately gets in front of me. "Who is this?" he asks in monotone.

"A house sitter. Obviously."

Bobby snaps his head at me, and I think that's a grimace. It's hard to tell when he has no skin. Nkura swoops down, headed straight for Bobby, and crashes into him. Bobby flies off the cliff. I gape down into the darkness, my knees shaking from the height. Not that I cared for the handmaid, but... I didn't even get a chance to say goodbye.

Nkura lands in front of me, and I stumble backward, but he grabs my wrist before I can fall. I'm panting as he shifts to his Ipani form, and Nkella's father's features come into plain view.

"Soren? What are you doing here?"

I hold up my other wrist to show my Death mark. "It's a long story... but Tetalla's army of dead is outside this place, and once Tetalla checks up on me here... which I'm sure he will, he's going to have questions."

Nkura's face grows rigid, fire burns in his eyes and I'm immediately reminded of Nkella.

"A lot has happened. Nkella is okay, but... he has to fight Tetalla for Danū. And—"

Confusion, then realization flickers over his features. "Tell me inside." I nod and follow him down.

"Your father, and your friend are living here as well."

My heart skips a beat. "Sehu? And AJ are here?"

"Yes." He walks briskly inside the castle, and I'm at a half run to catch up. I look over my shoulder in the direction Bobby fell, wondering how soon for Tetalla to reanimate him, and come here to take care of Nkura. Will he see him as a threat?

"H-how did you reclaim your castle?"

Nkura glances down at me from the corner of his eyes. "I do not need for the royal fires to speak to me in order for me to enter my own home."

I nod. I guess that's true. Tetalla hadn't ordered the royal flames until way after he lived here for so long.

"They hear me, still. They respond from time to time, but it does not matter here in the Deep. In order to have rein, one must be alive and above ground."

That must be why Nkella was able to move them here in the Deep, and then had to prove himself in Ipa.

Once inside the castle, he turns and lowers a huge lock that echoes through the palace walls.

"My love? What is happening that you need to lock the doors?"

I stare at a tall Ipani woman, decorated with light stripes up to her collar bone. She has long, straight black hair, and cheek bones just like Ntaoru. I hold in a breath as her eyes move sharply to mine, and her brows furrow.

She's stunning.

"Who is this?"

I swallow.

Nkura taps a gentle finger on my shoulder. "This is our son's aovate, Soren. And she has for some forsaken reason taken up the Card of Death. Which means she is away from Nkella and has come with news of war."

Her eyes widen briefly, then she nods, as if already accepting a new fate. I can tell by her grace and posture, that she receives news as it comes, no matter how traitorous. "Come then, Soren. I'm Maruñe, Nkella's mother." She guides me gently with a soft push toward the great halls. "You must tell me everything about my son. And Ntaoru too. Have you seen her?"

"Yes. She is... so much better."

"We might be in trouble, soon, my love," Nkura interrupts. "Let her speak of the news she brings first." We enter a room I've never been in above ground, and laughter makes my hairs stand on end. I pick up my pace until I go through an open archway, passing tall lit candelabras, and start running, not caring that I probably just scared the hell out of Nkella's mom.

AJ stops talking and jumps a foot high off the ground when he sees me coming for him.

"What the—"

I jump on him and he catches me, swinging me around.

"Soren! How? What are you doing here?"

A ball is caught in my throat, and I can hardly speak. Tears are flowing down my cheeks, and I hold onto him for dear life. He holds me tighter and I shut my eyes.

"They are friends," I hear Nkura tell Maruñe.

I reluctantly pull away from AJ, and stare at his beautiful face. His half smile is worried as he pulls my hair from my eyes.

"I mean, it's good to see you but... how?"

Someone clears their throat next to us, and I turn to see Sehu, my biological father, standing there awestruck. "Yes, how are you back?"

I let go of AJ and walk over to him. My nose itches from me trying not to cry. Do I... do I hug him?

Sehu reaches out and holds me close. I let out a shaky breath, and then slowly step back.

"There's no easy way to say this, but..." I hold up my wrist, and AJ gasps loudly.

"No, Soren. Why?"

"It's a long story, but you're all going to have to hear it. Also, Tetalla will know his castle is being occupied, and might come down here. Or, more than likely, will send his army instead. He's kind of busy with a big war right now."

AJ points to a pile of large plushy pillows on carpet, for me to sit. "Spill it. And also after that tell me how Lāri is. And Tessa, and Kae. And—"

"I will," I promise him, then I tell them the entire story from the moment Nkella and I left the Deep to Tetalla's trick and me living in the east tower, to the quakes ripping the worlds apart and bringing in refugees from my world.

They stare at me with gaping expressions, disbelief going from each one of them.

"This is terrible," Nkella's mother says. "My son has lost his aovate. What a great pain he must feel." She holds her hand to her heart and her eyes sulk. Then she quickly looks to Sehu. "Wait. This is your daughter?"

Sehu nods and something flickers through her features, like she's remembering something of the past. Her gaze trails to the far end of the room, and a moment of silence passes between us.

AJ steps toward me. "Soren, did you really die?"

I shrug.

"No, please tell me you're not actually stuck here until Tetalla comes for you?"

A shallow breath escapes me.

"Oh Lordy," his voice trails to a whimper. "Now what are we going to do?"

"I haven't thought that far."

We sit in silence, taking it all in. They listen to everything I tell them. But I'm finally taking a breath, without skeletons and sirens wailing. I wonder how long until Tetalla decides to try and see me through Bobby's eyes, and finds him swimming in lava.

Without the Empress there to directly oppose him, how much time does he have in his hands now? Hoping Nkella doesn't take her place as his sole focus. I can't help but feel so afraid of him ending up here.

At least we'd be together. But I want him to live.

"We cannot let my son fight Tetalla on his own," Nkura breaks the silence. I flick my gaze to him.

"I agree," AJ chimes. "It won't just be them two fighting. It'll be his entire undead army fighting our crew, all while the worlds are ripping?" His voice rises an octave at ripping. "Not to mention, Tetalla plays dirty. He's tricky. In fact," he looks at me, "I don't believe you're really dead. I think he just said that to you."

I blink at him.

"When was the last time he was reliable?"

My brows raise, but my frown deepens. "You're not wrong, but... I don't know. I don't feel my own pulse."

"Of course you don't, you're in the Deep. Did you feel it when you were here last?"

"No..."

"And you're a Fate. Plus, I would think the Death Card acts as some sort of immortality drink."

"He said the Death Card takes my life."

"That's what *he* said."

"Look." I stand. "I don't want to get my hopes up on being alive, and going back up there. Seeing Nkella—being able to touch him." I swallow the ball lodged in my throat.

AJ quiets, shutting his eyes as he pinches the bridge of his nose.

"But I do agree that I don't want to let him fight alone. He's liable to hurt everyone else he loves, so that he gives up... or—" I steady my breathing. "Nkella will be too late, and Tetalla kills half the population while the Arcana kill the other half—given the Empress makes it back from the Deep, as she is alive somewhere here. The Empress doesn't care about Nkella, or the Ipani. It's a war out there."

"What can we even do?" AJ asks. "It's not like we can go up there..."

Nkura's gaze falls on me. "Where did you say you thought the Empress was?"

"Possibly here somewhere. Or up there. We don't really know."

"But there was a rip between here and above ground?"

I stare at him. "...Yes..."

"What are you saying, My King?" Sehu asks.

"What if we can cross the planes?"

My lashes flutter. "Can that happen?"

"Consider the possibility that the Empress is here," Nkura continues. "She is like you. A Helāni. If she is alive, and if you are alive, like AJ here suggests, and there is a rip..."

"Then maybe you can go back up," AJ finishes.

I shake my head. "Right, but what about the rest of you? Last time I was here I needed the Ace of Cups to bring one person back with me, and that person was Nkella. One," I hold up my dampeners, "Tetalla put these on me to prevent me from using my magic, so I can't reach into the past and grab that card, and two, it could only bring back one with me anyway."

"Yes, but there hadn't been a rip through the barrier. If, in fact the Empress fell through."

...Oh.

Oh!

And the rip is only going to get bigger with the quakes getting worse. I lick my lips and stare at everyone.

"If she's here... and it's a big if. I would need to find her, and I have no idea how. Not even as Death did Tetalla have the ability to hear her heartbeat."

Silence befalls the room.

"And there's the possibility that she could have already picked herself up and left..." Sehu adds. "She is Helāni, after all."

I squint at the floor. "I'm not sure if she would know how. And she was injured." I won't rule it out though because she could spin herself from one place to the next as the Present Fate.

AJ perks up. "Wasn't that serpent her pet?"

"Apeiron? Yeah... until he got cozy with Tetalla."

"Aw, a pet is always a pet."

"Okay, so?"

"What if you find Apeiron and get her to find the Empress?"

I gape at him. "Find the giant serpent? With what? Dead sardines?"

"Maybe."

"And how would I talk to her? Last time I was here I killed her and he became a spirit serpent. I don't think I'm his favorite person right now." A fragment of a memory of being pulled down by the serpent comes to mind.

"Soren, this might be your only chance. Make a connection with him."

"That's insane." Yet, he might be onto something.

Sehu lets himself fall to a plush pillow and he wipes his face. "Let's say that plan works, daí? And she finds the Empress we all want dead, to take her back above ground. To what? Fight alongside our enemy?"

"Koj," Nkura says. "We use her to get out of here together, as an army. Soren will then have access to her, and has the power to kill her after they stop the dimensional ripping."

"Can't use my magic. I'm only as powerful as she is with these off."

"Maybe she can help you take them off, if she thinks you're on her side," AJ says. "Isn't that what she's always wanted? For you to be her fake sister?"

"Yeah, but she didn't know how to take them off when she first saw them on me. In fact, she was worried about him getting close enough to her to put them on her."

Maruñe stands. "Why don't we worry about one thing at a time. There must be something in the archives to undo magic like that." She walks toward me and gently takes my wrists. "This is Aō ouma, daí?" her voice is soft as she studies the markings. The Empress will not know how to take this off. Let me see what I can dig up in our library."

AJ scratches his chin. "So in order to keep the worlds from colliding, you need the Empress alive?"

"And possibly my sister Talia, as the Future Fate... but I doubt it was working. She's not a Fate. The Empress was teaching her, but I think it was just to convince me to stay with her."

"And then we help Nkella take down Tetalla by being his back up to fight Tetalla's army, and the Arcana."

I give a nod, but it all seems impossible.

"And if we do get rid of Tetalla, then we're back at having the Empress to deal with."

"And possibly all of the Deep above ground," Sehu ads.

"Let me handle the Deep," Nkura says. "I will start gathering an army. We just need to figure out how to take them all.

I scratch my cheek. "Do we have ships?"

"Yes," Maruñe says looking over her shoulder from a shelf of books. "We have a fleet."

A wide smile slides on my face. "That'll do."

25

NKELLA

THE CRACK ACROSS THE PANORAMIC WINDOW OF MY quarters traces a jagged path between sea and the night sky. A reminder that the world is splitting apart.

The sea hasn't stopped churning since Rutavenye fell. Tower debris is scattered across the water, like a vast graveyard. And somewhere below it all, the serpent took her.

Images of her play over in my mind, no matter how many times I try to shove them down. Reaching for the Death Card and allowing the Deep to have her. I keep seeing her silhouette disappearing beneath the surface.

Something told me she would choose the Death Card. I know Soren. In many things we are alike, and what wouldn't we do for our family?

The only solace I have is that our aovate connection is alive. Because she is alive. I have to remain calm and focus so I can bring us together again. But with the duel and the challenge from the royal flames before me, I have to shove Soren out of my mind and prepare to fight. Only after beating Tetalla can I stop to figure out how to get her back, and it is driving me mad.

I press my palms to the map on the table. If I don't hold something, I might break the whole room.

Tetalla left me burning on the sand with royal fires inside me but it won't be long until he learns I survived and am ready to fight him again. The crew knows we're not going to be away from shore for long. We attack in the morning.

"Well, isn't this atmospheric," Gari drawls from the doorway.

I don't turn around. "You pick the worst moments."

"I pick the important ones." He slinks closer, his voice bubbling as it always does. His body winds like smoke through the lantern glow. "And oh, Captain, you're going to want to hear this."

I glance at him, my impatience rising.

"She's alive!" he giggles. "Or, we hope she is."

I straighten. He knows I declared feeling Soren's life within our connection. "Who?"

"Talia."

The name stills the breath in my throat.

"Impossible. No one could have survived that fall."

Gari circles the edge of the room, tail flicking lazily. "The snow drakon saw her. Just before the island split in half."

I narrow my eyes. "She was in the Tower."

"She was," he purrs, "until the Empress plucked her from the air like a falling flower. Used her own body to shield her."

I stare at him. "The Empress *saved* her?"

"Just caught her... and vanished but Talia was seen falling and disappearing into the waves. "

"Hn. That's not like her. Why didn't the snow drakon save Talia from the fall?"

"She couldn't find her." He spins on his head. "But she is still looking."

"That does not fill me with confidence, Kategaris. How do you know then that she is still alive?" But my mind is already racing with what ifs—calculating distance, tide, wind. Talia's alive. Somewhere out there, adrift, Soren's little sister is alive.

"Krua assured me it wasn't a high fall from where the Empress grabbed her. She was moving fast with the current. I do hope she's still alive."

I step away from the table. "The Tower fell hours ago. How far could she have drifted?"

"Who knows."

"This is not good. If Tetalla has sensed her alive, he will know where she is and take her." I turn call out, "Iéle."

My wolf is already rising from her spot at the foot of the bed. She pads toward me, ears pricked.

"Find Soren's sister," I say. "Track whatever scent remains. Katergaris will fly ahead."

The drakon bows and vanishes out the window. Iéle bolts after.

My hopes of finding her are low. It would be a Fate's doing that Tetalla would be too preoccupied to take her, or not care enough to. He could leave her to die, and I would still want to find her before that happens.

For Soren's sake.

I throw open the cabin door and the wind rushes in. The crew turns from their tasks. I head straight to the helm. "Kaehante, we're changing our heading."

"Captain?"

"Talia's alive," I call out. "The Empress saved her when the Tower fell, but she is lost somewhere at sea."

They go still.

Tessa reverses her chair to face me. "But who could have survived that?"

"I won't rest until I know for certain," I say. "This ship is on a rescue mission now." The cry of a gull makes me jump, and I stare up at the sky, but see nothing. I spin around, my eyes narrowing. Gulls don't come out at night.

"Brother?" Nta asks.

"I thought I heard a gull." I wipe my eyes, tiredness obviously getting to me. "Never mind."

"Well, I agree. It is only fair we try," Ntaoru says rising up from below deck, with the refugees.

Tessa nods, and then stares past me. I turn to see Lāri leaning on a barrel for support as she tries walking the main deck.

"Lāri, you should be resting," Tessa says.

"If Soren's sister is alive, I have to help look for her."

"Koj, Lāri," I tell her. "You are still injured. You should not fly yet, daí?"

She shifts form with ease, wavering a little, but holding herself still.

I shake my head. "Kategaris and Iéle are out searching, you do not have to go."

She tilts her head at me, and then at Tessa before taking off, ignoring my order.

"Let her go," Tessa says. "You know Lāri has never been one to sit out a fight. Besides, she can take care of herself."

I stare after her as she disappears into the dead of night. Iéle will smell her scent and keep her safe.

"What about your fight with Tetalla?" Kaehante asks me from the wheel. I turn to face him.

"I may not be here for most of the rescue."

His eyes narrow, not understanding how I mean to leave the ship to go fight Tetalla. "We will not leave you to fight him alone, daí?"

"Then let us find Talia quickly."

Kaehante sails while I study the Tower's location on the map. Only because Ntaoru forced me inside saying it was no use watching each wave pass us by, turning the minutes to hours. I trace the area on the map where we are headed, toward where the Tower used to be. It's somewhere we barely ever travel through to avoid the Arcana army. The Empress was always after me, so why journey those waters?

West past the black rocks… that is not on the map.

Where could she be?

We sailed for hours into the night. Tessa has come in twice already, worried about me not getting sleep. She is right to worry. My body feels tired and at any moment, the fires could call me to fight.

Iéle is a good tracker so I'll admit I was expecting this to be quick. Each minute that passes could be a minute too late. I slap my face and gaze into the map, but my eyelids grow heavier by the second, and I yawn into my hand. I stretch my legs under the table, and when my feet plant on the ground, sand makes me pause. I blink.

I hiss behind my teeth, prepping my mind to fight. What I need is a nap.

The ground beneath my feet spins into a pink hue until I am surrounded by a sandy beach in Danū. I tense, ready for Tetalla to appear for our duel.

The waves crash on the shore under the night sky. Wind blows through my hair and my ouma reacts to it playfully. For a brief moment, my guard is let down.

Circular motions of sand form in front of me and I scoff. This is some sort of trickery.

"Such theatrics before a fight is not necessary, Death. Stop stalling and face me."

A feminine chuckle bites through the sand as the wind carries it away to show Soren, stepping out of it. I squint at her stepping up to me. Do my eyes deceive me? "Is this a dream?"

"Sort of," she says. I tense as she walks up to me, not sure if I should trust this or not. She is wearing the green tunic I bought her back in Sagirang. It was the first time she ever wore something Ipani and it took away my ability to speak. I swallow at how it fits her curves perfectly. Her large beautiful eyes are sad as she stares at me with regret.

This does not feel like a dream.

I am too aware to be dreaming.

"How?" I ask. A soft wind brushes past us, carrying her fiery hair away from her face. Her perfect lips tease me as she half smiles like she does when she's about to explain something long.

"My new powers have started to come in." She raises her wrists to show her dampener cuffs. "Maybe slower than they should have because of these, but apparently my Fate powers are still useless."

Now I reach for her cheek, pulling her toward me and she lifts her chin for me to kiss her. I lick my lips before brushing them over hers, our aovate connection stirring, letting me know this is not a normal dream.

"I miss you, my aovate." I kiss her lips and she leans into me with her body. It feels strange, like I can feel her, but she is still distant. Like a whisper, almost a dream, but conscious. It is not enough but I kiss her anyway.

She pulls away. "I'm sorry for everything. It was a waste; I was fooled. Talia is alive."

I caress her cheek and stare into her eyes. "I know."

"You do?"

Sighing, I nod. "We are searching for her now. I hope we find her alive before Tetalla does."

"Tetalla was the one who told me she's alive."

"Does he have her?" I ask.

"I don't know. He didn't tell me and I didn't have time to ask." She stares at me, a longing in her face only I can understand.

"I knew you were alive," I tell her. "I could feel it."

"I could feel you too. So you didn't rage out?" She narrows her eyes at me accusingly, but with a slight mock in her voice.

"You would be proud to know, Neyuro, this time I did not. But I need you. Come back to me."

"I'm working on it."

"How?"

She hesitates and her face goes distant, as if she's listening for something, but then she says, "I found your parents… and AJ, and my father."

"And they are safe? And you? Are you safe?"

She nods. But her forehead wrinkles. Hn. "What are you not telling me?"

She licks her lips.

"Soren?"

She purses her lips now, her voice lowering. "Remember Tetalla can always hear a heartbeat, and now so can I. We might be safe as long as he doesn't see me as a problem. But we share the same power, so if he hears me talking to you, he'll know everything."

"Everything."

"I wish I could tell you…" she stammers, "but he's already sent my handmaid to find me, and your father threw him into the fire pits. The moment Tetalla decides to come check on me and finds Bobby is gone, I'm in trouble.

I nod in understanding. She has to keep this plan of hers secret from me or risk Tetalla hearing how she will escape. An idea comes to mind. "You say your powers as Death are coming in slowly?"

"Yes, why?"

"Tetalla can reanimate the dead. Have you tried this?"

She shakes her head, "No... but there's dead all over the place here, I don't exactly have to do that."

"But he can reach their minds, make them do things."

She gasps. "You mean the skeletons. Like Bobby."

"Listen to me. Try to reach this Bobby. And the others, get them on your side. Soren, you are persuasive, daí? Use your skills to win them over like you won over the people in Danū. If you can make them see a Helāni is not all bad, you can shift the mindless skulls of an army of skeletons."

Her lips part, an idea lighting in her eyes as she stares at me. "I'll try... If this works, we'll have the upper hand against him."

"You can do it." I bring her in close and whisper in her ear. "This cannot be the only way I'll ever get to see you, my aovate."

"It won't be," she whispers back.

"Promise me."

"You have me forever. I promise."

I bring my hand up and squeeze her chin for her to look at me. "Koj," I say, "it is I who promises that to you. Just make sure you stay alive, daí? Because once this is all over and I am king of Danū, you will be by my side as queen." Her eyes widen and I kiss her before she can answer me.

It isn't like she didn't know that would be coming.

She takes a deep breath as I let go of her face. A dark storm forms overhead, and she gasps. She doesn't need to tell me, I already know it's time for her to leave.

"I have to go," she says. "This isn't a safe place. Nowhere is safe from him..."

"Wait," I say. I bring out the royal coin around my neck. "This was the Ace of Pentacles all along."

She blinks as though remembering the last moments before she took the Death Card. "That's why the barrels were filling with food."

"Suitable that you had it all along. My Queen, already caring for her people."

She swallows, staring at the coin. Thunderclaps loud overhead and she steps back. "Goodbye, Nkella."

"How can I call on you if I want to see you?"

"You can't," she admits. "But you'll see me again."

Sand forms at her feet, and spins above her head before everything around me fades, and I awaken in my cabin. Rain patters on the windowsill, followed by another thunderclap. The skies break out in a roar of rain, and I stand from my desk to check on the crew.

Kaehante stands at the wheel, fighting the waves.

"Have you thrown the anchor?" I rush past him as he calls out not yet, and I jump the steps to give Ntaoru and the refugees directions. "Secure the hatches!"

"Already on it!" Ntaoru shouts back as I make my way to the anchor and throw it over board. Winds whip past me, and I aim to collect them with my ouma. I glance at the refugees who run to toss loose items below deck. Kennedy stares back at me, worry crossing her features.

"We've survived worse storms," I say, meeting her gaze. My voice is low, almost lost in the howl of the wind. "We'll outlive this one too, whether we walk out of it alive. Or crawl out of it undead."

26

SOREN

Our conversation runs through my mind. So much has happened in the last twenty-four hours, and I feel as though I should be a lot more exhausted. But I guess being dead means I don't need sleep.

I'm mentally tired though. That's for sure.

Swinging my legs out of bed, I stand in the dimly lit room that was once mine above the Deep. Finding my way through the darkness to get here was eerie. It was familiar, but it felt different. Like the castle belonged to someone else, like the walls were watching me, but with different eyes than when I lived with Tetalla. More like curious spirits watching over me. Knowing that I'm here to try and protect them.

There's a silence in here that, despite having lived alone in this big palace with Tetalla, is almost deafening. But peaceful. There's no rattling of bones, or me getting annoyed over Bobby following me around, or any of the other guards coming in here.

Part of me still worries they will. Or worse, Tetalla comes storming in.

I leave the room and make my way back down to meet the others. Another part of me feels bad about not telling Nkella my plan, after I was furious at him for keeping me out of his. But I hope he understands. I can't risk Tetalla hearing our conversation.

Back at the living quarters where I left everybody, Sehu stands when I walk into the room. I smile back at him, knowing we're both appreciative to get another chance to spend time together, but understanding we have a mission ahead of us.

Maruñe and AJ are huddled together, flipping through old texts, presumably trying to find a way to release me from my cuffs.

Nkura turns from the table his wife sits at. "Have you rested?"

"I don't need rest. I was able to visit Nkella in his sleep."

Everyone stops now to look at me. His mother's eyes widen.

I avoid telling them how he's doing given he's about to fight the warrior legend of their songs. They have to know he's dealing with a lot. I turn to Nkura. "Can you take me to where Bobby fell?"

"The skeleton that was with you? What for?"

"Nkella and I have a plan. If he survived the fall, maybe I can reprogram him the way Tetalla does. That way, as long as Bobby is with me, I can pretend to just be sitting here, waiting for him and doing nothing, so Tetalla won't have a reason to come and stop us."

Nkura smiles. "Tetalla's downfall might be his own ego and underestimating you."

"I'm counting on it. So you'll take me?"

"Why don't you all go to the fleet, and I alone will find this skeleton. If he is intact, I will bring him."

AJ stands. "I'll board with my captain, if that's all right with everyone else." He smiles at me and I roll my eyes at him but smile in return.

"Hnn..." Sehu walks toward me. "It is wise for you to have a first mate who knows you, but the rest of us should each captain a ship. I would not just allow anyone to lead a crew above the Deep."

I squint at him. "I didn't know you knew how to captain a ship."

He smiles at me. "Learning to paddle a boat is Ipani life, but you forget I was raised here, with the best teachers." He passes a look back to Nkura. He had been adopted from the Oleanu royals by the Mikiroro royal family. I guess ships run in their blood.

Maruñe walks over with some old pages in her hands, she moves swiftly, a lot like Ntaoru. Anyone could tell they're related. "I've found something, but it's only half of what your cuff says. Let me see it."

I hold my wrist out to her and she takes it, raising it up to the torch on the wall. The light reflects on a scripture, and she looks at it carefully.

"We need Helāni magic to take it off completely."

I swallow. "Tetalla was somehow accessing this power from the Aō."

"Yes." She nods. "When the Helāni came to Ipa, and the Aō absorbed the strange magic within itself, it learned."

"That's how the Tarot marks spread on everybody," I confirm.

"While true, Helāni magic was never accessible for Ipani use. Especially with the ouma dampeners the Empress put on everyone for so long, keeping us away from our own Aō access and using our ouma. We can help as far as ouma is concerned... but with Helāni magic, we need another Helāni."

Sehu walks up to stare at my wrist. "Yet, somehow Tetalla has accessed it. Is the Empress the only one able to help with releasing my daughter from this then?"

I glance at him. "Yes. If she's here and we can find her."

He grimaces.

Maruñe looks at him. "But if she is not here, we have a bigger problem."

"Right. I need her in order to save the worlds from collapsing in on each other. If she's already left the Deep, I'll find her once we're out. So the plan is to acquire crews of the dead, find the Empress, and leave through the rip."

"We have to find it first," AJ says.

"There's no time to waste," Nkura says, orange torchlight tracing his wings as he shifts into devil form. "I will meet you at the fleet."

We follow Maruñe to a tunnel that leads to some kind of dungeon. From there, we creep through a series of interconnected caverns that lead away from the castle, until a pinkish light greets us at its wide-open mouth. Five ships are docked at the beach. AJ whistles. "They all look like the *Gambit*."

"With some changes, but yeah," I say.

"Well, this was prior to Tessa and the Hermit's tinkering. These ships won't have anything for potions. No transparency. No speed."

"That's true," I say. "I forgot about that."

"And they're old," AJ points out. The ships are covered in algae, but are they workable?

"It's all we have," Maruñe says.

I turn to her. "They'll work. But we're going to need a crew just to get them out of here, aren't we?"

"We may manage to get them to the water with my husband's strength, but sailing them by ourselves will be difficult."

"There's really nothing like the *Gambit,* is there?" I muse.

AJ shakes his head. "There isn't."

I'm lucky Kaehante and Nkella taught me how to sail one of these.

Wind musses my hair and I stare back at Nkura arriving from the tunnel. He drops a pile of bones at my feet as he shifts back to his Ipani form.

"You found him."

"He is slightly singed, but should be well enough to stand."

"Don't get too comfortable, husband," Maruñe says, "we need your strength to push the ships."

AJ helps me lay out Bobby's bones, placing him on his back so that his face stares straight up.

The others haul the ships to the water, with Nkura doing most of the work. I sit with Bobby's bones still beneath my hands, as I reach into the power of the Death Card, trying to reanimate him. A fall like that would only temporarily knock him out, so I better work fast before he comes to.

With the other Tarot cards, there was always a sort of magnetic pull, something telling me it's working. With this one, buzzing just started screaming in my ear.

I bring my hands to my lap. Tetalla does this effortlessly; he doesn't even look their way. They just rise and do what he tells them to do.

"The ships are anchored," AJ says running over to me. I glance past him and sure enough, five ships are facing the Dead Sea, and I'm still trying to get this magic to work.

"How's it going with Bobby?" he asks.

"What's it look like?"

"Sorry." He crouches beside me, and places a hand on my shoulder.

"No, I'm sorry. I shouldn't take it out on you—"

"Hey. You're glowing."

"I'm what?" I look to where he's staring. My Death mark is pulsing. "That's weird."

"Maybe it hears you? How are you trying to make it work?"

"I've tried putting my hands on him and focusing my energy. I don't know how Tetalla does it. He just tells them to move, and they do."

"So have you tried telling him to move then?"

I squint up at him. "I mean, not really. It has to be more than that though, doesn't it?"

"Or not? You're Death now." I blink at him. "I'm going to get one of our ships ready for us." He gets up and runs back to shore.

My gaze drops to Bobby. "Well, get up, you old pile of bones. You wouldn't stop following me around in the castle. It's time to do it again. But for me this time. Not for him."

Bobby doesn't move. I stand and dust myself off. It was worth a shot. Nkura walks toward me and I meet him half way.

"Are we ready to go?" I ask.

"We are. But we're going to need another captain later, or AJ won't be able to sail with you. It will be bad enough us all doing it on our own."

Nkella's mom walks toward us. "Will you try to awaken the rest of the skeletons?"

I give her an apologetic stare. "Even if I could, I don't think that would be a good idea. Bobby would be enough to keep Tetalla convinced I'm not up to something, so long as he doesn't try to act through Bobby. Me commanding Bobby is still a risk. Tetalla is be able to see through his eyes as if they're windows, but he wouldn't be able to know I'm in control. He can't feel my magic, just like I can't feel him doing magic. But if he can't reach his own army, that'll make him come down here."

She nods, and Nkura points behind me. I scrunch my face and turn to see Bobby rising and scratching his skull.

Dread swirls in my chest. Did I bring him back, or is it Tetalla checking up on me? "Bobby?"

He groans and looks up at me. I take a few steps toward him, and hold out my hand. He stares at it.

"Come on, let me help you up." He takes my hand and I help him stand. "Who do you work for?" Might as well cut to the chase and see how he responds. He points at me and my eyes narrow. "Not Tetalla?"

He shakes his head.

How can I be sure?

My breath catches in my chest as my vision blurs; a magnetic force grabs at me from over my head, and it feels like my spirit is leaving my body.

I— I can see myself. My hairs stick to my forehead, and my eyes are wide.

I'm literally looking at myself, but I'm also staring at Bobby.

I snap back to my perspective and the ground moves, making me lose my footing. Nkura catches me.

"Are you okay?" he says. "I've got you."

I gasp. "Thanks..."

"Can you stand?"

"Yeah..."

AJ comes running back with Sehu. "What happened?"

"I—"

"I think she was successful," Maruñe says, and my eyes widen. She's right.

"I have Tetalla's power," I tell Bobby. "If Tetalla tries to look through you, let him. But make him think we are alone in the castle."

Bobby stands at attention, and I take it as an understanding.

"Do you know how to do that?" I stare into his wide eyeless sockets. "Make it look like we're inside my room in the castle?"

He stares blankly at me, and I reach into a memory of us back in my bedroom. Me sitting on the bed, staring at the wall, and Bobby sitting on the chair next to the door, watching me. I pull Bobby into it, just like I had pulled Nkella into my dream space at the beach. Then I go into Bobby's view and watch me, sitting on the bed.

"That should be enough," I say to him, pulling out of our dream space. AJ stares at me, confusion written on his face. "If Tetalla tries to talk to me in that space, it might give us away though. So, we need to hurry."

Bobby follows us to the ship AJ prepared, and I have him climb aboard to bring down the gangway.

"What's the plan, Captain?" AJ leans his hand against the gangway rope.

I flick my gaze between him, Sehu, Nkura, and Maruñe. "We're going to have to split up. You all probably shouldn't come with me to find the Empress." I glance at Nkura. "And your people will most likely look to you and your wife for guidance, and not me."

"I wouldn't be so certain of that," Nkura says. "You released everyone from eternal torture. I have no doubts they will follow you once they hear of who you are. Still, it would be wise for us to split up and reconvene."

His wife nods in agreement, and I take in his words. I hadn't thought about how they might respond to me, especially given how the ones in Danū received both me and Nkella...

"I'm still not leaving you," AJ says, and I give him an appreciative grin.

"We do not know how long it will take you to find the Empress," Maruñe states. "Where do we meet you if you don't?"

"Right back here. And without the Empress, the plan continues the same way. We find the rip and make it through. If the Empress isn't here, it means she's up there, so the worlds won't collide yet. This will get both her and Tetalla's attention either way. But if she's here, she can hopefully take off my dampener, and we can make sure the worlds don't collide."

Which means me taking the seat next to her, or taking the Empress throne all together. *Queen of Danū.*

I shake away that memory. That's a lot of responsibility. Can I take up the Empress Card, and be Queen of Danū, now that there's no Tower?

"We must be off," Nkura interrupts my thoughts. "No matter the delay, we return here."

Sehu stares at me. "Be careful."

"I will, and you too be careful of the minotaurs."

He holds his hammer over his shoulder and I nod nervously. A shaky breath escapes me. This is happening fast.

AJ and I stay behind as the three of them leave back through the tunnel.

"Any ideas on how you're going to locate the Empress?" AJ asks me, now that we're alone.

Lowering my voice, I lean into him. I know I have Bobby on my side now, but just in case. "I've never been able to see the Empress's past, and she could never see where I am because our powers cancel each other out. Last time I was here, I had the World Card to move around, and the map of this place works in reverse."

"But the only card you have on you is the Death Card, right?"

"Right. Which isn't going to help with the Empress. Tetalla isn't able to access her either."

"How come he can access you but not her?"

"I think that's just her power... Being the Present Fate, she can control which ones of the cards can access her whereabouts. When it comes to me and her, it's more because we're distant relatives of the Fates."

"Can she see where Tetalla is?"

"I think so. He just became too strong, getting the Aō on his side tipped the scales."

He scratches the back of his head. "The Aō is probably desperate to get rid of the Tarot magic."

But hopefully not get rid of the humans. I swallow, hoping it's only Tetalla and the Empress, and not the whole Aō, working against us.

The only way to save the worlds is to get rid of the infection.

A low popping sound makes me practically jump out of my skin. AJ screams.

I gape down at the ground. "Sapphire!"

"Oh, Lordy," AJ says, clutching his chest.

I drop down to the sand. "What are you doing here? I thought Gari told you to steer clear of the Aō." She wiggles her little nose, her dark blue eyes staring up at me. I guess the Deep is beyond the Aō... so this is actually safer for her.

"This is good news," I tell AJ. "Sapphire can help us."

"If she doesn't eat me! Rabbits are vicious!"

"She won't; she remembers you."

He scoffs. "How can she help?"

A pull tugs me close to her, and I allow for her magnetism to connect. "She can help locate the Empress," I tell him as I focus on Sapphire.

Images coalesce:

Gari and Iéle with the pack of wolves flying over the sea. Debris from Rutavenye's crash flowing with the current. Gari coming into view. He doesn't say anything, but he's searching.

I pull away from Sapphire.

"Well? What did she say?"

"She just showed me Gari and the wolves searching for Talia. I think that was Gari trying to send me a message."

I refocus my thoughts on Sapphire, trying to get her to connect with me. "Can you help me find the Empress?"

"Does she even know who that is?" AJ asks. "She's just a rabbit."

"I know, but maybe she can help us cover more ground if I show her who to look for."

Our magnetic pull starts again when a shriek comes from the sky.

"It's the serpent," AJ says. "Be careful."

"Why is she here?"

"Probably smells the rabbit."

My shoulders drop. There goes thinking the Deep is safer for her. Sapphire is alive, but rabbits can cross dimensions. I grab Sapphire and hold her to my chest, to keep her safe. "Apeiron is the Empress's pet... maybe..."

Apeiron swoops down, his translucent skin shimmering in the pinkish hue of the Deep. Ever since I killed him, his spirit still remains to haunt the Deep. We all step back as he enters the cave.

"Uh, Soren, what was your plan? Spirit serpents are fast!"

"I didn't really have one!" I shout.

Sapphire disappears with a loud pop in my arms and I jump to the side as the serpent whips around me.

His long body slithers through the air, and makes a sharp turn at the tunnel entrance to head back around the mouth of the cave. Apeiron bumps me at my side and I'm shocked at how corporeal he feels against me.

He bows his head at my torso, and my jaw slackens.

"Is he hissing? Or purring? Do serpents purr?" AJ says.

"Don't drakons? They're kind of similar, aren't they?"

"Not sure Gari would agree with you, but I can see the resemblance. Except for the no feet, or gills." The serpent reacts to AJ's voice, and snaps at the air inches away from his face. AJ takes a sharp breath and dodges the bite.

Apeiron circles back to me, rubbing up against my back like a cat.

"Soren, I think he's acknowledging you're Death. You're one of them now."

"One of them?"

"One of the leaders of Major Arcana. Maybe he will show you where the Empress is."

Apeiron's translucent scales shimmer a soft green and blue as it moves around my body. This giant serpent would have once been too big to fit inside this cave. But now, after I slayed it, it's spirit stayed in the Deep. Not much changes here, so I guess he no longer eats spirits, yet still tries to eat live things that somehow end up here. But there is no real end of life for him. Not really.

I snap my gaze back to AJ. "Hey, don't call me one of them. I'm doing this for all of you, ya know."

"I didn't mean that. I just mean, maybe that's the way Apeiron sees you now."

"Well, I'm not feeling any kind of magnetic field with him."

"You probably wouldn't. Do you feel that with Gari?"

"No, but the drakons can talk... Oh, you're right. Apeiron isn't oumala." Apeiron nudges my hand and I tap his head twice, petting him. This is weird. I clear my throat. "Apeiron, do you know where the Empress is?"

I'm not exactly sure what I expect if he can't talk. He quickly wraps his tail around me and starts to constrict. Terror coils my insides while I wedge my hands between him and start to tug. "Oh no... AJ!"

"Oh Lordy, that's what you get for trying to talk to it." He starts tugging at the serpent's tail to get me loose. Apeiron lifts me up in the air, and I squirm uncontrollably, a scream lodged in my throat as he speeds out of the mouth of the cave.

I finally manage to scream AJ's name as I'm carried higher in the red sky, and my friend becomes small as an ant, the entire island growing farther away.

27

SOREN

"PUT ME DOWN!" I YELL THROUGH THE DEAD AIR. APEIRON swings his tail up and I start grabbing his scales, afraid he'll drop me. I clutch desperately, and he lets me go gently as I straddle his neck.

We're flying high, close to the surface above, and farther away from Danū. I'm thankful there aren't any more tortured spirits, or we'd be flying through their floating bodies right now. But I'm not ready to leave the Deep yet, so I'm hoping he doesn't bring us out. However, if the Empress is up there, maybe that's where he's taking me.

No sooner do I think that then Apeiron swoops down, heading for land. I hold on tight, squinting at where we're going. This has to be Sagirang by the looks of the wooded forest up ahead. There aren't any large waterfalls to be Oleanu, and it isn't covered in snow like Piupeki.

Apeiron lowers his body to glide over the sand, and now we have the Dead Sea to our right. Up in the living world, this beach is covered in Ipani skulls for miles, and bioluminescent plants and bugs light up the night. Here, there isn't any of that.

We start to slow down, and I spot a figure on the sandy shore. Apeiron stops a few feet away, letting me off. I pat the serpent on his head, still awkward over this unexpected interaction with the giant serpent that attacked us more than once on the *Gambit* and dragged Nkella to the Deep. I once saw her eat a man alive. After Nkella threw him overboard, but still.

We have a history together and it still haunts my nightmares.

Sobbing makes me turn to face the hunched-over figure. I take a few steps toward it before I recognize the black lace attached to a long cloak that can only belong to the Empress. She's weeping into her hands. I glance back at Apeiron who slithers in place.

Sand crunches underfoot as I carefully make my way to her. "Empress Aletha?"

She doesn't hear me, so I speak louder: "Empress Aletha?"

Something reflective catches my attention from the corner of my eye out in the waves. I walk over to it and pick it up; her gold mask. Striding over, this time, I tap her on the shoulder.

She jumps to her feet, her eyes heavy, and red from crying. Shock plasters over her burnt face.

"Don't look at me!" She rips the mask from my hand and turns around to put it on.

I don't say anything. I saw what happened to her in a vision of the past, when Tetalla burnt the Tower, thinking she killed her own sister. She burned trying to save her.

"I know what you did for Talia," I start. "Thank you. I thought she had died."

"D-did she survive?"

"We think she did. But I took the Death Card thinking she died. In doing so, I gave Tetalla what he wanted."

"Stupid girl," she huffs.

My fists clench, and when she breaks into another sob, I roll my eyes.

"I may have been stupid, but it was out of love."

"Love was the cause of all this, wasn't it? You should have taken my request to join me when we still had the chance. Now we've lost."

"We haven't lost yet. We still have work to do."

She gives a sarcastic chuckle as she sticks a finger inside her mask to dry her eyes. "There is nothing left to do. The Tower has fallen. My sisters are gone. I have led my people to war and destruction. It is all over for me now. I might as well build a home here in the Deep."

I blink at her. "Someone find me a violin."

"I beg your pardon?"

"Is this really what you've become? A sobbing mess that just gives up? Nkella is up there about to fight Tetalla for dominion over Danū."

"Oh, who cares about Danū? It's been Pentacles for hundreds of years, as this has been Wands. Things change. Get over it."

"Is this honestly what you're deciding to argue over? The worlds are colliding. If he fights Tetalla and wins—"

"Let them collide. I have nothing left worth saving."

I deadpan. "Have you always been this selfish? No wonder Asteria never wanted to come back here. She's afraid of you because you'd rather be entertained in your arena than help her save people."

"Don't you dare talk about my sister. You know nothing!" Her voice shatters my eardrum, but I hold my ground.

I take a deep breath before continuing. "If Nkella wins, Tetalla dies."

"He won't win."

"He will. The royal flames have acknowledged leveling the playing fields. He has a chance."

She quiets for a moment. "He still doesn't have the experience Tetalla has. Or the pull of the Aō. Tetalla is so much stronger now, and it's your fault."

My fault? Nope. Don't argue with ignorant people. Another breath. I open my mouth to speak but she cuts me off before I start.

"Had you taken the seat next to mine, the Tower would still be standing. The worlds wouldn't be colliding. Tetalla would have failed because we would have been stronger."

"You don't know that last part. Nkella has to be the one to fight him."

"Even if he does win, the worlds are still colliding. It's over, child. Make yourself at home."

She turns and starts to walk away from me. I walk after her.

"What is it you want, Aletha?"

She pauses. "What do you think you are doing? Calling me by my name like that."

"I'm making myself comfortable. You're not an Empress here. Or are you? Let me see your mark."

She starts walking faster, and I speed up.

"Aletha?" I keep going. "I bet it's reversed, isn't it? No one will follow you here. Not that anyone ever did. Not because they wanted to, anyway."

She spins around. "Yes, they did. When we first came here, they did. We were the first to lead our people to safety, away from war. I was the only one who stayed because I cared."

"Or because you were left alone, and had no other choice."

"If you are trying to change my mind, this isn't going to help."

"Don't you want to see Asteria again? Your only sister that's left?"

"She doesn't want to see me. She left me." Her voice quivers at the end.

"But you'll never get a chance if you just give up. What is it you truly want?"

She sets her hands down at her side and finally turns to look at me. "To finally be at peace. And yes, I would like to see Asteria again. I'm so tired of being alone. You would never understand it."

"I wouldn't? You killed my mother. You made it so I'd never know my real father and left me to be raised by bad people, because my stepfather didn't want me."

She stays quiet.

"Believe me, I know what it's like to feel alone."

A beat of silence passes between us and she stares at me from behind her gold mask.

"But you have your crew," she finally says.

"I fought for, and continue to fight for, my crew. You should do the same for your family. Especially with you being immortal. You being alone for so long is your choice. Is this really how you want to spend eternity?"

"Don't you see? This is why I've given up. There's nothing left for me to fight for. Let the worlds collide. I am finished with them. I wanted you to be my family, Soren. And even you rejected me."

"You killed my family. I could never forgive you for that. I could never be a part of yours."

"When you get to be as old as me, trivial things stop mattering."

"Trivial things, like people's lives? Everything you've done is for your own gain. That's what's kept Asteria away from you all these years."

We stare at each other in awkward silence. I hadn't noticed Apeiron had followed us and is coiling up beside us, his body reaching higher than my elbows.

"Do you think she could forgive me?"

I stare at her. "Asteria? I mean, she's your sister. At least allow yourself the chance to talk to her."

Aletha lets out a long, shuddering breath.

"This world is still worth fighting for, you know. You can change. Turn a new leaf."

She laughs. "If I show weakness, they'll revolt."

She's hopeless.

"Are you going to help me or not? Because I'm running out of time."

She straightens her spine. "After having spoken to you..." she lifts her chin. "Yes. For Asteria, I don't want her to die in the collision. Something like this would kill even us. And for mere spite, I cannot allow Tetalla to finish taking everything from me."

I won't argue with that last one to not be here forever, but she's taken everything from him too. I hold up my wrist. "I need your help taking off this dampener then."

"Let me see it again." She takes my wrist and studies it. "I can feel my magic in it, which must have been transferred to him through the Aō, but these scriptures are Ipani."

"Yeah, Nkella's mom has been looking up ancient scripts."

Her eyes snap to mine. "You're working with his parents here in the Deep?"

"Yes."

"And they agreed to work with me? They are going to want to kill me." She lets go of my wrist.

"Which we both know they can't do. And they're agreeing to work with you because we all need to work together." I turn to Apeiron. "Take us back to Danū."

"Perhaps then together, she and I can figure a way to take that off you. With it on, you won't be able to take the proverbial seat next to mine."

We climb on top of the serpent and lift off the sand. It feels weird having the Empress holding onto my shoulders behind me, but this has been a weird last few days. I still hate her, and I don't think I'll ever stop hating her. But for right now, I need to do what needs to be done to keep the worlds from collapsing. To make sure Nkella and I have a future together. To save everyone.

So far, my plan is coming together. Even if it means having this horrible person sitting so close to me.

"It won't suffice to show up at Tetalla's doorstep. It would be good to have the upper hand somehow, something to weaken him," she says behind me. I grimace at her breath behind my ears. Something about the Deep is how quiet it is. We don't have the strong winds to block out our voices, or the thrashing of violent waves. Everything is calm. Quiet. Dead.

"Are you hearing me?" she asks.

"Yes. And we do."

"Oh? What do we have then? It isn't enough to just stop the worlds from colliding. We'll still have him to deal with."

"You still think Nkella will lose, don't you?"

"I would just like to have security."

"We have an army."

"So does he. And I still have the Arcana, but that didn't help, now did it?"

I swallow. "We still need an army to fight his."

"Well, it is something, I suppose."

"... And with my new powers, I can turn his army against him."

"Oh, now that is interesting." Her voice actually sounds excited for just a minute. "Except, you're only sharing the card, he can take it back. You'll be tugging and pulling at that power the entire battle."

Shit. She's not wrong. "Then what do you suggest?"

"I'll think on it."

The mountains of Danū come closer, and Apeiron makes a turn for the caves.

"Aletha?"

"Empress Aletha."

She drags her voice, but I ignore her. "Where did Adara's spirit go?"

She quiets.

"Because, her spirit would be something that would catch Tetalla off guard."

I feel her tense behind me. Apeiron swoops down to take us to the mouth of the cave where I left the fleet.

"I always wondered where she went. But I could never find her, so I assumed her spirit returned to where we came from. Or to the past."

Ancient Greece. That would be unfortunate.

"I never had the Death Card in my power to find her here... but you do, Soren."

My head turns to my shoulder. Could I find her? I was able to zero in on AJ's voice. And I've seen Adara before in my past visions. What if I can? Then what? Bring her to Tetalla?

We enter the concave where the mouth of the cavern is, and Nkura is there with the rest, as well as what looks like fifty to sixty of the dead by the ships.

"It's not much, but it's what we have," Sehu calls to me as Apeiron makes it to the sand. "Mostly all pirates from different crews."

"This is excellent." I hop off.

Everyone stops working and stares at us. Sehu's eyes turn rigid at the Empress, and Nkura steps forward, his chin held high. Maruñe steps out next to him.

Aletha holds her ground behind me, but I know she's scared. She holds out a hand, a gust of black smoke appearing in her palm, I hold it down, letting the smoke singe my palm.

I lock eyes with her. "Do you really want to call the sirens over here because you're using magic? Remember, just because you have minotaurs and created a prison here, doesn't mean this still isn't Tetalla's domain."

She sets her hand down, and I turn back to everyone. "We're all going to work together for the same purpose. This means working with the Empress. She knows where the rip is so we can leave. She's our ticket to saving those we love. Anyone who has a problem with this, can stay behind. We need all hands on deck if we're going to go into battle against Tetalla together."

I search the quiet crowd. Some faces I recognize. Nangraku and his lover, they nod to me, and I nod back. My gaze falls on Nkura who turns to them.

"Tetalla is about to fight my son, if he wins, any humans, and half-Ipani will perish, whether the Helāni come together to keep Ipa intact or not. He may have once been the legends we sung about, but now, he is the ending to those we care about."

Sehu climbs aboard one of the ships and others begin to follow. AJ walks over to me.

"Any problems with Bobby?" I ask.

He shakes his head. "Seems quiet."

"Good. Let's board."

AJ licks his lips; hesitation marks his forehead as he looks up behind me.

"I know Nangraku is here, AJ. Long story, but I got to know him... and remember what Nkura said."

"It's not that." He shrugs. "And he's going to captain one of the ships to allow for Nkella's parents to stay together. That way you and I can stick with each other, and Sehu will take another crew."

"Then what is it?"

He nudges his chin toward one of the ships. "It was the only other captain we could find."

Up on the hull, stands the former Hierophant, Demitri. Staring down at me and the Empress.

28

SOREN

"Quite the crowd of misfits you've gathered," the Empress says, ignoring the ill stares shooting her way.

"Just come on." I head up the gangway with the Empress close behind.

"It's refreshing to find I won't be the only hated one on this voyage," she says.

Can't argue with that. "Where's the rip you fell through to get here?"

"Just south of Dempu Yuni, back toward Wands. Which makes it north here in the Deep."

Great, that narrows it down.

"It is not some rip in the sky; it's like a barrier. We'll know when we find it."

A barrier...

AJ loosens the ropes.

My eyes skim everyone else aboard, counting about fifteen of them, not including Bobby, myself, and the Empress. Not that she'll be helping us sail. It takes everything in me to resist glancing at Demitri on the ship next to this one, who's burning a hole through my skull with his gaze.

AJ catches my attention. "You all right, Soren?"

"It's going to be hard to ignore him." I motion for Demitri with my chin. "The Empress is right. He hates me. The last time he saw me, I killed him. And I don't regret it, not one bit, AJ. He used me for my power and made me kill Alec in cold blood. He's nothing but an opportunist who is probably on this mission to get back above ground, waiting for his chance." My blood rises and AJ squeezes my shoulder.

"If I thought we had someone else who could captain a ship, I'd say get him off."

"They won't survive the rip closing," the Empress snips.

AJ nods. "This is true. Once we go back to Ipa, however long you two take to do whatever you need to do to stop the worlds from colliding, is how long we have to fight in this war."

I stare back at him. I guess I knew that, but I didn't want to be reminded that my time with AJ is brief.

"Don't worry," he says. "Whatever he thinks he might be planning, I'll make sure he comes back down with me."

Maruñe walks up the gangway and stops in front of the Empress.

I pat AJ on the arm. "We'll cross that bridge when we get to it." I walk over to Nkella's mother who has a stoic look on her face as she faces her killer.

This is going to be the most awkward voyage ever.

The Empress turns to look at me. "Hold out your wrist."

I do as she says and both women study the markings. The Empress taps on the metal, and tries tugging on it. "Try tapping into your power."

I lean into Maruñe's past as practice, but I hit a blank wall. I shake my head. "I can't."

"I'm afraid that without communing with the Aō directly, our efforts will be wasted," Maruñe says.

I frown, but give her a slight nod.

She reaches for the sword strapped to her side and pulls it out. The Empress jumps back and I gasp. Maruñe hands it to me. "Seeing as you arrived without a weapon, Nkura thought you should have this one."

My lips part as I admire the craftwork. It has the Mikiroro crest etched on the hilt with four rubies around it. "T-thank you." I clear my throat as I stare into her eyes.

She nods with a tight smile. "I better get back to my ship. When do we leave?"

"Now," I tell her. She gives the Empress one last long stare before turning back down the gangway.

Pressure builds up in my gut as the time frame of all this is starting to crash down on me: Get through the rip, face Tetalla and his dead army, and keep them from destroying everyone while Nkella fights him. Take the seat by the Empress—which I'm hoping will be a quick ceremony—but not before Tetalla is dead. Because we need our army to do it.

And I really hope Nkella found Talia.

The Empress whips her gaze to me. "You better have that devil pirate of yours speak to the royal flames and get through to the Aō. Or do whatever it takes to get that thing off you, or all this is for naught."

"Great pep talk. Thank you."

She spins on her heel and starts walking away.

"Where do you think you're going?" I call after her as she heads for the steps that lead to the quarterdeck. I know she isn't about to take the captain's quarters. I scoff.

"To my room."

"*Your* room?" I laugh. "You're not going anywhere."

Slowly, she turns to me. "You best watch your tone with me young lady—

"Or what?" I step toward her with a loud echo of my boots on these floors, kicking away some of the algae. "You need me. Without me, you'll never see Asteria again because the worlds will collide, and you'll never wear a crown. So newsflash your greatness—you and I? We're on the same playing field now. Start acting useful, or I'll do what Demitri wanted me to do a long time ago, and just take the Empress Card from you the moment I find it." I'm bluffing, but it sure feels good to do so again. "I'm sure it'll choose me over you anyway," I add.

"That would never be enough to fix the rips. It needs us both—bad enough there's only two of us—"

I shrug a shoulder. "I'll figure it out."

"It is too late to keep it stable with just one of us."

"Don't care." I cross my arms. "In fact, once this dampener is released, I'll retrieve the Empress Card, and without you in the picture, I could probably go back and find Asteria. She'd come back here to help me if you're gone. I should have done that a long time ago."

This makes her quiet. Of course, I could never leave while all this is happening to find Asteria, not without the World Card to do so, nor my magic. There wouldn't be time for that, not without me going back in time—not that that's possible.

AJ's voice makes me turn to see the crew starting to leave. "Where are you all going?" he calls after them.

I walk past him toward a group of men standing in a corner with arms crossed, giving me dirty looks.

"Hey, boys, what's going on here?"

"Thinking we should leave."

"You want to stay here? In the Deep? When you have a chance to help stop Tetalla from killing your friends and family in Ipa?" I make it more a statement, but they get my drift.

"I would not have boarded a ship knowing she would be on here." He motions toward the Empress who's still standing by the steps.

I nod at him. "I understand that."

He quirks a brow at me.

"Trust me," I say, "I do. If you didn't hear my conversation with her just now, I was just telling her how much I hate her. She killed both my parents, and my aovate's parents. I know what she's done here. To all of you. But, you're not here for her. Or to work beside her. We're all here to save Ipa from being destroyed. It just so happens the Empress is part of that equation."

The man quiets, and AJ walks up.

"Just so you all know," he says. "Soren here is the reason why none of us are suffering in eternal torment. She killed the serpent and reunited our spirits." He points to the sky. "All of them came down, and it was because of her. I was there. So was Nkura and a few others on the other ships."

"We know," the other man says. "Our king spoke to us about you," he says, slightly bowing his head.

"Wait a minute." A tall man with two sharp stripes on either side of each eye walks up to me. "How do we know that wasn't just some stroke of luck or a byproduct of her own gain?" he says pointing at me.

"Either way, you're still dead, and supposedly at peace," I say, crossing my arms. "So what is it you want?"

AJ leans into me. "Not all of them know if they can trust you. They weren't here when you released their spirits. They don't know if you love the Empress... your family..."

"Not family. Ancestor if anything. But not family. I choose who my family is."

"I understand," AJ whispers to me, "but trust didn't come to you easily either. You're taking them to war."

I catch his gaze and stare into his eyes. With a nod, I step back and raise my voice.

"Anyone who doesn't want to be here, can leave. The rest of you, know you have a mission to save Ipa. Who on here have loved ones still alive?"

As far as I can tell, that's all of them raising their hands.

"Right, that's why you followed Nkura to the ships. So remember that. We are all in this together. For one purpose. Not Tetalla's purpose. Not the Empress's purpose. But to save each other."

They start to look at each other, and nod.

"When I first joined the *Devil's Gambit* and the Undead Crew—" This makes some of their heads turn, and I grin. "Some of you may have heard that name. You've all heard of the Devil Captain. My captain in fact, my love. Well, let me tell you, we didn't love each other at first. He called me an utwa, and stuck me in the brig. I'll spare you all the details of how we ended up together, but we realized something. He and I weren't so different, and our goals aligned."

The crew is all standing close to me now, listening to my words.

"I learned that we were pirates against the Tower. And now, our mission has become bigger than that. For all the people and animals we love up there, we're not serving some crown. Or some mask.

"We're fighting the tides against all odds, hell, against the gods! But we're doing it as one force. It's pirates against the throne."

Their cheers erupt all at once, and it catches me off guard. Did I really just say all that?

AJ grips my shoulder, and his smile reaches his eyes. He turns to them. "We live by the sea. Pirates against the throne!"

"By the sea! Against the throne!" They say at once.

Voices boom from all directions, as they chant, and I realize the other ships were listening in. The Deep is as quiet as the dead after all.

I turn to the Empress who's starting to make her way back up the steps, trying to hide away from all who despise her. I point at the two men who were just talking to me.

"Take her to the brig," I tell them. They exchange glances, and gape at me.

"I believe your captain gave you an order," AJ tells them.

Slowly, smiles spread on both of them and they rush toward the Empress, grabbing her at either side.

I step toward Aletha as she fights their grip.

"This is my ship now, and I'm the captain. Do as I say and go silently."

She stops fighting and they take her down a narrow set of stairs in the center of the main deck. I turn to AJ, a buzzing of excitement vibrating under my skin.

"Wow, you are not the same girl I knew before," he tells me.

"Guess I'm not."

"Take it as a compliment. How did that feel?"

"Pretty damn good," I confess.

"Wait till Nkella hears there's a new devil in town."

"Shut up," I chuckle, my nerves standing on end.

"So what are we going to call this ship?" AJ asks.

"I don't know, you pick a name." I turn to the crew. "Alright, get this place cleaned up and ready to go. We're late." The crew jumps at my command and gets to work on the sails, and cleaning the algae from the floors.

AJ stays close by as I walk up to the wheel. If the Empress can't take this dampener off me now, I don't need her taking up space. I'll deal with her after we close the rips and stop the worlds from colliding. But one thing at a time.

She was right to suggest we need some sort of distraction against Tetalla. And Adara could be the perfect one, but where and how do we find her?

AJ pulls out a scroll from beneath the wheel and unravels it to show a map. "Do we have a heading, Captain?"

"Dempu Yuni."

I leave AJ with the rest of the crew to lead the ships out of the cavern, and into the Dead Sea.

The damp air hits me in the face as I descend down the narrow ladder, carefully stepping on each rung. This ship makes me appreciate how spacious the *Gambit* is.

The majority of the layout is nearly the same. The brig is exactly where it is on the *Gambit*. I push the heavy metal door open to find complete darkness. There's no gas lamp down here below deck.

"Well, this is cozy," I say. Something shifts, the sound of her getting up off the ground.

"How do you expect me to help from here?"

"You deserve to be down here."

Silence, and then, "Was I really that bad?" Her voice sounds surprisingly heavy for someone who's committed all sorts of atrocities. But I guess royalty wouldn't see it that way.

"You tortured babies." I lick my lips. "Who does that?"

"That wasn't my fault."

"What do you mean that wasn't your fault? All those children, and babies... They were forcibly denied use of their ouma. They died from illness, and starvation, having been ripped away from their parents. And then when they died, they were stuck in eternal torture. Just like the rest of them. You caused that."

"No—" she sniffs. "You don't understand. Without Asteria here...

Without the future Fate, I had no control of any of their deaths... And I couldn't control the cards' magic anymore...it got too big for me to contain."

I tilt my head, listening to her excuses. It's true she probably couldn't control the cards anymore. That's become evident that the Aō and the Fate magic combined.

"So you took credit for it? Why?"

"Because if they did not fear me, they'd revolt."

"So lead in fear. Got it."

"You wouldn't understand—"

"You still killed my parents, and Nkella's parents, you kidnapped him, you restricted the Ipani's natural use of their ouma, which is like their lifeblood, you forced them to fight oumala animals in your rings, hell—you legalized fighting rings. The people were kept hungry, especially Danū through their siege.

"Fine then, enough!" She slams down against the bars.

"You deserve to be here," I repeat through the darkness. "The only reason why I came to find you is because I don't want the world to end."

I stand in the dark in awkward silence for a minute longer, before I turn to leave. "I'm going to find Adara, somehow. Once I do, I'm guessing she won't be happy with you either."

"Please..."

"Please? What is it that you want, Aletha? You're not going up there."

"But you're not going to let me go once we're back to Fateland, are you?"

I stay quiet. I haven't figured out how to keep her from roaming free and being terrible, but I'm not letting her go that easily once this is over. Killing her has always been the plan. I just need to preempt the collision of worlds, then take the control from her.

"I can tell you how to save your friend up there. What's his name? Ajax?"

"Save him? He's dead."

"But you can reanimate. You can bring to life more than just skeletons. You can have your father back too. Return Nkella to his parents," she says almost out of breath.

"Wouldn't that change the course of things? Isn't that against the rules?"

"Since when did you ever care about rules?"

I lick my bottom lip. "I'll think about it."

I leave her to her thoughts in the darkness as I shut the door behind me. Up on the quarter deck, AJ steers the ship, making a signal to Nkura who steers one of the four ships on either side of us. Up ahead, purple lightning strikes through the reddish hues of the Deep.

That's our heading.

As I reach the top of the stairs, the serpent flies above our heads. Some of the crew shout, afraid that they'd get eaten, but the serpent isn't here for them.

I bring my hand up, and Apeiron comes down to nuzzle my palm. "Find Adara, and bring her to me," I tell him.

With a swish of her tail, she leaves to do as I said. AJ's eyes are wide and on me.

"Being Death has its perks," I tell him. Now to try and hear her, somehow through the void. It's been hundreds of years for her, if she's lost somewhere at the bottom of the Dead Sea, will there be any noise to cling onto?

"Are you okay to keep steering?" I ask AJ.

"More than okay. Makes me feel like home."

I pat his shoulder. "Thanks. We might be making a detour if I can find someone under here. But for now, head straight toward those purple lights. It should be like passing through a barrier. Last time I went through, the entire ship spun in a whirlwind, so we'll all have to hang on tight."

"Noted, Captain. Who are we making the detour for?"

"The Empress's sister, the Past Fate."

29

NKELLA

The storm slams into us and the ship shudders. Rain pelts sideways. The rigging shrieks under the strain, and ropes snap taut, fraying against the wind. I can barely see beyond the rail, only the heaving of the sea opening and closing like it means to swallow us all into the Deep.

Iéle howls, and something hits the deck with a wet, heavy crack.

I spin around, sword half-drawn, but it is Katergaris, followed by Lāri landing on the ship as she shifts from her eagle form. The drakon sprawls across the planks, having swam in search for Talia. His talons scraping for purchase as his large yellow eyes pin me in place.

"Talia," he gasps out. His voice is raspy, like he swallowed mouthfuls of water.

"Tetalla has her," Lāri finishes for him as she holds onto the railing.

"*Rōkan.*"

Ntaoru runs to steady the mainsail. Kaehante curses as a coil of rope whips loose across the deck. The refugees cling together near the mast, with fear stricken in their eyes.

I push forward to keep my footing steady as I reach Katergaris.

"How do you know?" I shout over the wind.

The drakon's gurgling voice rises above the thrashing waves. "Krua saw her on a ship. He's keeping her in the brig!" He coughs up seawater. "I tried to reach Soren through her bunny, but I don't know if she got the message."

The storm rages harder, and the voices of my crew fade beneath it.

Lāri runs over to help them.

Iéle presses against my knee and her magnetic force draws me in. She shows me what she's seen...

Dark shapes shifting between wrecked ships. Bones dragging themselves upright. Hollow eyes meet my gaze as a dead army stands in formation.

Tetalla is preparing for my arrival. That ship must be headed back to the island.

We save her either on route, or at the cavern. It's time for our duel.

I whip toward the crew. "We take to the cavern on the south end. Stay on alert for a half-broken ship, where he has Talia. Her safety is our top priority. Leave Tetalla to me. The rest of you," I stare at Kae and Tessa, "be ready with raku, daí? His dead army will be waiting for us."

They move, none of them asking questions.

The ship rocks violently. I take the helm with Tessa, fighting to angle us toward the hidden inlet, while keeping my eyes peeled for another ship fighting the waves. The brig can easily be submerged in water. That won't matter to the dead, but the girl can drown.

The wolves, soaked and growling low, snatch at loose lines and drag them back into place. Iéle listened to my warning about them staying out of the Aō for about two days at most, but now I am thankful for it. Katergaris hauls himself into the rigging, his long body trembling with the effort.

I reach into my ouma in any attempt at steadying the *Gambit*, reaching into the spirit of wind to carry us through.

A soft light shines ahead as the winds spread around me, allowing us a clearer course. Out there, way ahead of us is a ship.

The question is whether Tetalla is aboard that ship. "Lāri!" I shout over the rain and wind. Both she and the drakon fly up the quarterdeck and land by my side. I hand her the scope.

"Captain?" she says, taking the scope from me and looking through. I direct her to where to look.

"I found Talia. She must be on that ship."

"We're on it." They turn to leave, and Iéle jumps up to follow them, but I call her back."

"I need you here, Iéle."

"Do you think Tetalla will be inside the inlet?" Tessa asks me, while she secures some cannon balls for her chair cannon on her bandolier. A row of raku potions flare a lime green under the lightning.

"I do not know, but it is where his ship is headed. Either way, that's where we're going, and if I need to get into the castle from there, I will."

I make a sharp turn with the wheel, and use my ouma to help us cut through the storm. A loud thunderous clap without lightning makes me realize I had made that sound. My winds clashed against each other.

"You are going to cause a cyclone, daí?" Kaehante yells.

"Mikiroro..." The royal flames seep into my mind, pulling me away from my task. *"He is waiting. It is time."*

And then they are gone.

My Devil stirs inside me. They told Tetalla where we're going, so he might be waiting in the inlet. This is our chance. I turn to Iéle and give her my instructions. She nuzzles my palm in recognition, and her ouma vibrates under my fingertips.

The other ship is nowhere to be seen. Hopefully, Katwergaris and Lāri stalled them and are keeping Talia safe. I tighten my grip on the helm and steer hard for the cliffs ahead, muscles straining as the ship fights the current.

We reach the inlet just as lightning cracks open the sky.

"Iéle... do it now."

The deck planks of the *Gambit* are splintering and breaking, the sails appear to be ripped. I stare at my hands, and bones appear instead of my skin. I turn to Tessa, and she screams, her mandible hanging low.

A low chuckle escapes me and scratch at Iéle's head.

"Take the wheel." I step aside and let Tessa steer the ship.

Kaehante stares at his arms as I walk down the steps. The rest of the crew—the refugees, and Ntaoru—stand as skeletons in clothing, gaping at each other, and screaming. I clear my throat, and they quiet.

"Iéle will hold this guise for as long as we need it. But it won't fool Tetalla for long. He will be expecting a ship he sent out to retrieve Soren's sister, but Lāri and the drakon are currently there. This will allow us to dock. But be ready for battle."

The wind dies under the overhang, but the rain keeps falling.

The ship scrapes against submerged stone, jarring the deck underfoot. Lanterns swing in the rigging, throwing thin, pale light over the ruined docks ahead.

I walk swiftly to the bow, ready to jump down, not bothering to throw an anchor.

Tetalla steps out of the shadows, purple flames crawling across his shoulders and arms.

He narrows his eyes when he sees the tattered ship and his glare swipes the exterior. He knows something's wrong, or he's waiting for his dead to bring Talia out.

Giving Iéle a slight nod, I drop my coat, and jump off over the rail, fully shifting to my devil form as I land on both feet in front of him. My tail whips from around me, and I duck my head to give him full view of my horns.

Shock plasters his face at the sight of me, and I can't help the smirk crossing mine.

He grimaces and pulls out his sword, the purple flames swiping down the blade.

I raise purple flames of my own off the sand with one hand. "We might as well fight without fire, daí?" I say. "We both control them now. It is a fight to see who keeps it. Devil to Devil."

He tosses his sword to the sand. And the dead start to rise from the ground and sea, causing a vibration under my feet. They begin to board my ship as my crew starts to fire.

Tessa fires her cannon, the blast ripping through two advancing corpses and scattering bone across the planks. Without missing a beat, she yanks a potion from her belt, pulls the cork with her teeth, and hurls it into the next wave.

Ntaoru follows behind her, blade flashing as she cuts a path clear for the refugees with her volcanic ouma lifting the ground.

We expected this to happen. I focus my gaze on Tetalla. The crew will take care of themselves.

Tetalla shifts forms, his horns coming out of his head, long and twisted. His fangs lengthen, as do his claws. He is bigger and stronger than me. And he has had years to control his Devil.

But I am smarter.

He rushes into me, and I jump back, sideswiping while pulling his arm to use his momentum. He flies to the side, but quickly takes hold of his balance with his wings.

"What is the point in this?" he screams. "Why challenge me instead of allowing me to rule?"

"Kh." I lunge for him, full force behind my wings, and this time, he too takes flight as we both take to the air. "You are no leader. Only myth," I hiss. I plow my fist into his jaw, and hear a crack.

Wind picks up before me, and at first, I think the storm has gotten worse, but as I lift up with no control of my wings, I'm thrown far back toward the mouth of the cavern. It happens so fast, it takes me a second to orient. I land hard on the main deck of my ship, back from where I started.

"Captain!" I hear Tessa cry out as I stand. The dead fight my crew around me, but there in front of the ship is Tetalla being carried by a small gust of wind.

My eyes widen. "Wind?" Tetalla's personal ouma is the same as mine?

This I did not expect.

He lands on the ship and kicks away a bone as he walks toward me. I straighten my spine.

Raku smoke explodes across the dock, thick and blinding, but I hold my ground as a grin spreads on his face. I cannot let this new revelation distract me. Tetalla is secretive. Of course he hid this; any warrior would. You don't show your enemy the full depth of your capabilities until it's too late. He kept his ouma from being known on purpose.

"Fire and wind is the Devil's domain," he says to me. "It is not your fault you never knew this."

My frown deepens. There's a lot of information stolen from me since birth.

A corpse bursts through the cloud, stumbling toward the cluster of refugees.

Amanda, still half-crouched behind Kennedy, moves without thinking.

She grabs a broken board from the wreckage and swings it wide, catching the corpse across the jaw. It stumbles sideways, long enough for Ntaoru to cut it down.

Amanda stands frozen for a breath, eyes wide, chest heaving, the broken board trembling in her hands.

I give her a sure nod. Good girl. Then I fix my gaze back on Tetalla.

Iéle barrels into another skeleton before it reaches me, her teeth snapping through brittle bone with a sickening crack.

I pull the wind hard into my chest and drive it outward. Only a Devil can fight another Devil. But can either win?

The blast knocks another line of the dead into the water, clearing a path.

Tetalla steps forward through the smoke, fire bleeding from his arms, his face hard with rage.

"You should consider who is more experienced to lead our people," he says.

"Kh. Stop talking and fight me."

He lunges.

I meet him halfway.

We clash fists, the impact rattling through my arms.

I snap my wind into his mouth, trying to rupture him from within, knowing he can do the same to me.

He stiffens, fire leaking from his skin in angry sparks.

Then he roars the air out in a blast of heat that rips across the dock.

I am thrown backward, skidding hard across the boards, pain flaring down my side.

Iéle lunges again, slamming a corpse aside before it can drag me down.

I push to my feet, blood in my mouth.

Tetalla watches from across the burning wreckage, his flames guttering.

His eyes are cold. Calculating.

"Captain!" Kae throws my bow at me, and I spit blood to the planks as I stretch to catch it. The wind coils tighter around me, and I lock my gaze on Tetalla.

I call on the royal flames, the wind dragging at my torn sleeves, straining to stay with me as I draw the string back. If he is using them, so then will I.

Every muscle burns.

Tetalla stands ahead through the smoke, blood leaking from his side.

The fire around him burns lower, but he does not fall back.

He gathers it in his hands again, pulling it tighter.

I tighten my grip on the bowstring and breathe against the rising tremor in my arms.

Tetalla lifts his hand, and the fire coils outward, aiming for outside the ship.

What is he doing?

"Lāri and the drakon are back with the girl!" Kae's voice rings through my ear.

I release my arrow.

It slices the thick air, the wind carrying it straight for his chest.

It cuts through Tetalla's flame blast and deflects it into the wreckage where it shatters.

Tetalla snarls, stepping forward, the purple flames alive on his arm.

I fumble for another arrow, but the dead turn toward me, coming forward. More dead rise around us, and I know Lāri and Talia are in danger. I lose sight of Tetalla. I fight my way through them.

Tetalla knows right now Soren's sister is my priority. He knows Soren would never forgive me if she died when I could save her.

Kaehante roars and charges into the dead, his oumalaarm shield smashing through two rotted bodies before they drag him down to one knee.

Tessa fires her cannon, the blast throwing a cluster of corpses into the sea.

I catch sight of Katergaris as he dives low over the wreckage, his talons knocking a dead knight off Kennedy's back.

If he is here, where are Lāri and Talia?

Iéle lunges at a corpse reaching for Gibby, her jaws locking around its throat, but two more fall onto her back, forcing her into the blood-slicked boards.

Adriel scrambles to shield Amanda, swinging a broken board with both hands.

Kennedy and Gibby brace Adriel, pressing their backs against the shattered rail.

The *Gambit* creaks under the assault, her mast bowing dangerously, the deck listing sharply toward the black water.

Tessa throws a raku potion into the center of the dock, the glass shattering, thick green clouds billowing out.

Amanda shrieks as a corpse grabs her arm, but Kennedy drives a boot into its side, wrenching it away.

I look furiously for Tetalla and I spot him aboard the other ship.

Iéle limps toward me, the other wolves dragging themselves between the refugees and the oncoming line of dead.

"Leave, Iéle. Get out of here, now. Save yourself."

She howls.

With heavy regret to leave her, I lift off with my wings and aim right for Tetalla. I land on the tattered ship, and he spins to face me. Lāri falls back to a metal cage holding Talia and tries to get it open.

I draw my next arrow and let it loose as Tetalla lifts both hands, gathering royal fire. It drives into his side twisting his torso with the impact.

The deck shudders beneath me, giving way under the combined weight of the dead and the storm.

I call my wind, barely able to feel my own ouma from exhaustion.

The gust strikes his arm just enough to throw the fire wide, burning a hole in the wreckage beside the cage instead of striking her.

Lāri stumbles back toward the dead, gasping for breath, blood seeping from her ribs. Tetalla advances toward the cage and pulls Talia out by her hair with her screaming and grabbing for his wrist. He walks off toward the railing and pushes her forward. Her body jerks as he digs his claws into her skin. I take a few steps toward them.

"Do you not think you will win, Tetalla?" I scream over the sound of my thundering heart and the rain still pattering against the wood. "You still need this poor girl for your leverage?"

"You do not matter. This fight means nothing!"

The dead pour in over the ruins of the dock, surrounding us from all sides.

I pull the last arrow from my quiver.

My arms shake. My vision swims.

Tetalla steps closer to the edge, blood running down his arm, the royal flames still lit on his arms, despite the rain. Talia tries to keep herself from getting burned by pulling away as far as she can as he holds her in place.

The *Gambit* is splintering under their numbers. For every corpse we cut down, two more climb over the wreckage. My crew is faltering, their shouts drowned by the endless groans of the dead.

If he escapes with her now, we're dead. Too many of his army swarm the dock, too many still rising from the sea.

I cannot let him jump overboard with her.

I fire. The arrow slams into his shoulder, but he catches himself against a shattered beam.

He loosens his grip long enough for Talia to break free and run. Lāri bolts after her to keep her safe.

My bow lands on the deck with a thud.

Tetalla lunges before I can take a full breath, fire bleeding from his fists.

We crash together.

The impact slams through my body, nearly knocking me off my feet.

I aim my fist toward his ribs, but Tetalla twists and smashes his fist into my side.

Heat explodes through my hard skin, and I stumble, pain flashing white across my vision.

I shove my wind into him, a burst of force meant to throw him back, but Tetalla braces through it.

Tetalla's face is bloodied, his fire flickering weaker with every swing, but he refuses to fall.

He stumbles into a broken piling but catches himself, rage burning the fiery specks in his eyes. The same type I have too.

I don't know why I didn't see it before... I didn't want to believe it when my people spoke of the legend as a prophecy. The fiery specks in his eyes... belong to me as much as to him.

I came back from the Deep, same as he did. Maybe the legends sung about weren't meant for Tetalla at all...but for me.

A roar leaves his throat as he swings back, a burst of purple fire exploding against my side.

The blast tears me off my feet. I crash to the deck, breath ripped from my lungs. My ribs scream as I drag myself upright.

Tetalla stalks toward me, dripping rain and blood.

The rain, now lessening, sprinkles across my face, and I blink against it as something familiar swirls in me through all this.

My aovate connection with Soren is hitting me stronger. But why is it happening now? It forces me to stare past Tetalla and out to sea. Large shadows of tall masts eclipse the rising sun emerging from the mist.

I shift my gaze to Tetalla. "Did you call on more of your dead to help you beat me? Kh?"

Tetalla spins around, now looking out to the fleet headed toward us.

A figure stands at the front of the lead ship, her stance strong against the turbulent waters.

Her hair flashes red under a lightning strike, and my heart nearly stops. Soren? How?

Behind her, the decks are packed with figures, standing shoulder to shoulder, their outlines holding weapons, sharp against the storm.

30

SOREN

THE RAIN HAS SLOWED TO A DRIZZLE BY THE TIME I GRIP THE rail, my fingers aching from how tight I'm holding on. Through the mist, a half-broken ship looms ahead, the *Gambit* rising just behind it.

AJ hands me a scope. "Found it in the captain's quarters."

I stare through it. Two Devils stand near the rail. One is Nkella, his short horns swept back against his head. The other is taller, and bears long horns on his head. A glow of purple fire skitters up his arm. Tetalla. He turns fast, fire flashing as he drives into Nkella. The hit slams him back against the rail. I can't help a scream escape the back of my throat.

AJ stands beside me and he draws his sword. I reach for mine too. "Full speed ahead!" I demand.

The crew pulls the sails wide, the canvas snapping hard in the gusts. The rest of the fleet follows our lead as Nkura and I share a knowing glance.

A sharp gust of wind rips across the deck as I turn toward the wheel. At first, I ignore it, assuming it's the aftermath from the recent storm, or us picking up speed. But it happens again, and with it comes the strong pull of our aovate connection.

Peering once more through the scope, I spot Nkella in heavy combat with Tetalla. The two Devils are destroying the ship they're on as they fight. Short bursts of wind pull at the waves, but each time they taper down, it's Tetalla who has a hold over Nkella.

It's like the wind is trying to build, but there's no strength behind it. Nkella reaches up, trying to pull something from the air.

"He must be trying to reach his ouma." I squeeze AJ's shoulder. "He's struggling."

"You think he's trying to make one of his tornados?" AJ wonders.

I stare at Nkella's body shaking with the effort. His jaw is locked, his blade gripped tight, but the wind just curls around him and then dies out.

AJ squeezes my arm and I glance at him. "The *Gambit...*"

I move the scope toward the *Gambit*. The others are also in mid-battle. Ntaoru's dragging someone toward cover. Kaehante swings wide with a half-broken shield. Iéle limps, her ribs soaked in blood. The *Gambit* has started to list, water climbing over the rails.

They're all going to die if we don't get there now.

"Take the wheel," I tell AJ as I jump the steps to face Nangraku's ship. Bobby groans behind me as I leave him to signal Nangraku to head for the *Gambit*. "Help them!" Nangraku gives me a sharp nod.

We get closer, so I reach for my borrowed sword, but drop it. It clangs on the hardwood and I gasp. AJ's eyes are wide.

"Soren, what's the matter?"

My fingers are trembling. Literally shaking. My heart rate speeds up, and my vision blurs. I press my hand flat against my chest. There's something building... pressure, heat. Am I having a heart attack?

My mark isn't glowing. The dampener is still on.

What even is happening? The pressure keeps rising, and now members of the dead crew are circling around me.

Something coils low in my gut, thick and heavy, drawing a rancid taste into my mouth, like something pulled from the sea floor. I try to swallow it down, force myself to breathe through it. But my lungs tighten. My fingers go cold.

The ship lurches. I brace harder. My heartbeat's gone somewhere behind my ribs now, and my bones start to shutter.

Then it rises. It feels like I'm about to hurl, but I'm overcome with a tingling rising from my stomach to my fingertips The sea shifts. A wall of water rolls forward across the waves, straight toward Tetalla's ship.

Nkella's winds kick again, and I gasp as the waters, which I think I just moved, clash with his ouma. I grip onto the rail as the winds make a loud clapping sound.

A sharp cyclone spirals into being above the ship. It slams into Tetalla's back and rips him off Nkella like he weighs nothing. The ship groans as it's shoved sideways by the blast. The whole battle line shifts and we brace ourselves for impact as my ship flies toward theirs and into a crash landing.

AJ grabs my arm. "Soren! What the hell did you do? How—?" He stares at me, disbelief written all over his face, and I shake my head.

"I—I don't know," I say. "I have no idea what the hell just happened to me. Give Nkura and the others the order. I'm going in."

As I run, my hand glides down my right arm, checking for anything different. Not my spiderweb mark or the dampener has changed. But I'll think more about what the hell happened later.

Bobby follows behind us as I move toward the rail, and I don't care now if Tetalla can see through him. It's too late for that, he knows I'm here. Swinging my legs over the rope, I possum my way down as quick as I can. The others follow suit.

The deck of Tetalla's ship hits hard beneath me. My boots skid. My knees nearly buckle, but I catch myself. Rain pounds across the boards. Tetalla is already dragging himself upright across from me, purple fire gathering again at his hands. Nkella is half-crouched, blood running down the side of his face, sword still drawn. His gaze finds mine, and for a split second those fiery specks illuminate his eyes, and our connection grows. Giving us both strength.

I start running.

Tetalla doesn't hesitate. He hurls the first blast of fire straight at Nkella, and I run faster. That same surge of power rushes through me again, but this time I don't question it. There's no time to figure it out, if it works, it works. I raise my hand out, but it doesn't come from my hands. It comes from the sea behind me, rising like it's been waiting for me this whole time. It hits the purple flames midair, and the two collide in a burst of steam that blinds us all. Tetalla flinches just enough for Nkella to launch himself forward at full strength.

Tetalla takes the blow, shoving through it, as two Devils in their full power fight, and for a moment I wonder if I should even be standing here. Heat surges off him, scalding the air between us. He kicks Nkella sideways, sending him crashing into the mast. The entire thing shatters and falls over him.

I resist the urge to check on him, and instead turn to face Tetalla. I know this fight is between him and Nkella, but I can at least slow him down. At my silent command, Bobby, with my sword in hand goes to help Nkella. Tetalla spots our exchange and he lifts his chin, a slight smile curling on his Devil face.

"Well look who's taken up the Death Card's powers." His voice is rougher, deeper in this form. "It was my mistake to underestimate you, Uoko yani. Good thing I brought insurance, daſ?" He motions behind me toward the stern, and I turn to find Talia who is standing over an injured Lāri. I freeze. I was so preoccupied with Nkella, I forgot to look for her.

Tetalla steps into me from behind, his hand pressing firmly over my mouth, and steps back with me. "Convenient you came to me at this exact moment."

My instincts kick in and I wedge my hand between his pinky and index, yanking down hard. At the same time, I kick my foot back hard and aim straight for his balls.

Devil or not, that'll still hurt.

He curses in Ipani and releases, but when he does, he strikes me on the back of my head and I lurch forward, tumbling onto the wooden deck. A searing pain shoots up my skull as I push myself off the ground.

With his father's sword in hand, Nkella comes at him from the side, still in his devil form, but slower now, ribs undoubtedly broken. Wind picks up around him and purple flames sear over his hands. His expression is dark, the royal flames now somehow have reached those specks in his eyes, and I blink at them. They both have the royal flames now, and are fighting to the death to keep them. But I've never seen the purple in Tetalla's eyes like Nkella has them now.

"You touched my aovate..." he rumbles, voice hoarse and low. And it's all he says before plunging into Tetalla.

Tetalla blocks the strike but takes a cut to the shoulder. He hisses and unleashes a pulse of purple heat that cracks the deck.

We all stagger and the ship groans beneath us. The fight shifts toward the edge.

Nkella ducks and drives his blade up from below. Tetalla bats it aside, but the movement leaves him wide open. Nkella doesn't back off. He pushes forward, planting his feet against the tilting deck, and throws every ounce of strength he has left into his ouma.

This time, I summon whatever the hell I summoned earlier, and a wave of water rises from behind Nkella, once again joining his air. A waterspout forms above the ship, and now Tetalla is backing up. Nkella slams down his ouma, and I feel mine coming down hard as it swallows Tetalla from the top of his head.

The purple lining around Tetalla's flames gutters out like a snuffed torch. His body jerks, the force ripping the heat from his skin, stealing the strength out of his hands. Tetalla stumbles.

With impossible speed, Nkella catches Tetalla square across the ribs with his sword, driving the blade deep.

Tetalla tries standing his ground as he wavers. He flicks his wrist, and I'm guessing he's trying to ignite again. Nkella hits him with another surge of wind. The air howls across the deck, throwing loose debris sideways, battering against the broken mast and torn sails.

Tetalla shudders and drops hard, coughing blood into the rain-slick boards.

The royal flames that were around him dies down. Only the ones covering Nkella's hands now remain. Steam rises off Tetalla's body, thin and colorless in the rising sun.

Panting in place, my hands are pressed firmly on the wet deck boards. Nkella and I stare down at him, both breathless, half expecting him to lunge up again. We glance at each other and lock eyes. A smile crosses my face, and he swallows. But we stay quiet.

Tetalla doesn't move, and all around the sea, the inlet, the dead soldiers drop to the ground.

My lips part... "He's dead."

Nkella stands with his father's sword and slams it right through Tetalla's chest, pulling it out clean. His body shifts back down to his Ipani form.

My hands shake.

He's really dead.

My boots skid across the broken boards, and I lock eyes again with Nkella. Blood pours down his arm, the sword half-lowered, his whole body trembling with the effort of standing.

I crash into him hard enough that we both almost fall.

He catches me, his grip bruising, desperate, and his forehead leans against mine, both of us too stunned to speak. But I let out a chuckle.

I tilt my chin up and kiss him, and he curls his hand in through my hair, and squeezes hard as he takes my lips. He kisses me furiously, like there's still a lot of fight in him. His hands tangle in my soaked hair, and his blood mixes with the rain starting up again.

For one moment, there's nothing else.

Just him and me.

"My aovate," he breathes me in. "I knew I would see you again."

"I'm so sorry, Nkella. I shouldn't have—"

"Shhh. You came back with a fleet." He can't help the chuckle in his voice, followed by a groan.

"How badly hurt are you?" I move my hand to his wound and he flinches.

"I will heal." He takes a deep breath. "Soren... when he touched you—"

"Don't. It's over," I say, holding a finger to his lips.

He kisses it. Something shifts behind me, and he glances past me. "Your sister—"

I pull back, breath caught in my throat, my head snaps toward the stern. "Talia."

The world crashes back into focus and I'm running. Talia is sitting in the corner, with Lāri badly hurt. She stares up at me as I lower myself to the ground. Nkella is right behind me.

"Talia—" My voice wavers, "Are you hurt?"

She shakes her head. "I'm fine."

Nkella bends down to sling Lāri over his shoulder. I help Talia up and stare out to the *Gambit,* but no one's aboard. Instead, I catch movement by the inlet, and my fleet is scattered across the sand and the waves.

Nkella steers this messed up ship as best he can, close enough to where we can get down and walk the rest of the way. We carefully make it down the split gangway, and reach the cavern. It's the exact same cavern this fleet was docked in down in the Deep.

Sehu crosses the sand and reaches me first. Realization of the power I used comes crashing down. The waves. The cyclone after Nkella and I joined... ouma?

My ouma?

"Soren," Sehu says. "I'm so glad you are alive."

"Yeah, you too." I blink at him, then stare down at my dampener. Nkella now stands beside me, holding Lāri up. "I'm not sure what happened." I look to Nkella too, and his eyes narrow.

"Yes. There was no time to question it but... that was not Helāni magic, daí?" He stares at me.

"We watched everything," Sehu says. "I..." now with a large smile blooming on his face, "I think... maybe with that dampener suppressing your Fate magic, your ouma... emerged."

31

SOREN

I STARE AT SEHU FOR A LONG SECOND, HIS WORDS NOT making any sense. "I don't even know how."

"It's from me." His eyes are glossy as he says it. "Our ouma is from Oleanu. You were always part of the sea."

Talia gasps at my side.

Nkella's expression softens as I glance up at him, in disbelief. "I—I thought I would never develop ouma..." The memory of us talking by the fire when we were together in the Deep comes into mind. He said what Demitri told me wasn't necessarily true. "So I have another power..." I stare at my dampener. Sehu's right.

"Go," Sehu says. "There's more to do before the worlds crash."

I give a tight nod, and turn to Talia. "Get the Empress out of the brig." She stares at me. "That's where I left her. I'll be right behind you."

She nods and takes off across the wreckage.

"Lāri!" AJ's shout makes us all turn. Lāri glances up from Nkella's shoulder, and gasps. She stumbles forward, trying to walk on her own but her leg is badly hurt.

"AJ..." she cries. He runs at her and they crash, arms holding each other tight. I swallow the lump in my throat. Even if this isn't permanent, no one can take this moment away from them. Ever.

Nkella grips my shoulder, holding me close. We turn, to give them privacy, but also, to get back to the imminent task at hand.

"Go to your parents," I whisper. "You don't know if you're going to get another chance." He kisses my forehead and lets me go, with regret in his face.

I need to take the seat next to the Empress. As a Fate. As her sister.

We'll decide what to do with her after the worlds are safe.

The weight of the sea is still humming under my skin. Back when I had drank the rikorō and swam as a mermaid, the way I felt underwater... it felt almost natural. I always thought it was only because of the ouma that belonged to that Ipani, but now, maybe there's more to it. I always wished for it back. I glance at my arms and legs. No scales have appeared, so this ouma is different.

It's mine.

I head to meet Talia, when the ground shifts under me, first starting as a rolling vibration, but intensifying into a violent quake.

I'm jolted onto the wet sand and smack into a broken beam sticking out of the wreck. The ocean sucks back hard, dragging ropes and splinters with it. I fight to grab a hold of something, anything, as the ground rips open with a deafening sound.

"Neyuro!" Nkella and AJ run toward me. I get myself up.

"I'm okay," I say. "But it was another quake. This has to happen now—"

We gape at each other as another deafening ripping sound comes from all around us. AJ grabs my arm and points to the sky as a sharp, white tear zigzags through the clouds.

Something crashes on the beach in front of us, a cloud of sand spraying toward us.

Silence blooms between everyone, now that the quaking has settled. I move to see what crashed here, thinking it's another refugee, but Nkella sticks his arm out holding me back.

A head of wavy black hair stirs on the ground, so I release his grip and run over to help whoever fell. She struggles to stand.

"Are you hurt?" I call.

The woman has long purple sleeves and an olive-green skirt. Her face is dug into the sand. I reach her, and grab her arm before she tips forward. She spits sand out of her mouth and moves her hair away from her face. I gasp. No way.

"Asteria," I say. "What the hell just happened? How are you here?"

Her breathing is shallow. "The boundaries are collapsing. We don't have long." She wipes her face. "Where is my sister?"

I gape at her, not really believing she's here.

"Quickly, Soren. I had to chase the rips and it's taken me too long. Where are the cards?"

I scoff. "The cards disappeared into the ocean when Rutavenye fell." All except for the Ace of Pentacles and the Death Card.

Her eyes widen. "The floating island fell again? The Tower is gone?" I stare at her, remembering what Aletha told me about Asteria leaving her to handle the Tarot inside the Aō. The Empress made her choices, but Asteria had a role in it too.

"And your sister is in the brig of my ship. So here we are." I cross my arms. "At least Tetalla is dead."

She narrows her eyes at me, and then tilts her head as if breathing the breeze. My brows furrow. "No. Something is off. I need to see Aletha now." She starts walking in the direction of the ships, not knowing which one is mine. I go with her, boots slipping in the wet grit.

Talia walks down the gangway with the help of some of the dead crew. She helps the Empress walk down steadily. Her gaze snaps our way and she pauses when she spots Asteria.

Asteria starts to run toward her, and then the Empress does as well. I slow down my pace and watch as they look like they're about to embrace, and then just stop in front of each other.

"You."

"Aletha... we don't have time—"

"You left me here. With all this!" she shouts, her gloved hands are shaking. She reaches for her face and peels off her mask. I've seen it before, but no one else has. Gasps come from around us.

Asteria's voice drops. "Oh, sister, you had become..." She shakes her head. "How could I have stopped you? I would have had to kill you. And I could never do that."

"What choice did I have? I was left here alone. With the power you and Adara introduced to this world." Her voice breaks. "You left me here. You left me!" she shouts and starts to sob, and she puts her mask back on, turning her face.

"I thought you hated me," Asteria says.

"How could I hate you? You are my sister."

Asteria walks over to her and wraps her arms around Aletha. "I should have stayed and helped you. Maybe this was all my fault after all. I never should have left you, Aletha. I'm sorry for my cowardice."

The rest of us don't move. We watch as two powerful beings come together. Another tremor hits and my pulse quickens. I take a step toward them, not wanting to ruin their moment but...

"Asteria, sorry to interrupt but—"

Asteria pulls away and faces me. "No, you're right. The world is splitting." She looks to Aletha, whose green eyes are red behind her mask. "Soren, with our powers together, we can call upon the cursed Tarot deck."

I shake my head and raise my wrist. "I still have this dampener on."

Asteria takes my wrist to inspect the inscriptions on the dampener. "Well, I can't say I know Ipani, but I can feel the power flowing through this, and—" She squints at it, turning my arm as she looks at the rest. "Hmmm."

"What?"

With both hands, she tries to pry it open.

"No, that won't work," I tell her. It snaps, and I gape at it. "Okay, I swear everyone has tried that already and it didn't work." I gasp and my head jerks back as my powers come crashing down on me at once. The magnetic force I feel when I look into the past drags me down, and images of things I missed rush past me. I catch my breath and blink, as she helps me stand upright.

"You didn't have me here to try it." She smiles. "You see, with all three Fates present, we outnumber whatever is trying to take over the Aō."

"Meaning Tetalla. And now he's dead." The blood is still rushing from my face.

She nods, holding out her hands for each of us. "So now, shall we? Before it's too late."

I swallow, nerves suddenly rattling in my bones. I look to Nkella who gives me a reassuring nod. His mother and father stand behind him. So does AJ, next to Lāri. Once we close the rip, all the dead, all our loved ones go back to the Deep.

"Wait."

Asteria stares at me expectantly.

"I have to say goodbye..." I turn to AJ and give him a tight hug. Then I let him go and let him have his moments with Lāri. She smiles at me as I pull away, tears falling down her cheeks.

Nkella is saying goodbye to his parents, and Ntouru throws herself into their arms too.

I smile and hug Sehu.

"This is our second goodbye," he says. "But it better be the last for a very long time, daí?" he whispers. A ball lodges in my throat. "You have ouma now, daughter. Use it wisely, but do not be afraid of it. One day, it will unite you with me in the Deep."

I nod against his shoulder. "Thank you for having my back," I tell him. I haven't known him for very long, but... he's the father I've always wanted.

A quake shakes us and we pull apart.

"It's time," Asteria says, urgency in her tone. Aletha whispers something in her ear, and they look past me to the rest of them.

I take their hands. "How do we return the refugees back home?"

"I will take them with me," Asteria says. "You're going to have to go into their minds and take those memories out of them like you would any object."

My eyes widen. "Oh. It'll be simple then."

She ignores me and raises our hands up. "Close your eyes. Feel for our central power."

Silence clears my mind. The seconds pass to minutes.

"What are we feeling for exactly?"

"Quiet."

A heavy pressure pulls me deep into my mind and I feel as though I become trapped inside my own head. Waves surround me, but there are two others with me. Two shadows stand beside me, and when I look to either direction, I see Aletha to my left and Asteria to my right. We're under the sea.

One of the cards glints before me, under a stone.

"This is the one we need to call them all." Asteria holds her hand out, palm facing up, and the card budges and flows to her. It's the World Card. "Attract the rest," she tells it.

She releases my hand and I nearly lose my footing. One minute I am under the sea, as if we can stand and breathe underwater, only one card in hand, and the next, Asteria pulls us out. Dampness fills the air.

I stare at her, the full deck of cards in her hands. Minus two. I reach into my pocket and pull out the Death Card. She takes it from me, frowning.

"Looks as though you've become more acquainted with these than I ever have."

"How did you do that? How did you just take one card—and then—"

Aletha chuckles. "I have been trying to tell you there is so much still to learn, and we are stronger together."

I frown at her. I still hate her. But I wouldn't mind working with her only if Asteria is here too.

"We are still missing one," Asteria says.

Nkella walks up and I pull away from the Fates and go to him. He undoes the necklace around his head and holds up the gold coin. I blink at it.

"My necklace?"

"It came off you right before you left to the Deep." He holds it out in front of me, and as I take it, the coin glistens with a purple sheen as it transforms into a Tarot card. The Ace of Pentacles. I gasp.

"You had it around your neck the whole time," he says. "And did not know it."

"I guess that was the burning on my chest right after the food started to appear in the barrels. Since the card was in the form of a coin, maybe it meant it was already working?" I suppose it could only work in

Danū, since I wore it for ages and didn't know what it was. Or I just hadn't learned to use it properly yet.

He shakes his head. "Thanks to your parents, it was only ever in the right hands," he says, glancing at Sehu.

Confusion flickers across Sehu's face, then recognition dawning as his eyes widen. "I confess not even I knew it was the Ace of Pentacles when I gave it to Diana."

A rumble shakes the ground. Another quake? No... My Death mark is pulsing. My pulse quickens and I search the grounds. "The dead are rising."

"What?" Aletha says.

Nkella snaps his attention back to me and we lock eyes. His brows furrow in question, and I shake my head.

A scream breaks through the air and I immediately recognize the voice.

Talia.

I jerk back, lifting my blade, twisting to see where she is, and my blood runs cold.

Tetalla stands there, lightning strikes the sky, and for a moment the skull in his face lights up. Nkella immediately shifts, and so does Nkura. I move forward to stop Nkella from doing anything.

"Stop!" I scream, fear in my voice that he'll do something to Talia who stands a foot away from him. She backs up, and he strides to her, slowly, with a sadistic smile on his face.

"Tetalla..." Asteria mutters. "He revived himself."

Revived himself?

The power of the Death Card. Tetalla, having had a deeper connection with the Aō must have twisted it on himself. Why didn't I see this coming?

My mark pulses and I remember my dampener is off. I raise my wrist and my webbing flies out, wrapping him in a thick sticky spiderweb. It feels good to have my powers back. I start walking toward Talia when the fact he doesn't move makes me wary. He's not even fighting it.

The webbing singes off him and he's completely unbothered.

Tetalla looks at me. "You were a bad girl, vicious one. I keep my threats, so now your sister will die."

I scream as he sticks a hand out, fire soaring out to Talia.

A blast of smoke emerges beside me and I jump back to see the Empress has disappeared into a gust of smoke, to reappear in front of Tetalla. His fire engulfs her as she stands in the way of Talia.

Asteria screams, and we both run toward our sisters. Tetalla's shift to his devil form is swift and sudden as he takes out a clawed hand and punctures Aletha through the chest. She cries out as she lands on her knees, just as he twists his wrist and tears out her heart.

I reach Talia and push her back. "Go to the crew. Run!" She takes off running in the direction of Kaehante and Tessa.

Asteria stops in her tracks, her screams echoing through the caverns. I'm shuddering. The Empress's body lays there, lifeless and burning. Tetalla holds her heart up for everyone to see, and then, he does the unthinkable.

He brings it up to his mouth, and he takes a bite out of it, then spits it on the ground.

No one, not even the dead who hate the Empress say a word. No one cheers. Because there is a new Emperor, and he's ruthless.

32

SOREN

Tetalla turns his attention to Asteria, his expression calm and collected. He's too poised, and that sends a chill down my spine. There was something always off about him before, but now there's something unnaturally off about him.

Asteria steps a pace back. I start walking to her, I don't know what I can do against him, but I have to try.

"Soren," she says. "Take the cards. Do what's right."

Tetalla moves his attention to me. "You know what is right."

I swallow.

"Take the throne," Asteria tells me. The cards are on the ground where she threw them before running to her sister. I run to them and leap to the sand, grabbing them in my hands.

"Become the Empress! Do it now, before the world implodes."

Shouts and yells surround me, but I block everyone out. Nkella's voice gets drowned out by roar of the dead. I rummage through the cards, and find the Empress Card. My eyes move up to Empress Aletha lying flat on the surface. I hold the card up to my face. The woman on the image wears a pearl mask on her face, a laurel crown on her head, and a black, militant-type dress on her body.

My gaze moves to Tetalla, who stares back at me. "You are vicious. That was a compliment. Use it to be cold, and do the right thing."

They both want me to take up the throne but for different reasons. Asteria wants me to stop the world from crashing down on itself, and ending everyone—and so do I. But after that? Ruling Ipa. Making things right.

And perhaps I can do better. Especially with Asteria by my side as two Fates.

Tetalla wants to destroy the world.

With a deep breath, I whisper the words into the cards, "I accept."

Asteria screams as Tetalla holds her by her neck, lifting her off the ground with impossible strength. He's in his devil form. His large body eclipses my view of what's behind him and I can no longer see Nkella.

I reach into my new Empress power, although I don't know how to distinguish which power from which anymore. But before anything can happen, Tetalla's eyes bulge.

His eyes go black, and his lips part. Black blood seeps out of his mouth, but he continues to squeeze Asteria's neck. Her legs shake uncontrollably. He's choking her.

I run at her right as he drops her. I land on my knees and spin her around. Her face is purple, and her eyes glossy. No... No! I look up, a hand—no, a devil hand has punctured through Tetalla's chest from his back.

He tumbles forward, and falls to the ground. Nkella steps on his back and holds his heart above his head. I gape at him.

Tetalla gurgles.

"He's still alive!" I scream. His arm shoots out and grabs my leg. I try to pry his claws off me but he's strong. He pulls me to him. Nkella drops the heart and jumps down to grab me, his body shifting back.

"Vicious one," Tetalla croaks.

That fucking Death Card. "Why won't you die?" My voice is hoarse.

He winces. "You have won."

"What?" I blink at him.

Nkella crouches down, releasing Tetalla's hand from my leg.

"I relinquish the Card," he whispers, barely audible. He reaches for Nkella, drawing him close. "Take care of Danū. Of Ipa." He looks to me. "Soren."

"Yes?"

"Do not be a fool now. You have the power to do what needs to be done. If you do not take them back, and never return, the world will continue to split. The Aō cannot handle it."

He lets me go. "I relinquish the Death Card so you can do what is right. They were never meant to be here." His head falls back, his eyes wide.

Purple flames ignite the perimeters.

"He is dead," Nkella declares, moving his hand over Tetalla's face and closing his eyes.

My heart is still lodged in my throat. I look to Asteria, who lies cold on the ground. The Empress is dead. I'm the Empress now.

What do I do?

Voices erupt around us and I look up. The serpent rises from the sea, but someone is on him. The spirit flies low to the ground, its body moving in an *S* close to us. I recognize her features instantly. The serpent lowers Adara, and she gracefully climbs down and grips Tetalla's body. She glances at me.

"Thank you for sending Apeiron to find me. My sisters will join me in the Deep." Holding onto Tetalla, the serpent drags them back down to the sea.

All around us, blood stains the beach.

"Neyuro... I am sorry for your friend."

I look to Asteria and close my eyes. He tightens his embrace around me. "Do not cry, Neyuro. We are together now."

Another tear falls down my cheek, and I pull away.

"I'm sorry, Nkella."

"Hn?" He lifts my chin. "What for?"

"I wasn't supposed to say goodbye to you too..."

"What are you talking about, daí?"

"What Tetalla was saying... he's right."

"What are you saying? Soren? What is it?"

I shudder a breath. "I have to go." Before he can keep asking me, I tell him. "As long as the cards are still here. As long as any of the Fates are still here... the Aō can't dispel the magic. It was never meant to be here, and as long as I'm here... everyone will still have a mark. The Aō will be..." I swallow, not wanting to say the word Tetalla used..." diseased."

Nkella's eyes widen as he realizes what I'm saying.

The Aō won't heal as long as I'm here. I have to go.

"Do you understand?" I raise my hand to his cheek. "If I don't go and take this magic back with me, your people will always suffer. The worlds will always want to split because the Aō is trying to get rid of the disease. Meaning me."

He shakes his head furiously. "Koj. You are not a disease. Get rid of the cards. Then come back."

"There's no way. Once I leave, the portal closes with the World Card. I can never come back. And even if I do, then there will be one Fate here, not two, not three."

"She's right," Demitri's voices rings through as he strides over to us. None of us bother to try and fight him. Once this is over, he goes back to the Deep. Everything goes to how it's meant to be. "You have to let her do this, Nkella. If not, all of us, including her people will die. You are the war hero who came back from the Deep to save them, not Tetalla."

"I do not care about some prophecy. I did what needed to be done."

"You are king of Danū now," Demitri shakes his head. "And you have a duty to protect them."

A pause, and then an agonizing growl comes from Nkella's throat. He grabs me and holds me tight. I break down in his arms.

His hair is plastered against the sharp lines of his face. "Neyuro... I do not want to let you go. You are my aovate. We are meant to be together. Forever, you promised." His dark eyes stare fiercely into me. Angry at me for leaving him.

Tears sting my eyes. "This is what has to be..." A dry chuckle comes from the back of my throat. "We never did get the Lover's mark..."

He scoffs. "I do not need some mark to tell me who I belong to."

An ear-shattering quake moves the ground, and boulders come

crashing down the cliff's edge of the cavern. Our Aō connection squeezes my gut as Nkella tenses his arms around me. And that's the moment I know he understands.

I pull away from him. Steeling my spine the best I can. "Where are the refugees?"

He doesn't let go of me, but tilts his head toward his shoulder and asks Kae to bring them.

"Soren," his voice is low, heavy, "there is nothing in this world or yours, that will stop me from finding you."

"Nkella, don't." I stare into his eyes. "Don't waste your life trying to get to me. I can never come back here."

"Then I will go with you."

"You can't." My voice rises slightly. He looks shaken. "You can't leave your people. Not this time."

His breath shudders and it rips my heart apart.

"I can't be the reason why your people suffer and are left without their king."

He passes his hand through my hair and squeezes it while he kisses my forehead. "As my aovate, you will always be my queen. No matter how far apart we are. You are always my roé yani. Light of my flame."

His dark eyes search mine. I stay quiet, memorizing his features. Sparks ignite inside his eyes. I touch his lips with my fingers, and he kisses them. He pulls me to him and takes my lips. I lean in, giving him everything I have. Breathing in his smell of embers and vanilla rum. One last time.

A quake causes everyone around us to scream. We should let go, but we hold on through it. I kiss him harder as if the world is going to tear us apart at any moment, because it is.

Pulling away, he whispers in my ear, "I love you." A gentle push, and he turns his head, commanding the fleet. "All of the dead who came from the Deep, get on your ships. Be ready to leave through the rip." He turns to the crew, who come walking out toward me. Kaehante urges the refugees out to me, and Talia joins them.

AJ runs over to me, and I wipe a tear off my cheek. "I know what to call your ship," he says.

I crack a smile. "Oh yeah?"

"*Fatebreaker.*"

I scoff. "Keep trying."

He shakes his head. "You won't even give me that one, huh?"

I laugh and hug him, but before he pulls away, I decide the Empress was right about one thing: I've never been one for the rules.

He quirks a brow as I hold his arm, frowning.

"Soren?"

Tuning into my power as Death, and as the Empress, I reach in for his spirit. When I find it, I hold onto it, and slowly blow smoke into his parted lips.

Lāri starts walking my way, eyes wide. "Soren? What are you doing?"

"Death isn't supposed to give second chances," I tell them. "But I've never been one to follow rules."

The crew also circles around us as the land shakes even harder.

I pull away from AJ. "Well, I'm not sure you can still taste food, but now you can stay." I look toward Nkella, but he's still not looking at me. "It's the least I can do before I go."

Shock is plastered on AJ's face, and Lāri screams as she throws herself over his shoulders. He mouths a thank you to me, and I nod. "One last thing to do."

"All Arcana survived by the Empress before me, I release you." I blow that to the wind, and something inside me, within my bones confirms it is true.

One of the rips in the sky disappears, and Ipani start pointing it out, and cheering.

I say my goodbyes to Kaehante, Ntaoru, and Tessa, giving them each a big hug.

The marks will disappear, but whatever magic was cast, will stay, so I know AJ will continue to live... undead. But I don't think he cares at this point.

I give Sehu one last hug and bid my goodbyes to Nkella's parents. Nkella walks off, giving me space to do so. Although, he still refuses to look at me.

Gari slithers toward me from the ship, his eyes big and weary, as I scratch Iéle behind her ears.

"Gari," I say. "You saved me that day in the brig. I'm going to miss you a lot."

"Don't cry, Soren." Gari turns over on his head in the air. "There are other portals you know."

I resist a sigh. "I can't go through any of them to come here, Gari."

"Not you, silly." He spins around. "I can still leave, you know."

I blink at him and his body sinews around me. "I'll see you around."

Shaking my head, I turn to Talia and the refugees. "I'm going to open a portal now, and when you get back, you won't remember anything about ever being here. Do you understand?"

"Wait!" Adriel shouts. "What if we want to remember?"

'Yeah," Kennedy says. "I don't want to lose my memories."

"Please, Soren," Talia says. "Don't take that away from me."

I glance at Talia. I was never going to take her memories. But Kennedy, Amanda, Gibby... they're already whispering to each other. If they went back with the truth, it would tear everything open. I can't let that happen.

"Sorry, guys," I tell them. "When I close the rip, it'll be like none of this ever happened for you."

They quiet. I look at my crew one last time, then to Nkella. My heart feels heavy. He still has his back to me. I understand. Ipa will remember though. The Aō will always keep these memories.

I take the World Card, and hold it out, hoping I can send everyone to exactly where they belong. Between my powers of my Past, powers of the Empress, and even Death, I believe I am precise enough to do exactly what I have to do. A window opens in the space in front of us, eclipsing the sky over the sea. One last breath to take in Ipa. Of Danū.

"Adriel, you're first."

Adriel steps inside.

"Kennedy and Gibby, you both go together." The images inside the portal change, and they step through. I do the same for each of them as I did for Adriel. I turn to the last one. "Amanda, right?" she nods. "Sorry we didn't get to really meet. But I heard you kicked ass. Be safe."

She steps through the next window.

I take Talia's hand and stare at her. "Ready?"

She nods.

Holding out the World Card, I direct it to open up to Tarotland Circus. Where this all started. It was the first place I thought to go, and I'll figure out what our next steps are once we get there.

We step through the light of the portal, and I let Talia's hand slip as she steps deeper in. For a split moment, I glance over my shoulder at the realm I'm leaving. Nkella stands at the end, his eyes heavy with regret as the portal closes.

33

HAROLD

Six months later

The limbs of the Yggdrasil tree slowly spins to a stop, and I turn to Kenjō, holding my hand out to her.

She shoots daggers at me. She's so beautiful. "Now what?"

"You did not tell me this was going to spin around in circles, á?" She straightens her hair out. "Please tell me we are home, and not going to a different place."

"I promise. Now do you want my help, or do you want to jump off?"

Why did I even ask? She's no sooner shifting to her jaguar form and leaping through the portal to avoid stepping on the tree's moving stepping stones that connect to the rainbow bridge.

We rush through before it closes, and I'm instantly hit with the humid air of… where the hell are we?

"Harold!"

I gape at her.

"I thought you said we were going back to Dempu Yuni."

Taking out a small bottle of translation potion, I pop the cork and swallow it whole. I should really learn Ipani, especially if we're going to live in Ipa, can't keep chugging these things forever. I swallow it. "Well, I said to take us back to the crew. I assumed that was at our tree hut."

Her eyes widen and peer past me, and I feel a pointed edge at my back.

Son of a bitch. Where did I take us to this time?

"Turn around, slow."

Someone else comes out from the trees holding a spear pointed at Kenjō. Now I'm pissed.

They have Ipani stripes reaching up their necks and arms, and my shoulders drop. Whew. At least we're in Ipa.

"No one is allowed to open a portal. No one comes in and no one comes out. Those are the rules." He shoves the point to my chest. "How did you get here?"

"Rules?" I ask, trying to peek a glance through my sleeve at my mark. To see if I'm still the Magician here.

"Wait a minute, á?" Kenjō says, lowering her hands. Her guard forces her to keep her hands raised as the spear stays on her. "Where are we?" Then she adds, "You do not have a mark. I do not have a mark!" She gasps. "Harold!"

Now I lift my sleeve up. Nope. No mark at all.

"This is Danū." His eyes are fixed on Kenjō. "And you are Ipani, daí? How did you come through with him?" Now she narrows her eyes at me. "You two will have a lot of answering to do. Move."

They urge us onward toward a pink-sand beach. Why are we in Danū? How long has it been? I estimated six months, last time we were here. Soren was going to the Deep. Cold dread sinks down my gut and I share a worried glance with Kenjō.

Kenjō's eyes widen. "Where are you taking us?"

"You will answer to our king."

Kenjō's face pales, but I search the perimeter. Would we be able to see the floating island from here?

"You are taking us to Tetalla!" she shrieks, now stopping, getting ready to shift. Damnit, just when I thought I could kick my feet up in our tree hut with a cup of garisi in hand and not have to fight.

"Kh." The guard looks at the other, then back to us. "Tetalla is dead. We are taking you to answer to King Nkella."

My jaw drops. The bastard did it.

"Why are you smiling? He is not kind to intruders, daí? He will most likely put you in a dungeon where you will rot. The Aō will not, cannot take, any different magic. Not anymore."

I process what he's saying. Seems like a lot has happened. "Well, we actually know him. And he'd be expecting us so... you can put your weapons down." They point them out harder. Right.

They lead us all the way out to an inlet, where the *Gambit* is docked.

"Are we going to the ship?"

"The king likes his ship more than his castle."

"Why am I not surprised?"

Kenjō laughs.

They guide us up the gangway, and have us wait with two guards on the main deck while someone knocks on the captain's quarters.

Nkella opens it, his face hard like he hasn't slept in weeks. His eyes land on me, and after about a minute, he squints.

"They say they know you, My King?"

Nkella's eyes go from me to Kenjō, then they widen.

I wave at him. "Long time no see."

"But... how could this be possible? The portals were closed."

I scratch my head. "You'll have to catch me up, but if the Tarot portals were closed, that has nothing to do with the runes."

Shock plasters across his face. "There is another way?"

"Yeah, of course there is. There's more than one way to my and Soren's world." I take out my pouch, and his eyes widen. He snaps his attention to the guards.

"Leave us."

"But, My King?"

"Leave." He stands aside to let me and Kenjō through. The stench of rum wafts under my nose as the door slams shut behind us. "Put that away. No magic outside of the Aō is permitted here. I cannot risk it consuming a different type again."

"I understand." I put my runes away in my jacket, and while I'm at it, take the damn thing off. Gods, it is hot! "By the way, don't expect me to call you your highness or king. I knew you before all that.

Kenjō smacks my shoulder. "Harold! He was a prince when you knew him, á? Be respectful."

"Kh." Nkella drops down to his seat.

Rubbing my shoulder, I scan the mess in his room, and my gaze lands back on his shirtless, unregal form. "Aren't you supposed to be in your castle... or something?"

Nkella pops open his flask and takes a swig. "I can protect my people better from the perimeters."

"Right. And the crew?"

He shrugs. "Around."

An awkward silence fills the space, and I glance at Kenjō who offers me a shrug.

"So," I look around the mess of clothes and weapons on the floor, "where's Soren?"

He takes another swig. "Gone." He glances back at me. "When do you leave?"

"Wow, want me to leave already?"

"I cannot risk your magic being here, daí? Now I understand why the Empress was after everyone with the Magician mark. The world was tearing apart and she could not stop it. It is why Soren had to leave me... she took the Helāni magic with her, and cannot come back."

I stare at him as he finishes up the rum in his flask.

"Well..." I glance at Kenjō who has worry creases on her forehead. I don't want to lose her. Not after everything. "I was planning on living here... with Kenjō."

"Then you must sacrifice your magic. Or you cannot stay."

I rub the back of my neck and stare at the floorboards. "Look, it's not like I wouldn't make a sacrifice like that for love. In fact, I have." I glimpse at Kenjō, and she smiles weakly. "But I can't give up my runes because I have a family back home. And I can't take Kenjō with me... she'll lose her power, and people aren't used to Ipani over there. It just wouldn't be fair to her."

Nkella doesn't even look in my direction, I'm not sure he's listening as he takes another sip of his rum, but I continue.

"What I'm saying is that's not going to work for me."

He glances at me, and those fiery specks I've seen in his eyes flare. Metal bumps poke out of his knuckles, but I hold my ground. I've fought Ice Giants. I'm not afraid of Nkella. Anymore. He slams a fist down on his table and it breaks in half.

I step back. Okay, maybe a little.

Kenjō's eyes glow yellow, ready to pounce for the door. But instead, she takes a few steps toward him and lays a hand on Nkella's broken table, bowing her head slightly. "Your rage is justified, My King. But let us speak plainly, not as enemies. Harold only means to help."

Nkella swallows, and stares at her.

"Clearly, you've gone through some stuff since we've been away." I back up. "I was planning on going home soon anyway," I say. Maybe I can sneak back? "I've been needing to check on my aunt. But listen... you can't stop the portals from opening and closing. Maybe the trick here is to reach the Aō... keep it from adapting or something. You can't protect the world like this forever. Not like this. Put up guards, yes. But keeping people out? And in? I'm sorry, Nkella, but... that's not right either. Is it? And this doesn't sound like you."

He's still staring at his broken table, but he finally shakes his head. "I agree with you."

"You do?"

"Tetalla reached the Aō to speak to it." He stares at me. "Perhaps we can help each other." He straightens.

"What do you need? I don't need anything in return from you, Nkella. You're my friend."

His features soften for a split second before returning back.

"You say you are going back?"

"I mean..." Kenjō shoots daggers at me. "Yes, I am. "

"Then take me with you."

34

SOREN

"WHY AM I SUCH A FREAKING MESS?" I MUTTER, FLIPPING over a stack of military recruitment brochures—Army, Navy, even one for the Coast Guard. And I am so late for work.

I shove aside a crumpled flyer promising *Adventure, Purpose, Stability.*

The only purpose I've got this morning is getting to work before my manager flips on me. I yank open the junk drawer. Gum wrappers. Tarot cards I swore I'd never touch again. I slam the drawer shut.

"Check the bathroom!" Talia calls from the kitchen. The sizzling aroma of bacon and eggs tickle my senses. She's humming off-key to that one ridiculous pop song she's played so much I'm starting to forget what silence feels like.

"I did! Twice!" I shout back, sweeping my arm under the couch cushions. Dust bunnies. Crumbs of an old granola bar. Not here either.

My phone buzzes on the kitchen counter.

Number Unknown. I grab it, thinking it's work.

I answer. "Hey—"

"Soren," he says, his voice tight with amusement, "uh, you might want to sit down."

Why does that voice sound familiar? I grab my bag, still looking for the keys. "Who is this?"

"It's Harold..."

I stop cold. "Harold."

"Yeah, uh, hi. Listen, we might not have enough time. Nkella is here, but—"

My spine straightens and all at once, the room starts spinning. I squint at the number in my phone, as if I would recognize the number, and bring it back to my ear. Am I hearing this phone call correctly?

"Wait! Harold? Like...*Harold* Harold?"

"We were in a different dimension together. Yes, I'm that Harold. Not sure how many Harold's you know, but—"

"What do you mean he's *here*?" My breathing picks up. Spots start to appear in my vision by how hard I'm staring at the wall. "That makes no sense..." Oh my God, "Harold, you brought him here? Where is he?" My pulse is flying right now. No, this has to be a dream.

"The plan was to open the portal to where you are but..."

My stomach knots. "Open a portal? What's going on?"

"I don't know where you live! And you know how he is... all intimidating and needing to come here. I remembered you said something about a Tarotland Circus, so I gave him your number... knowing he won't know how to use a phone, but figured he could ask someone, and before the portal closed to go to my aunt's... I heard sirens. There were flashing cop lights too... I can't imagine it went well to see a guy that looks like him just stepping out from who knows where the portal landed."

My mouth hangs open as I clutch my phone to my ear.

"Hello? You still there?"

"This can't be happening."

I hear him take a breath on the other end. "Oh, it's happening."

My breath hitches. Everything in me stutters, then launches forward. I'm already out the door.

I fly down the steps two at a time, barely registering the damp morning heat clinging to the air. I make it halfway to the car before I stop dead in my tracks.

The keys.

They're sticking out of the front door's keyhole. Just... dangling there. Mocking me.

"Are you kidding me?" I hiss, snatching them free. Of course. They've been here the whole time—just hanging there like an idiot's prize for getting her life together.

The car sputters to life on the second try, and I peel out like I'm late to a bank heist.

Logic crashes down on me, wanting to convince me this is all a ruse, or I'm dreaming. But Harold wouldn't lie to me. He wouldn't call me! So, this has to be real.

Nkella is here. On Earth. In Baton Rouge. Somehow.

And if he's really standing in some police station, in all his Ipani glory, trying to explain fate and death to a bunch of Louisiana cops?

I need to get there before someone tasers him.

The drive is a blur of yellow lights and near-stalled engines. I'm pretty sure I ran a stop sign, maybe two. I shoot off a text to work: *Family emergency. May involve extradimensional misunderstanding. Will explain later.* Then I toss my phone into the passenger seat before I can second-guess any of this.

I grip the wheel tighter. My throat feels like it's closing. I told myself I made peace with losing him. That closing the portal was the only choice. That love was sacrifice. That I could move on.

And now he's just... here.

I swerve into the cracked parking lot of the police station and park in the first space I find. I kill the engine and barely remember to yank the keys before I'm out the car.

The fluorescent lights of the front desk immediately take me back to when I got arrested at Tarotland Circus. A toddler screams somewhere in the back, and the disgruntled looks of government employees greet me as I come in.

I freaking hate this place.

I elbow my way to the counter, heart pounding in my throat. The woman behind the plexiglass window doesn't look up.

"Hi—uh, sorry—hi." I lean in. "Has anyone been brought in recently who looks like they walked out of a Renaissance Fair? Big guy, pointed ears, probably confused by traffic?"

She doesn't even make eye contact. "All new arrest bails need to be paid at window six."

"Arrested?"

She exhales through her nose, picks up the phone, and mutters something into the receiver. I glance around, catching fragments of conversation. Someone's arguing about parking violations. The vending machine's out of everything but pork rinds and despair.

Waiting in line at window six takes forever, and I really should have brought a jacket. Why didn't I bring a jacket? I knew where I was going.

A side door buzzes. A uniformed officer opens it, giving me a once-over.

"You the girl for the Pirate LARP guy?" he asks.

"Yep," I say. No hesitation.

If he used the word daí in front of a cop, I'd never get him out.

He gestures me through.

"Did he… hurt anyone?"

The officer shakes his head. "No. Mostly confused people. Those weapons were nothing like I've ever seen before. Not keeping someone in for a bow and arrow. He's in holding until someone vouches for him. And I hope you brought his ID, because we can't let him go without proof of identification."

I take out my wallet and flip through a few stolen IDs I still have from the days of the carnival. So much for straightening up this time around.

I follow him down the hallway, heart pounding louder with every step. My boots squeak over old tiles that smell like lemon cleaner.

When we turn the corner, goosebumps erupt all over my arms and legs.

He's seated on a bench, and has what looks like a paper towel someone gave him as a bandage on his face. Someone must've given him a hoodie, and it's three sizes too small, and he's wearing it like it might explode if he moves wrong.

But it's him.

He looks up.

And I stop breathing.

He rises slowly, careful not to tear the hoodie further. His frown is stoic, as he stares at me, and he looks like he hasn't slept in weeks.

"Nkella," I breathe.

For a moment, neither of us moves. We just stand there in the dim hallway of the Baton Rouge police station, surrounded by flickering lights and the low hum of air vents and bureaucratic chaos. Two worlds colliding again.

I take the first step toward him.

And it's all he needs.

He crosses the space between us in two strides. His hands are on me. Rough and primal. One curls around the back of my neck, the other wraps my waist like he's afraid I'll vanish if he lets go. We stare into each other's eyes as if we're still back in Ipa, like we're not standing in a police station's holding facility. Our lips crash and it's as if I'm not even standing. I'm flying, and we're back in Tarotland with the world spinning around us.

"Uh-ghuhuhum." The cop clears his throat beside us, and I reluctantly pull away.

"Time to go. What do think this is? A hotel room? Sheesh." He shakes his head and urges us to separate and move out.

My throat tightens. "You did all this... to find me?"

His brow furrows. "Do you really think I would let you go? Given the chance to come?"

"Now people." The cop pushes us toward the exit, and this time we leave in a hurry. "Freaking carnies. Don't forget your belongings."

After leading Nkella to grab the clothes he came in, we step out into the humid Louisiana heat. I stare at the bag he holds in his hands.

"What happened to your clothes when you got here?"

"Harold's portal landed in a swamp. Kh."

Now it makes sense. "And then someone lent you that?"

"Koj. People were staring. I found it behind a tree. Then guards were on me."

"Wait a minute. I can understand you. Did you—" I smile widely, "you took a translation potion, didn't you? I thought it didn't work on Ipani."

"Koj. It does not work on Ipani. But I speak Imboe too, and the potion works on that. You know this already. Kh."

"Well, glad to know it works here too."

He stops us on our way to the car, and pulls me close.

I let out a shaky breath, pressing my forehead against his chest. He smells like smoke and rum. Like him.

"I thought about you every day," I whisper.

He tilts my face up with one hand, eyes searching mine like he's making sure I'm really here. "Neyuro..."

A slamming door makes me jump. We're still in the parking lot. "Come on, let's go home."

"Home?"

"Yeah, back to my apartment..." Not worrying about explaining what one is to him, he'll see it when we get there. I open the door for him, and he stares inside. "Go on, you steer a pirate ship. You can handle a car." He narrows his eyes at me but doesn't say anything as he crouches down to sit. I hop in the driver's seat and buckle his seatbelt for him, causing him to raise his hands, startled. "It's the law here," I tell him.

"Hn." He scans his surroundings, intently noting every detail of my car, and of people walking by.

"Are you okay?" I ask.

He stares at me, a grin spreading on his face. "I found you, my aovate. Nothing in this land could scare me into going back home. Not without you."

I swallow. Not without me. "Nkella..." I breathe in, and rest my head back in the seat. I don't want to ruin this moment, so instead, I put my car in reverse and pull out of this parking spot. "Are you hungry?"

"Kh." Then he laughs.

"What's so funny?"

"I just stepped through a portal to find you. Ended up a gembella in your world. I just told you I will not live another day in Danū without you. And what you say in return is... 'Are you hungry?'" he guffaws.

I peel out of the parking lot and into the street, only to have to slam my brakes at a red light. Damnit. Although, I will admit him ending up as a prisoner when he first got here is funny.

Nkella grabs onto the dashboard and cusses. "This thing is fast, daí? Are you sure you can drive it?"

I narrow my eyes at him. "There's traffic. And people drive aggressive here. I have to move fast. You should know all about that."

He quiets, now too consumed with looking out the window. I can't help the smile spreading on my face. Never in a million years did I think I would have Nkella here, in my car, in Louisiana.

But the reality of the situation is... he can't stay here. Even if we just tell everyone he's a renny who had permanent surgery done, he's the king of Danū. And I can't live over there.

"What's the plan here?"

He glances at me, then goes back to looking out the window.

"Really? Nothing?"

He stays silent.

Okay, we're winging it, I guess.

"It's more of a hope," he finally says.

I shake my head.

"But before it's time to go, I want to see more of this land."

I smile at him. "We can do that."

We hit a stretch of road lined with chain restaurants and cheap motels before Nkella finally speaks.

"My ouma doesn't work here."

I glance over. "Yeah. It wouldn't."

He frowns. "You know this?"

"I grew up here, remember?" I say. "Magic's not real here. Not the way it is over there. No ouma. No curses. Just pavement, bills, and fried food."

My features twist while he sits with that. That's not exactly true.

"So your power's gone too?"

"No," I admit. "I can still feel it. But I don't touch it. I guess some magic is real here, but we don't have anything like the Aō here. Harold has magic because of his ancient ancestry from another world. And the Fates were from Ancient Greece, but that was a long time ago."

He studies me.

"I could've used it this morning when I was looking for my car keys, I tap on them hanging on my ignition so he knows what I mean." I continue, eyes still on the road. "But I won't feed the habit."

"Why not?"

"Because I'm not her anymore," I snap harsher than intended. I let out a slow sigh, calming my nerves. "What would be the point? The past should be left where it belongs. In the past. Look at everything that happened because of three selfish Fates? Just because we have the power to do something, doesn't mean we should abuse it."

He stays quiet as he sits in the passenger's seat, studying everything with that same sharp focus he used to scan the decks of his ship.

We pass a seafood place with a giant neon crawfish holding a beer. Nkella squints at it. "Is that the ruler?"

"It's a mascot," I chuckle. "For fried things."

His brow furrows. "It has a crown."

"They're sunglasses."

He leans back slowly, unimpressed. "Hn."

I shake my head, steering us into downtown. He leans forward when we pass the courthouse.

"What is this building?"

"That's a courthouse... meant for justice."

"It has pillars like the Empress's Tower did."

After giving him an extensive tour of the city, and stopping at Starbucks where people kept coming up to us to tell him his ears look cool. And ask him if he had his teeth sharpened—all of which I just said thank you, and yes. And also, yes, the stripes are tattoos, we make it back to my apartment by sundown.

Once inside, I lock the door behind us and toss the keys into the bowl by the door, the same bowl I swore I'd start using six months ago. He steps in slowly, taking it all in. The sagging couch, the crooked bookshelf, the laundry I'd half folded before rushing out this morning. It's not much. But it's mine.

"Talia?" I call out but no answer. Good, she's probably at her friend's house like she planned. I just want him to myself.

He brushes his fingers along the edge of the counter. "This is where you live?"

I shrug off my jacket. "Yeah. Welcome to civilization. Don't mind the smell, it's the neighbor's cooking. Or maybe the cat litter. Hard to tell."

I kick off my boots, grab my phone, and sink onto the couch. "I'm ordering pizza. You want meat or more meat?"

He raises a brow. "You have categories of meat?"

"Endless."

He sits beside me, cautiously at first, then leans back. The couch groans under his weight. He shifts, scanning the room again, when loud noise from the neighbors TV makes his head turn.

"That's normal," I tell him.

Slowly, he settles back. "I don't know how you survived here without going mad."

"I did," I say. "For a while, I really tried to forget it all. The magic. The cards... You." I swallow.

He turns toward me at that. His lips part, and I lick mine.

"Obviously, I can't forget you. I got good at pretending. I'd smile at my coworkers and rehearse normal life like it's a script..." My voice trails and I continue to scroll through the pizza app like it's any other night. Even though I know it's not.

I don't even know what to do with this.

I shake my head and place the order. A text message dings and I stare at my phone. A message from Harold.

Oops. I think I hung up on him before I ran out the house. I tap on it and it reads:

Harold
Did he tell you yet?

I'm a portal away. Spending time with my aunt, but my runes always work. Just tell me when and I'll be there.

I set the phone slowly down on the coffee table and stare at Nkella who has his legs spread wide on my couch. His gaze is dark as he looks at me, like he's getting ready to eat me.

My lips part, wanting nothing more. I climb over his legs. He takes me in, straddling me down on his spread lap. My breathing intensifies, already forgetting what Harold messaged me about. I'll just call him later. Right now, this is what's important. What has to happen before it gets taken away.

His places his hands firmly on my hips, and I lean in and press my mouth to his, and the second our lips meet, the rest of the world drops away. His kiss is passionate, deliberate, with that edge of restrained control just barely giving way. I feel the shape of his hunger in the way he draws me in, one hand sliding up my back, the other gripping my thigh like he's anchoring himself to this moment.

My fingers tangle in his hair. It's longer than I remember, and just as soft. I pull him in deeper, and he answers without hesitation, parting his lips, pulling me closer. Our mouths find a rhythm that's too familiar. His breath comes heavier against mine, heat building between us in the quiet of my living room.

It's almost weird not to feel our aovate connection stirring between us. But this silence is good too.

I pull back just enough to meet his eyes. "Let's go to my room."

He doesn't answer as he lifts me effortlessly, with one arm under my legs, the other cradling my back. I hook my arms around his neck, guiding him.

"Down the hall," I murmur, brushing my lips to his temple. "Second door on the left."

The floorboards creak beneath his feet as kisses my neck.

When he reaches the door, I lean in. "This is it."

He pushes it open with his shoulder, crosses the threshold, and closes the door behind us with the heel of his boot.

He sets me down on the bed with careful hands, but there's nothing careful in the way he looks at me. His eyes sweep over my body like he's trying to memorize it all at once, as if he doesn't trust this world not to take me away from him again. I sit up just enough to reach for his hoodie, and he lets me pull it over his head, dragging it free in one smooth motion.

The air shifts.

His chest is marked with the same lines I traced in Tarotland, the same stripes and tattoos I've memorized. I press my palm to his skin, right over the scar that curves beneath his ribs. He covers my hand with his.

For the first time ever, he doesn't have to worry about shifting to his devil form. Even though we conquered it together, and I stopped being afraid. This time, there's not a care in the world.

His weight eases me down into the mattress as he follows, one knee braced between my legs, the other still grounded beside the bed. His hand finds the hem of my shirt, lifting it inch by inch until he can push it over my head and toss it aside. His mouth is on my neck before I can let out a breath.

"This is for every day we lost, my aovate," he whispers.

I arch into him. My fingers scrape along his back, memorizing the tension in his shoulders, the way his breath stutters every time I press into him just right. His fingers skims along my ribs, then down, settling at the waistband of my jeans. He pauses, his sexy gaze staring up at me.

I lift my hips, and his gaze turns to hunger.

He takes my pants off with ease, like he already knows every line of me in this world too. My legs wrap around him, pulling him closer as his mouth returns to mine, more urgent this time. It's everything we've been holding back since the portal closed.

He groans when I slide my hand down the front of his pants, and the sound goes straight through me. His head drops to my shoulder for a second, breath hitching.

"You're going to kill me," he mutters.

I smile against his skin. "You found me. What did you think would happen?"

He positions himself between my legs, no fabric left between us. His palm cradles the side of my face, thumb brushing my cheek, grounding me in the intensity of us, and everything else we couldn't say before because there was no time before I had to leave.

And then he pushes into me, slow, steady, eyes pinning me down the whole time, and I swear, the world stops moving.

He fills me inch by inch, and a soft, involuntary gasp escapes me.

He catches my lips again, biting gently down. Our eyes meet as he goes in deeper, and I arch my back into him.

"My Neyuro...I could not live another minute without you."

I hook my legs around his waist, pulling him closer, deeper. "Then don't hold back."

His hips move in slow, deliberate strokes at first, like he's relearning the shape of me, the rhythm of us. Every thrust building pressure in waves, stealing the air from my lungs in slow drags. I arch into him, fingers sinking into his back, dragging down his spine just to feel the way his muscles jump beneath my touch.

He pushes deeper, harder now, the tension between us winding tighter with each breath. I press my mouth to his neck, teeth grazing his pulse, and he shudders.

His pace falters for half a second. "Who am I, Soren?" he breathes.

I blink up at him. "Nkella."

"Koj." He pulls back just enough to look at me. "*Say who I am to you. Who do you belong to?*"

My heart stutters. The way he says it. It's about remembering what we are, what we've been through to make it here.

"Aovate," I whisper.

He slams back into me, and my body answers him without thought, tightening, clenching, rising with him. His mouth finds mine again, and he kisses me with such intensity, as if it's the last time he'll ever kiss me again.

Because it might be.

I feel the edge building fast, my nails bite into his shoulders as I gasp out his name again, barely audible.

"Don't stop," I manage, voice breaking. "*Please don't stop—*"

"I won't," his voice is hoarse as he says it. "Not until you fall apart in my arms. Not until this body forgets every moment we were apart."

Oh God.

I come with a cry muffled into his shoulder, shaking hard around him as everything crashes through me—pleasure, grief, relief, everything I was refusing myself to feel, until now. He holds me through it, his arms gripping me tight.

Then his body tenses, trembling as he lets go inside me with a low, guttural sound that makes my whole body respond all over again.

He collapses over me, and I don't even care that it's hot in here. Soon, he'll have to leave me again, so I marvel in the comfort his weight gives me. We both catch our breath in silence, tangled and sweating and completely undone.

A minute passes. Maybe more. I don't care.

His forehead rests against mine, his chest still rising fast against my ribs.

Time feels like an eternity, but the daunting feeling that it will end lies in the back of my mind. He's still draped over me, one hand curled at my waist, the other smoothing down the side of my thigh like he's not ready to let go yet. I'm not either. I could stay like this for hours, body warm and all. Like this, my heart is full, and the ache of missing him finally dulled.

But he's too quiet now.

I feel it in the way his thumb stills, and his breathing slows, like he's bracing for something. Hmm...

He breaks the silence: "Are you sure you'll never want to use your Helāni magic again?"

I blink. "What?"

He lifts his head to look at me, eyes unreadable.

"You said you left it behind," he says. "But do you mean forever?"

I hesitate. "Yes." My brows furrow. "Why are you asking this right now?"

He doesn't move.

"But why?" he asks.

"Because it comes with too much responsibility, that shouldn't even be used," I say, barely above a whisper. "It made me into someone I had to be, but not someone I have to stay."

He studies me for a long moment. Then he shifts, pulling away just enough to sit up beside me, one leg still draped over mine.

"I have something to tell you," he says.

I sit up slowly, wrapping the sheet around myself. "Okay."

"When Harold came back from the world he speaks of..."

"Jötunheim?"

Nkella nods. "I remembered how Tetalla spoke with the Aō. Negotiated." When I say nothing, he continues. "I figured a way to do the same."

My jaw tightens. "You're going to have to spell that out."

"I negotiated," he says. "When Harold returned, I went with him. I found the place where the Aō meets. Harold called it the in-between. A passage between fates. It used to be guarded by a spider the size of a fortress, but it is no longer there."

I swallow, the hair on my arms rising. "And?"

"There's a way for you to come back. To live in in Ipa again. But there's a price."

I already know what he's going to say before the words come.

"You would have to relinquish your Helāni magic. Fully."

I stare at him. "Relinquish them? I didn't think that was possible.... It's who I am."

"It is possible," he says. "And you were you before you had that power, daſ?" His finger brushes under my chin.

I swallow hard. *Of course.* I saw Tetalla twist the Death Card on himself, bending fate where it shouldn't have bent. If he could force the Aō to let him live, then maybe I can ask it to take this power back.

"My Neyuro, you are powerful by your own wit. But I would need to know it is truly what you want. I do not want to be the reason you leave your magic behind."

I lick my lips and kiss his hand. "So how would I do this?"

"You'd have to pass through the in-between. Harold would hold you there, guide you to the Aō. You would speak to them yourself. Tell them you're giving up your Helāni power to be able to live there."

My lips part. I feel as if I'm waking up from a dream. Is this for real?

"Your ouma would be allowed back. You'd be free to live in Ipa with me... with the crew. Without the Helāni power."

I sit there, trying to process the *scale* of it all. Just when I thought I had to get my shit together here. The Empress and Asteria are dead. I wouldn't have any other connections to "home." Even though I've never felt at home here. And what about Talia?

Talia's getting her life in order too... She's no longer the child she was before. We can figure that out.

And I'm... half-Ipani. I still can't believe it. I'll have my own ouma. My breathing picks up. I press my fingers to my temple.

"Nkella," I murmur, "this is insane." But is it though? There's nothing for me here. Ever since my mother died, I've felt like I didn't belong. Like I've just been running from one home to the next, picking up skills to survive. It's as though I was being trained for Tarotland. To ride on drakons and have psychic connections with oumala animals. I want to feel the waves surge beneath my skin. I stare back down at him, into those dark eyes, that come alive in the other world. I want to see that again. I want to be with him.

"It's your choice," he says. "One I could never force you to make. I didn't even want to ask you... It is a big sacrifice to give up one's power. But either way, I had to see you again. I was not going to let Harold leave without me taking that chance." He grabs my arm as I move to get up. "Where are you going?"

I stare back at him. "Are you joking? To pack! And then to call Harold." He pulls me back onto him with a smooth, sudden motion, his smile breaking open across his face like light cutting through a storm.

"Mine forever," he says.

"Forever."

EPILOGUE

SOREN

One Year Later

I open the terrace door and the wind rolls in, thick with moss, salt, and woodsmoke. Below in the courtyard, half a dozen oumala wolf pups tear through the grass, their paws kicking up dirt as they chase each other in tangled loops. Iéle leads them, her movements swift and sharp. Rohaka stays just behind. He's bigger, with his gray coat catching the last light of the afternoon.

They herd the pups, and one veers toward the fountain only to be blocked by Rohaka's flank. Another jumps onto a barrel and slips.

Nkella steps up beside me. "One of them knocked over a tall candle this morning, catching a curtain on fire."

"Which one?"

"The one with the split ear."

"Troublemaker."

"He bit through a rope line. Twice."

"They're learning from the best," I say, nodding at Iéle.

"She denies everything."

Inside the halls behind us, voices carry. Tessa's chair clicks through a gear shift. Kaehante's boots echo against stone. Ntaoru is explaining something to AJ, who argues back over who knows what, followed by a laugh from Lāri.

It's the first time we've all been back at the Danū stronghold since the sanctuary finished construction. The final push to secure the other islands, clean up the remaining corruption, and reconnect the cavern cities have taken longer than any of us expected. We also have plans for the Hermit to come and implement his steam engineering here, but that will take him training a team to help do it. It's a work in progress, but we've gotten it fixed enough for a grand opening.

"They'll be waiting soon," I say.

"Let them wait," Nkella replies.

"We built it for them. We should at least show up."

He gives a low sound of agreement but doesn't move. His hand brushes against mine where they rest on the stone ledge.

A guard climbs the steps with a scroll in hand. "My King. Reports from the caverns are ready. The people are settling in. The council has requested a visit from both of you."

Nkella nods. "And the Kings of Oleanu?"

"On their way."

He glances at me. "Let's go."

A popping sound comes from my arm, and I glimpse at Philo waving her little arms at me. She dances on my skin, where my spiderweb mark used to be. It disappeared after I gave up being a Fate in the in-between.

I smile down at her. "Are you here for the grand ceremony? We're opening the previously destroyed areas of Danū for the ones who want to live above the caves." She slants her head at my voice. I was relieved to have Philo come back from the Aō after Tetalla had frozen her. I thought I had lost her forever.

One of the puppies howls in my direction, and now they're all running at me to howl at poor Philo. She turns her head, and pops back into the Aō. Welp, I guess that answers that question. I shake my head.

The pups shift direction again. Iéle cuts them off before they can get near the rose garden. Rohaka drives them back toward the orchard, and they fall into rhythm.

"Did you ever think it would end up like this?" I ask.

He glances at me. "Koj."

I look out at the fields again. There's still evidence of the war in places, burn marks, and gouges in the land, but the green is coming back. And so are the people.

"Do you miss your land?" he asks.

I think about it. "Sometimes. I miss certain things. The internet. My sister's playlists. Trashy TV."

He raises an eyebrow. "The one with the dating rituals?"

"That one. It was awful. I loved it."

"But do you miss it?"

I shake my head. "I never really belonged there. And none of that compares to this."

That sexy smirk of his appears on his face and he dips his head to kiss me.

Behind us, the hallway doors creak open, and the crew walks out in loud conversation. God, how I love them all.

Before we go inside, one of the pups breaks away from the group and trots up the stairs. It's the one with the split ear. He pauses at my feet, tongue lolling, his tail furiously wagging. I crouch and scratch behind his ears.

"Are you planning to cause trouble too?" I ask him.

He barks once, then bounds back down the stairs.

"They take after you," Nkella says.

"They're stubborn and fast and ignore direct orders. Yeah. They're mine."

He smiles, then sobers. "You're different than when I first met you."

"Yeah?" I say. "You carry things differently now too, you know." I slap him playfully on the chest.

A sharp cry echoes in the distance, followed by a deep, rattling bellow that shakes the stones beneath our feet.

We glance toward the upper ridge, just beyond the treeline. Gari soars into view, shining a silver glow over his blue fur beneath the sun's radiance. Just behind him, the snow drakon glides through the air, her body shimmering. They circle once before banking toward the cliffs.

"It's still funny to see Gari with someone," I say.

Nkella nods. "Took them long enough."

"I think she was waiting to see if he'd stop showing off first."

"They're aovate now. The sky won't be quiet for a while."

We stand there a moment longer, watching the light shift across the stone, hearing the soft call of birds in the distance and the quiet rumble of conversation behind us.

I take Nkella's hand, and he pulls me in closer to him.

We turn from the wind and head back inside.

The halls are warm and full of life. Tessa waves us over, a leather-bound journal balanced on her lap and three schedules open at once. "We're late," she says, but she's smiling.

Kaehate hands me a sealed satchel full of maps, reports, a handful of letters from the cavern children who'd started learning to write in both languages. I hold one up, marked with the Ipani scripture.

"Do you know what it says?" Kaehante asks.

"No," I answer. "But I'm going to learn."

As we pass through the corridor, a woman from the sanctuary staff nods in greeting, "King Nkella, Queen Soren."

I smile but look down at Nkella's hand holding mine. I don't think I'll ever get used to that.

Talia is leaning against one of the pillars overlooking the mountain range with a smile from ear to ear while she giggles at something one of the Ipani guards is telling her. I quirk a brow at them but continue walking. Like me, she never felt at home back in Louisiana, and she loves it here. I gave her the choice to come back, and she said I was crazy for me thinking she'd ever consider staying back home.

People don't bow to us. He hates that, and so do I.

We pass through the archway into the great hall. I pause just before the threshold, looking up at the worn stone above me. This place used to scare me when I lived here with Tetalla. Now it feels like home.

Nkella doesn't let go of my hand.

I stare up at my aovate. He meets my gaze with a mischievous smirk.

"What's that smile for?" I tease.

He reaches down to my ear and whispers. "My queen, wait until all these formalities are over, daí? And I'll show you just what forever means for us."

My eyes widen, and now I want to get this over with.

The air inside the sanctuary is cool, with a soft mist. Bowls filled with oumala moss, scented with fresh colorful herbs decorate the centers of all the tables.

I take a breath and let it fill my chest.

There were years where I didn't know who I was. Places I ran to just to keep moving. Faces I aimed to forget. But right now, surrounded by stone and light and the people I chose to stay for, I don't feel like I'm pretending anymore.

We walk in together, with my aovate by my side, and for the first time, I'm right at home.

The End

AUTHOR'S NOTE

Bet you thought I was going to leave you with another crazy cliff hanger. Be honest, when you got to the last chapter before the Epilogue and saw whose point of view it was, were you confused? Did you cuss out my name in frustration?

I think I heard a scream cut through the Aō and into my dream. Was that you?

If so, I just want to let you know, you inspired me to keep on writing this series, and I just wanted to keep you on your toes. The world building and characters of Tarotland has lived in my head for years, even years before I started writing it, and I want to thank you from the bottom of my heart for taking the time to read all of it!

I hope you stick with me. Harold and Kenjo's story is going to continue in their spin-off, where we get to venture into the realm of the Ice Giants. Be sure to join my newsletter at http://killianwolf.com/ for updates on when that will come out, and if you haven't read The Fool's Journey already, you can get the ebook free for joining my mailing list, and get to see how Harold and Kenjo meet.

GET IN TOUCH!

Come say hi in my Facebook Reader group. In there, every day is Halloween!

facebook.com/groups/killianwolf

Please feel free to get in touch with me.

Website: http://killianwolf.com/

instagram.com/killian_wolf_author
facebook.com/killianwolfauthor
tiktok.com/@killian_wolf_author
pinterest.com/killianwolf22
goodreads.com/killianwolf
amazon.com/Killian-Wolf/e/B07WHFB8FW
bookbub.com/authors/killian-wolf
patreon.com/killianwolfauthor

HONORABLE MENTIONS

To my contest winners at Literary Love Savannah in 2024, Adriel and Amanda, thank you so much for participating in my Career Fair game. Your participation showed encouragement in my work and I truly thank you from the bottom of my heart. Both your characters added that extra pazaz in finishing the series. Keep kicking butt!

To Rachelle, thank you for your unyielding support and for pledging the highest tier of my kickstarter. Your character Gibby was so fun to write and he brought comic relief in what an otherwise solemn scene.

To Kennedy, thank you for being my super-fan. Your character became an inspiration with her interests of crystals, that it inspired Soren's power to emerge.

To my ride-or-die critique partner, Christina, holy-cow—I could not have made this happen without you. Thank you truly, for being a text message or phone call away when I needed you, and for sticking it out during my crazy tight deadline to get this book published. This entire series wouldn't be what it is without your expert critiques, and suggestions. You got to know and love my characters, and would sanity check me when you felt something was off with one of them. With whatever you need going forward, you can count on me having your back, always.

I would also like to give my warmest thanks to Jackie Fitzpatrick. I'm honored to have you as a reader and as one of my greatest supporters at book conventions and on Patreon. Your encouragement inspires me to keep writing and to keep on world-building. From the bottom of my heart, thank you.

To all my readers, including those who have been with me from the very beginning, those who have created character art, and those who have supported me in countless ways, you are all amazing. I hope to see you again in the next series.

To my husband, Michael. Thank you for putting up with my writing shenanigans, and late night deadlines, and for putting up not only with me, but with our crazy wolfdog pup, Cairo while I worked on this book. You continue to support my dreams, and I love you for it—to the moon and back.

And to my mother, your innovation and artistry continue to inspire me every single day. Without you, and your teachings, my author career would not have been possible. Thank you, and I love you.

A special mention to my grandfather, who I lost shortly after publishing the Serpent's Deep. He inspired so much in me: the pursuit of knowledge, languages, history, and archaeology. He was a designer and an architect, and would work things into his designs like trap doors and hidden symbols. Without his influence, I do not believe this series would have become as intricate in detail as it is. Te quiero mucho, Abuelo.

FREE BOOK

Scan to get this free book and sign up for my mailing list.

"Don't kill" is a no-brainer. But what if it's for a good reason?

My name is Harold and my family is cursed. When my aunt made the tough call to pull my mother from life support, she enacted the curse of the Frost Giants, freezing herself from the inside.

To save her, all I had to do was step through the portal, but one wrong move sent me flying off to Tarotland, a place where the tarot cards have come to life. The good news is I still have my runes. The bad news? Magicians are illegal here. Not to mention, I haven't exactly come into my powers yet. . . and I can't get the portal to reopen.

My salvation is a breathtaking native. She makes me act like a Fool, but she also told me about a sword that cuts through any doorway. Power doesn't come without sacrifice, though. With a mysterious predator out for blood, and my name on every wanted poster, who knows if we'll make it before my aunt breathes her final breath?

ABOUT THE AUTHOR

Killian Wolf is a Miami, Florida, native who enjoys pirates, rum, and skulls as much as she loves writing about dark magick and sorcerers. She holds a Bachelor of Arts degree in Cultural Anthropology and Sociology and a Master of Science in Environmental Archaeology and Palaeoeconomy.

Killian writes books about obtaining magickal powers and stepping into other dimensions. She lives in Florida with her husband, a tornado of a cat, and the most timid snake you'd ever meet. When she isn't writing, you might find her at an archaeological dig, rock climbing, or sipping on dark spiced rum while working on a painting.

GLOSSARY

IPANI VOCABULARY

á: Sound often used by natives of Sāgirang, used to represent a sound made in speech in a variety of situations, often used to ask for something to be repeated or explained or to elicit agreement.

Aō: [a.ˈo] world spirit

Āngasoe: Minotaur

Aovate: (begisi aovate) [be.ˈɰi.si a.o.ˈva.te] soulmate, destined partner (lit. betrothed by the hand of the world spirit)

Bancha: [ˈbaɲ.ca] empty, free of, lacking, fool, idiot, stupid

Bayoa: turning light in the sky, northern lights/Nautilus

Besēla: [be.ˈseː.la] jerk, bastard

Daí: Sound often used by natives of Danū, used to represent a sound made in speech in a variety of situations, often used to ask for something to be repeated or explained or to elicit agreement.

Daekente: With horns

Drakon: Ancient Greek dragon with a serpentine body. Can both swim and fly, and pop in and out of the Aō dimension.

Garisi: drinkable potion, as opposed to explosive potion

gembella: [gem.'bel.la] from gembe, prisoner, inmate

Gichang: currency, money

gichang rīrō: money from Danu, pressed ruby

gichang riwao: money from Wands, pressed amethyst

gichachi: mark

guyuti: [gu.'ju.ti] shrivel-ear, derogatory term used to describe a human

Hn: A sound made by an Ipani when thinking out loud.

Helāni: Descendants of the Ancient Greeks who crossed the portal with the Moera

hū raku (raku): [hu: 'ɾa.ku] poison gas; poisonous breath

iá: [i.'a] hailing; hello, ahoy, greetings

Iéle: [i.'e.le] moon

Imboe: [im.boe] Ancient Greek-Ipani creole spoken in Ipa

Indakepoa: [ˌin.da.ke.'poa] translation potion, liquorice

Ipani: [i.'pa.ni] of the World; the language of the World. Ipani (singular and plural)

Iponónchi: [i.po.'noɲ.ci] cookie, pastry (lit.: little baked)

Kaehante: well prepared with a paddle (literal), or armed/prepared (figuratively)

Kaonī: Blacksmith

Kenjō: [keɲ.'ɟo:] (Open Sky)

Ko: Negative, soft no

Koj: [koej] No, none, no! don't!

Mei: Sound often used by natives of Oleanu, used to represent a sound made in speech in a variety of situations, often used to ask for something to be repeated or explained or to elicit agreement.

Mikiroro: Black palm tree, the Danū crest
Moera: The Ancient Greek Fates
Mūhī: [ˌmu,ˈhiː] footprint [in the] sand
Nangraku: [naŋ.ˈɾa.ku] poison tooth
Neyuro: [ne.yuro] brave girl
Ouma: [ˈow.ma] magic; magical
Oumala: [ow.ˈma.la] mage, practitioner of magic, magic user
Omute: magical sticky substance
Rikorō: [ʻdik.oro] soul thief, plant
Rikwa: [ˈdik.wa] thief
Rōkan: Curse word; used for anger, shock, or emphasis. Comparable in weight to the harshest vulgarities in English. Highly versatile, it can function as a noun, verb, adjective, or interjection depending on context.
Ruh: [ɾuo̯] wolf
saechi: peak berry, volcanic berry
solerie: [so.le.ˈɾie] soleri'g, solerigo (i) peppermint (lit.: ice-leaf), gives transparency, spectre; can be used for people and objects
Taevenye: [tae̯ ˈʋe.ɲe] cinnamon (lit.: cloud-wood), gives ability to fly, float; can be used in potions for people and objects
Tetalla: [te.'tal.la]: habitual dead-maker
Utwa: [ˈu.twa] scout, spy

PHRASES

Roē yani: Light of my flame
Pa chae: I love you
Uoko yani: My viscous one

PLACES

Danū: "Six suns." Farthest Southeastern Island. Currently called Pentacles, Danū by the rebels.
Dempu Yuni: trading post island
Dempu: foot; (i) standing, located; (i) river mouth
Ipa: [ˈee.pa] the global ocean, the World
Naó: Greek Temple
Oe Nū: [ˌoe̯ ˈnuː] «sacred water» (Ipani temple in Oleanu)
Oleanu: "Highwater" Island to the East. Currently called Wands, Oleanu by the rebels.
Piupeki: "Steelrock" Island farthest to the North. Currently called Swords, Piupeki by the rebels.
Rutavenye: "Cloudwall" The Floating island, location of The Tower

ALSO BY KILLIAN WOLF

The Van Tassel Witches

Of Headless Hollows

The Castillian Blood

Defying Demons

Escaping Demons

Lying with Demons

Blood of Demons

Queen of Demons

Dragons and Demons

Little Krampus

Little Krampus And The Magical Sleigh Ride

Little Krampus And The Christmas Secret

Little Krampus And The Mischievous Yule Lads

Little Krampus And The Christmas List Switch

Little Krampus And The Trick-Or-Treat Chase

www.ingramcontent.com/pod-product-compliance
Lightning Source LLC
Chambersburg PA
CBHW030537310726
48979CB00010B/1944/J
* 9 7 8 1 9 5 1 1 4 0 3 1 1 *